Winter '

A Polwenna Bay novel

by

Ruth Saberton

Copyright

All characters, organisations and events in this publication, other than those clearly in the public domain, are fictitious and any resemblance to real persons, living or dead, is purely coincidental.

The opinions expressed in this book are solely the opinions of the author and do not represent the opinions or thoughts of the publisher. The author has represented and warranted full ownership and / or legal right to publish all materials in this book.

Also by Ruth Saberton

Escape for the Summer

Escape for Christmas

Dead Romantic

Hobb's Cottage

Weight Till Christmas

Katy Carter Wants a Hero

Ellie Andrews Has Second Thoughts

Amber Scott is Starting Over

The Wedding Countdown

Runaway Summer: Polwenna Bay 1

A Time for Living: Polwenna Bay 2

Treasure of the Heart: Polwenna Bay 4

Writing as Jessica Fox

The One That Got Away

Eastern Promise

Hard to Get

Unlucky in Love

Always the Bride

Writing as Holly Cavendish

Looking for Fireworks

Writing as Georgie Carter

The Perfect Christmas

Chapter 1

The Reverend Jules Mathieson was exhausted. A violent gale had howled through the village all night, keeping her up until the small hours and she'd barely had an hour's sleep before the alarm roused her for an early-morning prayer group meeting. Feeling like something that had been dug up from the churchyard, and no doubt looking like it too, Jules had somehow led the session. Next, she'd dashed over to Polwenna Bay Primary School for an assembly. After that, she'd manned a bric-a-brac stall at the WI fundraiser – an experience that had made her understand just how Harry Styles must feel when mobbed by fans. When that was over with, she'd gone back to the vicarage to trawl through St Wenn's depressing accounts for the umpteenth time.

And she'd been worried that life in a rural Cornish parish would be dull? These days Jules counted herself lucky if she had so much as five minutes to herself; her mornings and afternoons flew by in a blur. By night she was usually out cold within seconds of her head hitting the pillow, and before she knew it the alarm was ripping her from sleep and hurling her into another day, just as busy as its predecessor. Jules couldn't remember ever feeling so tired.

It was probably better this way. At least when she was flat out working, there was no time to dwell on the dull ache in her heart or to miss those special conversations that had once flowed as easily as the River Wenn. Nor was there time to daydream about what could have been…

She wasn't going to allow herself to do that, Jules told herself sharply. Instead she was going to focus on all the wonderful things in her life and enjoy the autumnal beauty all around her. If she was becoming increasingly melancholic as the nights drew in, then Jules was determined to shake it off somehow. Perhaps she was suffering from seasonal affective disorder, or something of the sort. After all, it wasn't as though anything had actually happened between her and Danny—

Oh Lord, here she went again, starting to think about things she'd promised herself would remain out of bounds. Danny Tremaine was just a friend – and that was all he could ever be. He was married and, whatever he said about the marriage being over, that bond was a sacrament all the same. Apart from anything else, he'd never been able to give Jules a valid reason for the marriage breakdown, and she knew that Danny's wife still hoped they would manage to make it work. It was Jules's duty as their priest to help them mend their marriage, regardless of how she felt about Danny. Stepping away from him had been the right thing to do, no matter how painful it was for them both.

Nothing had happened between them and nothing ever would. Fact, as Danny's son Morgan might say.

It wasn't easy in a small fishing village to avoid somebody, though – especially not one of the Tremaines. They were the foremost and oldest family in Polwenna Bay, and were pretty much involved in all areas of village life. Still, Jules was working on it. She was professional and polite whenever she saw Danny, which was most days; even if the hurt on his face sliced her heart as sharply as the fishermen's knives gutted their catch, Jules was getting good at hiding it. Instead of their walks together over the cliffs or long chatty hours drinking coffee in the harbour tearoom, she'd changed her route to the wooded valleys behind the village and thrown herself into her work. Her waistbands were certainly looser as a result of taking a detour every day, and the bishop was delighted with the increased activity in the church Jules devoted so much of her time to. She supposed she had to accept her broken heart and Danny's reproachful looks as collateral damage, for the greater good. The future of his marriage was up to him and his wife now; Jules would have no bearing on any choice Danny might make. At least her conscience was clear, even if her heart felt as though it would never mend.

Why hadn't anyone told her that being a vicar would be this challenging? Would she have continued with her vocation if she'd known that it would come at the cost of losing the man she was in love with? She would have been answerable to God either way, of course, but the situation seemed so much more complicated because of her calling. It was a conundrum Jules wrestled with daily and was praying very hard about. She'd never realised until now how tough it could be to do the right thing.

Her friends in Polwenna Bay had spotted that Jules was unhappy and, although they had no idea why this was so, they were keen to cheer her up. Jules was touched by their extra efforts to fundraise for St Wenn's – the church's finances being an obvious cause of vicarly woe. Even Sheila Keverne, Jules's very difficult verger, had mellowed and now dropped by for a cup of tea on a regular basis. The Pollards had mowed the vicarage lawn for free, Kursa Penwarren had offered a discount hair-colouring session at the salon and Chris the Cod had taken to dishing up vast portions of fish and chips whenever Jules called in for supper. Jules was starting to feel a bit like Polwenna Bay's care in the community project; besides, she was concerned for her crowning glory (given that Kursa's hairstyling skills were notorious), not to mention her rocketing cholesterol levels. She knew she had to get a grip and keep her game face on.

This afternoon Alice and Issie Tremaine had called at the vicarage, convinced that fresh air and exercise were the answer. Jules, who'd previously had great faith in the restorative powers of the jam-filled doughnut rather than the five-mile hike, had found herself being bundled into her coat and frogmarched out into the autumnal sunshine. Her protests about having to write a sermon or prepare for the Parochial Church Council meeting were ignored. This didn't surprise Jules in the least. Individually, each Tremaine family member was a force of nature; when they got together they were unstoppable. Canute probably had more luck telling to tide to back off than Jules would ever have trying to say no to a Tremaine.

Now, as she followed her friends through the woodland, she smothered a yawn and tried to feel grateful she was so busy. Even though the storm had blown itself out hours ago and the day was now as warm and as golden as the pasties in Patsy Penhalligan's shop, all Jules really wanted to do was burrow under her duvet for an hour or two. Stomping through the countryside might be good for her figure, but her eyelids were becoming so heavy that she was considering snapping a couple of twigs from out of the hedgerow to prop them open.

"You're even slower than me today, my love," remarked Alice Tremaine, who'd paused and was waiting for Jules to catch her and Issie up. Jules didn't feel too shamed by this, however. Alice might be in her late seventies, but a lifetime spent walking the cliffs and steep lanes as well as running around after her brood of grandchildren had kept her fitter than most people half her age.

"I'm exhausted. The kitchen roof was leaking terribly last night and I was up for hours trying to catch the drips in saucepans," Jules explained.

"Can't you get the Pollards to patch it?" Alice suggested. The wily father-and-son builder team generally had the village sewn up; there weren't many jobs they didn't take on.

"They've given me a quote but it's pretty substantial. It would take quite a big chunk of our funds and I'd far rather we spent those on the church than the vicarage," Jules sighed. She'd pored over the books for at least an hour that morning trying to comprehend the accounts, before giving up. She could pay for some emergency repairs, but she feared it would be a false economy: she'd be better off waiting until the full job could be paid for. Unfortunately there wasn't enough money for that, though. Or at least, she supposed there wasn't. Right now the books didn't make sense. First an extra ten thousand pounds had appeared in the church's funds and then there had been several deposits of a thousand pounds each, made over the past two months. Neither Jules nor her treasurer, Dr Penwarren, could account for any of this. Handy as the extra cash would be, until she knew for certain that the money really did belong to St Wenn's and wasn't some banking anomaly, Jules didn't feel right about spending any of it.

"Do you want me to shag Little Rog and get him to do the repairs for free? He's been trying to chat me up ever since the Polwenna Bay calendar. I draw the line at Big Rog though, Jules, even for you," Issie joked.

At least, Jules hoped she was joking; you were never totally sure with Issie Tremaine. A law unto herself, whirlwind Issie partied hard, drank even harder and broke hearts right, left and centre. Half the young men in the village were in love with her and the other half were trying their best to get over her. It wasn't hard to see why. Issie shared the Tremaines' blessed gene pool and had the same hyacinth-blue eyes, high cheekbones and golden hair that reminded Jules so painfully of Issie's brother, Danny. Today, with her blonde braids caught up with a green ribbon on the crown of her head, and dressed in a flowing claret-coloured velvet coat and purple wellies, Issie looked like a modern-day pisky – and she was equally capable of causing havoc. The Pollards might be a sly pair, and they certainly weren't averse to making an extra pound or two where they could, but they didn't deserve an encounter with hurricane Issie. Besides, Jules was still trying to live down the Polwenna Bay naked calendar. In fairness it had raised a lot of money for St Wenn's, but the bishop had been less than impressed with the whole idea; he'd given Jules a stern warning about inappropriate ways of raising funds. Pimping out her parishioners in order to get the roof fixed would probably result in excommunication!

"Err, I'm joking!" Issie said, catching Jules's worried expression. "You obviously have a really great opinion of me. Little Rog? As if! In his dreams!"

Alice caught Jules's eye. "We're never quite sure with you, young lady. Let's be honest, you're not always the best behaved. Or the most sensible. I worry about you."

Issie tossed her head and snorted. "Please! I'm twenty-two, not two, Granny. Anyway, you're only saying all this because I'm a girl. It's actually quite sexist. You wouldn't bother if it were Nick. Or Zak."

Issie's brothers were just as golden and gorgeous as she was – and if village gossip was to be believed, they got through girls like Jules was getting through chips these days.

"Oh, I'm equally worried about them, believe me," said Alice grimly.

"And then there's Dad," Issie continued, squeezing between her grandmother and Jules and threading arms with them both. "He's as bad. I caught him on Skype talking to some woman in America. She must have been about my age. He slammed the lid down when he saw me. It was hilarious."

Alice's face clouded and she suddenly looked every one of her seventy-nine years. Jules's heart went out to her: she knew just how much Alice fretted about her son.

Jimmy was as charming and attractive as his brood but had never really grown up. Despite having been widowed in his early forties, he remained the Peter Pan of Polwenna Bay. He spent money as though it was going out of fashion and was inclined to pass his time propping up the bar in The Ship, pulling holidaymakers and generally squandering his talents as well as his cash. He liked to gamble, smoked too much and told stories taller than the Empire State Building. Still, he was so much fun and so good-natured that people tended to forgive him anything. Jules found Jimmy entertaining but she could certainly understand how he drove the more responsible members of his family to distraction.

"Dad was like a naughty kid. Oh, come on, Granny: it's funny," Issie insisted when Alice didn't comment. "You look just like Jake when you scowl. Dad doesn't mean any harm."

Alice exhaled and Jules squeezed her arm in solidarity. They'd had some long talks about Alice's fears that her son would gamble away the boatyard, and Danny had told her enough stories about his unreliable father to convince Jules that this was a very real possibility.

"He never means any harm, my love, but that doesn't seem to stop him causing it," was all she said.

Issie bit her lip. "I didn't mean to upset you, Granny. I was just messing about. I was going to say that it must run in the family, that was all. Like Black Jack Jago."

Alice laughed. "Oh, Issie! Whatever next? That's just a story."

"No! It's true! You know it is! You've got the necklace to prove it, haven't you? The one made from Spanish treasure."

Jules looked from grandmother to granddaughter, feeling more at sea than the Polwenna fishing fleet.

"What's all this? Who's Black Jack Jago? Something to do with Betty Jago from the village shop?"

The older woman nodded. "Somewhere along the line, I should think. This is Cornwall, Jules: we're all related somehow. Jack Jago was my great, great, great grandfather on my mother's side, as well a notorious Polwenna Bay smuggler and wrecker and, by all accounts, an all-round bad egg. Come on, it's getting late, so let's keep walking and I'll tell you the tale."

Although it was only three in the afternoon, the winter light was beginning to fade and wisps of sea mist were wrapping themselves around the trees like scarves. As Jules's wellies sploshed through the puddles she looked up at the canopy of leaves high above, the exact colours of toffee and treacle and caramel, and imagined that she was inside a giant jar of confectionery. It really was a magical setting, so still and ancient, and as Alice spoke Jules could easily picture another time. She visualised the smugglers' ponies, and could almost hear the muffled sounds of their hooves on the dank woodland floor as they were led through the cover of the trees and down to the beach below, where galleons waited to unload lace and brandy and tobacco.

"Black Jack Jago wasn't content with smuggling," Alice said. "He was greedy, and his heart was as black as those dark nights when he and his henchmen would set out onto the rocks with a lantern and lure ships onto the rocks. Once the ships had foundered, he and his men would wait for the cargo to wash up on the shore and spirit it away – after they'd finished with any survivors, that is."

Jules's mouth fell open. "You mean that really happened? People seriously wrecked ships on purpose? And murdered anyone who swam to shore?" She'd heard the tales, of course, and drunk the odd pint of Wreckers Ale in the pub, but she'd always imagined it was just folklore.

"Oh, it's true all right. Not one of the most glorious episodes in Cornwall's past, but it certainly happened. Times were hard and people were desperate. The locals believed that anything washing up on the beach was theirs by rights. You look at the beams in Seaspray next time you're up – they're made from teak that washed up in the bay in the nineteenth century."

"Some people still think that," Issie pointed out.

Her grandmother nodded. "Very true, my love. Anyway, the story goes that a Spanish treasure ship, *Isabella*—"

"That's the ship I'm named after!" Issie couldn't contain herself. She must have heard the story a thousand times and Jules couldn't help smiling at her excitement; it transformed her from a young woman to a wide-eyed child.

"Yes, indeed," Alice nodded. "Anyway, *Isabella* was supposed to have all kinds of treasure and when she was blown off course her captain headed to Plymouth to shelter and get the ship repaired. That was the last anyone heard of it. The story goes that Black Jack wrecked it and hid the treasure in the caves beneath the cliffs, then made his way home through the smugglers' secret passage."

"Wow," said Jules.

"It's only a story," Alice laughed.

"It might be true. There was a tunnel too," Issie insisted. "Jonny St Milton says he went through it as a boy."

"Jonny St Milton always was a fibber," Alice replied. The twist to her mouth as she spoke and the sharpness of her tone was so out of character that Jules was taken aback. Interesting. Was there history here?

"The legend goes that Black Jack was returning to the cave through the passage to collect his loot when the tunnel collapsed. Black Jack Jago was never seen again, and neither was his loot. The wreck was never found either, but they say that on a stormy night she can be seen out at sea and that Black Jack haunts the cave, guarding his ill-gotten gains."

Although she knew this was all nonsense, Jules shivered. That cave was cold and dank and shadowy. Who knew what was lurking in its dark depths? And whoever knew that Alice could spin such a good story?

"You've missed out the best bit," Issie complained. "Tell her about the proof."

Alice laughed. "It's hardly proof, sweetheart. Just a great family legend." To Jules, she added, "Although Black Jack was never seen again, a handful of gold coins were said to have mysteriously appeared in the family home on the night he vanished. Over the years most of them have been spent, but I still have one as a necklace. Or perhaps I should say that *allegedly* the necklace is made from one. Of course, it's just another tall tale. It certainly used to entertain Issie and the others when they were children, though."

Personally Jules thought it would have given her nightmares. Maybe there was something to be said for growing up on a featureless housing estate after all?

"You can call it a tall tale if you like but I totally believe it – and one day I'll prove it's true," declared Issie staunchly. "All legends have got some truth in them. Look, we're at St Wenn's Well, aren't we? That's another legend with some truth in it."

Her grandmother smiled. "Not quite as grisly as Black Jack Jago! St Wenn was a pretty peaceful woman, and I don't think she did much apart from sit by the stream and pray."

They'd reached a clearing in the woods where a small stream chuckled over pebbles, and where a moss-smothered Celtic cross marked a deeper pool of water. Although it was autumn, the leaf canopy was a vivid green here, and there was an odd stillness that Jules felt owed more to Cornwall's pagan roots than the Church of England might want to admit. Cornwall was crammed full of obscure saints, as many as sinners it seemed, and each had their own story. They tended to be linked to sites that had once been part of a much older religion.

In this particular place, little scraps of brightly coloured fabric were tied to the ash and willow trees that dipped their roots in the stream, as markers of wishes and prayers from people who had visited.

"They say that if you put your hand in the stream and make a wish here for true love then St Wenn grants it," Issie said, wide-eyed. "Everyone comes up here to wish."

Jules rolled her eyes. "Oh please!"

"You can laugh if you like but I'm having a go." Defiant, Issie crouched down and dabbled her fingers in the water. "Oh! It's cold! OK, St Wenn. Please bring me a fit man with a six pack and an enormous – wallet!"

Alice said quietly, "Do you know, I've not been here for years. I used to come here as a girl with—"

She stopped abruptly and her cheeks grew quite pink.

"Don't stop now. It's getting interesting, Granny!" Issie teased. "I take it we're not talking about Granddad? Who was it? Come on. Spill!"

But Alice wouldn't be drawn. "Have you been here before?" she asked Jules.

Jules shook her head. To be honest, she wasn't into superstition but now she was in the mossy dell she was curious about the saint who had lent her name to Polwenna Bay's church.

"She's supposed to be the aunt of St David, isn't she?"

"That's right," Alice said. "I'm not sure quite how she ended up in Cornwall, but then lots of people seem to wash up here eventually."

Issie glanced at her watch. "Make a wish then, you two. It'll be dark soon."

"I'm a bit too old for all that!" Alice objected.

"Don't be so boring. And Jules, before you protest all that religious stuff, this is a holy place."

Alice held out her arm to Issie. "You'd better help me, then: I'm not quite as agile as I was the last time I did this!"

Clutching her granddaughter tightly, Alice leaned over the stream and dipped her hand in. "And before you ask, I'm not telling you anything about who I may have used my wish for!" she called over her shoulder.

"Hope you used it on me. If somebody decent doesn't turn up soon Little Rog may start to look like my best option," grumbled Issie. "Go on, Jules, your turn."

Feeling awkward, and not wholly convinced that this was a great idea, Jules bent over the stream. There was no denying what she longed for, but she knew there was no way she should even be thinking of it, let alone wishing for it. She was utterly torn. And yet, from the moment her fingers dipped into the cold clear water, the words flowed from her soul as naturally and as freely as the stream flowed from the earth and into the sea.

She simply couldn't help it: Jules wished with all her heart for Danny.

Chapter 2

By the time the three walkers had returned to Polwenna Bay the sun was slipping below the horizon, casting a final ray of light that made the sea sparkle. Soon, though, the evening shadows would be draping themselves across the village. The sky flowered with hues of fuchsia and peony and poppy, lights began to twinkle in cottage windows, and on the chimney pots seagulls hid their heads beneath snowy wings. In the winter Polwenna Bay tucked itself up for the night early, its curtains closed against the darkness, and sent plumes of wood smoke rising into the starry skies. The fishing fleet was already in too: the chug of machinery landing the day's catch echoed up from the harbour, and voices drifted on the breeze as the men called to one another.

Jules dug her hands deeper into her pockets and shivered. Now that the sun had all but vanished the air was chilly and her breath was starting to cloud. Gradually, the sky was becoming bright with stars. A smile of a moon hung amidst them, hinting of sharp frosty weather to come. Yes, she was shivering from the cold and nothing more, Jules told herself sternly. Her goose bumps were not from Alice's tales of ghosts and wreckers, and they were certainly nothing to do with the ridiculous wish she'd made at the well.

Of course not! That was nothing but superstitious nonsense and Jules was bitterly ashamed for taking part in it. She really should have known better. Her only comfort was that nobody else had a clue what she'd wished for. She'd keep it that way too, Jules promised herself. She was busy already and in the run-up to Christmas her job was going to become even more demanding. There was the fundraising for the Christmas lights and the nativity play to organise as well. That was bound to be just as much of a nightmare in a rural parish as in an urban setting: no matter where the play, every parent thought their child should have the starring role. Then there was the carol concert and Midnight Mass too. Since this was her first Christmas as the vicar of Polwenna Bay, Jules was determined to make it memorable – in a good way, she hoped, and without a naked calendar in sight.

Yes, she'd be far too busy to spare Danny Tremaine a second's thought.

"Oh! Wow! Look at all the pumpkins lighting up the windows!" Issie's excited words snatched Jules out of her reverie. "Don't they look great? Really spooky!"

The steep lane they were descending snaked right and at once Polwenna Bay came into view, lying before them like a model village. Sure enough, in many cottage windows and porches the toothy grins of hollowed-out pumpkins grinned evilly into the twilight.

Of course. Tonight was Halloween. Jules had been so deep in refection that she'd almost forgotten about it, or at least forgotten as much as a vicar could forget All Hallows' Eve. This was always a tricky one for her; after all, Halloween was rooted in England's pagan past. Since she'd been living in Cornwall, Jules had become more aware than ever that those traditions were still very close to the surface. St Wenn's Well was just one example; the village's green man, a role played on festival days by Pete the Post decked out in face paint and foliage, was another. Then there was morris dancing, the village maypole and Padstow's famous Obby Oss – and that was before you even touched on piskies. All these things had their roots in pre-Christian times.

Where was the line drawn between some harmless trick-or-treating fun and the darker, occult ceremonies that were celebrated on the last night of October? And how did you draw that line, in a village that still insisted on celebrating May Day?

Jules wished she knew. Her solution to the Halloween conundrum had been to take an assembly at the local primary school this morning, and to make it all about hope and light. She'd suggested that if the children did go out trick-or-treating they should dress as something positive. One small girl had asked if she could dress up as Miley Cyrus. Privately, Jules had thought that sounded very scary indeed, for all the wrong reasons; Halloween or not, it wasn't *quite* how a seven-year-old should be going out on a cold October evening. Maybe a superhero, she'd suggested, or if they really did want to do something spooky, how about Harry Potter?

If the village was overrun by marauding Batmen and boy wizards this evening, she would know that the children had listened to her. Most likely her words had fallen on deaf ears, but she hoped all the little girls weren't out twerking.

"Apparently the village shop ran out of pumpkins by half nine this morning," remarked Alice. "Betty Jago said it was like a stampede in there."

"I heard that she'd doubled the prices too," said Issie. "They were cheaper in the supermarket, according to Summer."

Alice smiled at Jules. "What was I telling you about profiteering and wrecking earlier? Not a lot changes here."

"It seems not," agreed Jules.

"We're having a gathering at Seaspray," Alice continued. "It's not a Halloween party as such, just some nibbles and drinks. There won't be many of us, just family, so why don't you join us?"

Seaspray was the Tremaine family home; an old and stately whitewashed house with weathered blue shutters, it stood sentinel at the beginning of the cliff path, watching over the restless waves. Inside, it was full of scuffed furniture, faded rugs, tatty drawings, sand and odd gum boots – a true family home in every sense of the word. The Tremaine siblings still gathered there to squabble, drink tea and eat their grandmother's cakes. Some of Jules's happiest times had been spent sitting in Seaspray's kitchen, nursing a mug of tea and putting the world to rights with Danny.

Danny.

Of course. He would be there this evening, wouldn't he? Not a good idea, then, especially after this afternoon's slip of resolve.

"That's really kind, Alice, but I've got a lot on tonight," she hedged.

"Like what?" Issie asked. Her voice rang with challenge and Jules's heart sank into her wellies. She really didn't want to have to fabricate an excuse, although a night in with a glass of wine and Sky TV was on the cards.

"Just catching up on some stuff," she shrugged.

"Jules is busy with church business," Alice said gently. Her brown eyes met Jules's, and for a heart-lurching moment Jules saw such sympathy there that she was terrified Alice might have guessed the real reason she'd been staying away. But that couldn't be possible, not when she'd worked so hard to keep her feelings hidden.

"That's total bollocks," scoffed Issie. "Jules could leave all that for one night if she wanted to. And she bloody well should, because she's in her early thirties, not her nineties." To Jules, she added, "Chillax, Vic. We're not having a Black Mass, you know, just a glass of wine and some sausage rolls."

"Oh, Issie, honestly," said Alice, pulling an exasperated face. But Jules couldn't help laughing. Sometimes she needed the younger girl's irreverence to make her see the lighter side of life.

"How can I say no to sausage rolls?" she said. "OK, count me in. I'll only get pestered like mad for trick or treat otherwise, won't I?"

"Not a problem at Seaspray," Alice assured her. "The children are all far too lazy to climb all the way up to our front door. If they do there's never any trouble, they're all very good here. Most of them have their parents with them too. It's all harmless fun."

"I promise the closest thing you'll get to Halloween tonight is the wicked old witch who lives in *there*," Issie whispered to Jules, gesturing at a pretty cottage that overlooked the village green. "I'd bet you anything, Poison Ivy has a cauldron rather than a cooker. She's probably boiling up some children right now."

Issie was referring to Ivy Lawrence, one of Jules's most trying parishioners and known in Polwenna Bay as Poison Ivy. She'd only lived in the village since the summer but had already made her presence felt, complaining about children playing noisily on the green, calling the council when the live music from The Ship was too loud and refusing point-blank to replant the window boxes that had previously been a feature of her cottage (a matter that had cost Polwenna Bay a winning place in the Blooming Cornwall competition). With a face that could sour milk at twenty paces and a negative word for everyone, Ivy was pretty difficult to love – and Jules, despite praying for tolerance, was certainly struggling.

"She must be very unhappy to be that mean," was all Jules could come up with in her defence. Alas, Ivy's behaviour *was* poisonous and justifying it was far from easy, even for a vicar.

"Nobody could possibly be that unhappy," countered Issie. She shook her head. "Did you know that she even says the fishermen are making too much noise on the quay in the morning? According to Nick she's going to speak to the council about it. Unhappy, my arse! She's just a nasty old bag!"

Jules wasn't surprised; this sounded exactly like the kind of petty thing Ivy would do. But as for not being unhappy? She didn't agree with Issie on this. And neither did Jules think that Ivy was as old as she appeared, even if bitterness had twisted her face into a scowl and set her mouth in a permanent expression of disapproval. Her age and history were enigmas, however. Apparently she had sold the big family home in Falmouth and moved to the village for a quieter life – something that her behaviour was going to make very difficult. There were rumours that she was very wealthy although the dark and gloomy look of her cottage suggested a pensioner living on a tight budget. Jules suspected that the truth was somewhere in the middle but what she did know for sure was that there was more to Ivy than met the eye. She was at a loss as to what this could be and guessed that, as with all her flock, only time would tell.

"Isabella Tremaine, I didn't bring you up to be rude about your elders," Alice said firmly. "No matter what you think of Mrs Lawrence, I want you to show her some manners and respect next time you see her, because that's how you were raised. Never let it be said that the Tremaines behave badly."

Issie looked as though she was on the brink of retorting when, right on cue, Ivy appeared at her gateway. Brows drawn together in her habitual scowl and looking as disagreeable as always, she waved across the street at Jules.

"Reverend! Come here a moment, will you? I need some help."

"Manners and respect," muttered Issie. "Keep walking, Jules. Pretend you can't hear her."

But Jules couldn't do that. For all her faults, Ivy was still one of her parishioners, and Jules could no more walk past her now than she could tell herself that it was fine to let Danny Tremaine give up on his marriage. Sighing inwardly, she pasted a smile onto her face and waved back.

"Good evening, Ivy."

"It's not good at all," snapped the older woman, her thin lips pursed and her hands on her hips. "Young hoodlums have been banging on my door demanding sweets. I've a good mind to call the police!"

"There's no need to worry. That will only be the youngsters trick-or-treating. I'd just have a bowl of sweets by the door, and when they knock you can give them a few. They won't do any harm, I promise," Alice explained, but her attempts at reassurance fell on deaf ears and Ivy looked at her as though she was insane.

"I'll give them trick or treat, all right. How dare they trespass on my property and have the nerve to demand sweets? Over my dead body."

"The village children are very good natured and they won't do anything. Please don't be worried about trick-or-treating here," Alice began, but Ivy wasn't listening. She was far too busy complaining and threatening. Issie, catching Jules's eye, pulled a face.

"See?" she mouthed. "Horrible old bag."

Jules ignored her friend. Having lived and worked in big cities she understood only too well just how worrying pensioners found Halloween pranks. It could be frightening for them and she was prepared to do whatever she could to reassure the older woman.

"How can I help, Ivy? Do you want me to tell everyone to leave your house out?"

Ivy snorted. "It's a bit late for all that. Anyway, that's not what I need you for. When I came out to give those brats a piece of my mind the front door slammed behind me and now I'm locked out. I need you to help me get back inside."

Jules glanced at the door. It was solid wood with some serious-looking security fittings. The power of prayer was strong but she wasn't sure it could overcome a deadlock.

"I think you need a locksmith then, Ivy, not a vicar," Alice said gently. "Why don't you come up to Seaspray for a cup of tea while we call one out? It's getting cold and you haven't got a coat. I could even send one of my grandsons to see if they could help? Jake might be able to get the door open."

"I haven't got time for all that!" snapped Ivy. "I've left a saucepan on and the fire's going too. There's an open window around the back." She turned back to Jules and demanded, "Can't you just climb through it?"

Ivy's cottage had to be two hundred years old at least and the windows were pretty narrow. And then there was the small matter of the cottage backing right onto the River Wenn.

Jules wasn't in the habit of carrying a ladder around, either.

"She's a vicar, not Spiderman," Issie said, earning herself a look from Ivy that would have laid a more delicate personality out flat on the lane.

"Roger Pollard left a ladder round the side of my house when he was mending next door's roof. Their loose tiles blew into my garden and they're lucky I wasn't hurt. I had my solicitor onto them straight away, let me tell you!" Ivy said. "I must have told Pollard to move it fifty times but, like everyone else around here, he works at a snail's pace. Anyway, you can use that to get in."

Ivy wasn't asking Jules: she was telling her. Now one bony hand was clamped round Jules's wrist and Ivy was towing her down the narrow path to the back of the cottage. The path was shadowy and smelt of damp; barely beyond it the river rushed by, muddy and swollen by the rains of the previous night's storm. Sure enough, though, the top window of the cottage was wide open.

Jules gulped. She didn't like heights at the best of times. Scaling the cottage walls on the Pollards' dodgy ladder wasn't at the top of her list of fun things to do. In fact it wasn't even on her list.

"Well, go on then," snapped Ivy as Jules dithered, torn between her duty to help and her terror of heights. "My saucepan will catch fire at this rate."

"They always did burn witches," murmured Issie. She stepped forward and, grabbing one end of the ladder, began to drag it towards the back of Ivy's cottage. "Come on then. Better get this over with. Then we can go home and party."

Together Issie and Jules manhandled the ladder along the path before leaning it against the wall. The gap between the bottom rung and the rushing river was a matter of inches. One false move and Jules would tumble into the cold, brown water.

"Jules, you don't need to do this," Alice said, looking worried.

"Yes she does. How else will I get in?" barked Ivy. "Anyway, she's the vicar. It's her job to help me."

Jules swallowed back the huge lump of fear that was starting to block her throat. Now that the ladder was leaning against the whitewashed wall it seemed ever so precarious. The top of that wall looked higher than Everest.

"I'll go up if you like," offered Issie, catching sight of Jules's pale face.

Jules shook her head. She'd been asked do this. She had to do this because Ivy was right: it was her job to help her flock. Surely now that Jules was in her thirties she ought to be over her silly fear of heights?

"I don't care who goes up," Ivy snapped. "Just hurry up. I'm getting cold!"

Jules placed her feet on the bottom rung, first one and then the other. Her palms were clammy and her fingers were starting to tingle. Slowly, painfully, she climbed up, one rung at a time, the blood whooshing in her ears and her heart thudding. *Just don't look down*, she told herself. *Don't look down, don't look—*

Oh! Too late! She'd looked down and it was such a long way that her vision turned black around the edges and her head swam. Below her, Ivy, Alice and Issie's faces were just three pale and blurry ovals in a world that was growing ever darker. Jules clung to the ladder with all her might; her fingers tightened on the uprights in such a vice-like grip that she didn't think she'd ever loosen them.

"Jules!" Alice cried. "Are you all right up there, love?"

Jules couldn't answer. Her mouth had gone dry and, besides, every last bit of concentration she had was being consumed by the effort of clinging on and not passing out. The open window was just ahead of her but, now that she was closer, Jules realised there no way she could possibly fit through it. Even if she remained up here starving for a month, she'd still be too big. Her heartbeat accelerated. If she couldn't squeeze through the window and she couldn't move a muscle to get back down the ladder either, then she was stuck.

How on earth was she going to get down? The world began to spin around her, with the ladder as its axis.

"Jules!" Alice shouted.

"Hurry up!" cried Ivy. "My saucepan!"

"Bugger your saucepan," Jules heard Issie say. "Can't you see she's stuck?"

Jules tried to speak but the only noise she made was a strangled gasp. The sensation in her hands had changed from tingling to numbness and she felt faint. She couldn't faint. She'd fall off the ladder. How was she going to get down? Polwenna Bay didn't have a fire brigade to execute a Trumpton-style rescue and Superman was too busy trick-or-treating to help. Time seemed to run slow, the panicky conversation of the trio below rising and falling in the breeze and washing over her in a meaningless tide of sound until Jules wasn't sure how long she'd been up the ladder. It could have been five minutes or five hours. All she could do was cling on, as tightly as any limpet might cling to the rocks of the bay.

Help me Lord, she prayed.

Then a voice called up to her and it really was all she could do not to pass out. Surely not?

"Hold on Jules. I'm coming!"

It was Danny, and Jules could have wept with relief. It didn't matter anymore that she was supposed to be giving him a wide berth or that the atmosphere between them had been frostier than tonight's weather: all that counted was that he was her dear friend and she trusted him more than anyone else.

"You can't possibly climb up there," she heard Alice gasp. "You've only got one arm."

"One's better than none, Gran," Danny said mildly. "I can climb one-handed, anyway. How do you think we manage on manoeuvres carrying weapons? It's all in my amazing core strength. Watch and marvel."

"I can't watch," Alice wailed. "Hold the ladder for your brother, Issie, and let me know when he's at the top."

The ladder jolted and Jules inhaled sharply. Her fingers were claws now and her knuckles looked a very odd green through her white flesh. All the blood was no doubt sloshing round her head. She'd not felt this odd since the Pollards had insisted she sample their home brew.

"It's fine, Jules. It's just me on the first rung." This was followed by a couple more wobbles. "That's the second and the third. There's the fourth. You're doing really well."

Jules couldn't reply. It was taking every ounce of strength she possessed not to tumble to the ground. She was growing resigned to the fact that she might well spend the rest of her life stuck on a ladder propped against Poison Ivy's cottage. She'd be a phenomenon, a bit like one of those mystics from the Middle Ages who'd gloried God by sitting on the top of a pole for years. Admittedly Jules had never really understood the point of this before, but now she totally got it – they'd been stuck.

"So, what's a nice girl like you doing in a place like this?"

Danny was on the rung below her, his left arm brushing past her waist to hold the side rail. Although he wasn't holding her, Jules felt safe. Danny always made her feel safe.

"Don't answer that," he continued. "You've taken up a shady career as a burglar to raise money for St Wenn's, haven't you? Was the naked calendar not risky enough for you?"

Jules couldn't help laughing.

"That's better," said Danny, sounding relieved. "Just breathe as steadily and as normally as you can for a moment. In and out. In and out."

Jules did so and, to her amazement, her heartbeat started to slow. "Sorry, Danny," she whispered. "I don't know what happened. I feel so stupid. I've never liked heights, but nothing like this has ever happened to me."

"You had a panic attack," Danny explained. "And I think you've been incredibly brave to even try to help. Just breathe a bit more for me, OK? There's no race."

Jules nodded. Although she couldn't see him she knew that the uninjured part of his face would be etched with concern.

"How did you know I was up here? Did you walk past?"

"Err, not quite," said Danny. "Jules, you've been stuck up here for over twenty minutes. Issie and Gran are frantic. They phoned me thinking that my hostage-rescue negotiation skills might come in handy. I thought that Poison Ivy had you gagged and bound in there. It's quite a relief to see you up a ladder and know she's not joined the militant wing of the WI!"

Over twenty minutes? Jules was staggered. "What about Ivy's pot?"

"Sod Ivy and her pot. It's you I'm here for," Danny told her, "and it's all going to be fine. Now, we're going to make our way down really slowly, one rung at a time. Three points of contact at all times, OK? Which is going to be far easier for you than for me. I can't hold you, I'm afraid, but I can talk you down. Happy with that?"

Happy wasn't quite the adjective Jules had in mind but she nodded again.

"Great. Right then: left foot down, down, down. Perfect! Now right foot. Hey, have you lost more weight? Your bum looks much smaller."

"You're not supposed to be looking at my bum!" Jules said, shocked out of her fear.

"Says who? Anyway, can't help it. I'm a guy and genetically programmed to look at sexy backsides. Left foot again. Now the right. Good girl, that's it. Yep, all that walking has definitely toned and firmed you in all the right places. Those jeans are great. Looking hot, Rev!"

Jules was so busy blushing that she hardly noticed they'd descended three rungs now.

"Close your eyes," she told him.

"You want me to descend a ladder one-handed and with my eyes closed? What do you think this is? The circus? Yes, right foot there. Brilliant! You're doing well."

"I just don't think you should be looking at me from this angle," Jules said primly.

He laughed. "So what angle would you like me to look at you from? I'm open to all suggestions. Left foot, lower, lower! Brilliant! You've got it."

At the thought of Danny looking at her from above, his face only inches from her own and his lips just a kiss away, Jules almost had a very different kind of panic attack. One more accurately described as a surge of desire. Even the ends of her hair were blushing now.

"Right foot a little lower. Well done. We can slow down if you like? Make my fun last?"

Sure enough, Jules found that she was able to negotiate her way down more easily with Danny's cheeky quips helping to calm her nerves. By the time her feet touched the ground, her pulse was almost steady again and the horrible whirling sensation had passed.

"The eagle has landed!" cried Danny, pulling her against his chest and holding her close. "Well done, Jules! You were so brave. I'm very proud of you."

"Brave?" scoffed Ivy. "She was stuck there for ages. My pan's bound to have boiled dry by now and I'm freezing cold. I've probably caught a chill."

Jules hung her head. "Sorry, Ivy. I'm scared of heights. I always have been."

"Why on earth anyone would climb up a ladder when they're scared of heights is beyond me," muttered the older woman.

Danny spun around and glowered at her. "Just for once, why don't you try being grateful? Jules risked her neck for you, although I have no idea why, seeing as you seem to make it your mission in life to be as mean to everyone as possible. Why can't you just be nice?"

Ivy snorted rudely. "In my experience nice doesn't get you very far."

"It'll get you a lot further in this village than being unpleasant," Alice Tremaine said quietly – and Ivy stared at her in surprise, because Alice usually kept her own counsel. "People won't keep trying to help forever, you know. We're generally a pretty easy-going bunch here in

Polwenna, but people only have so much patience with rudeness and ingratitude."

"How dare you call me rude and ungrateful!" Ivy gasped, her mouth pursing like a cat's backside.

"Because it's true, Ivy, and because I care," Alice said wearily. "I don't know what's happened to you in the past that's made you so bitter, but I do know that if you carry on like this then you really will be alone. Even vicars can only have so much patience. Whatever it is with you, Jules was only trying to help. Don't take it out on her – or Issie, or even me for that matter. We only tried to help but, believe you me, we'll think twice about doing that again."

Ivy's mouth was wide open now. She looked like something Nick Tremaine would find in a trawl net.

Laying her hand on Danny's arm, Alice added, "Come on, love, don't get yourself worked up."

Danny was teetering on the brink of erupting, Jules could see that. He'd worked so hard to control his anger and there was no way she could bear an old boot like Ivy spoiling things.

"It's fine, Danny," Jules said.

Danny looked as though he wanted to point out that Ivy's behaviour was far from fine, and for a few tense moments he visibly struggled before exhaling slowly and nodding.

"You're both right. It isn't worth it. I should know that much. You might win a battle but unless you're winning hearts and minds you'll never win the war." To Ivy he added, "Mrs Lawrence, I still think the least you owe Jules is a thank you, but if you can't even manage that then just do us all a favour and keep out of my way. I'm 'mentally unstable', as you know. Or at least, my son overheard you saying that about me in the village shop. So I guess you realise that I could explode at any moment if I'm pushed!"

"Like the hulk! Grr!" added Issie, and Ivy stepped back hastily, muttering something that sounded suspiciously like an apology. She looked very pale and, in spite of Ivy's behaviour Jules couldn't help feeling a little sorry for her. There was always more to a story than met the eye. Nobody would choose to be as sour as Ivy.

"Thanks for rescuing me, Danny," said Jules. Her legs felt like boiled wool and she sagged against him. It was wonderful being held by him and for a moment she allowed herself to luxuriate in the comfort of his closeness.

"You don't need to thank me. You've saved my neck more times than you know." Danny said softly, into the top of her head. Then Alice was pushing him out of the way, hugging Jules and telling her off for being reckless. In the meantime Issie had scampered up the ladder and shot through the window with embarrassing ease.

"Don't be ashamed. She was Polwenna School's gymnastics champion when she was eleven," Dan explained, seeing Jules's stricken face. "She wanted to join the circus too."

"I should have just let her go up instead." Jules felt so stupid. "What was I thinking? I'm such an idiot."

"You were thinking about helping Ivy and not risking anyone else. That makes you one of the bravest people I know," Danny said firmly. "You'd have made a great army commander. Leading by example for the good of your men is what it's all about. Even if it doesn't always work out so well." He touched his right shoulder and shrugged. "If you're an idiot, then so am I."

"You're a hero!" Jules said hotly. She'd not hear anything else.

"Then you're one too," Danny countered. "OK?"

Jules was going to argue the point (after all, getting stuck up a ladder wasn't really on a par with fighting for your country in a war zone), when Issie reappeared to announce that the door was unlocked and the pan had been removed from the stove. Without even so much as a thank you, Ivy turned her back on them all and stomped back towards her front door, muttering under her breath and looking as though she only needed a broomstick and a pointy hat to join in with the Halloween revellers marauding through the village.

"You're welcome!" Issie called after her, and for once even Alice didn't remonstrate about manners.

"I think after this we all need to go to Seaspray and have a drink," was all she said. "Halloween or not, Jules, you're coming too. No arguments."

And Jules, too drained now that the adrenalin had subsided, simply nodded. A drink was exactly what she needed – to get her over the shock of the ladder episode and the even bigger shock that Danny Tremaine was back in her life scarcely two hours after she'd wished for him.

St Wenn's Well, it seemed, had a magic all of its own.

Chapter 3

An hour later and curled up on the sofa beside the Aga with a mug of tomato soup in her chilly hands, Jules was starting to feel more human. The walk through the village and back up the cliff path to Seaspray had passed in a blur of subsiding adrenalin and increasing embarrassment. Whatever had she been thinking, volunteering to climb up the ladder in the first place? She'd never liked heights. She even felt light-headed sometimes looking out of the vicarage window at the village falling away below. She must have been crazy to risk her safety like that. For the first time Jules understood what she'd been taught when she was a curate: sometimes it was in everyone's best interests for a vicar to set limits on what she was prepared to do for her parishioners. Only her sense of duty to Ivy had driven Jules up that ladder. Nothing else could have made her do it, not even if there had been a family-sized bar of Dairy Milk at the top held aloft by a naked George Clooney!

Jules had been even more embarrassed to learn that Issie had also climbed up behind her in an attempt to coax her down. She'd been so frozen by terror that she hadn't even registered this, and now she was mortified. What a lot of trouble she'd caused by wanting to help and not thinking things through first. A wise person had once told Jules that a vicar must always consider the consequences of her actions, but it seemed that this was still something she needed to work on. First of all there had been the naked calendar fiasco, then almost kissing Danny on the morning of his sister's wedding and now shooting up a ladder when she had acrophobia. It wasn't a great track record.

She'd pray hard about it, Jules decided. Yes, she'd ask for some help to be less impulsive.

OK then. A lot of help.

The stinging humiliation had been eased somewhat by having Danny's arm around her shoulder (although it now troubled her that she'd enjoyed his embrace so much) and Alice's sweet reassurances that being stuck up a ladder for twenty-five minutes really wasn't such a big deal. Once she was inside Seaspray, Jules began to feel better still. Alice's kitchen was so warm and welcoming, with its pools of cosy light and the soft hissing of the kettle from the hotplate amid the family's chatter. The mouth-watering aromas of home-made soup, sausages and jacket potatoes cooking in the oven certainly had restorative powers too.

"How are you feeling?" Danny asked. He was crouched down beside Jules, his hand resting lightly on her knee, and looking concerned. "You're still really pale. Maybe some sugary tea would be better than soup? Sugar's good for shock."

In Jules's experience sugar was good for most things, from celebration to feeling fed up. She was just about to agree, when a knock at the front door sent the family's Jack Russell into a fit of barking.

"That'll be the trick-or-treaters," remarked Alice from her seat at the kitchen table. Her laptop was open in front of her and, with her eyes still fixed on the screen, she added, "I'm just in the middle of something here. Can one of you get the door, please? There's a bowl of sweets in the hall ready for them. Only a few, mind, or we'll run out. Mo! Shut your dog in the boot room, for heaven's sake! I can't concentrate."

Danny caught Jules's eye.

"Told you," he whispered. "She's glued to that computer. It has to be online gambling."

Jules laughed but Danny pulled a face.

"I'm not kidding. Where do you think Pa gets it from?"

Mo Tremaine grabbed her dog's collar and dragged the animal, still barking and straining to get to the door, into the boot room. "Shush, Cracker. It's only trick-or-treaters! Shush, I said! Ashley, answer the bloody door before we're all deafened."

Mo's dark-haired husband raised an eyebrow. "Seriously? If I answer they'll run a mile, surely? Frankenstein's-monster property developer with the scar on his head and bald patch coming to get them? Arms outstretched as he tries to grab their parents' cottages? "

Ashley had undergone major surgery only weeks before, and part of his scalp was still shaven and criss-crossed with pink scars. With his stern, hawk-like profile and intense glittering eyes he was strikingly handsome. Shaven head and scars or not, he was hardly in the league of Frankenstein's monster. Still, Ashley did have a fearsome reputation in Polwenna Bay. Although it had been softened a little by his recent marriage to Mo, it might well send the youngsters scuttling back into the village.

"Stay put, Ashley. I'll get it," offered Issie, leaping to her feet and heading into the hall in a blur of braids and velvet.

"Don't you dare eat those sweets, Issie Tremaine! They're for the children," her grandmother called after her.

"You know she will. She always does," Mo grinned, and Alice laughed.

"Of course I do. Why do you think I stocked up with extras?"

Their family banter washed over Jules like a tide. The Tremaines were a noisy bunch, and were sometimes tricky and determined – but they were loyal to a fault, loved one another fiercely and always made her feel welcome. As she drank her soup she tuned in and out of the rise and fall of their chatter, broken now and again by more bouts of frenzied barking from the captive Cracker when there was another knock at the door. Family members flowed in and out of the kitchen, helping themselves to sausages and soup, and teasing one another. But throughout all of this Jules was so acutely aware of Danny that she could hardly concentrate on anything else.

How was it possible, Jules wondered, that one person could become the sunshine of your entire world? That as hard as you tried you just couldn't help longing to turn your face towards their warmth? Even when she wasn't looking at him she knew exactly where Danny was. Her ears seemed to be perfectly attuned to his steady voice, rich and deep as the seams of copper that ran beneath the Cornish landscape. She could picture just how his head would tilt as he listened carefully to Jake, knew that his brow would crinkle thoughtfully as he considered his reply, and saw the way he ran his hand over his cropped hair as he began to speak. Even the hand was etched into her mind's eye, large and strong, the back sprinkled with golden hair, the fingers square with short nails that had perfect half-moon cuticles.

She'd memorised his hand? That was ridiculous. *She* was ridiculous.

Jules bit into a piece of jacket potato, hoping that the hot buttery flesh would jolt her out of these thoughts, but instead managing to scald her tongue. Nothing, it seemed, was going to help her get over this foolish crush. She'd tried praying. She'd applied logic. She'd avoided him. Now she was even self-harming with steaming-hot food, but all to no avail. She was still totally and utterly in love with him.

The tears that sprang into her eyes weren't just from the scalding potato.

"Do you want some water?" Danny was at her side holding out a glass. "Those potatoes are so hot that you need an asbestos mouth to eat them."

Jules glugged a few mouthfuls down gratefully, wishing that her heart could be dealt with as easily as her burned tongue. While she drank he sat down beside her, his lean body sinking easily into the saggy cushions and his left arm resting on the back of the sofa just inches away from her shoulders.

"You've been avoiding me," he said quietly, "Don't answer, Jules. You don't need to. We both know it's the truth. I've hardly seen you since that morning we walked up to Fernside."

Jules stared miserably down at the glass of water. "Danny, I—"

"It's OK, I don't need an explanation." Danny's voice was low and steady. "I'm not an idiot, Jules. I know how these things work. I understand you're the vicar, and I totally respect that it's your job and your calling – of course I do. I also know when a woman is telling me one thing with her voice but another altogether with her heart. You wanted me to kiss you that morning. We both know that."

She turned her head and the intensity in his good eye took her breath away. His gaze was full of the same fire she'd seen there back in September when they'd walked hand in hand through the russet woodland and he'd made a move to kiss her. For a moment Jules had almost given in to the longing, had nearly let his mouth rest on hers, before her senses had kicked in and she'd stepped away.

"Danny, it doesn't matter what I want," she said gently. "I told you then that nothing can ever come of it."

Danny shook his head. "I think you're wrong, Jules. I think there's something between us that's special and wonderful and rare, and I'm not prepared to give up on it. You can tell me about my wife and my marriage and my vows until you're blue in the face, but none of that matters. Tara and I are over. We've been over for a long time."

"Your injuries must have been tough on her, on you both—" Jules began, but Danny wasn't prepared to listen.

"Don't you dare try and go into vicar mode on me! You don't know the half of it. We were over long before the Taliban decided it was their turn to have a pop. Christ, even they couldn't do me as much damage as bloody Tara."

Frustration was coming from Danny in such waves that the fishing boats at sea were probably rocking like crazy.

"We're friends, you and I – or at least I thought we were," he said bleakly.

"Of course we're friends," Jules protested.

"Friends don't hide from each other or run away when life gets tricky."

"I was trying to do the right thing." She was still trying but it was so hard, especially when he was this close and offering her everything she'd secretly dreamed of.

"You always do the right thing," Danny said wearily. "That's the problem."

Jules wasn't so sure. Wishing for another woman's husband at St Wenn's Well probably hadn't been the right thing to do.

"You're married," she said woodenly. "I care about your marriage."

He sighed in exasperation. "I know you do. You care about so many things, Jules, and I love that about you. But my marriage is over. There's no resurrecting it. Life isn't black and white. Can't you just trust me on this one? What about what's right for us?"

Jules was dangerously close to saying that she did trust him and throwing all caution to the wind, when Alice slammed her hand on the kitchen table. Her usually gentle face was taut with anger.

"Who's been booking flights to the USA and using the household account?"

"God, you almost gave me a heart attack," Issie gasped, her hand pressed theatrically to her chest.

"I'll give whoever it was more than a heart attack," her grandmother promised grimly. "Well? Who was it?"

There was silence while Alice glowered at her family.

"Well? It must be one of you. Nobody else knows the banking passwords."

"Don't look at me," grumbled Issie, looking wounded. "Bet it was Zak. He's always flying off somewhere."

"Or Symon?" suggested Nick. "Perhaps he has some business there? Or maybe it's a mistake?"

With shaking hands, Alice shut the laptop. "Zak and Symon have their own business accounts, though. And this doesn't look much like an error to me. The transaction was made this morning. I've checked the account twice, and over a thousand pounds has gone to British Airways. It can only be one of the family."

"Maybe the account's been hacked?" Jimmy Tremaine offered quickly. "Personal details get hacked all the time, don't they?"

His mother fixed him with a knowing look.

"Do they, Jim? How very convenient."

"And what's that supposed to mean exactly, Ma?" demanded Jimmy Tremaine. The tall story he'd been telling Summer about how he'd ridden a horse from Paris to Istanbul had halted mid-canter and he was looking unusually flustered.

"Shall I go?" Jules offered, awkward at finding herself flung into the midst of a Tremaine family crisis. She didn't know Dan's father particularly well but she'd picked up enough from Alice and other family members to know that he might be charming and a good raconteur but was also totally feckless. Jake was driven to distraction by his father using the boatyard like his own personal playground, and Alice had often hinted that she was considering whether or not she trusted him to manage the property when she was gone. He was fun and good-natured and his family loved him dearly, but Jimmy drove them crazy.

It was no secret who Issie and Zak took after...

"No, no need to leave. There's nothing here we wouldn't say to you," Danny said to Jules. He squeezed her shoulder and her heart did a forward roll at the heat of his fingers through her shirt. "Besides, you're practically one of the family."

Ashley winked at Jules. "Careful, Vicar. I'm not sure that's always such a good thing!"

Mo whacked him with a dog-eared copy of *Horse & Hound*. "Too late now, Carstairs. Unless you want me to divorce you and take half of your evil empire?"

"If you'll put on a leather Princess Leia style bikini and wear your hair in Chelsea buns for me I'll gladly give you all of my evil empire," Ashley drawled. There was a gleam in his eye as he grinned at his wife, and Jules could almost see the electricity crackle between them. "Hmm, know what, Red? That would actually be worth losing all my fortune to see!"

Issie made a puking gesture while Nick rolled his eyes and Danny laughed – but even Ashley's joking couldn't ease the atmosphere completely. Alice was still scowling at the laptop and Jimmy couldn't have looked guiltier if he'd sauntered through the kitchen in full burglar costume with a bag marked "swag" over his shoulder.

"So what's the problem, Ma?" he asked.

Alice sighed. "You know exactly *what*, Jimmy Tremaine. Small withdrawals here and there. Not usually enough to make too much of a difference, and I never normally say anything – but do you really think I don't notice? I may be old but I haven't gone gaga yet, you know! I can still cope with basic mathematics."

Jake stepped forward and laid a calming hand on Alice's shaking one. "Let's take it one step at a time, Gran. Nick's right: it's probably a mistake. If you show me the details we can probably trace who made the transfer."

"Oh, it's no mistake. Is it, Jim?" Her mouth set in a thin line, Alice looked across the table at her son.

Jimmy Tremaine pulled a wounded face. "I love the way you assume I'm to blame. I'm not the only person in this room who can access that account." His eyes slid from one child to another. "Am I? It could be anyone here."

"Did you take it, Dad?" Jake asked quietly. His words were spoken calmly but a muscle ticked in his cheek, indicating just how angry he was. To his grandmother he added, "How much has gone in total?"

"Nearly fifteen hundred pounds," Alice whispered. She looked utterly defeated.

Jake paled. "Fifteen hundred? The business can't replace that amount. We've a massive diesel bill to pay and the winch hydraulics need fixing."

Summer and Mo exchanged worried looks. Ashley was probably itching to reach for his chequebook, thought Jules, but he would know by now how proud the Tremaines were. According to Alice, his previous offers to help the business out had been rejected very swiftly. Summer's finances had been practically wiped out as a result of replacing her family's trawler and taking her ex to court, but she too had offered what little she did have left. Danny had mentioned that this gesture had caused the only row he'd ever witnessed between Summer and Jake. The family would find a solution without accepting handouts, Jake had insisted. That was the Tremaine way. Quite what this solution could possibly be, Jules didn't know. Holiday cottages and boats only paid dividends in the summer. The winter months were lean for everyone in a village that depended on seasonal trade, and the Tremaines were no exception.

Danny had risen to his feet now. "Dad, if you did take it just say so, for Christ's sake, and save us the arse-ache of calling the bank."

"OK, so I took it. What's the big deal? It's my money too." Jimmy glared at Alice, his grey ponytail bobbing in outrage. "So what if I have some now and then? The last time I looked I was the head of this family. It's technically my money anyway."

"It's money to pay the bills!" Alice cried despairingly. She looked close to tears. "Jimmy, isn't it bad enough that you use the business like your own personal cash flow? Have you started raiding the bills account now? What's next? Do you want to sell Seaspray? Or have you equity-released it all and not told us?"

"It's one solution," Jimmy shrugged.

"Dad, you can't sell Seaspray!" Issie wailed. "It's our home."

Jimmy blew her a kiss. "Of course I won't, baby girl. That was a joke. Don't worry about a thing. Granny's just making a fuss."

"A fuss?" Jake echoed in disbelief. "You call our being twenty grand in hock to the bank already *a fuss*?"

Jules fought the urge to clap her hands over her ears. Oblivious to her presence, the family were now happily airing all their dirty laundry, and doing some ironing and folding to boot. Resentments, old wrongs and grudges were flying everywhere. There were some things a vicar really didn't need to know about her flock.

"I've booked a holiday," Jimmy was now explaining, an aggrieved note in his voice. "I've worked bloody hard all summer."

This was news to everybody in the room. Although he was supposed to run the family's marina business with Jake, on most days Jimmy was more likely to be found in The Ship chatting to tourists than doing anything useful at Tremaine Marine.

"I deserve a holiday, don't I, Vicar?" Jimmy turned to Jules now, his eyes wide and guileless.

"Don't you dare try and drag Jules into this!" Danny thundered.

"Oh chill out, son," Jim said airily. Turning to his mother he continued, "I've booked a trip to California. So shoot me, Ma. There's some stuff I have to deal with and I need a bit of sun. Don't look so frightened. I'm not off to Vegas to marry a showgirl." He winked at Jules. "If I did want to marry one, I'd bring her back here and boost the numbers for the church, Rev, so don't worry. We'd make Mo and Ashley's bash look tiny!"

In spite of everything, Jules's lips twitched. Jimmy's irreverence was part of his charm. It was also what made him so frustrating to deal with. Even Jake laughed, although it was a very despairing sound.

"California! Cool!" Issie's eyes were wide. "Can I come too? Please?"

"Better pawn the silver first," Nick suggested.

"If Dad hasn't already," Mo muttered, glowering at her father, who merely shrugged.

"I loved being out in San Francisco back in the nineties," he continued, sensing that some of his audience were becoming ever so slightly less antagonistic. "After Penny died, only going out there saved me, you know? I wasn't myself when I lost your mum."

Danny exhaled impatiently. "None of us were. We lost our mum, and then our dad pushed off to 'find himself'. It was really considerate. None of us are at all fucked up by it, Dad. I'd never do that to Morgan and I'll never understand how you could do it us. Still, at least you 'found yourself', eh?"

"We're all different, son," said Jimmy sagely. "And I'm sorry if you still find what I did hard to accept, but I was grieving and I needed to come to terms with things my own way."

"In a Californian hippy commune?" Danny scoffed. "Smoking dope and dropping out?"

His father laughed. "It wasn't the sixties, Dan, although truth be told there was a bit of weed now and again. I just fixed farm equipment and helped out. It was a healing time."

"It sounds good to me." Suddenly Issie couldn't see anything wrong with blowing the month's bills money on a trip to San Francisco. "Please, Dad, can I come? I'd love to go with you."

"Another time, doll," promised her father. "I've got business this trip."

Jake's eyebrows leapt into his thick blond fringe. "Business? Come on, Dad, don't take us for idiots. You'll drink whiskey and smoke too much. What *business* could you possibly have out there?"

"I can't tell you that, son, but it's important and you'll just have to trust me on this one."

Danny and Jake glanced at one another. It was clear that they didn't trust their father as far as they could throw him; even that short distance would be pushing it.

"Jim, we really can't afford that kind of expense," Alice said wearily. "You'll have to cancel the ticket and get a refund."

Jimmy, busy pulling his ponytail out of its rubber band and running his hands through his grey locks, frowned. "I can't do that, Ma. The tickets are non-refundable. If I don't fly then I've lost the money. I'll have to go, with or without your blessing."

Alice closed her eyes in despair. "Where did I go wrong with you? What don't you understand about paying bills?"

"Can't Summer help with all that?" Jimmy asked Jake hopefully. "She's got loads of money surely?"

Jake's jaw clenched. "It's not my girlfriend's job to pay this family's bills."

"I'm happy help out," Ashley offered hesitantly. He was holding Mo tightly and his chin rested on her bright red curls. Everything about his body language said that he would protect her from all this nonsense no matter what it took.

"You'll do no such thing and neither will Summer," Alice said hotly. "This is a family matter and we'll handle it as a family."

"Ashley's part of our family now, remember?" Mo pointed out, waving her left hand at her grandmother. Her wedding ring sparkled as she did so.

"He's not a Tremaine though," Danny said. "No disrespect, Ash. We appreciate the offer but this is our business and we'll sort it ourselves. That's the Tremaine way."

Ashley nodded. "I understand. I'd feel exactly the same – but the offer's always there if you change your minds. You're Mo's family and there's nothing I won't do for Mo."

"Are you lot mental?" Issie said, looking from Danny to Jake in disbelief. "Ashley's bloody loaded. Why can't he help us?"

"Because we have our family pride," Alice told her staunchly, "although your father's doing his best to destroy that. And besides, it isn't Ashley's job to bail us out of financial trouble."

There was another knock on the door, followed by more furious barking.

"I'll go," said Jules quickly, glad of a pretext for stepping away from the argument. She'd make her excuses and slip away once she'd answered the door, she decided. She could always plead urgent sermon-writing or a prayer meeting. Nobody tended to argue with those.

Leaving the family deep in discussion, Jules made her way to the front door, pausing only to scoop up the entire bag of mini Mars bars from the hall table. It was a cold and murky night and any child who'd made the effort to climb all the way up to Seaspray deserved a good haul.

"Coming," she called cheerily, as she fiddled with the latch and gave the heavy door a good hard shove. "Give me a minute: the door's stuck! Ah! Here we go!"

With one more concerted push, cold night air laden with the scent of woodsmoke came rushing inside. The door swung open but, rather than the gaggle of excited costumed children Jules was expecting, there was just one child on the doorstep.

One child holding the hand of a pale-faced woman who had two suitcases set at her feet. Jules's mouth fell open.

"Happy Halloween, Vicar," said Tara Tremaine.

Chapter 4

The last person Tara had expected to answer Seaspray's front door was the vicar. For a brief moment she was lost for words. She'd considered all sorts of possibilities – it was hard not to when you were about as popular with your ex's family as a bout of diarrhoea – but the chance that Jules Mathieson would be in situ hadn't featured on her list. Rather than the confrontation she'd been expecting, here was a smiling, if rather surprised, face and a warm welcome. Tara was completely thrown.

Maybe returning to Polwenna Bay wasn't going to be quite as dreadful as she'd feared.

As she'd walked through the dark village, only half listening to Morgan's endless chatter about pumpkins and fancy dress, Tara had been psyching herself up to face Issie – or, even worse, Morwenna. Neither of them would be thrilled to see her. Issie would probably slam the door in her face, Tara had decided, while Mo was bound to make some biting remark about tricks rather than treats. As she'd lugged the two suitcases up the steep path that led to the elegant whitewashed house, Tara had prayed very hard that Alice or maybe Nick would answer. Alice would be gracious even if she was horrified, and Nick would probably be in such a hurry to get to the pub that he'd scarcely care who was calling.

The thought that Danny might answer the door was one that Tara hadn't dared contemplate. She hadn't seen her estranged husband for months, but this hadn't stopped her heart from skipping a beat whenever she caught sight of a tall blond man in the street or saw from the corner of her eye somebody she thought for a split second might be him. The inevitable surge of despair when it turned out to be a stranger was overwhelming. Tara wasn't sure how she would handle the reality of being near Danny again. The last time they'd met, the ice in his voice had almost been enough to give her frostbite. He'd loved her so much once – they'd been everything to each other – and it was painful beyond belief to see this turn to indifference.

It was even worse to know that she had nobody to blame for this but herself...

"All right, Jules?" Morgan said as he charged past into the lamp-lit hall. Her son didn't seem at all surprised to find the vicar at Seaspray, thought Tara. So she was a regular here, then. Interesting. Jules certainly looked at home in the hall in her socked feet and clutching a bag of Mars bars. She'd lost weight since the start of the summer, though. She was still very full-figured – way bigger than Tara's own slim size-eight frame – but defined cheekbones and killer curves were starting to emerge. Jules had changed her hair too: it was definitely longer, with soft tendrils curling around her face, and that awful maroon home colour had been replaced by a glossy brunette shade.

A ripple of unease spilled down Tara's spine. What else had changed in her absence?

"Tara, hi! Come in out of the cold!" Setting down the packet of Mars bars, Jules pushed the door wider open and reached for the bags that Morgan had abandoned in his haste to reach the kitchen. She was smiling warmly and didn't look at all upset to see the unexpected visitor.

Tara took a deep breath and pushed her paranoia aside. Dragging her suitcases behind her, she stepped into the hallway and into a rush of warm, soup-scented air. Alice's cooking, of course. Tara's mouth watered. When had she last eaten? Not today, at any rate. Her Visa card had been declined and what money she did have had been spent on breakfast for Morgan and their journey to Polwenna Bay. Right on cue, her stomach rumbled loudly.

"Hungry?" asked Jules.

Tara shrugged. "I've not eaten for a while."

"We both know Alice will happily sort that out," Jules smiled. She had a nice smile. It crinkled the corners of her eyes and made dimples dance in her cheeks, so that you couldn't help smiling back. Tara thought this was probably one of the things that made her so good at her job.

"Don't struggle with all that lot: leave your bags by the door. Dan and Jake can fetch them," Jules protested as Tara wrestled with her baggage. "Let's get you warmed up and find something to eat."

Maybe her worried prayers had been answered by having Jules answer the door, Tara reflected as she abandoned her suitcases and followed the vicar's more generously proportioned backside along the hall and into the kitchen. The family would have to behave themselves if the village vicar was present, and even Mo would have to button it. Having psyched herself up for a confrontation, Tara felt relieved now. Confrontations would come, that was inevitable, but at least she could prepare herself and hopefully talk to Danny first.

Seaspray was blissfully warm after the bitter chill outside, and every inch of it was achingly familiar. Tara glanced around as though reacquainting herself with an old friend, one she'd known for years and maybe taken for granted sometimes, but that she loved dearly nonetheless. Yes, it was a place she'd very much missed. Seaspray had seen some of Tara's happiest times and her most unhappy ones too. She'd grown up in this house, studied for her GCSEs at the kitchen table, had her first kiss in the garden, been carried over the threshold by Danny, brought Morgan home here, drunk tea with Alice and cooked dinner on the temperamental old Aga. Every corner of the place rang with echoes of the past. That John Dyer painting on the wall opposite had been a wedding present. Over there were long scrapes on the skirting board, made by Danny attempting to manoeuvre their garage-sale bargain sleigh bed through the back door. The frame of Morgan's pram was probably still in the cupboard under the stairs, buried like a metal dinosaur skeleton beneath old wellies and coats. Tara knew without having to look that there was dust on the tops of the door frames, that the kitchen tap leaked and that a kettle would be boiling away on the Aga.

How was it possible that nothing and everything had changed?

On this bitter October night, unemployed and down to the last few coins in her purse, it was hard for Tara to remember exactly why she'd walked out on her life here. In the months that had passed since she and Danny had last flung accusations at one another, the sharpness of their angry words had dulled. The reasons that had driven her away, so intense and so pressing at the time, now cast only faint shadows. A broken relationship, a lost job and several very hard lessons on, Tara was no longer so convinced that she'd made the right decision.

How much life could change in just a heartbeat: all it took was a drink or two, a rash choice, a foolish mistake, the wrong words spoken…

Now isn't the time to dwell on all that, Tara told herself sharply. Seaspray might have been her special place for years, and these people staring at her now with expressions of mingled horror and surprise on their faces might have been her family once, but all that was in the past. It didn't matter to them that she'd stood by the Aga a thousand times waiting for the kettle to boil, or that she and Danny had spent many an evening kissing on that battered old sofa, or that she'd sat with him to eat supper while the baby laughed and cooed from his high chair. Even though the tide of nostalgia breaking over her now was as powerful as any waves rolling into the bay below, she was the only one feeling it. The others were bristling with antipathy. She was no longer wanted here, that was a given, and it was a measure of her desperation that she'd even thought of returning, let alone made the journey back.

Tara raised her chin. Well, whether or not they liked it she was still a member of this family. Danny hadn't filed for divorce yet, had he? For months she'd expected to hear the heavy thud of legal paperwork falling from the letterbox to the doormat, but it hadn't materialised yet. Surely that had to mean something? Dan wasn't lazy or forgetful, so why hadn't he served a divorce petition? Could it be that he too was having second thoughts about ending their marriage?

Tara glanced at Danny, who was perched on the arm of the sofa. The black look on his face suggested that this wasn't the case at all: there were no second thoughts on his part. Disappointed, she was hoping to catch his eye – but he was too busy wrestling Morgan out of his coat to pay her any attention. In fact he was making a concerted effort not to look at her.

Fine. Danny was still angry. Tara got that, of course she did, but since none of the others had yet screamed at her/slapped her/thrown her out/trampled her with a horse (delete as appropriate to whichever family member), Tara knew for certain that he hadn't told them the whole truth. For that she was grateful. She hoped he never would tell them, but that was a decision only he could make. Still, Tara reminded herself, it was in Danny's interests too that some things remained a secret…

It felt so odd to be a stranger in the place that had once been her home, to wait to be asked to sit down when before she'd have been making the tea and fetching the dented biscuit tin from the old dresser. She knew this kitchen as well as everyone else here, and certainly better than *one* person in particular; she could tell without even looking which mugs were chipped, knew that the wobbly table leg was resting on the folded-up page of *Cosmo* she'd put there years ago. Tara clenched her hands and fought back another surge of regret and nostalgia. She needed to keep her temper and her nerve. Any moment now Volcano Morwenna was bound to erupt.

Three, two, one…

"What the hell is she doing here?" Right on cue, Mo Tremaine leapt up from the table, her chair scraping the floor loudly. "Talk about treat or trick!"

If only everything in life could be as predictable as Morwenna Tremaine, thought Tara. Fiery Mo always shot from the hip, was one for the quick explosion and the drama, whereas Danny – the Danny she'd once known, at any rate – was the opposite. He simmered slowly, tolerated and forgave a great deal; but when he finally lost his temper, that was it. It was white hot and burned for a long, long time. He might not shout the odds like his sister, but he felt things just as deeply.

However calm he seemed right now, there would come a time when he'd want to have more answers.

Tara swallowed. It was not a conversation she was looking forward to.

"We weren't expecting you," Danny said quietly. "It's the middle of the week, Tara. What's going on?"

The undamaged part of his face was turned towards her and for a moment it seemed as though the past two years had never happened. The injuries, the hospitals, the words she'd said that couldn't be taken back – all of it could have been a bad dream. Then he stood up to hang Morgan's coat and the bright kitchen light illuminated the full extent of the damage, shocking her as much now as it had the first time she'd first seen his wounds. The taut pink skin, the twist of his soft sexy mouth, the closed and puckered eye. She must have flinched, because scorn flickered in his good eye before he turned back to his son.

"Go and sit at the table," he said gently. "Grand-Gran's made some soup. We'll get you a bowl."

"Can I go trick-or-treating?" Morgan asked. "We couldn't go in Plymouth because Mum's card didn't work when we tried to buy a costume and then Anthony said we had to move out. We're homeless. Fact."

Tara wanted to sink through the slate floor. So much for her planned and measured explanation – the one that wouldn't have put her in too much of a bad light or made her seem like an irresponsible parent. Things were far more complicated than her son's summary of the situation implied, especially the whole fallout with her boyfriend, but Morgan had a talent for cutting through details. That didn't always make him popular with his peers, and it often made situations a little awkward.

This was one of those times. Everybody in the room now knew she was broke and dumped. Great. Still, Tara supposed that if anyone deserved to be humiliated for their past crimes then it was her. Maybe the vicar could help her deal with the guilt.

"I'm really sorry to turn up like this, Alice," Tara said calmly, doing her best to ignore the flush creeping up her neck. "I would have called but it was a last-minute decision."

"Yeah right," Mo snorted. "Like you never do anything without working out what's in it for you, Tara. Now you're desperate, you've crawled back."

Tara chose not to respond to this comment; there was some truth in it, she supposed. She was relieved to notice that Mo's handsome new husband was holding his wife's arm tightly, as though trying to stop her leaping forward like a spitting cat.

"Mo, that's enough," said Alice. There was a warning note in her voice, honed from years of raising her grandchildren. "Morgan and his mother are always welcome at Seaspray. This is our family home."

"Unless Dad pawns it," Jake remarked, shooting a look at Jimmy, who just grinned.

"I'm going to San Francisco, man, not Mars," he said.

There were more undercurrents flowing through this kitchen than around the Shindeep rocks beyond the bay, Tara realised. Jimmy had obviously upset everyone. Another thing that hadn't changed at Seaspray.

"Can I have some bread too?" Morgan was asking, plonking himself down at the table between Issie and Nick. "I'm starving. I haven't eaten since breakfast."

Issie pushed her plate towards Morgan. "Have mine, Rug Rat. *We* won't let you starve."

Tara flinched at the implied criticism. Maybe coming here was a mistake. Perhaps she should have taken the train to Reading and to her own parents. Their terraced house might be small and their disappointment in her might weigh Tara down like concrete, but at least there she wasn't hated.

She bit her lip. *Come on*, she told herself, *don't be so pathetic. You knew how Mo and Issie would be. It could have been a lot worse.* Besides, Danny wasn't in Reading. He was here in Polwenna Bay. And he was still Tara's husband.

That had to mean something.

"Morgan, take your bag up to your usual room and get changed," Alice said quietly. "You can take the bread while I get you some supper, and afterwards Issie will take you trick-or-treating, won't you, Is?"

And then we can talk, said the look she threw Tara.

"You can go as Black Jack Jago," Issie told Morgan. "In that pirate's outfit Nick had for New Year? That'll be cool."

"Black Jack Jago was a wrecker, not a pirate," Morgan said pityingly. "Don't you know that?"

"Pirate, wrecker, whatever," said Issie airily. She was used to her nephew's quirky ways, Tara realised. "I'm going as a cyber fairy, but up to you. It's all in the dressing-up box. Want to come or not?"

Morgan nodded quickly, just in case his aunt's offer was withdrawn, and shot upstairs. Tara's heart clenched with love so intense that it hurt.

Morgan adored being here with his family around him. Already he was a thousand times more animated than he'd been in Plymouth. What did it matter that they all hated her? If being here made her son happy then Tara was more than willing to take whatever Mo or Issie threw at her. Even Danny's cold disdain could just about be borne. Nothing mattered more than Morgan.

She turned to Issie. "Thank you for taking him. I really appreciate it."

Issie's pretty nose crinkled as though the smell of rotting seaweed had drifted into the room. "I'm not doing it for you, Tara."

Tara sighed wearily. All this antipathy was exhausting. "I know, Issie, but thank you for doing it anyway and in spite of what you think of me."

There was a heavy silence, broken only by the ticking of the kitchen clock, Alice slicing a crusty loaf and the distant crashing of waves on the rocks below. Tara wondered who would speak first. Would Alice offer her some food? Or perhaps Mo would make a sarcastic comment? Or maybe Jules, who looked about as comfortable as somebody kipping on a bed of nails, would swing into vicar mode and try to smooth things over? This idea almost made Tara laugh out loud. Not even an industrial lorry load of Botox could smooth things over with this lot.

Nick mopped up the last of his soup. "I'm going to the pub," he announced thickly through a mouthful of baguette. "Anyone coming?"

"I will." Jimmy was on his feet and practically out of the kitchen before Nick's spoon had even clattered into the bowl. He seemed very keen to escape.

"Me too," Danny said, and Tara's heart sank. She'd been wanting to catch him alone for a quiet word, for yet another apology. As always, the small flame of hope that this time he'd forgive her had started to burn deep inside that stupid part of her that never learned. Had she really thought that she could just turn up, find the right words and then life would go back to normal? As if it would ever be that easy. Now Danny would hit the booze as usual and create a scene, and things would be even worse.

"No, don't do that. I'll go." Tara forced herself to sound as though walking out into the cold dark night really wasn't an issue and she had a choice of places to sleep. She stood up. "I don't want to cause any problems. That was never what I intended."

"Don't be ridiculous," Danny said impatiently. "You've already said you've nowhere to go. Don't look so worried either. I'm not about to go on the lash and cause a scene. I haven't had a drink for months."

Tara's eyes widened. The last time she'd been in Polwenna Bay Danny had been drinking heavily and was regularly being thrown out of The Ship. That he'd managed to stop completely was hard to believe.

"Jules has helped me," he explained, seeing her incredulous expression. "I couldn't have done it without her. She's been amazing."

The vicar's face coloured at this praise and Tara felt another prickle of unease. Was there something going on between Danny and Jules? Surely not?

"So you don't mind if I stay?" Tara asked him. She wanted him to say *no* so much that it almost hurt. His indifference was unbearable.

Dan shrugged. "It makes no odds to me either way. The main thing is that Morgan's safe. Besides, I'm not such a bastard that I'd turn you out when you're down on your luck, Tara."

He was reaching for his jacket. Her heart ached as she watched him struggle to put it on. Once, not so long ago, he'd been the fittest and most agile man she'd ever known.

"Coming, Jules?" he was saying. "I'm buying, so you needn't raid the collection."

"Dan, don't you want to talk Morgan?" Tara said quickly.

"Morgan seems quite happy to trick-or-treat with Issie this evening." Danny's coat was on now. Everything about him was poised for flight. "We can talk about what's been going on tomorrow and I'll chat to him then."

Tara bowed her head. It was a polite but very clear message: as much as he loved his son, Danny wasn't prepared for Morgan to be the lifeline that would bring him and Tara closer together.

"I'll join you for an hour," announced Jake. "If that's OK, baby?" he murmured to Summer, dropping a kiss on the top of her head. To Jimmy he added darkly, "We've got a few things to discuss, Dad, remember?"

His father rolled his eyes. "Why do I feel as though I'm the kid here?"

"Because you behave like one?" Jake suggested wearily.

With Ashley and Mo opting to head home and Issie taking food up to Morgan, who must have got sidetracked by the dressing-up box, the kitchen suddenly felt very empty. Jules had made her excuses too, hurrying after Danny perhaps, which left only Alice and Summer in the kitchen. Neither were her greatest fans and Tara stared bleakly into her bowl of soup. The ravenous hunger of earlier had suddenly disappeared and now she just felt sick. Nobody wanted her here.

"I shouldn't have come here. I've ruined your party."

"Of course you should have," Alice said staunchly. "No matter what happened between you and Danny, you and Morgan are family."

Tara shook her head. "I know how you all feel about me. I'd hate me too if I was in your shoes. I get it. I'm the bitch of a wife who walked out on a war hero."

"We don't hate you," Summer insisted. "Do we, Alice?"

"Of course not," Alice said.

"Mo does," Tara pointed out. "And so does Issie. I can't stay here. I'll go."

Summer looked at Alice, helplessly.

The older woman shrugged. "Mo is Mo, Tara. You know how she is. She has her own way of handling things and she's devoted to Danny. But you and Morgan are family and of course you can stay here if you need to. None of us would ever have it any other way."

"Even Danny?" Tara said quietly.

Alice sighed. "I can't speak for Danny, Tara. He's never told me what happened between you two, but he loves Morgan and I know he'll be thrilled to have him nearby again. The rest will have to resolve itself in time." She rose to her feet and reached for the laptop. "It's been a long day and I'm going to have an early night. The guest room is all made up, Tara, as it always is. You know where it is."

Tara certainly did. She'd sneaked Danny into the narrow single bed many times when she'd stayed there as a teenager. The memories of his kisses, of the way his lips had once traced her skin and turned her blood to lava, would probably keep her up all night tossing and turning. It saddened her to think that there was no chance he'd sneak in tonight. Or maybe ever again.

I've ruined everything, thought Tara miserably. Why hadn't she just kept her mouth closed that night in the hospital? Why had she felt compelled to tell Danny everything? Sometimes the truth was better left unsaid. Once the words were out they could never be unspoken. Knowledge could never be unknown. It was a whole Pandora's box of horrors.

Earlier that summer, when she'd first noticed how close Jules and Danny were becoming, Tara had been terrified that he might have confided in the vicar. She'd lived on a knife edge for weeks and had even visited Jules to try to gauge whether or not she knew anything, but nothing in Jules's manner had suggested that she had any inkling. Now, sipping the tea that Summer had made, Tara told herself that there would have been some clue in the vicar's demeanour this evening if Jules had known the full story. A look? A nuance of her voice? A glance exchanged with Danny that spoke of a secret shared? Something, surely?

Which meant only one thing.

Danny hadn't told a soul. Nobody knew why they'd really split up. Nobody knew the truth.

Tara wrapped her hands around the ceramic mug, feeling its warmth against her palms, as comforting as the knowledge that was now warming her heart. Danny didn't want anyone to know the truth, and by remaining silent he'd contained the damage. Was he hoping that one day they could go back to how they were? Was there still a chance that he could love her again?

Well, if there was, then Tara Tremaine was determined to take it. And absolutely nobody, vicar or otherwise, was going to get in her way.

Chapter 5

"Danny! Wait up!"

Clutching at the stitch in her side, Jules stumbled down the shadowy garden track that snaked through the grounds of Seaspray to the cliff path. Although she was a lot fitter now than when she'd first arrived at Polwenna Bay, she still had her work cut out catching up with Danny when he was on a mission. He'd only left the house a few minutes ahead of Jules but he'd managed to overtake his father, who'd stopped to roll a sneaky joint. Already Danny was fumbling with his gloved hand to unfasten the gate; his haste to escape from Tara couldn't have been more evident.

"Bloody stupid gate," Dan was muttering as his hand struggled to release the catch. "Open up, for Christ's sake!"

He made several more failed attempts, swearing furiously under his breath, and then kicked savagely at the gate with his booted foot. Jules frowned. She hadn't seen Danny this upset for a long time – in fact, not since the evening they'd first met, when she'd had to talk him down from a colossal scene in the pub. On that occasion, though, alcohol had been involved, whereas tonight he was stone-cold sober. Knowing that he hadn't had a drink made Jules feel even more worried. Usually when he was sober Danny was an easy-going guy, with none of the famous Tremaine temper that Mo and Issie had in spades. Something about Tara upset him profoundly, and instinct told Jules that there was far more to this than a broken heart.

"Hey, you," she called. "What's the hurry? Is there a worldwide Diet Coke shortage that I don't know about? Is The Ship about to run dry? Or even worse, is there only one packet of pork scratchings left?"

Usually Danny would laugh at her jokes, however lame, but this evening his good humour had vanished faster than the sweets being dished out to the trick-or-treaters all around the village. His tension was palpable, and he vibrated with nervous energy from it. No wonder he couldn't open the gate: his fingers were trembling so much that each time he reached for the catch his leather glove slipped away from it.

"Oh damn it all to hell," Danny cursed, rattling the gate furiously. "Why did she have to turn up this evening? Bloody, bloody woman."

Gently, Jules reached under his arm, slid her fingers onto the catch and loosened it. The gate swung open and together they stepped out onto the path. With Seaspray and Tara now behind him, and the gate closed with a firm click, Danny exhaled raggedly and passed his hand over his face.

"Sorry."

"You don't need to apologise to me," Jules said softly. "It was a huge surprise to see Tara tonight. Even I was taken aback, so it's bound to knock you for six."

Danny laughed harshly. "Knocking people for six is what Tara does best. She'll have planned this for maximum impact."

"Come on, Danny, you can't really believe that. She's been made homeless."

He snorted. "So she says. That's all very convenient, isn't it?"

Jules opened her mouth to say that carrying two heavy suitcases halfway up a cliff on a freezing cold October night looked the very antithesis of convenient to her, but then thought better of it. Something told her Danny wouldn't appreciate that comment right now. Besides, why was she sticking up for Tara? The woman might have looked exhausted and unhappy but she had a track record of hurting Danny – and at the end of the day he was Jules's friend. She didn't have any loyalty towards Tara.

The problem was, Jules couldn't help feeling that Tara Tremaine really was desperate. The confidence and the gloss Jules had been so struck by the last time she'd met Tara had vanished entirely. Jules reflected that if she had to sum up Tara's demeanour this evening in a word, then that word probably would have been *broken*. Tara looked like a woman who'd lost everything and, even worse, realised it too.

"Don't look at me like that, Jules," Danny snapped. "I'm not the bad guy here. You have absolutely no idea what that woman is capable of."

He was right: Jules really did have absolutely no idea. As far as she was concerned, the whole Danny-and-Tara relationship was an enigma right up there with Stonehenge. She knew the bare bones of it and had gleaned enough over the past few weeks to have put some of the pieces together, but there still seemed to be a substantial chunk missing somewhere along the line. Dan's smouldering anger towards Tara seemed out of proportion at times. Yes, she'd let him down when he was injured, but Jules understood that things must have been difficult for her too. They'd both had enormous changes to adjust to. As much as she adored Danny, Jules wasn't blind to his faults. He was stubborn and single-minded and hugely proud. These were all qualities that must have made him an incredible officer – but also, she suspected, an appalling patient. How would his wife have handled witnessing her husband suffer? And Danny would have bitterly resented anyone seeing him in what he'd consider to be a weakened state.

"You think I'm exaggerating," he said. It wasn't a question.

As she searched for the right words, Jules watched their breath cloud and rise into the starry sky. She felt torn. Was she speaking here as Danny's friend or as his vicar? As his friend she was wholly on his side and could have throttled the woman who had given up on him when he'd needed her the most. Yet as a vicar Jules had been touched by Tara's side of the story, and she wasn't oblivious to Danny's shortcomings. Tara and Danny were both human and, as such, fallible.

As was she, of course.

Jules bit her lip. This kind of situation was the very reason why she'd been warned during her training about getting too close to her parishioners. It was also yet another reminder of why she had to fight her growing feelings for Danny. How could she possibly give him the right advice about his marriage when she was falling in love with him? She hadn't a chance of being objective.

"You have no idea what being near that woman does to me," Danny continued bleakly when Jules didn't answer. "I can't stand having her around. It makes me feel sick; everything comes flooding back when I look at her. You probably think I'm exaggerating, Jules, but just the sight of her kills me inside."

There was a tight feeling in Jules's throat, as though somebody had taken the ends of the scarf that was wrapped snugly round her neck and given them a sudden yank. If she'd ever wondered whether Danny still had feelings for his wife, then he'd just provided the answer she needed. How could she tell Danny that she understood completely the pain he was feeling? That every day, having to acknowledge that she couldn't be with him, a little piece of her died too? It was as clear as the night sky that he still had very strong feelings for Tara, no matter what he might tell himself.

"I'll sleep at the marina while she's here," he was saying, almost to himself. "There's no way I can be at Seaspray if Tara's there too, but I won't make a scene – for Morgan's sake."

"Won't Morgan expect you to be at Seaspray?"

"I'll get up early enough to be there when he wakes up. The last thing I'd ever do is upset Morgan. Tara knows that."

"But Seaspray is your home!" Jules hated to think of Danny camping out in the damp marina office. "You'll have to come back at some point. Besides, Morgan's smart and it's only a matter of time before he notices you're sleeping there and starts asking questions. He'll want you to tell him why things can't be the way they once were."

Danny laughed contemptuously. "That's what Tara's counting on. She thinks Morgan's the key to worming her way back into the family. She knows I can't tell him the truth, but I'm damned if I'm going to give her the satisfaction of playing her games. "

Jules was confused. "What do you mean? What truth? What games?"

"The kind she always plays," Danny said wearily. "Emotional blackmail. *Poor little me, I'm lonely. Morgan misses you.* You name it, Tara can play it. Trust me on this one. I'm the world's expert when it comes to her."

"Dan, I don't think tonight was an act. Tara looked pretty desperate to me."

His top lip curled. "Don't be so naïve, Jules. Surely you haven't fallen for the poor and abandoned single mum act? That's classic Tara. I have no idea who this Anthony was – the latest sucker, I suppose – but he obviously worked her out pretty fast and gave Tara her marching orders. Smarter guy than me, that's for sure. I'm the stupid one who actually used to believe her."

Jules had never heard Danny's voice so acidic with loathing. His entire face was twisted with it, too. That Tara could still have such an effect on him spoke volumes.

What should she say? Jules wondered. How should she handle this? The fallible, human part of her wanted nothing more than to agree with him, to unite with him in a good old bitch about Tara and to keep him close for herself. The other part of Jules, the part that she hoped was better than that and who had been called to serve God as her true vocation, knew that this was unfair. Marriage was a sacred bond in the eyes of the church, and Jules was supposed to do everything in her power to help uphold it. A line from the wedding service flittered through her mind:

Those whom God has joined together, let no one put asunder.

She shivered. How many times had she spoken those words when marrying people? Now it was time to put her faith in them and stand by what she believed. She was not in a position to judge Tara or speak ill of her. Not when God had joined Tara to Danny in holy matrimony.

"I don't know if that's fair, Danny," she said quietly. "Throwing herself on the mercy of her estranged in-laws couldn't have been much fun for Tara, and the huge slice of humble pie she'll have to eat would be enough to give anyone indigestion for years. I think she needs your help, not your judgement. She hurt you, and I'm sorry for that, but maybe it's time you were the bigger person and forgave her? If not for her or you, then maybe for Morgan?"

Danny spun around and his hand grabbed her shoulder so tightly that Jules felt each finger bite into her skin even through her thick winter coat.

"You don't know anything about it," he said fiercely. "Not the first thing! Do you hear me, Jules? You don't have a bloody clue what that woman is capable of. You can say whatever you like, chuck God at me all day if you want to, but I'll never forgive Tara for what she did, never. I'll rot in hell before that ever happens! If you only knew just what she's done—"

He paused; words unsaid filled the darkness between them.

"So tell me what she did!" Jules demanded. "Help me to understand, Dan. If it's more than I already know then tell me!"

But Danny only shook his blond head.

"I can't, Jules. You'll have to trust me on this one. My marriage is beyond all repair. Just believe me when I say that I can't have that woman anywhere near me. Sometimes I think I could kill her."

There was such black rage in him that Jules shrank back. Gone was the gentle friend she adored and in his place was someone dark and brooding and dangerous – the same ruthless part of Danny, she imagined, that had been able to go into battle and destroy his enemy. A man who was trained to kill. The two personalities were flip sides of the same coin, and recalling this now her pulse began to skitter. The rumours and gossip she'd heard about him when she'd first arrived in Polwenna Bay yawned and stretched back into wakefulness: *unstable, dangerous, post-traumatic stress, keep away from Danny Tremaine!* Even Danny's family had tiptoed around him. Had her feelings for him blinded her to the reality?

Danny's face, drained of colour, was paler than the moon – and as Jules stared up at him he seemed just as far from reach. He was keeping secrets from her. Maybe he had been all along. Just how well did she actually know Danny Tremaine? Who was he really?

"I don't understand," Jules whispered. "What's so awful that you can't tell me? Don't you trust me?"

"I trust you totally," Danny said miserably. "But there are some things that I just can't speak about, OK? Not even to you. Maybe I don't trust myself. Besides, this isn't just about me. If it was then it wouldn't matter."

They stared at one another and although they were only inches apart it might as well have been miles. In the cold moonlight the angles of his face were sharp and harsh, the scars cruel pale slashes. He felt like a stranger and Jules was close to tears. Then his fingers slipped away from her shoulder and she felt as alone as a ship that had slipped its anchor. She rubbed at her shoulder and felt the flesh throb.

"Sorry," he said softly. "I didn't mean to hurt you. I think I need to be alone. I'm no good to anyone in a mood like this. The last place I trust myself to be right now is the pub."

Jules swallowed. "I agree. The pub's not a good idea. I'm fine, but where will you go? To the marina?" She wished she could invite him back to the vicarage, but that just wasn't appropriate. Apart from the danger of her own feelings there was Sheila Keverne, St Wenn's nosey verger, to worry about. Sheila would have a fit if she brought Danny back; she'd probably call the bishop, and Jules already had enough black marks in his book for one lifetime.

Dan patted his pocket. "There's a couch in the marina office and I have a key. I'm not going to make a scene at home but I meant what I said. I'm not sleeping under the same roof as Tara. God, I'm sorry, Jules. What a horrific night. First Poison Ivy and now this. Who needs a Halloween party?"

Jules tried to laugh but it was an odd, strangled sound. "Maybe I should have just stayed up the ladder?"

"I bet you wish you had," Danny sighed. "My bad temper makes Poison Ivy look like Mary Poppins."

Footsteps and muffled voices behind them signalled that Jake and Nick weren't far away. Further back, that red glow in the dark and the scent of skunk must be Jimmy. She caught Danny's eye and knew the last thing he needed was a family interrogation.

"Go and have a few drinks with them; it's the least you deserve," he suggested before leaning forward and brushing her cheek with his cold lips. "Happy Halloween, Jules. I guess it was the perfect night for the past to come back and haunt me."

Jules stared after him as he headed down the cliff path and into the village. She was confused and concerned in equal measure. Once the darkness had swallowed him whole, she rubbed her shoulder again and drew a shaky breath. Whatever secrets Danny Tremaine was keeping, it was abundantly clear that he wasn't prepared to share them with her. They were between him and his wife.

The message couldn't have been clearer: she had to step away.

Chapter 6

In the light that streamed through the big bay window, Tara gazed into the dressing-table mirror, checking her reflection. She tucked a strand of dark hair behind her ear and narrowed her hazel eyes thoughtfully. All things considered, she didn't think she looked too bad for someone who was nearly thirty. Her recent weight loss had sharpened her cheekbones, drawing attention to her heart-shaped face – and a good night's sleep had gone a long way towards erasing the smudges under her eyes. Still, she was not as confident as she'd once been.

Tara didn't usually do nerves, but as she left the spare bedroom and made her way downstairs she felt a prickle of anxiety. Seaspray might not have changed – the clanking water cistern and the creaking timbers that had soothed her into sleep were as familiar as her own heartbeat – but everything else in her world was utterly different now. *I'm different*, she reminded herself sharply. She'd learned some tough lessons over the past two years and paid an extremely high price for a mistake. She was no longer the thoughtless, selfish girl that she'd been before.

This was her new start, Tara thought as she paused on the half-landing and looked out at the view from the window. November the first had dawned bright and sunny, with that crisp cold that made the sea sparkle and the sky a deceptive summery blue. She couldn't help taking this as a good omen. Tara had lived in Cornwall for long enough to know that the weather was as fickle as a teenaged girl's love for the latest boy band: one moment sunshine was the flavour of the month, the next louring leaden skies and driving rain held sway. Nevertheless, she felt her spirits rise. It was a glorious day and she was home at last.

There was everything to play for. Thank goodness she'd ignored the doubts that had gripped her when she'd fallen into bed. As the waves had crashed onto the rocks below her bedroom and the moon had poked a cold white finger of light through the crack in the curtains, Tara had been tempted to snatch Morgan from his bed and steal away, never to come back. What was the point of staying? Danny would never forgive her, the family hated her and nobody in the village really cared whether she was there or not. Why put herself through it?

What a difference a good night's sleep could make. Now, as the sun poured through the windows and the gulls called merrily as they performed their aerobatics, Tara was glad she'd held her nerve. She could hear Morgan chatting away in the kitchen with an ease he'd never had while they'd been staying in Plymouth. Even if Danny hated her until the day she died, and even if every time she saw Mo she was bombarded with scornful looks and comments, Tara knew that it would be worth it all to see her son this happy all the time.

She took a deep breath. Everything was going to be just fine. She'd done the hardest bit by coming back and breaking the ice. She'd known it would be difficult. Of course Danny was angry with her; Tara understood that completely. She'd known, too, that his family would close ranks and protect him. She wouldn't have expected anything else from a tight-knit clan like the Tremaines. Having Jules and Ashley present had certainly smoothed the way, though – and Jimmy had clearly just pulled another stunt, which had helped to dilute the impact of her arrival. *Yes*, Tara decided as she descended the final flight of stairs, *it could have been a lot, lot worse.*

Since her unexpected return last night Tara had been doing a lot of hard thinking. The row with Anthony had just been the latest in an escalating succession of disagreements and, if she was honest, Tara hadn't been sorry to leave him behind. What had seemed like a lot of fun on a Saturday night in a Plymouth club had looked very different in the cold light of the working week. Once the initial rush of excitement had worn off, Tara had been drumming her fingers in boredom on his black marble worktops while Anthony had been driven to distraction by Morgan's need for order and his distress when a routine was broken. Right now he was probably driving to work in his Ford Focus and heaving a sigh of relief that she was gone. Tara was interested to find that this idea didn't hurt in the slightest.

Was she really a hard and unfeeling bitch, as Danny had once accused her of being? Tara explored this idea gingerly. It was the emotional equivalent of probing the gap where a tooth has been extracted: she wasn't quite sure what she'd find and whether it would be painful. She'd moved in with Anthony very quickly, uprooting Morgan from Polwenna Bay in the process. Tara had been prepared to make a whole new life with this man but now, and with the twenty-twenty vision that always came with hindsight, she could see that she'd simply been running away. Anthony, with his shiny car, shiny shaved head and shiny house on a shiny new estate in the city, had been a distraction from the car crash of her marriage. She'd been looking for an escape and he'd seemed to offer it.

No, Tara decided, Anthony hadn't been her Mr Right; he'd only been *Mr Right for Now*. Her rebound from Danny. Her stupid mistake. She'd only been thinking about her own anguish and the driving need to put as much distance between herself and her failed marriage as possible. Maybe a stupid part of her had even hoped that Danny would be eaten up with jealousy and come tearing after her. Even when Anthony had driven her away to Plymouth she'd pulled down the passenger sun visor and kept a lookout in the vanity mirror, just in case the Tremaine Marine truck should come racing after her. The disappointment when it hadn't had been like a physical blow.

So making Danny jealous didn't work. Neither did pretending she didn't care. The same went for yelling back at him. Tara had slowly and painfully come to the conclusion that nothing she ever said or did would be able to change the way Danny felt about her. All she could do now was be here in Polwenna Bay, and hopefully with time he'd remember the way he used to feel about her.

Provided nobody else came along, that was.

Tara pushed this thought firmly aside. *She* was still Danny's wife, on paper anyway, and the mother of his son. For the moment that would have to be enough as she worked out how to build a life here again for her and Morgan. Maybe that life would eventually involve Danny – she certainly hoped so – but right now Morgan had to be her priority. She couldn't put him through more changes. Change wasn't good for a child with his specific needs. The educational psychologists were already concerned about Morgan, and Tara was well aware that what he needed most was stability. Having his family around him and the security of a small school again was another of the reasons she'd come back to Polwenna Bay. She had to make this work, for Morgan's sake.

Squaring her shoulders, Tara walked into the kitchen. Apart from Summer, who was stacking the dishwasher, it was unexpectedly empty.

"You've just missed Alice and Morgan," Summer explained when Tara expressed her surprise. "Alice has taken Morgan to the church to help her with the flower arrangements – although to be honest he was more interested in taking photographs of the stained-glass windows.

I've no idea where Nick and Issie are, but I think Danny's down at the marina with Jake."

"Oh." Tara was deflated. Her spray-on skinny jeans, tight sweater and carefully applied make-up were going to be totally wasted on Summer and the family cat. She wished now that she hadn't bothered at all; compared to Summer, who was currently make-up free and clad in simple yoga pants and a vest top, she surely looked as though she was trying far too hard. Which of course she was.

Tara had known Summer long ago, when they'd been teenagers dating the two eldest Tremaine brothers, so she was used to the other girl's beauty. All the same, it she remembered now that it had been hard to contend with sometimes. What had taken Tara hours to achieve by sitting at the mirror with her make-up brushes in one hand and straighteners in the other had always looked harsh and contrived in comparison to Summer's soft ringlets and dark-lashed green eyes.

"I've just made some coffee. Do you want one?" Summer asked her.

Fighting the urge to dash back upstairs and scrub her face, Tara nodded and sat at the table. Then she laughed out loud.

"I've ended up in the same seat where I always used to sit," she explained, seeing Summer's puzzled face. "Some habits die hard, don't they?"

Summer smiled as she poured hot coffee into a mug. "They certainly do. I did exactly the same thing when I first came back. Isn't it weird?" She pushed the mug across the table to Tara. "We're both a dozen years older, but we can't help reverting to the same patterns we had as teenagers."

"You've had a more successful decade or so than me," Tara said sadly. "You're a successful model with a glittering career and an adoring partner, whereas I'm just a dumped wife nobody wants to have around."

Summer's dark brows drew together thoughtfully. "Don't believe everything you read in the papers, Tara. I wouldn't say all of it was successful. In fact, I made some pretty big mistakes along the way – and now I've got my ex trying to sue me. As for Jake? I guess I'm very lucky that he was prepared to give me another chance."

Tara stared into her coffee cup. "I wish Danny thought like that. I don't think the words *second chance* are in his vocabulary."

There was a brief silence, broken only by the call of the gulls outside. Summer cradled her coffee in her hands. Her forehead was crinkled with thought. Oh dear. If even Summer couldn't tell her that Danny would find it in his heart to try again, then she really was in trouble.

"It's OK, you don't have to try and find something to say that will make me feel better. I know I messed up," Tara said.

"We all mess up." Summer's emerald eyes were full of compassion. It was just as well that she didn't know the real reason why Danny was so angry, Tara thought. Summer might be the closest thing Polwenna Bay had to a saint, but even she would struggle to get past *that* particular gem. "Whether Danny and you can make it work is something only you two can decide." She paused, her white teeth worrying her full bottom lip for a moment, then asked, "Is that why you've come back, Tara? To try and sort things out with Danny?"

Tara shrugged one shoulder. She found it hard to discuss her feelings and had never been the kind of woman with close girlfriends that she confided in. If she had to describe herself, Tara supposed she would say that she was a man's woman rather than a girly girl. She was only just beginning to realise that this was a lonely way to be.

"Do you still love him?" Summer asked gently.

Tara shrugged again. "I know that we were happy once, and I don't see why we couldn't be happy again one day. And I know he adores Morgan. It would mean the world to him if we could all be together again."

"We all adore Morgan," said Summer warmly. "He's brilliant. If he hadn't had his camera with him when my ex turned up to launch another one of his attacks, my lawyer would be having a much harder job building a case."

Tara felt the same thrill of pride that always came when she thought of her son. Morgan was on the autism spectrum and sometimes struggled to make friends and negotiate school life with the ease that came naturally to most children – but he was kind, funny and original. He'd been so unhappy in Plymouth and it broke her heart to know that she'd unwittingly caused this.

"I know that he's happier here with his friends and family around him," she said slowly. "I've come back for his sake as much as my own. When things didn't work out with Anthony, coming back to Polwenna Bay felt like the right thing to do."

Summer nodded. "I'm sure you're right. He seemed full of beans this morning. He ate a bowl of Rice Krispies and two rounds of bacon sandwiches as well. With no butter and the ketchup underneath the rashers, of course."

Tara smiled. "See? That's exactly what I mean. You *get* him here, whereas that kind of thing drove Ant wild. He thought it was weird and he was always trying to make Morgan do things *normally*. I couldn't even start to describe the meltdown we had when Anthony insisted that the sauce went on top. Morgan was beside himself."

"Anthony sounds like an idiot, if you don't mind me saying so," said Summer bluntly. "What's normal, anyway?"

Tara had no idea. What she did have, however, was a huge collection of paperwork, including numerous educational psychologists' reports and statements attempting to put Morgan into a box in which he was never going to fit. In the past few years since his diagnosis, Tara had become something of an expert on autism – or at least, on Morgan's particular challenges. It had been a learning curve as steep as Everest. In spite of Tara trying her best to explain her son's needs to the teachers at his new school, the experience had become more and more stressful for Morgan. He happened to be exceptionally bright too, and the work had been far too easy for him, which had frustrated him beyond belief. At the end of her tether with it all, Tara had even started to consider home schooling, an idea which had sent Anthony off on yet another rant about Morgan needing to toe the line and fit in.

I should have stood up for Morgan more, Tara thought guiltily. Why had she kept quiet rather than telling Ant that people with autism didn't always fit a set mould? Why hadn't she challenged him more when he'd been critical? Who knew what wonderful things her son would achieve one day? What did it matter if he had to run to a timetable, was obsessed with photography and ate his peas one at a time?

You're so weak, she told herself scathingly. *You were too scared of being alone and of having nowhere to go, and guess what? It's happened anyway.*

Maybe this was exactly what she deserved. Was it her punishment for what she'd done all those years ago?

"There's a brilliant teacher at Polwenna Primary," Summer was saying now, fortunately oblivious to Tara's stream of self-critical thoughts. "She's called Tess Hamilton and all the kids are bonkers about her, or according to Mum anyway. I bet she'll have lots of ideas how to engage and support Morgan. She goes to the village yoga class – it's Silver Starr's latest thing but it's pretty good. I'll introduce you, if you want, and maybe then you could have a chat about getting Morgan back into the school. If you're staying, of course."

Tara's head was spinning. Was she staying? Was it a possibility? Enrolling Morgan into school here again meant that she really would be putting down roots and staying in one place, didn't it? She would have to make up her mind; it had been half term this week, but it would probably take a few days to organise things and she didn't want him to struggle with settling back in. Once Morgan was sorted out and secure, then Tara guessed she would need to start thinking about what she was going to do too. If Danny couldn't forgive her, she didn't think she could remain at Seaspray indefinitely. She already suspected that he hadn't come home last night; the thought of being under the same roof as her had probably upset him too much. That was classic Danny behaviour, and she'd already done enough to her husband without driving him away from his home as well.

"Tess is full of ideas and she's really creative," Summer continued. "I should imagine she's giving old Mother Powell all kinds of headaches."

Recalling the old battleaxe of a school teacher who'd been at Polwenna Primary since baby Jesus was in the reception class, Tara grimaced.

"She's not still going? Seriously?"

"At full throttle, apparently," said Summer. "Hopefully by the time Jake and I have kids she'll have retired, but who knows? She's probably drinking the blood of virgins to keep herself alive!"

"That won't be easy in this village," said Tara drily, and the two women giggled as though they really were teenagers again.

"Talking of yoga, I'm supposed to be off to a class right now," said Summer, glancing at the kitchen clock. "In fact, I'm running late. Are you all right to clear up here?"

"Sure," said Tara. "I know where it all goes."

Summer left the kitchen, and for a moment Tara sipped her coffee and watched the waves roll across the bay. Then she heard the front door slam and the scrunching sound of trainers running down the path. She was alone. The old house seemed to shift and stir a little as though missing Summer's presence, before it settled down again into a new rhythm.

The clock ticked, the cat purred from the sofa and the gulls squabbled on the kitchen roof. Tara exhaled slowly, feeling the stress of the past twenty-four hours start to ease. For the first time in ages she didn't have Morgan to worry about or Anthony's moods to contend with. She closed her eyes and basked in the autumn sunlight streaming through the window. Tension slipped from her body like a discarded coat.

She was home.

Of course, technically Seaspray wasn't Tara's home, but she'd started going out with Danny when she was fifteen and had spent so much time at the Tremaines' house that it had always felt like home. She and Danny had married very young and had started their life together in the old house. She could still picture the girl she'd been then, arms twined around her new husband's neck and shrieking with laughter, being carried over the threshold. Confetti was in her hair and she'd been protesting that he was smudging her make-up every time he kissed her

– but then Dan had carried her upstairs and she'd forgotten everything else. The bittersweet memory made her eyes fill with tears. Tara blinked them away impatiently. *That was all a long time ago*, she reminded herself sharply. *You're a different person now. You both are.*

Looking back, Tara sometimes wondered what she'd been thinking. The answer, she feared, was that she hadn't been thinking much at all. Danny was gorgeous, the village's golden boy, and she'd been crazy about him. He'd been in the army, and if she wanted to join him then they needed to be married; it was that simple. While Danny had focused on Sandhurst and his army career, Tara had thrown herself into planning their wedding. Her days had been occupied with choosing flowers and place settings and fabric samples, and she hadn't really thought any further ahead. Did anyone at that age?

Somewhere in this house there was an album full of pictures of the big day, hastily shoved into a drawer or a cupboard along with some silver-framed pictures too, out of sight in a way that reflected how the family had dealt with the break-up of the marriage. Maybe Danny had even binned the pictures, Tara thought. Who knew? Anyway, it didn't matter whether she had the photographs in front of her or not: that day was etched in her memory forever. One perfect moment frozen in time, a day when life had seemed rich with promise and possibilities. The idea that anything would ever be otherwise had never crossed her mind. She'd got married in her dream dress, a riot of frothing lace and pink ribbons, and Danny had been heart-stoppingly handsome in his ceremonial uniform. Mo and Issie had been trussed up in fuchsia ruffles (was this why they hated her?), and their respective sets of relatives had been beaming proudly. It had been a huge wedding, the Polwenna Bay event of the year, and exactly what Tara had wanted.

The sun slipped behind a cloud and Tara shivered as the warmth vanished. She'd felt something similar a few months after her wedding. Once the excitement of the big day had gone and the novelty of her new name had worn off a little, Tara had focused on her beautician's job at the Polwenna Bay Hotel and lived for the times when Danny came home on leave. Each of these visits was like a honeymoon, and Tara had basked in the glamour of having a gorgeous soldier husband – especially when Danny was promoted swiftly to Second Lieutenant. At this point Tara had quit her job and flown out to join her new husband at his army base in Germany, full of excitement about going abroad for the first time. The elation was short-lived. Their married quarters were small and Spartan, and life as an army wife was nothing like she'd imagined. There were no glitzy balls or parties, and the other wives operated within a strict hierarchy. As she was bottom of the heap, she was generally ignored. Tara's German was on a par with her Klingon, which meant that any trips into the nearby by town were pretty limited. Meanwhile, Danny had been working long hours and was rarely home. When he was, all he wanted to do was sleep; partying and exploring the local nightlife weren't high on his list of priorities. Tara had been lonely and bored, and if young wives on army bases got lonely and bored it was a sure recipe for trouble.

And when that trouble came in the form of a six-foot cadet with eyes like rain-washed violets and a great line in banter, things could only end badly...

Tara got up and carried her mug to the sink. Sometimes reliving this next part of the story was more than she could bear. She'd tried her hardest not to think about it, had pushed it to the furthest and darkest part of her mind, but from time to time the memories rose to the surface like bloated corpses drifting up from the sea bed.

Bloated corpses? Tara shook her head at this analogy as she rinsed the mug and watched the water swirl down the plughole. Talk about a sense of the melodramatic. And yet, in a way her story did resemble a horror movie: it haunted her and caused her to wake in the night with a racing heart and dry mouth. The difference was that the past that haunted Tara wasn't dead. It was very much alive. She lived with and regretted it every day.

It was, after all, the reason why Danny had stopped loving her.

Chapter 7

For the past few minutes, Tara had been standing at one of Seaspray's upstairs windows, leaning her forehead against the glass and watching the clouds scudding across the sky. Beneath them, the white-tipped waves galloped onto the pale slice of beach. Winter mornings in Cornwall had a cold beauty all of their own, she thought. Something about the bright sunshine glancing off the sea, the harsh cries of the gulls and the knife-edge wind that slashed one's breath away was always capable of luring people from their cosy cottages and out onto the cliffs.

A man was walking at the water's edge, throwing a stick into the surf for a bouncing chocolate Labrador to fetch, and the rocks at the far side of the bay were dotted with children searching the rock pools for treasure and nature's curiosities. Morgan had loved that, Tara recalled. It had been one of his early passions – and there had been nothing he didn't know about the creatures that inhabited the cracks or lurked in the bottom of the seaweedy pools. He and Danny had spent hours clambering over the slippery shore with nets and buckets, returning with tales of crabs and tiny fish and, once, a rare sighting of a basking shark. Recollecting the innocence of those days was painful now. She turned away, almost unable to look at the ever-changing scene.

With all of the family absent, Seaspray felt as though it was holding its breath and watching to see what this interloper would do next. Tara's every nerve was fizzing, and once she'd cleared the kitchen she'd wandered from room to room, her fingertips brushing surfaces and skimming over furniture as though trying to reacquaint themselves by touch alone. She'd breathed in the familiar smells of polish and lavender and salty air. The house was still glorious, with scoured light pouring in through the big windows. The beeswaxed floors glowed and the threadbare rugs that covered them told of generations of feet crossing the rooms. There was still a scattering of sand too, a gritty memento of days spent on the beach, and in the back porch she'd been touched to find that her wellington boots were still standing to attention beside Danny's.

Home and yet not home.

Unable to settle or shake off the feeling that the old house was watching her and waiting to see what she did next, Tara returned to her bedroom and peeled off the ridiculously tight jeans and the clingy sweater, before padding into the bathroom and scrubbing off her make-up. As she wiped the cotton wool across her cheeks and watched the carefully applied contours melt and blur, Tara laughed at herself. This was Polwenna Bay. Who was there to impress here? The seagulls? A few bored fishermen? The old biddies from the church? Danny certainly wouldn't care about make-up, not if his taste in women tended towards those who looked and dressed like Jules Mathieson.

She paused, mid-wipe, and frowned at her reflection. Was Danny involved with the vicar? Surely not? Although Jules seemed nice, and Tara supposed that she was quite pretty if you liked that kind of thing, she was a vicar. Would Danny seriously date a vicar? He'd never been into religion before, but then again maybe his injuries had changed more than just his physical appearance.

I'm being paranoid, Tara told herself. Besides, the vicar had reassured her in the summer that Danny and she were just friends – and vicars didn't lie. There was still a chance that Tara could make things work with Danny. She just had to play the long game and be patient.

Faded Levi's and a soft red sweater, teamed with stripy socks and a thick cream scarf were far more like it, Tara decided as she pulled her hair into a ponytail. A lick of neutral lipstick and some black mascara brushed across her lashes and she was good to go. She looked less sexy now, perhaps, but it was the perfect outfit for a walk up on the cliffs. Just what was needed to blow away the cobwebs and hopefully find herself some headspace.

Tara went back down the stairs and through the kitchen to the porch, where she liberated her old wellingtons, carefully shaking out a few sleepy spiders, and dug out a waxed jacket from the selection hanging above. Wrapped up against the November chill, she set off through the garden and headed down the path towards the village. If nothing else, at least the bitter cold and the exercise would take her mind off all the drama of the past few days and burn a few calories. Her membership at Anthony's gym was now a thing of the past, and if she indulged in too much of Alice's cooking she'd end up twice the size.

The village was quiet on a Sunday morning. Although a few walkers were about, most of the locals were either in church or curled up by the fire with the papers. Woodsmoke scented the air as it drifted lazily from chimneys, and fishing boats rode the gentle swell of the tide, their mooring ropes creaking softly. Across the harbour, the lights flickered on as The Ship opened for business. Tara might have been away for a few months but she would have placed money on the probability that the same locals were still heading inside to sit at the same seats and play dice. Big Eddie Penhalligan would be there for sure, and Chris the Cod from the chippy. And without a doubt, her father-in-law, Jimmy

Tremaine, would be in there too for a pint and the chance of winning a few pounds.

Elsewhere, too, the same familiar people would doing the same familiar things in the same familiar places as always.

It was this continuity that Morgan needed, Tara concluded. There was comfort in it and safety and routine; all the things that were necessary for him to be happy and secure. The same things that a few years ago had driven her almost to distraction. When Danny had phoned and said that there was a vacancy in the officer's accommodation, and that if she wanted to come to Germany she could fly out that month, Tara's feet had hardly touched the ground. She couldn't escape Polwenna Bay quickly enough. If she could turn the clock back, she would do things so differently, Tara reflected as she crossed the bridge and headed past the huddled cottages that jostled for space on the quayside. Yet there was one thing she could never regret, and that was Morgan. He alone made everything worthwhile. She would never, ever regret having her son.

Deep in thought, Tara took the steepest path out of the village and over the cliffs. Her breathing came in sharp gasps and before long she was unwinding her scarf and pulling off her coat. The sea glittered and boiled around needle-sharp rocks, dizzyingly far below now as the path climbed higher and the land fell away dangerously to her left. Tara paused for a moment to catch her breath before continuing on her way. Walking the cliffs required more physical effort than all the treadmills and steppers in Ant's gym put together, and by the time she turned away from the water and followed a merry stream into the woods, her lungs were burning.

But at least she wasn't thinking anymore – and that had to be a good thing.

Slowing her pace so that she could recover her breath, Tara followed the stream for a mile or so until the trees opened out into a clearing. The branches high above were knitted together less densely now, allowing the light to filter through their vibrant green canopy. The stream had widened out too, tickling the tree roots that had crept closer over time to dip themselves into the water. Gradually it flowed into a deep pool around a weathered Celtic cross. Nearby, little scraps of fabric flickered in the breeze and a string of bells draped over a lilac bush chimed softly.

"St Wenn's Well!" Tara said, in surprise. She hadn't expected to find herself here. Goodness, she'd walked miles if she'd reached this isolated spot. Wasn't there supposed to be a myth about making wishes here? Something to do with wishing for true love?

She laughed out loud. She could wish all she liked for that. Tara was starting to wonder whether true love even existed. Once upon a time she'd thought so, but life, and her own stupidity, had soon put paid to that belief. Danny, Ant and… well, never mind him, they'd all done their bit to prove to Tara that true love was right up there with the tooth fairy and Santa.

Sunlight dappled the dank woodland floor, turning the chuckling stream to diamonds and making the shadows dance. A wood pigeon's trembling call floated down from high above her head and the bells tinkled again as the breeze toyed with them. Tara stopped and crouched down at the water's edge. It was certainly a pretty spot and, judging by the numerous rags and scraps tied to the branches, enough people still believed in the power of St Wenn to make the long hike up over the cliffs and through the woodland. The pagan past was never far away in Cornwall, she remembered. Enough people still dressed up as green men or had fun morris dancing, didn't they, so why would making a wish in a sacred stream be any different?

Tara wasn't quite sure why, but she found herself leaning over the stream and trailing her fingers through the cold water.

"OK then, St Wenn," she said aloud, "if you can bring me true love then I'd be very grateful. It might be a bit of a big ask though, even for a saint, but any help I can get would be nice. I haven't done so well by myself."

Just as Tara was pulling her hand out of the stream, and feeling incredibly foolish for talking to thin air, a squawking pheasant burst from the dense undergrowth, its wings flapping wildly and its eyes bulging as it flashed through the clearing. And no wonder: a chocolate Labrador was in hot pursuit. The abrupt noise came as a shock after the stillness. Tara shrieked with surprise, her heart hammering in her chest. She scrambled backwards, almost losing her footing, clutching at a sapling to steady herself and catch her breath.

"Watson! Watson! Jesus Christ, you stupid hound! Come here! Now!"

A man came charging through the trees, his waxed jacket billowing behind him like a superhero's cape and with his sandy hair standing on end. He seemed every bit as surprised and flustered as the pheasant. His wire-framed glasses were slipping down his nose and he paused for a minute with his hands on his knees to gulp some air. His face was much the same colour as his cherry-red scarf; from the look of him, he'd been pursuing his errant dog for quite some time.

"You made me jump out of my skin!" Tara exclaimed.

The man stood, then grimaced and doubled up again, clutching his side. He seemed to be having trouble breathing. Tara hoped he wasn't having a heart attack. Her own heart rate was only just returning to somewhere almost normal, and although she'd done some basic first-aid training when she'd worked at the Polwenna Bay Hotel she was pretty rusty now. Giving a total stranger the kiss of life wasn't quite what she'd had in mind when she'd wished for true love just a moment ago.

She stepped forward and took his arm. "Are you all right?"

He was panting. "I am, but Watson won't be when I catch up with him! Bloody dog, taking off on the cliff path like that. I haven't run this far since school."

That was obvious from the state of him, Tara thought privately. He was tall and lean but it was a cold day and being wrapped up in all those layers would have made running just a few feet hard work, let alone the mile or so from the coastal path.

"Do you need to sit down?" she asked.

The man straightened up. "What I do need to do is join the village gym and take my own advice about diet and exercise. I'm a doctor," he explained, when Tara looked puzzled. He held out his hand. "Richard Penwarren. My mother's Kursa, the hairdresser."

Tara didn't know much about Richard, who must have arrived just a month or two before she'd moved to Plymouth, but his mother's skill with the scissors was notorious. Most villagers had suffered a disastrous scalping by her at some stage. Luckily the new doctor, with his long floppy fringe the same colour as the wet sand of the bay, appeared to have escaped his mother's hairdressing. Richard pushed his hair out of his grey eyes and smiled down at Tara expectantly.

"Oh, sorry!" Suddenly aware that she'd been staring at him while lost in thought, Tara took his hand and shook it. "I'm Tara. Tara Tremaine."

Richard's eyes widened behind his glasses. So he'd heard of her, then. No doubt the usual tales of the heartless bitch who'd walked out on her war-hero husband.

But Richard wasn't thinking about Danny. "So you're Morgan's mum? He's a super little character, is Morgan. Often walks Watson for me, and probably has the sense to have the bugger on a lead. He'd despair of me – and quite right too."

Tara smiled at the warmth in his voice. "Morgan would have assessed every inch of the walk before he let the dog go. He likes to have all eventualities covered."

"I'll take a leaf out of his book the next time I take the bloody mutt out. He'll be on the lead all the way to Fowey," Richard promised. "I guess I'd better be on my way. Watson will be miles away by now. Maybe I should book him in for some obedience classes?"

"I think it's a bit late in the day for that," Tara told him, and Richard Penwarren smiled ruefully.

"Yes, I think you may be right. Always too late. Story of my life, that."

He fell silent and for a moment sadness shadowed his features, before he collected himself and smiled.

"Anyway, nice to meet you, Tara. Hopefully the next time I bump into you it won't be quite so literal and," he glanced in confusion at the fluttering ribbons and tinkling bells, "in quite such a strange place. What is all this, anyway?"

Embarrassed at being caught here herself and in the act of wishing for true love, Tara decided to be economical with the truth. Richard was a doctor and no doubt a rational man; he would probably think her as bonkers as Silver Starr from Polwenna Bay's mystic shop if he knew what she'd been up to.

"I think it's an old well," she hedged, crossing her fingers deep in her coat pocket and hoping that he didn't ask anyone in the village.

"It's pretty," Richard said thoughtfully. "There's a nice energy too, isn't there? It feels like a place where good things happen. Apart from being flattened by mad dogs and doctors, obviously!"

His eyes crinkled when he smiled and he looked much younger.

Tara smiled back. "Yes, apart from all that commotion, it was a very peaceful spot."

"Well, I won't disturb you for a second longer," Richard promised. "I'd better find Watson before he creates even more havoc. Nice to meet you, Tara. Say hello to Morgan and tell him any time he wants a dog I've got one going spare!"

"Hmm, I may not remember all of that message," said Tara. "Stick insects are about my limit."

"Can't go wrong with a good stick insect," nodded Richard. "It'd look a bit daft on a lead though!"

And then he was gone, crashing through the undergrowth and yelling his dog's name so loudly that people could probably hear him in Devon. Tara couldn't help laughing as she retraced her steps to the village. She was still smiling when she walked back through the narrow streets. Sunshine, fresh air and exercise as well as the feeling that today was a new start had put her in a much more optimistic frame of mind. Richard's comical behaviour had amused her, and she'd been touched by his fondness for Morgan. Despite her doubts about coming back to Polwenna Bay, hearing someone speak so positively about her son had certainly helped to soothe her anxieties. Nothing mattered as much as Morgan's happiness.

Tara was still thinking about her son as she passed the village green and the brightly lit window of Silver Starr's shop, Magic Moon. The scent of pasties wafted across the street and her mouth watered. It must be almost lunchtime by now. Maybe she and Morgan could have a pasty picnic on the quayside and throw the crusts to the gulls like they used to do. That would be fun.

"Mum! Mum!"

As though she'd magicked him just by standing outside the mystic shop, here was Morgan now, scurrying down the road towards her. As always, his camera was in his hand – but, unusually, it was out of its case and bashing against his leg. Morgan had a very intent expression on his face. There was no sign of Alice either, which was odd. He was never far from his great granny.

Something was wrong…

"Mum!" Morgan gasped, hurling himself at Tara's legs and almost felling her. "Don't let her take my camera, Mum! Please!"

His eyes were wide with terror and, pulling him close, Tara felt him shaking. What on earth was going on? Her son was petrified.

"My camera!" Morgan kept sobbing. "She's going to take my camera!"

"Who is?" Tara asked, but Morgan was too beside himself to answer. All Tara could do was cast her gaze around for any teenaged thugs who might have been terrorising her child – but she drew a total blank. There was one spotty youth sprawled on a bench texting, and across the village green a pair of girls were looking longingly into the window of the clothes shop, but of camera-snatching yobs there was no sign.

"No one's going to take your camera, Morgan," Tara said, tightening her arms around him. "I promise."

But Morgan wasn't convinced. "She will! She said so! Even Granny Alice can't stop her."

"Who says they're taking your camera, sweetheart? Are you sure that was what they meant?"

Having a tendency to take things literally meant that sometimes Morgan got things confused. Tara hoped that this was just one of those times, but instinct told her otherwise. She wished Danny was here. He was fantastic at keeping Morgan calm, whereas she tended to get far too upset, which only made things ten times worse.

"Her!" Morgan cried, pointing down the road to an elderly woman who was scuttling closer and yelling. Her face was pinched with rage and her mouth was pursed up tighter than a cat's bottom. She was waving a fist at Morgan and shrieking more loudly than the seagulls.

Morgan ducked behind Tara and wailed, "Poison Ivy!"

Tara looked up and down the street, half expecting to see a Marvel supervillain appear. But no, Morgan really did seem to be terrified of this rapidly approaching old woman. What on earth?

"Mum, she's going to throw it in the river! She said so! Please don't let her!" Morgan wept.

Tara had no idea who this elderly woman was or why she was so angry with Morgan, but there was no way she was letting any adult, old or otherwise, frighten her child like this.

"You give me that camera right now, you little tyke!" Morgan's pursuer shouted from further down the road. "How dare you take pictures of me without my permission? That's against the law, I'll have you know! I'll call the police and they'll lock you up!"

At this threat, Morgan really began to panic. "I don't want to be locked up! Don't let them lock me up, Mum!"

"No one's locking you up," Tara promised him fiercely. "Of course they're not."

"Ivy, calm down, for heaven's sake!" cried another voice. "He didn't mean any harm. He's just a child!"

Granny Alice, pink in the face and with her hand on her heart, was trying in vain to catch the other woman's arm and slow her down. Unfortunately each attempt only met with her being shaken off. It wasn't long before Ivy was within spitting distance of Morgan and Tara.

"You're the mother, I presume?" demanded the furious old woman. She stood with her hands on her bony hips and looked at Tara as someone might look at something nasty on the sole of their shoe. "This is *your* child?"

Tara tightened her arms around Morgan. "Yes, I'm Morgan's mother."

"Call yourself a mother? Pah! You're a disgrace, that's what you are!" the elderly woman hissed. "He's been spying on me! Spying! What do you say to that? Hmm?"

"Spying?" This accusation threw Tara, and her angry retort evaporated on her lips. "That doesn't sound like Morgan. Are you sure?"

This question enraged the other woman even more. "Are you calling me a liar?" Saliva flecked the corners of her mouth and splattered her chin as she spoke.

"No, of course not. But spying?" In desperation Tara turned to Alice, who had just caught up. "What on earth's going on here?"

"Morgan took Ivy's picture outside church," wheezed Alice. "He shouldn't have done, of course, but you know how he is about taking pictures."

Tara certainly did. Photography was Morgan's pet obsession, and he was pretty good at it too. This seemed a huge overreaction just for snapping a photo.

"Did you, Morgan?" she asked gently.

Her son nodded miserably.

"Without my permission!" screeched the old woman. "I know all about little perverts like him! It'll be all over the Internet in minutes! On that Book-Face thing! Give me that camera now, you little rat!"

She dived towards Morgan, but Tara stepped forward. Not for the first time in her life she was glad to be taller than average. Crowded pubs, getting served at the bar, fending off mad old bats… Other people – like Mo, for example – might fight with words, but somehow Tara didn't think this character would be stopped by semantics. Like all bullies, physicality intimidated her.

"Don't you dare call my son a pervert," she said, her voice dangerously cold. "He loves photography and, as I'm sure Alice has tried to explain, there are good reasons why he likes to do things a certain way. If he took your photo without permission then he'll certainly apologise and delete it, but I won't stand for you bullying an eight-year-old. That isn't appropriate. Do you understand?"

Ivy glowered at her. "Appropriate? As if spying on people is? Of course he didn't have my permission, you stupid woman. As if I'd let a brat take pictures of me!"

Ignoring these insults, Tara crouched down until she was face to face with Morgan. He was pale and shaken but this, she knew, was more from the fear of having his camera taken and nothing really to do with Ivy's shouting. Morgan didn't respond to shouting or any extremes of emotion. These just perplexed him.

"Sweetie, did you take this lady's picture without asking?"

"Yes."

"OK." Tara took a deep breath. "Can you tell us why?"

Morgan looked up at Ivy. "Don't be cross, Mrs Lawrence. I had to do it. It was an important scientific experiment. I was trying to help you."

"A scientific experiment?" Alice echoed. "Darling, whatever do you mean?"

"Issie told me that if I took a picture of Mrs Lawrence my camera would break," Morgan explained, deadly earnest about this. "I said that was rubbish but Issie promised it was true. She said that if you take a picture of a wicked old witch your camera will break, but I said there's no such thing as witches. Fact. So I took a picture of Mrs Lawrence to prove it."

Alice clapped her hand over her mouth, and Tara didn't know whether to laugh or cry. Bloody Issie!

Ivy's jaw was swinging open in disbelief at what she was hearing.

"It was a good experiment because my camera still works," Morgan said proudly. Turning to Ivy, he added kindly, "Which means you're not a witch, even though you are really nasty to everybody and make all the children scared. Is that why you don't have any grandchildren? Because you were nasty to them? Did they run away?"

"I… I…" spluttered Ivy. She'd suddenly run out of words.

Poor Alice was mortified. "Ivy, I'm so sorry. Morgan sometimes takes things very literally. Like in this instance, Issie saying something very rude and very silly when she ought to know better."

Issie really was twenty-two going on six, thought Tara wearily. To Ivy, she said, "I think this has been a very unfortunate misunderstanding. I'll delete the pictures right now and maybe we can draw a line under it all."

"I'll do it for you," said Morgan helpfully. "Unless you want them as proof you're not a witch?"

Ivy scowled at him. "Just delete them, you stupid little boy!"

Morgan fiddled with his camera and his brow pleated. "I'm not stupid actually. I have a very high IQ. Fact. You shouldn't call people stupid either, by the way. It's very rude and my teacher says it makes people sad and then you have no friends. Is that why you have no friends? Because you've been unkind and made everyone sad? Will you die all alone like Mr Scrooge nearly did?"

Ivy stared at him. "I..."

"Because you probably will and I think you really should be nicer," Morgan told her. "Then people might like you. But they all hate you now. Fact."

"Right, that's enough," Tara interrupted him, jolted out of her shock and into parent mode. "You are being rude now. Apologise!"

"But I was telling the truth!"

"Morgan," Alice said gently, "remember how sometimes we need to think about whether the truth makes someone happy or sad?"

Her grandson nodded. "Sometimes when something is true we shouldn't say it," he told Ivy gravely. "I'm sorry if telling the truth about you being mean has made you sad."

Time to nip this apology in the bud before it gets any worse, thought Tara.

"The pictures are all gone," she said quickly, taking the camera from Morgan and holding it out to Ivy. "Do you want to check?"

But Ivy seemed dazed. "What? No, no. If you say they're gone, I may as well believe you."

That was big of her, Tara thought. What a nasty piece of work. She didn't usually agree with Issie, but Ivy Lawrence really was a wicked old witch; Tara wouldn't be at all surprised to see her zip by on a broomstick.

Without uttering another word, not even so much as a grudging apology, the old woman had turned her back on them and headed back to her cottage, where she'd probably stick pins in a few dollies and boil up a hex or two.

Tara shivered. It was all nonsense, of course it was.

So why did she feel as though she'd just made a terrible enemy?

Chapter 8

"So what do you make of the Wicked Witch of the South West rocking up?" Issie asked Jules over an enormous plate of cheesy chips. Dunking one in ketchup and biting down hard on it as though wishing it were Tara, she added, "I take it you're as shocked as we are?"

It was Monday and officially Jules's day off. Even so, she'd spent most of the day so far worrying about work. She'd already planned a sermon and spent several hours puzzling over the mystery money that kept appearing in the St Wenn's account, before chewing her nails to the quicks as she stressed over the bishop's impending return visit. Still, it was good to keep busy, Jules decided, because that way she didn't have time to think. While she was supervising the Pollards or listening to Sheila Keverne's moaning she couldn't dwell on her own private unhappiness, whereas all alone in the vicarage it was a different matter entirely. When Issie had called and suggested lunch in The Ship, Jules had leapt at the chance of some distraction. Of course, she should have known that Issie would want to dissect in minute detail the very subject that she was desperate to avoid…

"Well?" Issie demanded when Jules didn't reply. "What do you make of Tara coming back?"

How on earth could Jules respond? The real answer would be "horrified, jealous, afraid and torn", but Jules wouldn't dream of saying this. She hardly dared admit it to herself.

"I think it must have taken a lot of courage," she said carefully, avoiding Issie's beady eye and focusing her attention on her mackerel salad. Healthy and slimming. Danny would have been proud.

Issie snorted. "No shame, more like. She's got nerve, I'll give her that. What does Danny say?"

"Danny?"

"Yeah, Danny. Six feet tall? Scars? Blond hair? Arm missing? Irresistible to women, apparently, and can belch *God Save the Queen*? Spends a lot of time with our local vicar?"

"Danny can belch the national anthem?"

"Don't change the subject," Issie said sternly. "We all know how close you two are. We've hardly seen him at Seaspray since Thursday. Jake thinks he's still kipping in the office at the marina, unless he's up at yours?"

Jules felt her face grow hot, and not just from the peppery fish. "He certainly isn't at mine and I have no idea what Danny thinks. I've not seen him since Thursday either."

"Blimey," Issie spluttered. "I nearly choked on my food then! You two are normally joined at the hip."

"We are not." Jules pushed her plate away. She wasn't hungry in the least today. Her appetite had vanished on Halloween and at this rate she'd be a size zero by Christmas. "As for how he feels? I should imagine pretty upset, especially since he's still got feelings for her."

Issie goggled at Jules; the ketchup-laden chip she was holding halted on its final journey. "What? Did he tell you that?"

"Tara's Danny's wife," Jules said quietly. "He's upset because he still loves her. I know she hurt him pretty badly—"

"That's an understatement. She must have said some pretty unforgivable things to him when he was in hospital, because he wouldn't see her after that. No," Issie shook her head and her blonde braids swished in agitation. "I think you're totally wrong, Jules. Danny doesn't love Tara. No way."

Jules said nothing. Issie hadn't seen the state Danny had been in on Thursday and neither had she been party to Tara's confession to Jules, back in the spring, that she still loved him. It was one of hardest parts of Jules's job: people confided in her, but who could she confide in? God, of course – that went without saying – and Jules usually told Danny everything too, but how could she share her conflicted feelings about all this with him? He had his marriage and his son to think about, and they had to come first. The last thing he needed was Jules's feelings colouring his decisions.

"Things are complicated," was all she said. "Tara and Danny have history and a child. They need time to work things out. Maybe we should give Tara a bit of support? It can't have been easy for her."

"Are you mad?" Issie shook her head. "Or are you trying to get some kind of promotion by being a total martyr? St Jules of Polwenna? Don't be a muppet. Danny doesn't want to be with Tara."

Ignoring the jibes, Jules said quietly, "I just think we should let them have some space, Issie, and give Tara a chance, OK? Doesn't everyone deserve that? If you won't do it for her, then at least do it for Morgan. You're always telling me how much he needs stability. The last thing he needs is his family arguing and making it clear they don't want his mother around."

"Now why do I feel guilty? She's the bad guy, not me," Issie grumbled. "Honestly, you're so annoying sometimes, Jules. You always make people think about stuff."

"All part of the service," Jules said, thinking privately that nobody knew better than her just how annoying that *stuff* could be.

"Especially after all the upset with Poison Ivy the other day," Issie added thickly through mouthfuls of cheese and potato. "Morgan was really upset."

Jules nodded. The story had filtered back to her, no doubt heavily embroidered in the retelling, but from the gist of it she gathered it was standard Ivy behaviour.

"And if she ever upsets Morgan again then I won't hold back," Issie promised. "She can't go around being so horrible, Jules. Somebody needs to tell her."

"I know," Jules agreed wearily. "I'll talk to her."

Issie grimaced. "Good luck with that. She's a horrible old bag and even you, Jules Mathieson, won't change my mind on that one. Some people really are just born nasty."

Jules feared that Issie was right. Try as she might, there really wasn't a positive spin that she could put on Ivy. She hadn't a clue why the woman was so relentlessly unpleasant. Ivy just seemed to revel in making everyone's life a misery. While Issie fetched more drinks, Jules gazed thoughtfully out of the window at the wintry village. It was a dreary day; November had chased away the last golden days of the autumn, and it was hard to see where the leaden line of the sea met with the grey sky above. It was only early afternoon, but already the daylight was starting to die and lamps were shining in cottage windows as smoke coiled lazily from the chimneys. Winter's chilly breath was in the air now. Even the seagulls were huddled up on the rooftops, their feathers fluffed up against the cold.

The fire had been lit in the pub. It crackled merrily in the hearth, sparks fantailing upwards into the chimney, and every now and again the landlord added another log. A man was sitting in the chair beside the fire, a notebook held loosely in his hand as he stared into the flames, deep in thought. He had a striking, hard-boned face, hooded eyes and a strong chin. An emerald bandana held his thick long mane of silvery hair away from his lived-in face, a roll-up was tucked behind his ear and both of his wrists were looped with leather bracelets. All in all, the look was an intriguing mixture of a young Dumbledore and Jack Sparrow, Jules thought with amusement. Even his clothes were a mishmash of fantasy and historical costume; a purple shirt was tucked into tight black leather trousers and his outstretched feet sported cowboy boots. He couldn't possibly be a local, Jules thought. Compared with the fishermen standing at the bar in their jeans and sweaters, he looked like a lost parrot surrounded by a flock of sparrows.

Sensing her watching him, the man glanced up and smiled politely before returning to his writing.

"I leave you for one minute and you're on the pull!" Placing two pints of cider on their table, Issie cast a glance at the stranger who, Jules noted, smiled at Issie a lot more enthusiastically than he had at her.

"I am not on the pull!" Jules protested.

"Shame," said Issie. "He's not bad for a crumbly, and it's about time you had some fun, Rev." She slipped back into her seat and reached into her bag to pull out a creased paperback. "Never mind; here's the next best thing," she said, passing it to Jules.

"*Blackwarren*," Jules read. The scarlet cover bore just a title, and the paper felt thin and cheap. It looked like a self-published book, the kind that Betty Jago often sold in the village shop as a favour to locals with literary aspirations. Flipping it over, she scanned the blurb and felt her face turn the same cover as the book. "Issie! What is this? Porn?"

"*Porn?*" mimicked Issie. "How old are you, Jules? It's called erotica now, FYI, and anyway, this is hardly up there with *Fifty Shades*, although it is pretty steamy."

"So I can see." Jules handed the book back. "I'll stick to the Bible and the odd romance, thanks."

Issie's nose crinkled. "Like those pink books you try and hide?"

"My Cassandra Duval novels?" Jules shrugged. These bestselling bodice-rippers were her guilty pleasure and she'd devoured every one. From passionate pirates to headstrong highway men, there was always an alpha male sweeping the heroine off her feet. Jules guessed it was the closest she'd come to this in real life, unless some serious weight loss happened or her hero had a crane.

"That stuff is so lame!" scoffed Issie. "Honestly, Jules, you should read this. Everyone else in the village is."

"Are they?" Jules hadn't noticed but she guessed she'd been lost in her own worries. People also had a habit of hiding anything they thought might offend the vicar, as though she was an elderly Victorian spinster.

"It's got to have been written by a local because it's definitely set here. The hero even has a birthmark the shape of a starfish below his left buttock, just like Teddy St Milton's," Issie told her.

"I'm not going to ask how you know about that!"

Issie winked. "My lips are sealed! What I can divulge is that apparently it's a family birthmark and his grandfather has it too. But I agree, whoever wrote this book must have seen Teddy very close up."

Teddy St Milton, heir to the Polwenna Bay Hotel, was the local playboy. With his fat wallet, expensive car and floppy hair, he was irresistible to the local girls and holidaymakers alike.

"I know, I know, that doesn't really narrow the field much," grinned Issie. "Tell you what, I'll read you a bit and you can tell me what you think."

Jules took a big gulp of her cider. "Please don't. I've just eaten."

"Don't be such a wuss," her friend said airily, flipping the pages. "Anyway, don't you think you ought to know what your flock's reading? Ah! This is a good bit. Lord Blackwarren has just come back from the Battle of Waterloo and seduces his arch-enemy's fiancée—"

Hands over her ears, Jules cried, "I'm not listening! La, la, la!"

"Where would that kind of wussy attitude have got E L James?" Issie asked, despairingly.

"Go on, Issie," piped up Little Rog Pollard from the far end of the bar, where he was supposed to be fixing a light fitting. "We're all listening. Is it the bit where he picks her up, throws her over the desk and—"

"Don't give it away! Issie said. She began to read: "'Lord Blackwarren's midnight-black eyes narrowed dangerously as he saw the twin globes of Amelia's snow-white bosom.'"

This really had to stop!

"E L James isn't a vicar!" Jules reached out and plucked the book from Issie's ring-crammed fingers and stuffed it into her bag. "And I am confiscating this!"

"Spoilsport," said Little Rog. "That's one of the best bits."

"Confiscating it, or saving it for later?" grinned Issie, then held her hands up in mock surrender at the look on Jules's face. "OK! Just kidding! You hang onto it if you like. I've got to run anyway. I promised Gran I'd give her a hand this afternoon cleaning the holiday let. Happy reading!"

As Issie breezed out of the pub Jules closed her eyes wearily. Spending time with her friend was like hanging out with a minor hurricane – exhilarating, exhausting and never, ever dull.

"Excuse me, but I couldn't help overhearing your conversation. Do you mind if I join you?" asked a male voice.

Jolted out of her thoughts, Jules looked up and saw the man who'd been seated by the fireplace standing beside her table and smiling at her hopefully. Used to meeting strangers and having to try to figure them out fairly swiftly, Jules instantly liked what she saw. It was a face as weathered as the granite rocks outside, one lined with smiles and life and strong emotions, and his eyes were twinkly and warm. He was somebody who'd lived, Jules decided – and he probably enjoyed every second of his existence, if the near-empty whisky glass held loosely in his nicotine-tipped fingers was anything to judge by.

"I'm a writer," the man added. "I heard you talking about literature with your friend just now and I was intrigued."

"I'd hardly call that literature," Jules laughed, but her new companion didn't join in. Instead he nodded vehemently.

"I totally agree, but that kind of thing seems to be all anyone wants to read these days. Those of us who write books of merit are sadly out of fashion." Placing the whisky on the table he held out his hand. "Caspar Owen."

"Jules Mathieson," said Jules as they shook hands. "Please, sit down."

Caspar lowered his long frame into the window seat and exhaled theatrically.

"It seems a crime to turn my back on such scenery, especially since I've come all the way from London to be inspired by it."

"It is stunning," Jules agreed. Although it was a cold day and the sun was currently sulking behind a bank of thick cloud, the picturesque old harbour and whitewashed cottages clustered around it still drew the eye. "I often find myself staring out of the vicarage window when I really ought to be working."

"Ah! The village vicar." Caspar raised his glass and Jules chinked hers against it. "So tell me, Reverend Mathieson, are there lots of interesting events going on in Polwenna Bay that a humble wordsmith might find inspiring?"

"How many plots do you need?" Jules asked. She'd never heard of Caspar Owen but she was pretty sure that if he approached his editors with storylines inspired by events in Polwenna Bay, they'd tell him it was all too far-fetched.

He sighed and raked a hand through the ends of his silver mane. "One would be enough for me right now. I've got writer's block, Reverend, and I haven't been able to write a word for months. It's an absolute curse."

"I bet. Poor you." Jules did her best to look sympathetic, although she didn't really know if she believed in writer's block. Having to pen two sermons a week, or otherwise look like a real numpty at Sunday services, this seemed a bit of a luxury to her. Self-indulgent even.

But Caspar was nodding, his eyes wide and mournful. "It's awful. I've got a book to deliver at the end of December and I haven't written a word. I've rented a cottage here to see if a change of scene will help."

Jules hadn't lived in the village long but she'd already learned that artists and writers flocked to the place for inspiration.

"And has it?"

"Not yet." His mouth drooped. "The muse has well and truly deserted me, I'm afraid."

And would continue to do so if he kept looking for her in the pub, Jules thought privately. Aloud she said, "Well, then we need to find her for you. What genre do you write? Would I have read any of yours?"

"I'm pretty, err... niche, so probably not. They wouldn't be your kind of thing," Caspar said quickly, and Jules had the distinct impression that she was being fobbed off. "I'm far more literary than that book you and your friend were reading earlier."

"Literary fiction's fine by me," Jules said. She would have been offended by his swift assumptions about her reading habits, except that she could tell from the way he was chewing his lip and from the rapidly vanishing whisky that Caspar was truly worried – and worry, Jules knew, often made people tactless.

At least, that was what she told herself when members of her flock were rude and thoughtless...

"Actually, you might be able to help me," Caspar was saying. "Your friend? The one you were having lunch with? She might be able to get me writing again."

"Issie?" Jules frowned. "I don't see how."

"*Isabella and the Pot of Basil.* Issie. Issie." Caspar rolled the name around on his tongue just as moments before he'd been savouring the ten-year-old Macallan. "Yes, she could be my muse. The Fair Isabella. Would you ask her?"

Personally Jules though Caspar had as much chance of Issie being his muse as she did of becoming a supermodel.

"You'll have to ask her that," she said diplomatically. Then, as an idea occurred to her, she added, "But why don't you take the book she was talking about earlier? I know I have no real literary appreciation and can't possibly understand your niche, but it might give you some ideas, you never know."

Her sarcasm washed over Caspar like the tide was starting to wash over the beach.

"That's not at all a bad idea," he agreed, looking far more cheerful.

Jules plucked the book out of her bag. Was it her imagination or did that scarlet cover burn her fingertips? Either way, she felt very relieved when Caspar slipped the paperback into the pocket of his long black cloak. It would be just her luck if it had fallen out of her bag the next time she saw the bishop.

"So Issie will be my muse," Caspar was saying to himself, dreamily. "The beautiful maiden with eyes of sapphire blue and laughter like a peal of bells. A goddess whose sweet feet float above the ground."

Was this the same Issie? The one who swore like a trooper, drank pints and wore DMs? Jules bit back a smile. If this was an example of Caspar Owen's writing then maybe it was just as well he had writer's block!

Having emptied his glass, Caspar was on his feet again and heading for the bar.

"Can I buy you another cider?" he asked Jules. "Go on, the sun's over the yardarm somewhere!"

She shook her head and pulled her purse out. "No thanks. I'm going to do some work on the church accounts, and as much as that makes me long for another drink I'd better stay sober. It's time I went home."

"At least let me pay for your lunch," Caspar insisted, waving a twenty under Kelly the barmaid's nose. "A salad in return for inspiration and a book seems a fair exchange."

"The Rev's lunch is already paid for," Kelly told him with a toss of her newly dyed red head and a swish of her false lashes. "But I'll not say no to a drink if you're buying."

Jules was confused. "Did Issie pay?"

This seemed highly unlikely, since Issie was always broke. Still, stranger things had happened, especially in Polwenna Bay.

Kelly snorted. "As if! No, it's really weird – and I meant to say earlier, but we were so busy – but when I opened up this morning there was an envelope pushed under the door. It had thirty pounds in it and a note saying to buy the vicar lunch and a drink. So you're all square."

Jules was taken aback. Things like this never happened to her. "Really? Who was it from?"

She held her breath because, stupidly, she was hoping it was Danny.

"No idea." Kelly pushed Caspar's glass underneath the optic, filling it with a good three fingers of whisky before he gave her the thumbs up. "It wasn't signed."

Jules was thrown. Who would want to buy her a secret lunch? And why? Danny would just say so, and the members of the Parochial Church Council would take her out so that they could all join in.

"Why would someone do that?"

Kelly giggled. "Maybe you've got a secret admirer? Maybe he's a lonely millionaire like Christian Grey in *Fifty Shades*. It might be red roses to the vicarage by moonlight next."

Jules hadn't read the book in question, but from what she'd gathered about it, red roses didn't feature as prominently as red rooms full of pain. The latter sounded a bit too much like a WI meeting in the village hall's back room to be escapism. Anyway, roses and moonlit declarations of love only happened in Cassandra Duval novels, didn't they? Her admirer was probably just embarrassed.

Caspar's eyes were glittering like the pub's fairy lights. Turning to Jules, he said excitedly, "You weren't kidding when you said there were lots of plot lines for me in this village, were you? You have an angel watching over you!"

Jules raised her eyes to the beams.

"You're a writer?" Kelly couldn't have looked more thrilled if he'd said he was the new member of One Direction. "Will you put me in a book?"

"If you pop another tot of whisky in that glass, sweetheart, I'll write a book all about you!" he promised.

This had to be one of the most cringeworthy lines Jules had ever heard. Kelly, however, seemed delighted with this answer; moments later, Caspar's glass was practically full to the brim. Jules had a sneaking suspicion that Caspar Owen got a lot of drinks this way, which probably helped to account for his writer's block.

With the glass safely in his hand and Kelly assured of her impending immortality in a work of great literature, Caspar strode across the bar and sat back down opposite Jules.

"A toast is called for!"

An escape was called for, Jules thought darkly, but to humour him she raised her empty glass and pasted on her best polite-vicar expression. Caspar was as nutty as the WI fruit cake, which meant that he was bound to fit into Polwenna Bay beautifully.

"What are we toasting?" she asked. "Writing books? Muses?"

"We'll toast writing books," he nodded, his glass glittering in the firelight, "and muses and vicars too. But most of all, let's drink to a new and exciting mystery. Raise your glass, Jules! To my book, my new muse and an exciting new enigma. To the Polwenna Bay Angel, whoever he or she may be!"

Chapter 9

Jules didn't have time to dwell on the identity of her mysterious lunch-buying angel or Caspar Owen and his writer's block. She was too busy poring over the church's tangled finances. She'd fallen into bed late the previous night, her eyes gritty and her head spinning from hours of trying to make sense of numbers that flatly refused to add up. She was still trying to makes sense of them the next day.

"It's not your maths, Jules," Richard Penwarren said when, driven to despair, she swung by the surgery to ask him for help in his capacity as the PCC treasurer. Her desperation was clear – not many people would willingly brave the waiting room and its battalion of germs – and he'd instantly sacrificed one of his rare afternoon breaks to scrutinise St Wenn's books. "Trust me. These figures really don't add up."

"Nice to know I'm not going mad," Jules said. She certainly felt like it. The only positive was that at least her mathematical troubles took her mind off Danny.

Richard slid his glasses off and ground his knuckles into his eyes. Then he replaced them and peered blearily at the printed spreadsheets.

"You're certainly not going mad, but somebody somewhere is behaving very strangely. See all these deposits I've highlighted?"

She nodded. "They're the same ones I can't make sense of. I've been through the paying-in book a thousand times and there's no record of any member of the PCC paying them in."

"Which means that somebody else is paying money into the church account," Richard concluded.

Jules was puzzled. "Why would anyone do that? All they have to do is come and see me or put it into the collection."

"Maybe they want to remain anonymous?""

"That's fair enough, but I don't understand why they'd need to do it this way. The collection is anonymous."

"You'd still know who's been in the service though. Giving the money this way means that our mystery benefactor can make sure nobody's able to guess their identity." Richard pushed the paperwork back across the table.

"That's a good thing isn't it?" Jules folded the pages up and pushed them into her bag. "They must mean well."

"They're paying money into the church account, so I'm sure they have wonderful intentions," Richard said slowly. "However, my granny used to say that the road to hell is paved with good intentions."

Jules stared at him. "That doesn't sound good, Richard. I take it there's a problem with this?"

He sighed. "Well, I'm still new to all this, of course, but I'm afraid there could be. This kind of thing looks very fishy. I'm wondering if it might cause problems for St Wenn's further down the line – questions about money laundering and so on, I mean."

Jules felt cold all over. "Money laundering? Richard, tell me you *are* joking? The bishop will have a fit!"

But the doctor was deadly serious. "Jules, we have no idea where that cash is coming from. Yes, it could be a genuine person who wants to give to the church and not have any fuss made, but presumably we have a duty to know where those funds are coming from. What if it triggers some sort of investigation by an authority?"

Jules felt sick. An investigation was the last thing she needed. The bishop was due to visit again in a month or so and, although she'd worked hard to increase the activity of the church, she knew that the future of St Wenn's was far from secure. Would someone's misplaced kindness end up being the reason for closure that she feared the Church of England had been looking for?

"What can I do?" she asked.

"There's only one thing you can do," Richard said. "You need to find out who our mystery benefactor is, and as soon as possible too. This needs to all be above board and legitimate, Jules, or I'm afraid we really could have a major problem on our hands."

Jules nodded – although, short of staking out every bank in Cornwall, she had no idea how she could find out who the donor was. As she left Richard to his afternoon surgery and meandered back through the village, Jules wondered whether this could be the same person who'd bought her lunch the other day. Might it be Caspar Owen was Polwenna Bay Angel? It was all a mystery and one that she wasn't sure how to solve. She wished she could ask Danny – he was always a brilliant sounding board – but she hadn't seen her friend for days. He wasn't walking on the cliffs or drinking coffee in the harbour tearoom. He'd missed yesterday's PCC meeting and Alice said he'd not spent a night at Seaspray since Tara had returned five days ago. No matter where Jules went in case she accidentally bumped into him, Danny just wasn't there. Her friend seemed to have vanished into the drifting sea mists.

Or else, and this was an unbearable thought, he was avoiding her.

Outside the warm fug of the surgery the late afternoon was bitterly cold. As she walked, Jules pulled up the hood on her coat and dug her hands deep down into her pockets. The streets were quiet and even the seagulls had retreated to the cliffs, leaving the rooks caw-cawing in the skeletal trees above the village. The tang of woodsmoke laced the air and Jules's breath rose in little clouds. Lost in thought, she walked past the village shop, skirted the green and crossed the narrow bridge before turning towards the harbour. The boats were all out and the quay was deserted for once, apart from a doughty pair of walkers braving the cold to stride across the cliff path. Most likely they would soon be diving into the pub to warm up.

"Afternoon, Vicar!" Big Eddie Penhalligan called over from the fish market, where he was loading the fork-lift truck with old pallets and the splintered remains of ancient furniture. "Have you come to help?"

"Help?"

"With the bonfire?" Eddie jerked his bobble-hatted head in the direction of the beach. "Everyone's down there dumping anything they don't want and gathering up driftwood. I'm going to chuck this lot down onto the beach if you care to give a hand?"

Of course, today was November the fifth, Guy Fawkes Night. The village was quiet because everybody was down on the beach building the bonfire and getting ready for the fireworks display. Jules thought about the spreadsheets nagging at her from the depths of her bag. The idea of tossing them onto the bonfire was incredibly tempting.

"It should be bloody good tonight," Eddie hollered as the fork-lift spluttered into life and whizzed him along the narrow quayside. "One of the best nights of the year, Rev!"

Jules followed, breaking into a jog to keep up. She remembered now that Ashley had donated a huge lump sum of money towards the fireworks display and was allowing it to be set up in the grounds of his home, Mariners' View. Big Rog had done a fireworks course and had supposedly become the village expert. By the time Jules was helping Eddie to lob sections of pallets and broken chairs onto the beach below, he'd also filled her in about last year's event. Apparently, several mothers had fallen out with Jules's predecessor over the results of the Best Guy Competition.

"Don't look so worried," Eddie said, his huge ham hands making light work of tossing a table top onto the wet sand below. "We've banned the competition this year. You're safe."

"Glad to hear it," said Jules, who knew just how upset parents could become if they felt that their little darlings had been slighted. It was one of the reasons she was planning to let Hamilton take charge of the nativity play – that, and Danny saying that he might have survived a war zone but he'd rather face military action than a group of Polwenna Bay mums on the warpath.

Oh Lord, no. Anything but that. Even manning the cake stall at the Christmas fayre was preferable.

"You could collect money or draw the raffle if you like," Eddie said kindly, mistaking the look of horror on her face for disappointment. "Being a vicar we'd trust you not to cheat. Ashley's donated a good chunk of cash towards the prizes as well as paying for the fireworks."

Jules's ears, pink with cold, pricked up. Was Ashley her mysterious benefactor? He was certainly rich enough and probably felt as though he owed God one. On the other hand, he was also a businessman and smart enough to know the headaches that unexpected lump sums appearing in a bank account would cause.

"And as you know, he's letting us have the display at Mariners," Eddie continued. "The Pollards are there now setting up."

Jules hoped that the Pollards would do a better job of rigging a fireworks display than they did of fixing the church roof, or the village would be in big trouble. Glancing up at the steep grounds of Mariners she saw several figures, swaddled against the cold wind and scuttling around the garden.

Having deposited the firewood, Eddie trundled off to fetch the next load. Brushing splinters and flakes of paint from her coat, Jules headed down the worn steps that led to the beach. No wonder the village was empty; all the locals were hard at work heaping junk and timber into an enormous mound at the bottom of the cliffs. Already several Guys were sprawled at the foot of the pile, awaiting their gruesome fate.

"They look like I feel," said a voice over her shoulder.

Jules turned, her heart racing, to see Danny standing beside her. He was wearing faded Levi's tucked into battered country boots, and was swaddled in a thick Arran sweater that smelled faintly of damp sheep and salt; Jules recognised it as the same jumper that she'd often seen on one of the pegs in the Seaspray boot room.

Neither of them spoke, but simply gazed at one another. As always Jules was struck by the intensity of him, the incredible blue of his uninjured eye, the way it almost seemed to burn with a light of its own. His close-cropped hair was golden in the sunshine and his face was flushed from his exertions building the bonfire.

"Hey you," he said, in a tender voice.

The fine hairs on Jules's forearms rippled. "Hey," was all she said back.

Still they stared at each other; the only sounds were their breathing and the hiss of the waves. Jules found that for once she really didn't know what to say. When did their friendship get so complicated?

About the time his wife came back, she supposed.

"Morgan looks like he's having fun," Jules remarked eventually.

The bonfire was growing bigger with every minute that passed. Morgan, easy to spot in a scarlet hat and gloves, was dragging an enormous branch across the wet sand with great concentration. His mother stood a small distance away, arms crossed tightly across her chest, watching him intently. Although Tara's back was turned to them, her tension was evident in the rigid way she held herself; in spite of everything, Jules's tender heart went out to her. Returning to a village where you'd been painted as the bad guy couldn't be easy.

"Morgan's thrilled to be home," Danny agreed. He watched his son heave the branch onto the pile, determination written all over his serious little face, before racing away to collect another from the bottom of the beach steps. "And I'm delighted to have him here, you know that. I've really missed him."

She nodded. "I know you have."

"But I haven't missed Tara, before you start drawing all the wrong conclusions," Danny stated, turning his attention back to her. "Well? Go on, say it. I know you're dying to."

"Say what?"

"How am I? How do I feel about Tara coming back? Am I all right? Will I try again? Et cetera, et cetera. Take your pick. I'm ready for the inquisition. Isn't that what the Church does?"

"Other team – and, anyway, I haven't said any of that," Jules said, stung. She thought she'd been doing a great job of *not* saying these things, even though she'd been longing to. Only lots of prayer and a gallon of willpower had prevented her from hammering on the door of

Tremaine Marine's office for the last few nights and demanding to be let in to see if Danny was all right.

"You're thinking it though, admit it. Everyone is, but they don't dare say so. I might have lost an arm and my devastatingly good looks but I haven't lost my mind. It's like a whole troupe of elephants are dancing through the village."

"Lord," said Jules picturing this. "Sheila would have a fit. Imagine the mess. She's bad enough if one of Mo's horses craps in the village! Anyway, isn't the saying supposed to be 'elephant in the room', not 'elephants on the rampage in a Cornish fishing village'?"

Danny laughed. "Thank God you speak to me like I'm normal, because nobody else seems to. You're the only one who ever does and I've missed it." He paused. "I've missed you, Jules. Can't we just hang out like normal?"

Jules looked up at him and was taken aback to see a kind of hunger in his expression, as though he hadn't seen her for weeks rather than just five days. It was exactly how she felt.

Stamping out the hope that had flared at the words *I've missed you*, she said quickly, "Danny, you know how awkward this situation is for me. Polwenna's a small village and people like to gossip. Things are tricky enough with the bishop and St Wenn's future without any rumours about marriage-wrecking lady vicars being added to the mix."

"My marriage was well and truly wrecked before you turned up," Danny pointed out reasonably. "Anyway, it's nobody's business but ours."

Jules shook her head. "That's not the case, Dan. I'm the village vicar and I have to set a standard, otherwise how can I stand up in the pulpit and try to guide others? You're not free and neither am I. Fact, as Morgan would say."

"Excuse," Danny shot back.

Jules decided to ignore that comment. "Anyway, you made it very clear what you thought the other night, so I haven't been speculating about anything except maybe where you've been."

He smiled. "So you have missed me a little bit then?"

"Of course – there was no one to take the minutes at the last PCC meeting. Big Rog did it and he's got even worse handwriting than you. Sheila Keverne's having kittens trying to decipher his scrawl in order to type them up. The accounts are driving me mad and I could have done with some help. The vestry tap is dripping too, but apart from that, I've been far too busy to miss you, Danny Tremaine."

"Ah yes, chatting up writers in the pub! Don't think I don't know all about that," said Danny darkly. "It's the talk of the village."

Honestly, MI5 ought to recruit the Polwenna Bay busybodies, thought Jules in awe. No terrorist cells would stand a chance if Kelly from the pub and Sheila Keverne were on spy duty.

"I was not chatting Caspar up!" she protested.

"*Caspar.*" Danny rolled the name around on his tongue before pulling a face. "Yep, of course he's a Caspar. That's just the sort of stupid name a writer would have. Bet it isn't really his name though. He's probably an Alan or a Malcolm. What does he write? Vampire novels?"

She grinned at this. Actually, with his flowing locks and swirling black coat Caspar did look a bit *Interview with the Vampire*.

"Niche stuff, he said."

"Niche stuff?" Dan's brow crinkled. "What's that supposed to mean?"

"No idea. I think he thought he was far too highbrow for the likes of me," Jules laughed. "I can't blame him though, because your sister left that dreadful *Blackwarren* novel with me and he caught us flicking through it."

"The sexy one that somebody local has written? Vicar, I'm shocked at you. Especially after that sermon you just gave me about setting an example," teased Danny. "Or are you the author? Are these your deepest fantasies immortalised in fiction?"

Jules flushed. "Don't be ridiculous! I haven't even dared read it. In fact, I gave it to Caspar." Then, as an idea occurred to her, she asked, "I don't suppose you know who the author is, do you?"

Danny tapped the side of his nose. "Information like that will cost you."

"Do you know?" Jules was intrigued. Who was Polwenna's answer to E L James?

"If I tell you I'll have to kill you," Dan said, and then yelped when Jules punched his arm. "OK! I'm just teasing you. I haven't a clue either, but after the naked-calendar fiasco my money's on Sheila Keverne. She probably has an entire wardrobe full of whips and crotchless panties."

"*That* is an image I do not want to have," Jules shuddered. "Thanks, Danny. Now I'll not be able to eat for a week."

"It's good to know I have some uses. Danny Tremaine's Diet Tips at your service."

"Talking of diets, I've missed my walking buddy. I'm far too good at talking myself out of exercising at silly o'clock." She gave him a stern look. "Some personal trainer you've turned out to be."

He reached out for her hand. The teasing atmosphere melted away and Jules's breath caught in her throat. "I've been waiting to catch you away from everyone," he said softly.

Jules was sorely tempted to twine his gloved fingers with her own cold ones but, catching sight of Tara and Morgan dragging a drunken-looking Guy across the beach, she stepped back and instead rested her hand on his arm.

"We're hardly alone here, Dan. Half the village is on the beach."

"I meant away from Seaspray and from the church." He sounded exasperated. "Anyway, we've got nothing to hide because we're doing nothing wrong! Jules, I just want to talk to you. I'm not about to drag you into the cave and kiss you until you can't breathe." He paused and then grinned at this thought. "Actually that sounds like a great idea. Fancy exploring the cave with me, Rev?"

Embarrassed, Jules said, "No, I don't want to explore the cave with you!"

The left side of Dan's mouth quirked upwards and he stepped closer. "But kissing me is OK? Happy to do that bit?"

"I didn't say that!" Heart racing, Jules snatched her arm away. "Stop teasing me like this, Danny. It isn't fair."

There was a pause and she raised her eyes to look at him. In the afternoon sun his fine bone structure was beautifully lit, and her stomach went into free fall.

"Who says I'm teasing?" Danny asked quietly. "What would you say if I told you that kissing you is all I can think about?"

Jules felt exactly the same way.

"You've got to stop saying things like this," she whispered.

He shook his head. "I don't think I can, not when I mean them. Why can't you just trust me, Jules? Tara and I are finished and nothing you could say or do will change that. We can never get back together."

"Why not?" Jules asked, feeling increasingly frustrated. It seemed a simple question. After all, nothing about Danny's reaction to his wife's struggle to come to terms with his injuries really made sense to her. It seemed like grudge-holding, and this wasn't Danny at all. All Jules could imagine was that Tara really must have broken his heart for him to still be so bitter. And how did the old saying go? Love and hate were just two sides of the same coin.

Dan looked across the beach and sighed wearily. "I can't say."

She crossed her arms. "Can't or won't?"

"Both, I guess. Like I said, you have to trust me on this one, Jules. Sometimes things break and even if you glue them together carefully they'll never be the same again. The cracks are there and every time you look at the thing you've tried to mend, all you see are the flaws and the damage. You know that you'll never feel the same way about it again. It can never, ever be repaired. That's my marriage."

His expression was hard, his mouth set in a tight line.

"What makes you so sure?"

He reached again for her hand, his grip strong, and held her fingers against his chest until she could feel the steady beat of his heart through the scratchy wool.

"This," he said quietly.

Jules's mouth was as dry as the tinder piled up for the village bonfire. This was the point where she knew that she should say something, make a protest about his marriage and her role as a vicar, but instead silence grew between them. She simply couldn't find the words. When she was with Danny all her objections seemed to vanish. It would be a huge lie to say that she didn't long for him to pull her into his arms and kiss her until she didn't have any breath to protest. They stared at one another and Jules felt the unmistakable tug of longing, a current that would snatch them both up and drag them under just as surely as the rip tides beyond the bay could. All Jules needed to do was step forwards and she would be totally and utterly lost in her love for him.

A love that she had no right to feel.

"I can't," she said bleakly. "I'm sorry, Danny, but it's not enough of a reason. Not to throw a marriage away, anyway."

Danny stared at her. The rosy flush had fled from his cheeks now and he was as pale as sun-bleached driftwood. Jules's fingers slipped from his grasp as he stepped away, shaking his head sadly.

"It's not my secret to tell," was all he said. "If you can't trust me then just walk away now because, believe me, Jules, without trust there really is nothing worth having. Nothing at all."

And then Danny was gone, striding away from her across the rippled sand. Jules watched him go, his lean figure blurring with her tears, and she pressed her fist against her lips to stop herself from calling after him. The truth was that Danny was only half right: Jules trusted him entirely. She always had done and she knew that she always would.

The person she didn't trust was herself. When it came to Danny Tremaine her feelings were in as much danger of bursting into flames as the Polwenna Bay bonfire and, Jules knew, every bit as likely to burn anyone who came too close.

Chapter 10

The evening of November the fifth couldn't have been more perfect if the Polwenna Bay Fireworks Committee had managed to arrange the weather as well as everything else, Tara thought as she huddled deeper into her coat.

The day itself had been one of those perfect crisp autumnal days. When she'd first pulled open the curtains that morning, the sky had been a bright Wedgwood blue; frost had glittered on the rooftops and bushes, and the shrubs in the Seaspray garden had sparkled with lacy spiders' webs. Morgan had already been up for hours and was itching to join in with the building of the bonfire and to make a Guy. Although they'd been back in the village for less than a week, already he was losing the pinched worried look that had broken her heart, and his cheeks were a healthy pink from the wind and fresh air. How could she regret coming back, Tara asked herself now, when her son was so happy?

If Morgan had slotted straight back into village life, Tara was finding it a little harder. Although Alice was being nothing but gracious and Summer was always friendly, Mo and Issie were avoiding her and Danny obviously wasn't sleeping in Seaspray. Jake and Nick were cool with her too, and whenever she walked through the village Tara had the impression that people were whispering about her.

Now, standing on the quay and watching the tide of visitors flowing into the village for the fireworks display, Tara couldn't help laughing out loud. What did she mean, the *impression* that people were talking about her? Of course they were! She was the scarlet woman who'd walked out on her war-hero husband, wasn't she? The one who'd come scuttling back with her tail between her legs. Gossip and scandal didn't come much better than that. Sheila and her coven would be loving every minute.

Tara shivered in spite of her thick scarf. Thank goodness nobody knew the real story – and double thank goodness that Danny was a man of his word and had never told a soul. Once he kept a promise he would rather die than not keep it, a quality that she appreciated far more now than ever. If the truth ever leaked out, the villagers would probably throw her on the bonfire in a Polwenna Bay version of *The Wicker Man*.

The bonfire was burning brightly against the darkness, crackling and spitting and showering orange sparks into the night. Morgan was thrilled with it and was jigging up and down by her side, his camera constantly in his hands as he tried to figure out the best exposure and shutter speed to do the spectacle justice.

"Isn't it just the best bonfire, ever?" he asked Tara, tugging her sleeve to drag her out of her thoughts. "Do you think it's the biggest one the village ever had?"

"Absolutely," Tara nodded, although to be honest one bonfire looked pretty much like another to her. This one was huge though, and to Morgan's delight she'd helped to build it too. Dragging old pallets and sticks of scrapped furniture across the beach had worked wonders when it came to taking her mind off everything. Or rather, it had until she'd spotted Danny and Jules deep in conversation across the beach. They'd only been talking, but there was an intensity between them that had made the hairs on the back of Tara's neck prickle with unease, a feeling that worsened when she saw Dan try to take Jules's hand. The vicar hadn't reciprocated or given any indication that she wanted to, but Tara's every cell was on red alert; the attraction between them was palpable. They hadn't spoken for long before Danny was walking up to Mariners to help the Pollards, while Jules's plump figure was crossing the beach to join in the fire-building activities. Nevertheless, Tara had felt on edge for a long time afterwards.

What if this couldn't be her place anymore and Danny really meant what he said and couldn't forgive her? This thought made her chest constrict, and Tara wrapped her arms around herself tightly. Everything was going to be fine. She would make sure it was.

"I can't wait for the fireworks," Morgan was saying excitedly. "I'm going to take lots of pictures! Maybe the *Cornish Times* will publish one?"

Looking down at his excited face, blushed crimson by the bonfire, Tara felt such a rush of love for him that for a moment she could hardly breathe.

"Your pictures will be fantastic, sweetie," she said finally, but by then Morgan had scampered down the steps to the beach to join Issie and Nick who, cans of lager in hand, were watching the dancing flames. Knowing that they'd not welcome her presence, Tara stayed put on the quay and watched from a distance that was almost metaphorical.

She couldn't remember ever feeling quite so lonely, especially on Bonfire Night. It was among the highlights of the year in Polwenna Bay and had always been one of her favourite occasions. As she watched the crowds begin to gather on the quay and line the narrow streets, memories overlapped the present. The stirring notes of Holst's *Planets* suite, the green and blue blurs of glow sticks, the scent of woodsmoke, the rattle of collecting tins… All these were entwined with images of standing here a lifetime ago with Danny's arms around her and his lips pressing kisses onto her cold cheeks. Usually by this point she would have been hungry for the hot soup and baked potatoes after working all day to build the bonfire. Hand in gloved hand, she and Dan would have explored the stalls erected on the village green for the evening. Tara didn't need to visit these stalls now to know that beneath the striped awning one of them would be selling mulled wine, another would house a barbeque and the third would boast the same tombola that was wheeled out every time the village had an event. When she'd lived here the routine of village life had made Tara want to scream; now she found it comforting.

What was it they said about not knowing what you had until it was gone? If only she really could drift back in time with the bonfire smoke and catch the Tara of ten years ago. She'd tell herself to hold onto Danny, to love him and to never let him go…

It was only six-thirty, but the clocks had gone back just over a week ago; inky darkness bled over the rooftops by five o'clock in the evenings now. The horses in Mo's paddocks huddled in their rugs and stood in muddy gateways. In the harbour, the trawlers rolling in from the sea cast shimmers of emerald and ruby from their starboard and port lights, and the cottage windows glowed with warmth.

It felt as though winter had arrived.

Despite this, the Bonfire Night celebration had the power to entice people from their snug houses. Wrapped up warmly in their thickest coats, they had stomped down to the harbour to enjoy the spectacle. All around was chatter and laughter. The people who owned houses overlooking the bay were having their own parties in their gardens with friends and family; right now they were settling onto their terraces to watch the show with glasses of mulled wine in hand.

Tara checked her watch and waved at Morgan.

"Morgan!" she called down to him. "The display's going to start any minute and you'll get a really good view of it from here."

This year the fireworks display itself was set up in the grounds of Ashley Carstairs' house. This was far enough away to ensure that no rogue rockets or bangers strayed near the crowd but, because the garden stretched out onto the headland that rounded the bay, it was also just the right distance to afford the perfect view and fill the harbour with trembling reflections of the spectacle.

Torches flickered across the dark garden as the Pollards and their helpers made the final checks, and in spite of her melancholy thoughts about gloved hands and winter kisses, Tara felt a familiar fizz of excitement. This was going to be stunning.

"Are you ready, Mum?" Morgan was asking, beside her now and busy setting up his shot.

She ruffled his hair. "Absolutely!"

"Mo says that Ashley paid for extra fireworks too, including a huge fierce tiger rocket," her son continued. "Isn't that cool?"

"Very cool," agreed Tara. She had no idea what a fierce tiger rocket was, but it was clearly very exciting.

"Money for the fireworks!" A rattling bucket announced the arrival of Danny. Clad in a fluorescent vest marked *Steward*, he stepped up beside them and shook the bucket again.

"How come you got landed with this job? I didn't know you were on the fireworks committee?" Phew, at least her tongue was still working, thought Tara as she recovered from the shock of seeing Danny again after five days' absence.

"They daren't let me lose on the explosives," he deadpanned.

But Morgan, who didn't do deadpan, was confused.

"Why not? You know more about explosives than anyone else," he said proudly.

"Not really, mate. That was a joke," said Danny. "I'm not much help stumbling about in the dark with one arm."

"It's not a very funny joke," Morgan told him. "A joke goes like this: a cowboy walks into a German car showroom and says 'Audi'! Get it, Dad? Audi. It's a car."

"Ha ha," said Danny dutifully. He caught Tara's eye and smiled, a real smile this time. It warmed her far more than the heat from the bonfire. He rattled the bucket again. "Come on, cough up."

"We don't have any money. We're poor. Fact," Morgan reminded his father, to Tara's mortification. Great. Now Dan would think she was even more useless and, worse still, not fit to look after their son. First thing tomorrow she'd swallow her pride, brave the gossips and trawl the village in search of a job. She'd take whatever she could find, even washing up or pulling pints.

Danny delved into his pocket and pulled out a handful of loose change. "Chuck that in," he said. "And you're not poor. I'm here to look after you." He looked over Morgan's head straight at Tara. "Both of you."

Before Tara could reply or even think about how these words made her feel, the frosty night sky was filled with dazzling fireworks: golden stars, peacock blues and silver sparkles soared and fell as the sparks from the bonfire leapt into the dark. The ground beneath her feet shook with each burst, and beyond the silhouettes of onlookers the inky sea shivered with golds and greens and vivid scarlets. The crowd gasped and clapped, Morgan snapped photo after photo, and even Poison Ivy seemed to be impressed, although her hands were clamped firmly over her ears. Danny watched the display intently, but it didn't escape Tara's notice that every explosion made him start. She guessed that the horror of war was never very far away.

I wish I could turn back time, she thought sadly. If only they could travel back two years to relive their lives before everything had gone wrong and the secrets had been spilled out in the hospital like blood. Was Danny's heart as damaged as his body? Was he even the same man she'd first fallen in love with all those years ago?

She stole a peek at him but there were no clues in his expression; he was even less decipherable when he turned and she saw again, with the same jolt of shock that she never failed to feel, the scars and the brutal injuries. *Do I still love him?* she wondered. Perhaps it was just a ghost of the past that she was clinging to. After all, how well did she really know Danny Tremaine these days?

Tara was still deep in thought when the display ended, to rapturous cheering and applause from the crowd that was acknowledged by flickering torchlight from the firework technicians high up the sloping land of Ashley's garden. The crowds began to thin as visitors made their way back to the car park or into the pubs and restaurants. On the beach children were being given sparklers, while the WI were doing a roaring trade dishing up jacket potatoes that had been cooking in the embers of the fire.

"The stalls on the green will have a fit," Danny remarked. "Alice was cooking all day for the barbeque. There's enough honey-mustard sausages and coleslaw to feed my entire unit."

"The money all goes to same cause, doesn't it?" Tara recalled that every year the village raised money to cover the fireworks and then donate to charity. This year it was the Air Ambulance. The year Danny was hurt it had been Help for Heroes.

"Come on T, you've not been away that long. You know how competitive those ladies are over whose bucket has the most money in it!"

He'd used his old name for her and Tara was taken aback. He'd not called her T since... well, since he was in the hospital.

Morgan was down on the beach with the other children. He'd turned down a sparkler and a potato and was busy taking yet more pictures. Nothing else mattered to him, and Tara's heart twisted with love. As long as he didn't snap Ivy by mistake things should all be fine. Luckily the miserable old woman had left a few minutes earlier, but not before she'd complained bitterly about her ears ringing and told Danny she didn't believe in charity. What a nasty piece of work she was.

"Morgan! Come and have some food!" Tara called.

"I'm taking a picture of the bonfire with everyone standing by it!" Morgan shouted back. He was fiddling with the lens as he spoke and heading across the sand as far as his little legs could carry him. "I'm using a wide angle!"

Now he was climbing up the rocks at the furthest side of the beach, still trying to screw the lens onto the camera. This was a dark and slippery spot and Tara's stomach lurched. It was the hardest thing in the world, to give your child freedom despite seeing dangers lurking everywhere; it was a tightrope act of love, trying to balance both her instinct to protect him and his need for independence.

"Careful, Morgan," Danny called. "Use both hands!"

But Morgan was so focused on the picture he was trying to take that he didn't reply. Sometimes people thought he was ignoring them, when actually he was just very single-minded. When he had an idea, there was no stopping him. With alarm, Tara realised that this was one of those times. Morgan was climbing much higher than he usually did.

"He's getting too far up," Tara cried, clutching Danny's arm. She was shocked anew to find an empty sleeve.

"Morgan! Get down!" Danny yelled. "That's high enough!"

"He's not listening." Tara was heading towards the beach steps now with Danny at her side. "We'll have to get him down."

The next two seconds seemed to happen in sickeningly slow motion. One moment Morgan was scrambling over the rocks; the next he was tumbling down them until he lay at the foot like a rag doll.

Tara didn't register running down the steps or tearing across the beach. Nor did she have a clue that Danny was right beside her until they reached Morgan and he was crouching down next to his son. All she could see was her baby, in a heap and with blood running over his face.

Her body was cold all over. How was there so much blood? What had happened?

"Mum!" Morgan's voice was weak but he was speaking. Tara's knees turned to soggy seaweed with relief. "My camera's broken!"

"Never mind your camera," Danny told him. "Just stay there for a moment and don't move. We need to check you over."

Tara's vision filled with ghastly images of broken necks and shattered bones. He looked pale and the amount of blood made her head swim. It was like a scene from Macbeth.

"There's an awful lot of blood, Dan," she whispered, not wanting to alarm Morgan, who was very white.

"That's because he's cut his forehead," Danny assured her. "It looks a lot worse than it is, I promise. Cuts there bleed like mad. He's had a bit of a fright and a few scrapes but he'll be all right."

"Let me through! I'm a first-aider!"

Sheila Keverne, clad in her St John's garb, was elbowing her way through the crowd like Moses parting the Red Sea. "Let me examine him! It might be a head trauma! He could be having a brain haemorrhage!"

Head trauma? Brain haemorrhage? The scene dipped and rolled like a fairground ride and Tara began to sway. Morgan's blood became Danny's blood, then became a burned-away face. She saw again the nightmarish injuries that still caused her to wake up in the night, her limbs shaking and her sheets soaking with sweat. She heard ragged sobbing from somewhere and then, appalled, realised it was her. The world had begun spinning so fast that she thought she was going to be violently sick. Doubling up, Tara retched onto the wet sand, before an arm pulled her close and her hair was gently pushed back from her face.

"Morgan's OK," she heard Jules Mathieson saying over and over again. "It's going to be fine, Tara. He's just cut his head."

"My camera!" Morgan was saying over and over again. "Where is it? I've dropped it."

"Never mind your camera, young man," Sheila said sternly. "I need to look at you."

"Sheila, he's bumped his head," Danny pointed out. "I think we can take it from here – and Dr Penwarren's only just up the road."

But Sheila wasn't having this. She was the First-Aider for the Polwenna Fireworks Committee, which was A Very Important Job. Drawing herself up to her full five feet three and puffing out her chest, she fixed him with a steely glare.

"Now you listen to me, Daniel Tremaine! I'm the official first-aider and I have to record any incident and decide if further medical attention is required." Whipping out a medical kit and a torch, she began to peer into Morgan's eyes and examine him – and before Danny could protest, she was enthusiastically mopping up blood.

"Dad!" wailed Morgan.

Danny shrugged. "If you will insist on climbing rocks, son, be prepared to take the consequences."

Now that it was clear nobody was dead, the crowd of onlookers began to thin. Feeling better, Tara crouched down beside Morgan and winced when she saw the cut on his forehead.

"Oh baby," she said sadly, kissing his head. "Does it hurt?"

"It may need stitches," said Sheila hopefully. "I've called Dr Penwarren."

"Cool," Morgan said. "I'll look just like Harry Potter."

Harry Potter had been his previous passion and Tara laughed, although it probably sounded like a sob.

"Don't hassle poor Richard. Morgan will be just fine as he is," Danny said firmly. "The bleeding's stopping and he'd not concussed. I know enough to spot any problems, so we'll just take him home."

"You'll do no such thing!" Sheila barked, pulling a wad of bandages from her first-aid kit. "This isn't a battleground, Danny Tremaine. Now, let me dress that wound, young man."

Moments later Morgan was swaddled up like something from the British Museum's Egyptian rooms and Sheila was wondering aloud whether they might need a neck brace or X-rays, the mention of which sent Tara into a state of panic.

"Blood type?" Sheila barked, her pen hovering over her pad.

"Seriously?" Tara asked.

"Do you need his shoe size too?" teased Danny.

"You can mock all you like, young man, but I do things properly," Sheila huffed. "There's no point with half measures. I'll also have to fill in the accident book. This is very important, I'll have you know."

"Maybe just hurry up a bit," Jules suggested gently. "I think Morgan needs to go home."

"Once this paperwork is done," said Sheila firmly. "Who witnessed the fall?"

"You did," Jules reminded her. "What's next?"

Sheila checked her paperwork. "Name, age and weight, I have. Now I need to know Morgan's blood type."

Tara hesitated. "Why?"

"In case he needs emergency surgery, of course," said Sheila, with evident relish. "Do you know it? Don't panic if you don't, dear. We can always find out at the hospital."

"The hospital?" Tara echoed. She was feeling as though she was having a very bad dream.

"Don't panic, T. Morgan won't be going to hospital unless Dr Penwarren thinks he needs to go," Danny told her. He was always so calm in a crisis, Tara remembered. It was one of the things that must have made him such a good officer.

"He might," huffed Sheila.

Jules laid a warning hand on Sheila's shoulder. "You're doing a fantastic job, but I think that Richard's the only one who can make that call."

"Fine," muttered Sheila, looking mutinous. "We'll see what he says."

"My blood group's A," announced Morgan. He looked at Tara. "That's right, isn't it, Mum? That was what the doctor said when I had my appendix out."

"That's right." Tara had the horrible sensation that the earth was moving beneath her feet, and not because of the shock. She waited for a thunder clap or lightning bolt, but the only sound was the gentle hiss of waves breaking on the beach.

"Do I hear somebody talking about doctors?"

Richard Penwarren had arrived, his black bag in hand. He looked as though he'd come running. He must run a lot, Tara thought abstractedly. If he wasn't chasing dogs then he was tearing about after his patients. This evening his hair was standing on end and he was dressed all in black from lighting the fireworks up at Mariners. Seeing Tara, he smiled warmly.

"Hello again, Mrs Tremaine. I hear that Morgan's taken a tumble. Can I see the patient?"

"I've cleaned and dressed the wound, Doctor," said Sheila proudly, stepping back to reveal her handiwork in the style of Gok Wan doing a reveal.

Richard did a double take and the grey eyes behind his glasses widened. "Err, right, good job," he said. He caught Tara's eye, and his lips twitched. "Would you be so good as to remove the dressing, Sheila, so I can see the injury?"

Once the bandage was unravelled and the cut had been revealed, Richard examined Morgan thoroughly. Tara watched, admiring the way he explained everything to Morgan, who as always had about a thousand questions. Richard was gentle and patient as well as kind, she thought, and those were great qualities in a man and a doctor.

He was obviously better at dealing with humans than animals!

"Fit and healthy," declared Richard finally. "Just keep an eye on him and if there's any change or he looks a bit groggy then give me a call at once."

"He's OK? After all that blood?" Tara needed to hear this confirmed, because it had looked dreadful to her.

"Any wound near the eyebrow always bleeds a lot. It probably looked horrific but it's not too bad. Keep it clean and pop some antiseptic on it again tomorrow and it'll be fine." Richard shut his bag and gave Morgan a stern look. "No more rock climbing with your camera, young man."

"My camera's broken," Morgan said sadly. "It didn't bounce."

"Neither did you," pointed out the doctor. "Next time you might not be so lucky. Mrs Keverne can't always be here to bandage you up!"

Sheila was so busy puffing up with pride that she missed his swift wink, but Tara did and it made her smile. As Richard packed his bag and headed up the beach, Sheila was hard on his heels and describing in minute detail her every action.

"Even I didn't get this much fuss when I was blown up," Danny said to Tara. Maybe Sheila ought to work in a field hospital? The Taliban would run a mile if she showed up armed with those bandages."

Tara laughed. "Yep. She's pretty scary."

They smiled at one another.

"Let's go home," Danny said.

"Seaspray home?" Morgan's voice was full of hope. "Are you coming back too, Dad?"

Danny paused momentarily before resting a hand on his son's head. Tara found she was holding her breath. There was nothing she wanted more than for Danny to be coming home with them. Then he looked at her and her heart rose with a sudden helium gust of hope.

"Yes, Morgan," he said quietly. "I'm coming home. We all are."

Chapter 11

"There you are, Vicar! I've hardly seen you since I arrived. Can I drag you away from this fascinating pile of jumble to join me for a coffee?"

Caspar Owen waved at Jules over the huge pile of clothing she was sorting through, or at least attempting to sort in between having to fend off villagers eager for a bargain. Lions taking down gazelles on the African plains were positively restrained in contrast to WI members on the hunt for a bargain. Although she'd only been manning the stall for an hour, Jules was already frazzled and Betty Jago's earlier dive for a fringed scarf had practically dislocated her wrist.

Anyone who thought that being the vicar of a rural parish was a doddle ought to spend some time running St Wenn's monthly bring-and-buy sale, Jules reflected as she smiled back at Caspar. Coffee sounded great, especially if she could stick a brandy in it.

"This isn't jumble: it's consignment goods," Sheila Keverne was scolding Caspar before Jules could reply. Hands on hips and lips set in a slash of outrage, she glowered at the writer. "Jumble! The cheek!"

In his patched black coat, threadbare scarlet waistcoat and faded silk cravat, Caspar looked as though he was more than familiar with the nature of jumble, but wisely he chose not to argue with Sheila.

"Apologies, madam," he said, lifting off his fedora and giving the outraged verger a theatrical bow before reaching for her hand and kissing it. "Of course these are *consignment* goods. And very fine ones too, sold by two even finer young ladies."

Jules rolled her eyes. Any cheesier and Caspar Owen could be whacked onto a Jacobs cracker and served up after dinner. Still, however corny she found his charm offensive, it clearly worked with older generations: rather than walloping Caspar with her pile of crocheted doilies, Sheila was blushing and giggling like a teenager.

"Oh, get on with you," she said, more breathlessly than Marilyn Monroe singing happy birthday to the president. "Although, we do have the best bring-and-buy sales in the area, you know. The ladies from St Issey's WI don't make half as much as we do."

"I can believe it," nodded Caspar. Then, catching Jules's eye, he added, "Although, I must admit I had no idea that jum— I mean *bring-and-buy* sales were a competitive sport."

"You'd better believe it." Jules rubbed her tender wrist. "If this was an Olympic event, Sheila and her team would bring home the gold."

"It's certainly busy." Caspar was glancing around the village hall where, on a drizzly November Saturday, most of the villagers were sheltering in between dashing to the paper shop and the grocers. Trestle tables were heaped with clothes, books and bric-a-brac, and the villagers had descended on them like jumble-loving locusts. The shoppers were just as eclectic as the goods they were rummaging through. Silver Starr from the hippy shop was unearthing all sorts of treasure; Jonny St Milton the wealthy hotelier, dapper in his pinstripes, was chatting to Alice Tremaine at the tea stand while his grandson Teddy chatted up Issie Tremaine; and a group of burly fishermen were wiping out the cake stall. Even Ashley Carstairs had put in an appearance. He'd spent a fortune on raffle tickets to win a meal at The Plump Seagull, while outside his wife was giving pony rides to excited but soggy children. Jules felt a little glow of pride at how everyone always came together to support the church. Surely if the bishop could see this he'd realise just how much St Wenn's meant to Polwenna Bay? He couldn't possibly want to close the church then.

"So, have you time for a coffee?" Caspar prompted when Jules, who was lost in thought, didn't reply to his initial question. "Surely you get some time off for good behaviour? And being a vicar I'm assuming you're always good?"

Afraid so, thought Jules sadly. It was proving to be very hard though. Morgan's accident on Bonfire Night had highlighted just how much Danny's family needed him, and Jules had made a conscious effort to keep away. It hurt terribly but she knew it was the right thing to do.

There was no way she could share any of this with Caspar, though.

"Of course I am," Jules said lightly, "but there's no such thing as time off for me, I'm afraid."

He pulled a face. "Not even after sorting all those *consignment* garments? Come on, Rev. Even God took Sunday off – I'm sure He'd be happy for you to have ten minutes?"

Jules glanced at the village hall clock. It was coming up to eleven, and she'd been up since six that morning setting out all the stalls before lugging the ancient tea urn back from the quay, where it had been abandoned after fireworks night. A break was way overdue.

"Throw in a slice of walnut cake as well and you've got a deal," she said.

Leaving Sheila in command, Jules bagged a table at the back of the hall and checked her phone while Caspar joined the queue. There was the usual stack of emails, plus a Facebook message from her mum and two texts from Danny. For a second her finger hovered over the keypad, but then she took a deep breath and deleted both of Danny's text messages without even opening them. She was like a drug addict, and the only way to handle her withdrawal was by going cold turkey, Jules decided bleakly. Quite how long this process would take was anyone's guess, though.

"Coffee and a slice of walnut cake and plenty more where this came from because apparently two of these have been donated anonymously, which must be the work of our angel again." Depositing the spoils of his trip to the refreshments stall, Caspar lowered his lanky body onto the folding chair next to Jules and shrugged off his flowing coat. "Eat up," he commanded, pushing a plate containing the most enormous slice towards her. "From the looks of this lot you're going to need your strength."

The bring-and-buy sale was in full swing around them and the village hall was certainly rammed. To Jules's surprise, Poison Ivy was here too. She was busy trawling through precarious piles of paperbacks on the book stall, her nose wrinkling in distaste whenever she came across a stray Jackie Collins or E L James. *No doubt I'll be in for a telling-off for having unsuitable books in a church fundraising sale,* Jules thought wearily. Ivy generally found something to moan about.

Caspar tipped several heaped spoonfuls of sugar into his coffee and stirred vigorously. "Thanks for taking some time out, Jules. I appreciate it. I've been stuck inside my cottage on my own for so long that I'm in danger of starting to talk to the wall like Shirley Valentine."

"You'd probably get more sense out of the wall than me. I'm shattered," Jules sighed.

"Drink that coffee. It should wake you up a bit," he suggested. "Besides, I don't know anyone else apart from you, and Issie is far too busy to talk to me."

"Ah, yes. Isn't she supposed to be your muse?" Jules asked, recalling their last conversation. Personally she thought Caspar's chances with Issie were slim to nil. Issie, although supposedly helping Alice with the teas, was far too busy flirting with Teddy St Milton to pay Caspar any attention, and Jules hoped he wasn't too hurt. Writers were supposed to be sensitive souls, weren't they? It had been a while since her A-levels but she could still recall learning about Petrarch mooning over Laura and Dante pining for the long-lost Beatrice. Unrequited love seemed to be a common literary theme. Besides, who knew better than she how painful it was to love someone hopelessly and from afar?

Fortunately, Caspar Owen seemed to be made of sterner stuff and merely looked at her blankly.

"You said in the pub that Issie was going to be your muse?" she reminded him.

He took a swig of his drink and smiled sheepishly over his mug. "I did, didn't I? Ah, the muse is a capricious mistress, Vicar. Issie is very sweet but she wasn't the one I'm looking for."

Just as well, thought Jules as she watched Issie merrily flirting now with one of the young fishermen. Amusing as he was, Caspar was more likely to fly to the moon than catch Issie's interest, which wouldn't help his writer's block.

"No," Caspar continued, swirling his coffee dreamily, "I need a real woman, not a young girl, to inspire my craft – and I found my true muse last night."

"Great," Jules replied, hoping she sounded more convinced than she felt. She didn't know Caspar very well but she already suspected that constancy wasn't one of his strongest character traits. While he enthused about the virtues of the latest object of his affections, a mysterious woman who sounded like an unrealistic cross between Mother Theresa and a Victoria's Secret Angel, she gently tuned him out and cast an eye over the happenings in the village hall. All seemed to be going well until she looked over at the book stall, where, true to form, Ivy Lawrence was giving an unfortunate WI member a hard time. She was brandishing a paperback and making such a fuss that Sheila Keverne had even abandoned her post to try to defuse the situation – a solution on a par with amputating a leg to cure an ingrown toe nail. Jules sank down in her seat, hoping that Caspar was shielding her from view. Surely having five minutes of peace wasn't too much to ask?

"She's an angel with hair like spun silk and a voice like music," Caspar was saying with an expression that Jules was more used to seeing in the eyes of some of her more evangelical colleagues. "I just know that she'll cure my writer's block. I've already written her a sonnet."

"Wow," said Jules dutifully. As Caspar rambled on about the object of his affections she wondered what it would be like to be the sort of woman who inspired men to write poetry and wax lyrical. The guys she'd dated in the past tended to be more the kind who might write a limerick – but only after several drinks, when rhyming *vicars* with *knickers* struck them as hilarious. It might be a sin of pride, but Jules thought she'd like to know what it was like to be tall and skinny and blonde, even for just a few minutes. Surely it had to be easier than life as a short and rather too plump brunette?

"The problem is that I don't know who she is," Caspar concluded sadly. "Any ideas?"

"Err," floundered Jules, who'd been deep in a very pleasant daydream. "Not really. Where did you see her?"

"Up at the hotel. I went there for supper last night. I think she must work there. My heart is totally set on her, Jules! She's the perfect heroine."

The penny dropped and Jules only just managed to stop herself laughing out loud. Caspar's latest muse had to be Ella St Milton, one of the snootiest and most unpleasant women in Cornwall, if not in the entire world. With her golden hair and willowy figure she might well look like an angel, but that was where the similarity ended. If Caspar was counting on Ella to help cure his writer's block then Jules feared his novel would be a long time coming.

She was trying to work out how to say this tactfully when Ivy Lawrence charged over, slamming a book onto the table with such force that coffee sloshed everywhere.

"You should be ashamed of yourself, peddling filth at a church event!"

"For heaven's sake, Ivy! Now look what you've done!" Sheila Keverne, hot on Ivy's heels and armed with a wad of serviettes, started mopping the table and dabbing ineffectively at the huge coffee stain that was spreading across Jules's jeans.

"What *I've* done?" Hands on her bony hips, Ivy glared at Jules. "I'm not the one selling porn!"

For one awful minute Jules feared that the St Wenn's naked calendar was back to bite her on the backside. Then she caught sight of the book that had outraged Ivy.

"*Blackwarren,*" Ivy hissed. "You should be ashamed, having that filth in here!"

Jules bit back an impatient sigh. It was typical of Ivy to make such a fuss about something so minor. The book was definitely spicy, but it was hardly pornographic. Fascinated in spite of herself, Jules had downloaded it to her Kindle and devoured it in a few hours – all in the name of finding out what her flock were reading, obviously! The tale of the dark, handsome and brooding Lord Blackwarren rattled along at a furious pace and the hero certainly got his share of sword action, both literal and metaphorical. Even more intriguing was the fact that the book was set in a Cornish fishing village spookily similar to Polwenna Bay, and several of the lead characters were rather too familiar to be coincidental. Somebody local had to be the author and most of the villagers were busy speculating. Last night while in the pub Jules had been alarmed to hear even her own name in the frame. She'd had to scotch that rumour pretty fast. The bishop had forgiven her for the naked calendar, just, but if he thought for one minute that she was the author of *Blackwarren*... Jules shuddered to think what might happen.

She had to nip this particular misunderstanding in the bud. Fast.

"I take it you've read the book?" Caspar asked Ivy. His face was innocent but there was an amused gleam in his eye as he posed the question.

Ivy's mouth hung open. "I beg your pardon?"

"You clearly know the book is racy, so I'm assuming you've read it?" Caspar said.

"How dare you!" Ivy's face was almost the same colour as the book jacket. "I most certainly have not!"

"So how do you know it's filth?"

"Because I've heard everyone else talking about it!" Ivy shrieked.

Jules was just about to step in and calm the situation when Sheila snatched up the book and stuffed it into her bag.

"I'll take it," she announced, thrusting a five-pound note at Jules, who was staring at her in amazement. "Oh, don't give me that look, Vicar. Somebody around here needs to know what the fuss is all about."

"Somebody around here needs to show some moral fibre," snapped Ivy.

"Sounds like something you'd eat for breakfast," Caspar murmured, which incensed the older woman even more. Arms folded, she glowered across the table.

Jules knew from bitter experience that she'd need a whole oil well to smooth these troubled waters now. Ivy wasn't above phoning the bishop's office to complain.

"Ivy, I'm very sorry that the book offended you. I certainly didn't put it on the stall, but whoever donated it had good intentions, I'm sure."

"The road to hell is paved with those," Ivy shot back.

"Yes, because people get things wrong sometimes," Jules pointed out gently. "It's part of being human and it's often only through God's grace that we can forgive those errors, just as He forgives us."

Ivy stared at Jules as though she was speaking Chinese. Forgiveness probably wasn't in her vocabulary, and it was with a sinking heart that Jules pressed on.

"Look, what I'm trying to say, and saying badly, is that we're all trying to do our best here to raise money for the church. Can't you just focus on all the good things we do at St Wenn's rather than this one mistake?"

But apparently Ivy couldn't; instead, she just huffed and scowled before spinning on her heel and stomping away, her indignation evidenced by the rigid set of her shoulders. Jules sighed. She'd better prepare herself for a difficult conversation with the bishop.

"My God, what rattled her cage?" whistled Caspar.

"Oh that's just Ivy, don't mind her," said Sheila. "She's always a little grouchy."

He raised his eyebrows. "Grouchy? I'd hate to see her in a really bad mood."

"Stick around and you will," Jules promised him.

Their coffee was cold by now and Caspar went to fetch more, muttering about putting a drop of brandy in the next ones. Jules half hoped he wasn't kidding. She stared thoughtfully after Ivy. Why was she always so determined to be as objectionable as possible? There had to be more to her behaviour than met the eye, and Jules knew that she needed to get to the bottom of it if she was to stand a chance of helping the elderly woman.

The trouble was that Ivy made it so difficult to help.

"That's a long face. Is there anything I can do?"

Looking up, Jules was jolted to find Danny standing at her side, close enough for her to touch, close enough to smell his aftershave. As she inhaled that familiar scent Jules experienced a pang of longing so intense that she could hardly stand it. It must be raining heavily outside now because his hair was plastered to his scalp like a dark gold cap and his long eyelashes were starred with raindrops. Struck by the beauty of him, she gulped and looked down at the table top. She had to fight these feelings and she had to win.

"Let me guess," he continued, pulling out a chair and sitting next to her, "the lovely Mrs Lawrence again? Do you want me to have a word?"

Seeing him so unexpectedly had made the words dry up on Jules's tongue, and all she could do was shake her head.

Danny grinned. "Thank goodness for that. She bloody terrifies me!"

"You're not alone there." Jules was relieved to find that her vocal cords were working again. She took a breath to steady herself. "I'll go and see her."

"Rather you than me," said Danny. "Seriously though, if you want a wing man for support I'll be there. After what happened with Morgan the other day she isn't on my list of favourite people, but I promise I could keep my cool. Not like in my bad old drinking days."

The allusion to his behaviour on the night they'd first met made Jules smile.

"Not even Ivy deserves a dose of that."

"That's debatable! I could always bring an emergency six-pack of lager?"

"Tempting, but I'll speak to her alone," Jules said. "I know I have to. Her behaviour's been really unacceptable recently. I'm sure there's more to it – and hopefully this," she touched her dog collar, "will help her feel that she can share whatever it is."

"You always see the good in people, Jules," Danny said warmly. "It's one of the loveliest things about you."

They stared at each other momentarily. His hand on the crumb-covered table top was only inches away from hers and it took every drop of self-control Jules possessed not to reach out and touch his fingertips.

"Why aren't you answering my texts?" he asked quietly.

Jules couldn't look at him now. "You know why."

"Are you seeing someone?"

Her head snapped up. Danny's uninjured eye was trained on her with such a deep blue intensity that she was floored.

"What?"

"You heard me. I'd have thought it was a simple enough question, Jules. You haven't been to the house. You ignore my messages and you're drinking coffee all over the village with some handsome arty type. Are you seeing him?"

"Caspar?" The idea was so absurd that Jules just stared at him. Was Caspar handsome? Maybe in a poetic and long-haired way, but she couldn't say she'd noticed.

"Yes, Caspar," Danny said, and there was a savage note in his voice that she hadn't heard before.

"I haven't been drinking coffee all over the village." Coming from the city, Jules never failed to be amazed by the swift nature of village gossip. It certainly gave the tabloid press a run for their money. She could sneeze in the churchyard and reportedly have developed pneumonia by the time she reached the quay. "One drink in the pub and a coffee just now is hardly *all over the village.*"

His blue eye narrowed. "So you are seeing him. Thanks for letting me know."

Jules was stung by the accusatory tone. "Dan, I'm single and I can drink coffee with anyone I choose. We've been through this a thousand times. You're married to Tara – no!" She held up her hands. "Don't tell me again that it's over. I saw the way that you guys came together on Bonfire Night."

"Because Morgan bloody well hurt himself!"

Jules saw her chance. "How is he?"

"Fine, it was just a nasty cut. Don't think I don't know you're trying to change the subject." Danny reached out to grab her hand and Jules pulled it away just in time. If he touched her she knew she'd be lost.

"I'm not changing the subject. I'm talking about Morgan and Tara – your family," Jules said firmly. "The three of you are a family, Dan, I saw that for myself and it's important. Maybe things are going to sort themselves out for you all, now that Tara's moved back?"

Danny made a strange strangled sound. "How many times do I have to tell you? Things will never sort themselves out. Tara and I are over."

"But you've moved back home again." Alice had let this detail slip, and although it felt like a razor blade to her heart Jules had tried her hardest to be happy for Danny.

"Because I'm bloody sick of kipping on the couch in the marina office! You might not have noticed but I'm a sodding cripple these days and it hurts to sleep there. I'm sleeping in my own room, in case you want to know. I'm not with Tara."

His voice rose and several heads swivelled.

"I don't need to know that. The details of your married life aren't my business," Jules said.

"When it suits you, right?" Danny's face was black with anger. "Normally you can't wait to stick your nose in and tell me just how great my marriage could be. You're happy to keep your secrets too, aren't you?"

"I don't have any secrets!" Jules protested. "If I think you should make your marriage work then it's because I happen to believe in those vows that people take in front of me and God."

"Yeah, well maybe you should just bear in mind that not everyone keeps them," Danny shot back. "You keep talking all you like, Jules, but one thing's for sure and that is I am *never* taking that woman back. Never."

Stung by the fury in his voice and the sticking-her-nose-in jibe, Jules felt her eyes fill with tears. Oh Lord, there was no way she could cry in the middle of the village hall and in front of everyone. It would be the most talked-about event of the year. Furious with both herself and Danny, Jules blinked them away as best she could – but one solitary tear still rolled down her nose and splashed onto the table.

She couldn't cry. Not here. Not now.

"Oh Jules, sweetheart, please don't be upset. Not because I'm being a prick," Danny was saying, aghast. "I'm so sorry. None of this is your fault. It's not you I'm angry with, I promise. Look, what you need to know about Tara and I is—"

But Danny's words were drowned out by a sudden shriek of excitement from the far side of the room.

"Vicar! Vicar! You've got to see this!" cried Sheila, elbowing her way through the crowds until she was at Jules's side. Her right fist unclenched slowly to reveal a fifty-pound note. At least, Jules thought this was what it was. Being a vicar she didn't often see notes of that value. The last one she'd seen had appeared in one of the collecting buckets on Bonfire Night, an occurrence so out of the ordinary that the postmistress had opened the post office especially so they could check it was genuine, which it was.

"Where did those come from?" Jules asked in surprise.

"There were in the book stall float," said Sheila. "I hadn't turned my back for five minutes and there they were. Oh, Vicar! It's like a miracle!"

But Jules wasn't so sure. First her meal in the pub, then the collection bucket and the cakes and now this. Was it the same person who was making the mysterious donations into the St Wenn's account and causing her so many headaches? And why on earth would they choose to do this all anonymously?

"It's the Polwenna Bay Angel!"

Pushing through the villagers who were rapidly gathering around Jules's table, and with his black coat billowing behind him, was Caspar.

"Polwenna Bay Angel?" echoed Sheila. "What on earth are you on about?"

"The mystery benefactor who bought the vicar dinner and donated the cakes today," Caspar explained in his theatrical voice, full of more plums than a Christmas pudding. He flung his arm around Jules's shoulders and pulled her tightly against him. "There's an angel in the village and this is their way of doing good! They love this lady here, that's for sure!"

At this there was uproar and it took Jules a good five minutes to calm things down and to try explaining the odd events of the past few days. She even pleaded with the mystery benefactor to come forward. The hush that fell while everyone waited was even tenser than that well-known part of the marriage service that required an answer, but it was no use. The Polwenna Bay Angel, whoever he or she was, wished to remain a mystery.

And talking of mysteries, what had Danny Tremaine been about to tell her? Jules turned back to him in the hope of picking up the thread of their earlier conversation, but then saw that his chair was empty. Her stomach felt as though somebody had kicked it and she had a horrible sensation that something fragile had just slipped from her grasp.

Danny Tremaine had gone, taking with him whatever secret he'd been on the brink of sharing.

Chapter 12

If this is what it feels like to be a celebrity then I'll leave it, thanks, Tara
Tremaine thought as she made her way through the village. Huddled
into her duffle coat and with her head practically tucked into her chest
to avoid the driving Cornish drizzle, she might not be able to see the
villagers watching her from behind their net curtains or from the shop
windows, but she could certainly feel their curious gazes burning into
her back. They'd be sizing up her outfit and what she looked like, and
they'd probably be judging her as the kind of flighty and appalling
mother who not only unsettled her child by dragging him to the distant
reaches of The Big City but allowed him to fall off the rocks and cut his
head open to boot.

Tara sighed. It was one thing being Angelina Jolie, or even Summer
Penhalligan, with a team of publicists and stylists behind you to ensure
that your image was spun to perfection and that you looked fabulous
wherever you ventured, but it was another altogether to be cast as a
scarlet woman, friendless and looking an absolute state in a borrowed
and ancient wax jacket that smelled strongly of horse. Catching a
glimpse of her reflection in the window of Kursa's Kozi Kutz was
enough to make Tara want to weep. Gone was the woman with the
glossy bob and carefully applied make-up, and in her place was a
bedraggled mascara-smeared fright. Maybe she was vain and shallow,
just as Mo had once accused her of being, but for Tara looking
beautifully groomed and well dressed was her armour. The villagers
could say what they liked about her being a bad wife and a useless

mother, but at least if she felt confident about her appearance she could hold her head up high. Without that, what did she really have? Tara thought bleakly. No education to speak of, no job and a broken marriage.

She was a total failure. Nobody really liked her or wanted her here. Alice and Summer were kind enough, Jimmy as always was affable albeit preoccupied with whatever madcap schemes he was up to, and Mo was fortunately far too busy being loved-up to pay Tara much attention. Issie and Nick, however, had made their antipathy very clear, and their cold-shouldering was starting to give Tara frostbite. None of this would have mattered if Danny had shown any signs of being pleased to see her. He was obviously thrilled to have Morgan home but he'd hardly spoken to Tara since Bonfire Night, and it was now the second week of November. As much as she hated to admit it, Tara was starting to fear that her plan to win him back wasn't going to be as straightforward as she'd hoped. Danny had made it clear that there would always be a place for her and Morgan at Seaspray, but this seemed to be about as far as things went. There had been none of the late-night chats or nostalgic moments that she'd hoped for; in fact, Dan had been in a very strange mood for days now and was hardly talking to anyone. Even Alice had been snapped at for asking him what was wrong – which was a very bad sign indeed, because Danny adored his grandmother.

I haven't helped at all by coming back, Tara reflected sadly. *I've only made everything worse.* If it wasn't for seeing how happy Morgan was to be back, she would have been sorely tempted to catch the next bus towards Reading and throw herself on her parents' mercy. Even their long, disappointed silences, the endless Radio Four and the strain of them having a lively eight-year-old in a fussy house crammed with figurines from Sunday newspaper supplements had to be better than this.

If the weather mirrored moods, then today was fitting her dismal one perfectly, Tara decided as she made her way to the village shop. The clouds hung so low over the village that even Ashley's house was hidden from view and the sea was just a pewter line beyond the grey harbour wall. Relentless drizzle blew up the valley to soak everything from flower beds to fishing gear and seagulls dripped silently from their chimney-pot perches. Now and again a car swished through the village, its headlights turning the wet roads to gold, and the odd brave soul armed with an umbrella splashed to the shops, but other than this the village was quiet. Tara's hair dripped down her neck and her nose was running with the cold. Even the tissue she'd stowed in her pocket was nothing more than a useless mass of pulp now.

Sniffing like an A-lister with a coke habit and sporting a red nose that would put Rudolph to shame, Tara almost laughed out loud at the stupidity of coming back here. Cornwall in November. No tourists, no sunshine and no hope of escape. It had driven her mad before, so what on earth had she been thinking? It was an indication of just how desperate she was that she'd even contemplated returning.

The rain was growing heavier, driving up the narrow street in icy torrents, and with relief Tara ducked into the village store. She noticed that the usual gaggle of matriarchs had clustered around the counter at the far end. However, they were deep in conversation and, despite the loud jangle of the shop bell, blissfully oblivious to who was coming in. Tara was thankful for this; she'd come to buy some sausages for Morgan's dinner and not to be grilled herself. Picking up a wire basket, she began to choose some groceries. As always, she looked carefully at the prices, selecting the special offers, the marked-down veg and the budget ranges rather than the higher-end items. There was money in her purse – Dan was always more than generous with child support – but Tara hated feeling that she wasn't paying her own way and it was a point of honour now to eek any funds out for as long as possible. This hadn't been too difficult in Plymouth when she'd been doing a few hours here and there as a beautician and when she'd been able to look for bargains in Aldi or Lidl, but it was proving tricky in a small village shop where things tended to be more expensive.

I need to find a job, Tara decided as her hand hovered over some tempting pork and cider sausages before plumping for the cheapest ones in the cabinet instead. She dreaded to think what might have gone into these – probably not a great deal of meat, anyway – but at two whole pounds less it was a no-brainer. Of course, Alice would cook for them if she asked, but Tara wanted to pay her own way and provide for her son herself. Maybe it was a case of being too proud for her own good. Tara wasn't sure, but she did know that it didn't feel right to be living on the charity of her estranged husband's grandmother. Living in Seaspray wasn't going to be a long-term option either, not if things continued to be this difficult with Dan. There was an atmosphere you could cut with blunt kiddy scissors, never mind a knife, and it was only a matter of time before this began to affect Morgan.

No, Tara concluded as the alarmingly pink sausages landed in her basket, if she and Morgan were to stay and if there was any hope of rebuilding her relationship with Danny then she had to have her independence. Maybe this would make him respect her again? So it might be November, the worst time to find employment in a village so highly geared to the tourist trade, but there was bound to be something about. There were always jobs going in the pub or up at the hotel. At least with family nearby to take care of Morgan it would be possible to work to more unsociable hours. As soon as the shopping was done she'd walk over to The Ship and see if there were any vacancies.

Buoyed by having some kind of a plan, Tara threw caution to the wind and swapped the low-cost sausages for the more expensive ones, then added a tin of Heinz beans and some Cornish butter to her selection. With the basket feeling pleasantly heavy she was just in the process of getting some local King Edwards from the vegetable rack when the strains of conversation from the counter froze her so completely that she no longer registered the cool potato mould against her fingers or the dark earth crusting her nails. Instead there was a loud rushing sound in her ears, as though the River Wenn had burst its banks, and all she could focus on were the ugly words from the other side of the vegetable display.

"Well, if you ask me she's come back with her tail between her legs because yet another man saw right through her. If Danny Tremaine's got any sense he'll give her one pound fifty and kick her back across the Tamar Bridge," Betty Jago was telling her acolytes. "A girl like her just means trouble. Look how she treated him before. And him a war hero too! Shocking!"

There was a murmur of agreement, amidst some fairly energetic tutting.

"I heard that she's pregnant," said somebody else to a ripple of shocked glee.

"I heard she had a gambling problem," added another, who sounded just like Sheila Keverne. "Sandra on the fish stall told me that she'd heard in the pub that there are huge debts that the Tremaines will have to pay."

"Nothing would surprise me about that one," Betty Jago said darkly. "Did you hear what happened to that poor little boy on Bonfire Night? She wasn't looking after him at all and he fell off the rocks. I ask you! What kind of a mother lets that happen?"

"There was a dreadful lot of blood. I thought it was a hospital admission and stitches, but that new doctor wasn't nearly as thorough as he should be." Yes, definitely Sheila.

"Perhaps Danny should go for custody? She's clearly an unfit mother," mused another voice.

Tara couldn't listen to another word. Her heart was hammering and her hands and feet had turned icy cold. The potatoes slipped from her grasp and bounced across the shop floor. Before she even registered what she was doing, she stepped out from behind the vegetables and slammed her basket down on the counter so hard that Betty Jago's feet nearly left the floor. Staring in horror at Tara, the shopkeeper drained of colour and her mouth fell open. The other women instantly dispersed around the shop, busying themselves with magazines or pretending to be interested in the tinned fruit, but Betty was trapped behind her counter.

"Don't stop the conversation on my account," said Tara coldly. "I was absolutely fascinated. I'm an unfit mother and a gambler, am I? That's all news to me. Keep going, please. I can't wait to find out what's coming next. It's better than an episode of *EastEnders*. Actually, don't tell me, I'll guess. Alice is secretly Danny's mother? Issie is actually a boy? Or maybe I'm on drugs? That would be really juicy, wouldn't it? A big fat heroin habit for you all to gossip about. Maybe I could shoot up on the quay or in the pasty shop?"

"Tara, dear, I had no idea you were in the shop," Betty said faintly.

"No! Really?" Tara's lip curled.

Betty stared miserably down at her counter. If she hadn't been spreading such poison Tara could almost have pitied her.

"Anyone else the rest of you want to add?" she asked the others, glancing around. Nobody was able to look her in the eye. "Come on, ladies. Don't be shy. Sheila's already given her medical opinion – congratulations on qualifying from medical school by the way, I must have missed that one – and Betty, if you catch me playing the fruit machine in the pub, please do make sure to call Gamblers Anonymous, won't you?"

Sheila and Betty didn't know where to look. It was awkward enough for them to have been caught in full flow of their malicious gossiping, but being challenged by the very subject of their spiteful speculations had wrong-footed them all the more.

"Well? Anyone want to add something?" Tara repeated, glancing around at them. She was so angry that she felt she might explode like one of last week's fireworks. "Come on, don't be shy. You were all happy enough to voice your opinions just now, so please, don't hold back on my account."

Betty's face was an exact match for her scarlet pinny.

"Honestly, Tara, I had no idea you were here, love," Betty said again.

"Yes, I got that. So what you really mean is that you were gossiping about me behind my back?" Tara couldn't keep the sarcasm from her voice. "How very unusual! Well, do you know what? How about in future you just keep your pathetic, small-minded opinions to yourselves and leave me and my family out of it? And here's another thing—" She shoved her basket hard towards Betty. "You can keep your sodding overpriced sausages too!"

Shaking with fury and adrenalin, Tara stormed out of the shop. She was so blinded by outrage that she only registered the tall figure who was about to enter when she cannoned straight into him. Two strong hands caught her shoulders and steadied her, otherwise she probably would have fallen over and straight into the puddles. Yes, that would have topped today's crappy morning off perfectly, she thought grimly.

Grey eyes behind rain-speckled glassed crinkled at her. "Steady on, Mrs Tremaine! I'm not used to beautiful women throwing themselves at me!"

"I'm so sorry!" Tara gasped, shocked out of her rage sufficiently to realise that she'd barged straight into Dr Penwarren, he of the badly behaved dog and lunatic hairdresser mother. "I wasn't looking."

"Then I'm totally disappointed. I thought my luck had changed," Richard deadpanned. When she didn't laugh, he added hastily, "That was a joke, by the way, albeit it a pretty inept attempt at one. I didn't meant to imply… say that I thought…" He ran a hand through his tufty hair and his face began to turn pink. "Oh Christ. I'm just digging myself in deeper here with every word. You're upset, aren't you?"

"It's fine," Tara told Richard quickly, before he could grab a shovel and really go for broke. "You've not offended me, I promise. In fact, that's probably the nicest thing anyone's said to me for weeks."

"Seriously?" Richard looked shocked.

She nodded. "Seriously. Come on, Dr Penwarren, you might be new but surely you've noticed that I'm not exactly popular around here? If I look upset then it's because I've just had a run-in with the vicious old biddies in the village shop. I'm doing a runner before they fetch the ducking stall."

His kind grey eyes were troubled. "I do my best not to listen to village gossip and I'm constantly telling my mother that she really ought to do the same." He frowned as a thought occurred to him. "My mother isn't in the shop, is she?"

Tara shook her head. "Just Betty, Sheila and their cronies. I ought to know better than to let them get to me, but today…"

"Today the weather's rubbish, you're having a hard time readjusting to village life and their small-mindedness just touched a nerve?"

It was on the tip of Tara's tongue to tell Richard that calling her an unfit mother was more than just touching a nerve, but a small part of her was scared that maybe they'd been right. After all, hadn't she let Morgan slip on the rocks? And hadn't she been the one to walk out on the marriage? She didn't want one of the few people who'd been friendly towards her to think badly of her. There was something so warm and so kind about Richard that you just wanted to pour out your troubles to him. It was probably what made him such a good GP.

"That's probably it," she agreed.

He glanced at his watch. "Look, it's nearly lunchtime and I could do with something before afternoon surgery. How about we head to the pub for some food and a warm-up by the fire? My treat," he added quickly. "I could do with the company of someone who understands how it feels to be an outsider here."

"I'm worse than an outsider. I'm an insider who blew it," Tara said bitterly.

"To err is human; to forgive, divine," Richard quoted. "I think Alexander Pope said that. I don't see many gods and goddesses stomping around Polwenna Bay, but I do see lots of normal human beings just trying to make the best of things and sometimes getting it wrong."

She looked up at him. "So you're saying we all mess up?"

"I guess I am. And if I don't have a good lunch I'll be far too hungry to concentrate on my patients this afternoon, and then who knows how awful my mess-ups could be? I have an ingrown toenail to attend to and several other things that I won't mention before we eat. You'll be doing me a favour by helping make sure I can focus!"

Tara almost made an excuse about needing to get home to put the sausages for Morgan's dinner in the fridge. Then she remembered that all her food shopping was left on the shop counter and, unless she was prepared to eat a huge slice of humble pie, there was no way she could go in and collect it. Besides, Morgan would be thrilled to eat whatever Alice had made. His great grandmother was a fantastic cook, whereas Tara pretty much burned water. There would be nothing for her to do at Seaways except hide in her room, watch the raindrops trickle down the windowpane and fret about just how thoroughly she'd managed to sabotage her own life.

It was not a happy prospect. Lunch with Richard could be fun and it would be a good opportunity to find out if there was any bar work going too. There was no time like the present.

"I'll even throw in some of their sticky toffee pudding," Richard said, sensing her weakening.

"Now you've got me," Tara said. "I can't resist that. Lunch sounds great, thanks."

The Ship was busy with lunchtime trade: a mixture of villagers and the last resilient tourists had crammed into the tiny low-beamed building to enjoy bowls of soup, ploughmen's lunches and creamy fish pie packed with the spoils of the local trawlers. Richard and Tara managed to squeeze themselves into a window seat overlooking the quay, where they enjoyed piping hot minestrone and watched the grey waves churning beyond the softly misted-up windows. The log fire in the grate soon dried Tara's damp clothes and she found herself starting to relax, as much from Richard's easy company as the warmth. Before long she found herself opening up to him. Richard was no fool and had lived in the village just long enough to have heard the story of the local war hero's runaway wife, but he didn't probe to know more. Tara was surprised to find that she was able to divulge some of the true story to him. Of course, she could never tell him the whole story, only Danny knew that, but she was able to share some of her concerns about needing to be independent and to do the right thing for Morgan.

"I can't believe I've told you all that. What's in this sticky toffee pudding? The truth drug?" Tara said, glancing down at her empty plate and the gleaming spoon that had been licked clean. Lord, and she never ate stuff like this. She'd be the size of Jules Mathieson if she carried on.

"Damn. They told me that it left no taste," said Richard.

She laughed. His dry wit amused her – and beneath that quiet and gentle exterior something deeper was lurking, she was sure of it. There was a sharp sense of humour and a naughty glitter in those eyes that spoke of emotions Richard Penwarren kept hidden far below the surface. Mild-mannered doctor? Yes, maybe, but instinct told her that passion ran beneath the surface too.

"You're very easy to talk to," she said thoughtfully. "A bit like a priest."

Richard pulled a face. "Sexless and getting people to confess sin? Oh dear."

"OK, not the best analogy. What I meant was that you have this way of putting people at ease and making them feel comfortable. You've let me rabbit on all through lunch."

"You certainly don't rabbit on," Richard said firmly. "I could listen to you all day."

"Hmm," said Tara who wasn't so sure about that. "Anyway, you know loads about me but I don't think I know anything about you at all."

He shrugged. "That's because there's nothing really to tell. I'm a very boring country GP with a mad mother and an even madder dog. That's about it, I promise. There are no mad wives in the attic just to complete the picture!"

"Talking of having mad wives in the attic, I need to find somewhere to rent so that Dan can have some space," Tara remarked. "Maybe some of the chalets up at the campsite will be free for the winter. I might make a call."

"You can't live up there in the winter. You'll freeze." Richard looked horrified.

He had a point. The chalets at Polwenna Park were designed for the summer months and although they had little electric heaters these wouldn't be a match for the gales blowing in from the sea. Plenty of locals did hire them off-season though – and they survived somehow, so it had to be possible. Perhaps she could sell it to Morgan as an extended camping trip? A few years ago he'd been obsessed with all things Bear Grylls, so he might be up for it.

"Look, I may be speaking out of turn and you can tell me to butt out if you like," Richard continued, dragging Tara back from thoughts about electric blankets and fan heaters, "but why don't you rent my cottage? You'd be doing me a favour by keeping it warm and dry. You know how damp places get here if they're not lived in. It's right on the slipway, so it's bad enough even in August. If it's left empty over the winter it'll be a state."

Tara stared at him. Waterside Cottage was one of the prettiest properties on the harbourside. Although very small, it looked straight out onto the water, and the kitchen door led to the slipway steps, where a little bench basked in the sunshine and boats bobbed against their moorings. In other words, it was every Cornish seaside cliché made real. There was no way a place like that would be empty, even out of season, and her proud hackles rose. Was he offering charity?

"Won't you be in it?" she asked.

"I'd love to be, but my mum's place is really big and I don't trust her to heat it and look after it. To be honest I don't think she could afford to; the salon doesn't bring in that much."

Tara understood. Kursa's dubious skills as a hairdresser were legendary. The only person who raved about her was Summer.

"And don't get me started on my useless waste-of-space father, who left her pretty much penniless," Richard continued with a grimace. "Since she won't accept any help, the only way I can ensure my own mother doesn't catch pneumonia is by moving in myself, cranking up the night storage heaters and stockpiling logs. If you could take the cottage then it would be one less thing for me to worry about."

There was a strange feeling in Tara's chest. It felt dangerously like hope.

"Really?"

"Really." Richard drained his half and smiled at her across the glass. "The rent will be cheap, I promise."

"I'll pay going costs," Tara said quickly. "I'm not a charity case."

"No, but I might be a charity case myself if that place gets damp again! It cost enough to renovate the first time around. So what do you say?"

"I'd say yes, but I'll need a job first to even cover the bills." She got to her feet. "Give me one moment."

"One lunch and I've driven you to drink?" Richard asked as she made her way to the bar.

Tara laughed. "No time like the present to find out about work," she called back over her shoulder. She was weaving her way through the lunchtime drinking crowd and waving at Adam, the landlord. A good friend of Danny's, or at least he had been until Danny had started drinking heavily and causing scenes, he was someone she knew well. They'd even double dated in the past; she'd been friends with Adam's wife Rose too. The friendship had soured a bit when she and Dan had split up, but Tara was old enough to know that this was how these things tended to go. Divorcing couples divided up everything from pensions to pets, and friends were no exception.

"Lunchtime drinking, Tara?" This softly spoken question came from the lithe man with deep damson ringlets who was leaning against the bar and nursing a whiskey. Although his eyes were bloodshot they were unmistakably that bright periwinkle blue shared by all the Tremaines, along with the high cheekbones and full sensual mouth.

"Playing truant from the restaurant, Sy?" Tara teased, knowing that her brother-in-law was the ultimate workaholic.

"As if! No, we're closed today for some work on the kitchen," Symon Tremaine said. "That's why I look like the undead; we're working flat out to open again at the weekend."

"Licence to print money, that's your place. Beats me why people want to eat all that fancy foreign muck," teased Adam as he pulled a foaming pint.

Sy laughed. "Yeah right. I'm loaded, me. I never work a day in my life."

"You keep pinching all my bloody staff, mate, that's why. Now even Kelly's done a runner. Thanks for stealing my best barmaid. I ought to bar you," Adam complained.

Tara saw her chance and took it. ""If Kelly's left, is there a job going here? I'd be really interested, Adam. I need some funds to rent a place and I'm happy to do pretty much anything. Bar work, kitchen chores or even cleaning."

There was an awkward pause. Adams's round face had never been very good at concealing what was going on inside his simple skull, and Tara's heart sank. He didn't want to employ her. The battle lines had been drawn up and he and Rose were clearly on Team Danny.

"I'm really sorry but I don't think I can help," Adam said finally. "It's nothing personal, Tara, but I don't think my Rose would like it."

And she'd never sleep with me again was the unfinished part of the sentence.

"It feels pretty personal to me," said Tara bitterly. "Cheers, Adam. Thanks a lot."

She stared down at the bar and bit back tears. What an awful day. Talk about getting signs. How many other locals would feel the same way about her? If nobody wanted to employ her then what possible hope did she have of being able to give Morgan the security of staying here and Danny the space that he clearly needed? She'd have no choice but to move in with her parents.

"There's a job at mine if you want it?" Sy said quietly. "It's nothing glamorous, just a bit of waitressing and some prepping in the kitchen, but it's yours if you want it."

Tara looked up at him. "Really? You're not just saying that to be kind?"

Sy gave her his sweet lopsided smile. Out of all the Tremaine siblings he was the most sensitive and there was no way Tara wanted pity from him.

"Once you've seen the scrubbing and worked the hours I demand, there's no way you'll think I'm kind. In fact you'll think I'm such a pain-crazed bastard I make Christian Grey look easy-going!"

Tara held out her hand. "I've given birth. Pain doesn't faze me. I'm up for it."

Sy shook Tara's outstretched hand. "That's just as well, because you're about to witness a whole new level. If Gordon Ramsay came to my kitchen he'd soon be crying like a girl."

But Tara couldn't have cared less how tough it was in Sy's kitchen. And as for crying? Well, she'd done more than her fair share of that over the years, but now she had a new job and a beautiful place to live – and both things had come to her in the space of less than an hour. Perhaps her luck was starting to change.

And maybe, just maybe, now that these things were in place Danny might start to come round. Was her wish at the well going to come true after all?

Chapter 13

Thank goodness the weather had cheered up, thought Jules with relief. For the past few days the rain had been unrelenting and she'd been holed up in the vicarage catching up on paperwork and doing her very best not to drive herself crazy worrying about the future of St Wenn's. She'd continually glanced up to look out of the window but the usually pretty view had been distorted by the raindrops blurring the pane, creating a smudged seascape of pewters, leads and greys. If it had carried on for much longer she'd have had to consult the book of Genesis for instructions on ark-building.

This afternoon, though, a falling tide and sharpening wind had driven the rain away. Weak, lemon-hued sunshine was seeping through the low clouds, and outside her office window a chaffinch had started to sing. Jules had decided it was time to abandon her paperwork and do her best to push all her worries aside by setting off for a walk. As she'd laced her walking boots she'd smiled. How on earth had she become somebody who actually relished the thought of a stomp outside? Not so long ago her idea of a walk had been pushing her trolley along the sweetie aisle of Tesco's; she would have been horrified at the mere suggestion of cliff paths and steep hills.

She had Danny to thank for this change.

Jules felt a pang: every time she thought of Danny it was still just as painful. She hadn't bumped into him since the jumble sale – sorry, she meant *consignment sale* – but she guessed he too was hiding from the elements.

Or her.

The village was quiet for this time of day, Jules thought. Cottage windows flung golden light into the grey mid-afternoon, and down on the quay the fish truck was revving into life. Seagulls heckled above, stretching their wings and scraping the stillness with their harsh calls. Jules took the path from the vicarage down into the village, along to the quay and then down the slippery stone steps that led to the beach. The tide was out and the pale sand was hemmed with seaweed as far as the grey rocks at the very end of the bay. Inhaling the sharp salty air and picking up pace, Jules strode along the wet sand, enjoying the feeling of the cold air against her warm face and the way the exercise made her muscles ache. The beauty of the Cornish seascape never failed to move her; even the louring skies and white-tipped waves were part of the wild and breathtaking beauty here.

Jules had just reached the jagged rocks at the furthest end of the beach when her mobile began to ring. Plucking it from her fleece pocket, she saw Caspar's name flash up on the screen.

She tried not to sigh. Caspar was proving to be quite a needy addition to her flock. This was the fifth call of the day. Whether or not this was something all writers had in common or just a quirk of his own rather intense personality she wasn't certain. One thing Jules did fear, however, was that Caspar had brought his quest for a muse a little closer to home. She would have been flattered, except that she strongly suspected it was only because everyone else had turned him down. Sending up a swift prayer for patience, Jules took the call.

"Hello?"

"Jules? Is that you on the beach? I'm waving from the quay!"

She looked up and, sure enough, a figure clad in swirling black was waving enthusiastically at her. He looked dangerously close to the edge.

"I can see you, Caspar," Jules said, waving back and adding a PS to her earlier prayer, that he didn't take a tumble. The last thing she needed was Sheila storming down onto the beach with bandages and the air ambulance on speed dial.

"When you're back, how about coming to my place for afternoon tea?" Caspar was saying. "I've bought scones and jam and I've lit the fire too. It's very cosy!"

"I'm pretty busy," she hedged.

"Too busy for scones? I've bought saffron buns too. It's a proper Cornish cakey tea!"

There was a hint of loneliness in his voice and, even though for once she didn't feel inclined to stuff her face with clotted cream and scones, Jules was moved. Nevertheless, it seemed wise to turn down the offer. "I can see that you've already got the hang of life in Cornwall. I've just been exercising, though. The last thing I ought to be doing is eating afternoon tea. I'm on a diet!"

"I've never heard anything so ridiculous." Caspar tutted. "You're perfect as you are. Absolutely perfect. Like a Rubens come to life."

Uh oh. Parishioner With Crush alert.

"I'm not sure quite how to take that," Jules told him briskly, hoping to defuse the compliment. "Aren't they fat and cellulitey?"

"Not at all! They're voluptuous and womanly and sensual," Caspar declared. "Pillowy bosoms and soft arms and—"

Jules got the picture. They were the sort of girls who might eat cake and take pity on a blocked writer until he found a tall skinny blonde muse instead. She made a mental note to ask Issie if she had any friends who might be interested in being immortalised in literature. If Caspar really was a writer, that was. Googling him hadn't revealed very much.

"Cake sounds wonderful," she said, interrupting him in full flow. "I've just got a couple of errands to run and then I'll pop in."

"Wonderful." Caspar gave her a thumbs up from across the beach. "I'm at Tide's End Cottage – the second one along by the slipway. I'll put the kettle on."

The call ended and he waved once more before vanishing in a swirl of billowing black fabric. Jules sighed. So much for sneaking into the pub for a quiet half by the fire and a swift read of the *Western Morning News*. She slid the phone back into her pocket and frowned. She'd have to find a tactful way of nipping this in the bud or things could become very complicated very fast. She could certainly do without the extra stress though; there was quite enough on as it was with the run-up to Christmas and the bishop's impending visit, without having to wade through Caspar's purple prose and suffocating attention.

She turned back for the village, walking at the water's edge this time and pausing to watch as her own footprints were smudged away by the lapping waves. The air was thick with the smell of the rotting seaweed tangled around the exposed chains of the moorings. The cottages above watched her, and up at Mariners a bonfire was burning, sending sparks dancing into the greyness. Beyond that was nothing but low cloud rolling in from the Channel, thick with spray and the threat of more bad weather.

Jules stomped back over the sand, deep in thought. The scene was unusually quiet and, except for one dog walker, the beach was empty. The last cold fingers of sloping sunshine were being ambushed by clouds; by the time Jules was back in the village, the sunlight had been smothered altogether, until the world looked as grey and as bleak as she was starting to feel. In the past she would have been with Danny, laughing about something or listening to him tell a tale of the Pollards' latest antics, and then they'd have headed up to Seaspray together to drink tea with Alice. Jules hadn't set foot in the Tremaine family home since Halloween. The dynamic had changed with Tara's arrival, and going there no longer felt easy or right. It was Tara's place now, not hers. At least tea with Caspar was a distraction from the dull ache in her heart.

Jules laughed despairingly at this thought. Now she was even thinking in clichés! Caspar was not a good influence. She needed to read less of her Cassandra Duval books and get stuck into the more racy stuff like *Blackwarren*. Lord Blackwarren was far too busy having sex with a bevy of willing maidens to worry about aching hearts – although he got so much action that surely other bits of him must ache! Jules was rereading the eBook and still trying to figure out just who the secret author was. It had to be a local, but who? She'd already worked out that the shopkeeper character was based on Chris the Cod and that Lord Blackwarren was probably Teddy St Milton, while the sneaky wreckers were poorly disguised Pollards. Jules was now trawling through the book again, just in case she'd managed to miss a plump vicar. As for Blackwarren's feisty stable wench Alicia, the true love of his life and the only woman who was his equal, well the jury was out regarding her identity. No wonder most of the villagers were reading the book. They were all trying to work out whether they were in it!

Caspar's home was a crumpled building that looked as though it was sliding down the slipway and in danger of sploshing into the harbour. Once a hovel dwelt in by poor fisherfolk, it had been given a chichi facelift by a second-homer and was now a picture-postcard Cornish cottage, complete with sage green window frames, potted bay trees and a cherry-red front door. The adjacent cottage was owned by Richard and, although not quite as twee, was in Jules's opinion far more authentic with its piles of crab pots, its weathered bench and its tubs of die-hard geraniums. Richard hadn't owned the cottage for long but he was head over heels in love with the place and Jules could see why: it had views to die for and a boat mooring. What more could an ocean-loving doctor ask for?

Since the slipway was on the opposite side of the village, Jules had to trek all the way around. She went past The Plump Seagull and the village green, ignoring the delicious smells from Patsy's Pasties, and crossed two bridges. She was just turning into the next street, to make the final loop to the other side of the harbour, when a taxi came hurtling towards her at speed. Jules had only seconds to flatten herself against a whitewashed cottage wall to avoid being run over. Cold spray from the road splattered her jeans and splashed onto her face. As she mopped her eyes on her sleeve, the taxi's passenger window hissed down.

"Sorry about that, love!" called Jimmy Tremaine, looking anything but repentant. He was wearing a stars and stripes bandana and blue-mirrored Ray-Bans. "In a bit of a hurry! Got a plane to catch!"

Then the window shot up and the cab sped away. So Jimmy really was off to California. The last Jules had heard of this was that Jake and his father weren't speaking because the trip had all but cleared out the marina's account. Alice must be in despair. I ought to catch up with her, Jules thought guiltily. In avoiding Dan, she'd also been staying away from her friend. Maybe she should take Alice up to the Polwenna

Bay Hotel for lunch. Then they could have some time together on neutral territory.

Jules was still musing on this idea when she knocked on Caspar's cherry-red door – which was flung open almost as soon as her knuckles met the wood.

"Come in, beautiful lady! Come in! Don't let's dally upon the doorstep!"

In his leather trousers, frilly cerise shirt and flowery waistcoat he looked like an aging Russell Brand, Jules thought – although Russell probably wouldn't be seen dead wearing fluffy slippers or a Cath Kidston pinny.

"The stone floors are terribly cold," he explained, seeing her look. "Under-floor heating isn't standard here, I take it?"

Thinking of the superannuated storage heaters in the vicarage, Jules just laughed.

"You're not in Kansas now, Toto!"

"Indeed I'm not," he agreed, his eyes twinkling down at her. "And very happy to be here with a Cornish maid come to visit me!"

"I'm from Basingstoke originally. I haven't even lived here all that long; I was based in the Midlands this time last year," Jules pointed out, but Caspar wasn't going to let a minor detail like the truth get in the way of a good storyline. He was still busy spouting forth about *Poldark* and du Maurier as he took her fleece. Then he grasped Jules's shoulders, and a rather moist kiss landed on her cheek as his liberally applied Aramis almost asphyxiated her.

"Come and sit down," he said, taking her hand and towing Jules into the small sitting room and gesturing to a laden table. "Let's have afternoon tea."

"How many people have you invited?" Jules asked, taking in the piles of scones, the Victoria sponge oozing jam and cream, and the stack of sunshine-yellow saffron buns.

"Just us," said Caspar, which was as Jules had feared. "Make yourself at home. I'll just finish making the tea. I've only got Earl Grey. Is that all right?"

One of the lesser-known dangers of being a vicar was extreme tea-drinking. Some days Jules was literally awash with the stuff; people seemed to get offended, or at least very insistent, when she declined. Moreover, being more a builders' brew kind of girl, there was nothing she hated more than dishwater Earl Grey. Still, she tried her best to be tactful at all times.

"Lovely," she told him dutifully. Hopefully fibbing about tea didn't count as a lie and, if it did, surely the Boss would forgive her?

While Caspar clattered away in the kitchen, all the while keeping up a steady monologue of his writing woes, Jules admired the pretty sitting room with its thick walls, Cath Kidston print soft furnishings and cheerfully glowing wood burner. Every now and then she threw an "mmm" or an "absolutely" in his direction, which seemed to keep Caspar happy, but mostly she tuned him out. There was only so much doom and gloom about not being able to write that she could handle, especially when her Sunday sermon was still waiting to be penned. Somehow Jules didn't think that her congregation would be very sympathetic to the notion of writer's block.

Surely just staying here would be enough to inspire anyone to write? The view from the window was breathtaking even on such a gloomy day. The small boats lined up on the harbour floor, the sparkle of fairy lights from the pub and the cottages sprinkled on the hillside opposite were just crying out to be included in a novel. Jules had lived in the village for almost nine months now, but even so she never took Polwenna's beauty for granted. On a summer's evening when the light was long and golden and the sky arched over the harbour the view from this cottage must be incredible. Wanting a closer look, Jules perched a buttock on the window seat and leaned forward. She was trying her hardest not to disturb the heaped papers or touch the laptop balanced next to them, but her backside was a little more generously proportioned that the seventeenth-century equivalent and she inadvertently nudged the computer.

The screen of Caspar's laptop flared into life. Jules didn't mean to pry but the sudden brightness was hard to ignore and her eyes were instantly drawn to it. The problem was that, once she'd seen what was typed at the top of the blank Word document, there was no way she could *not* look. It would have been easier to stop the tide from seeping back into the harbour.

The Duke's Dangerous Bride

by

Cassandra Duval

Not a great deal in life surprised Jules these days – being a vicar opened your eyes to all sorts – but this discovery really did knock her for six, partly because she'd rather unkindly written Caspar off as a wannabe author and partly because she loved Cassandra Duval. There wasn't a novel of hers that Jules hadn't devoured within hours. Cassandra's books were romantic and escapist, with heroes just the right side of the alpha male/dominating sadist line and feisty heroines who always ended up being the ones to reform the confirmed rakes. It was all total nonsense, of course, but Jules and thousands of other readers like her couldn't get enough.

And these books were written by Caspar Owen? A self-absorbed dandy in fluffy slippers and a pinny? Seriously?

"Here's the tea. Do you want milk or lemon— Oh!"

Caspar stared at Jules. His face was as white as the cottage walls.

"I'm really sorry. I was looking out of the window and I brushed against the computer," Jules said, feeling as though she'd been caught rifling through Caspar's wallet.

"I take it you've seen what's on there?"

She bit her lip. "I'm afraid so."

Caspar nodded and then glanced at the laden tea tray. "I think I need a brandy rather than a cuppa now."

"Me too," Jules said. Her head was spinning from the discovery. "So you're Cassandra Duval? Really?"

Caspar didn't reply but the tea tray was set on the table with a clatter. It was only once two generous measures of brandy were poured into tumblers that he seemed ready to speak. He leaned against the mantelpiece, raised his glass and gave her a weary smile.

"So now you know the truth. Yes, Cassandra Duval is my nom de plume, for my sins."

Jules's eyes were wide. "But you're a man."

He raised his eyes to the beamed ceiling. "And that's exactly why I have a pen name. Call it reverse sexism if you like, but men who write romance only sell well if they pretend to be female. Darling, you'd be amazed how many romantic novelists are guys."

"I guess that makes sense," Jules agreed. "Well, don't worry, Caspar. I won't say a word. I'm a priest, after all, so everything is in total confidence."

Caspar looked relieved at this and, feeling a little star-struck, Jules added, "You're one of my favourite authors! I've read everything of yours and I love them all. Honestly, I can't wait for the next one."

"You and several million others," Caspar said wearily. "Along with my agent and my publishers and my publicist. Everyone wants that sodding book."

"But isn't that a good thing? You're super successful. A real bestselling author, right up there with Jilly Cooper and Dan Brown! That must be great."

In answer he knocked back the brandy and poured another, before drinking that too and then abandoning his glass in favour of the bottle.

OK, maybe not, thought Jules.

"Can you imagine the pressure I'm under to deliver this book?" Caspar asked her finally. "It's got to be as good as, if not better than, the last one – or else my career is over."

"But it *will* be good. All your books are brilliant!" Jules assured him. "Goodness, I've had this one on pre-order for months."

He groaned. "That's just great to hear. You can see for yourself just how much of it I've written."

"The title? There's nothing else? That's it?"

"That's it. Now can you see why I'm so desperate? I'm already three months late with it and the publishers are starting to talk about calling in my advance."

"So can't you just sit down and write it?" Jules was stumped because the answer seemed obvious.

"Hah! That's what they say too! That's what they all say! I can't write a word, Jules! My muse has left me!"

More brandy was knocked back and Jules was worried. This was worse than she'd thought.

"All this muse stuff is way too metaphysical. You need to treat writing like any other job. Just sit down and get on with it," she said sternly.

Caspar passed a despairing hand across his eyes. "If only I could. The thing is that I need a muse to write and for the past five years it was my girlfriend, Imogen. She was the inspiration for all my heroines. When I looked at her it was all I could do not to write odes."

Privately Jules thought this must have been quite annoying for Imogen. Odes were all very well but after a while the novelty must sure wear off?

"When Imogen left me last year she took my gift with her too," Caspar explained sadly. "I haven't written a decent word since, and I know that I won't be able to write another either until my muse returns. I had hoped that a change of scene would help me write – but I knew within moments of arriving here that my hopes were misplaced. I need passion in my life. Without it I'm nothing!"

"Oh dear," Jules said lamely. So his writer's block was caused by a broken heart. That would be trickier to fix than she'd thought.

"You know I'm not muse material, don't you?" she said hastily.

"There's no way I could have you as my muse now. You have uncovered the secrets of my soul. I have laid my ego bare. I have flayed myself raw, I have—"

Jules held up her hands. "Yes, yes, I get the gist. But Caspar, if you sit around waiting for too long for this muse you'll never get the book written at all. Can't you love a woman from afar? A bit like the troubadours did in the olden days?"

"Unrequited love?"

"Absolutely! I think it was supposed to really inspire writers." Jules was frantically dredging up her A-level Lit and wishing that she'd listened harder. "Think about it. Petrarch loved Laura from a distance and Dante was the same with Beatrice. They wrote great poetry. And how about Shakespeare's sonnets to the Fair Friend?"

"Or Catullus for his Clodia?" Caspar said, a note of excitement creeping into his voice. "Yeats and Maud Gonne!"

"Err, yes," said Jules, who was really wishing she'd listened harder at school. "Or Peter Parker and MJ!"

"Pip and Estella?"

"Them too!"

"*I grant I never saw a goddess go; My mistress, when she walks, treads on the ground,*" Caspar breathed. "Of course! Jules, you are a genius! I shall love her from afar! Once I find her, of course."

"You can take your pick now," Jules pointed out. "Maybe they don't need to reciprocate as long as they inspire you."

At that exact moment, Tara Tremaine just happened to pass the window. As she did so, the sun peeked out from behind a cloud and the light caught her chestnut hair, turning it to pure flame. Haloed and unearthly, she could have stepped straight out of one of St Wenn's stained-glass windows. Jules heard Caspar gasp.

"My God! There she is!"

A greyhound after a rabbit couldn't have moved faster than Caspar did to grab his laptop. Within seconds, his fingers were flying across the screen and the document was filling with words. Tea, scones and cakes were all forgotten.

Jules's work here was done. She slipped out of the cottage and left him to it, laughing to herself that even curing writer's block was all in a day's work for the vicar of Polwenna Bay.

If only it were as easy to cure broken hearts.

Chapter 14

"How is it possible that three nine-year-old boys have so much energy? I'm shattered after just ten minutes, so God knows how you must feel having had them here all evening!"

Danny leaned against the Rayburn in the tiny cottage kitchen, a bottle of J20 held loosely in his hand, and smiled at Tara. The room was lit by lamp light and the string of red heart-shaped LEDs she'd pinned across one of the beams; in the soft glow he didn't look a day older than when they'd got married. He certainly didn't look like a man who was celebrating his son's ninth birthday.

Tara smiled. "I think they were high as kites on pizza and fizzy drinks. Or maybe we're just getting old?"

Danny shook his blond head. "Never! You didn't see me thrash one of them on the Xbox earlier. I've still got it, even with one hand."

"I don't doubt it for a moment." Tara opened the fridge and poured herself another glass of wine. After the whirl of the last few days – which had included moving into the cottage, working two shifts at The Plump Seagull and hosting a birthday party for a very excited nine-year-old – she figured that a drink was the least she deserved.

She raised her glass. "To Morgan."

Danny chinked his bottle against her wine glass. "Morgan, his ninth birthday and seeing him being so settled."

Tara smiled. "He does seem settled, doesn't he? I was thrilled he wanted to invite friends over this evening."

"The new camera was a hit too. I think he's fallen asleep with it in his hand," Danny told her.

"Sounds about right to me," Tara replied. "After losing the last one there's no way he's going to let the new camera out of his sight. I spoke to Tess, his teacher, and she says they're going to set up a photography club at the school next term. Morgan's in charge apparently."

"So you're staying here then?"

"I've got a job and I'm renting this house, aren't I?" Tara couldn't help it if she sounded defensive. She was painfully sensitive to any implied criticism that she might do something to unsettle their son.

"At the moment, yes, and you've made a fantastic home for him," Danny said. Although he spoke quietly there was an edge to his voice, an edge that she had put there. He didn't need to say any more; Tara knew what he was thinking.

"But you think I'm going to get bored and take off again, don't you?" she asked bitterly.

"Will you? It wasn't so long ago that the village was too small for you and you needed to get away." Danny's steady blue gaze met hers across the kitchen. "You've uprooted Morgan once before, which we both know isn't great for a kid with his needs. Before he gets too settled here, don't you think that you really ought to make sure it isn't going to happen again?"

Tara's hands curled into fists, her nails scoring little half-moons into her palms. She felt guilty enough about having moved Morgan to Plymouth, without Danny making her feel even worse.

"It isn't going to happen again," she promised him. "Dan, I don't know what I can say to make you believe me."

Her ex shrugged his broad shoulders. "I don't think there is anything you can say, T. You just have to prove it I guess."

Tara raised her chin. So far she'd been insulted in the village shop, snubbed by most of Danny's siblings and let down by one of her oldest friends. Clearly, she was the subject of some very juicy village gossip. And yet she was still here, wasn't she? In spite of everything she'd found a house to rent, moved herself and Morgan in and started earning some money. Just how much proof did Danny need?

Then she remembered what it was that had made him doubt her so much in the first place, and regret knifed her. She'd do whatever it took to show her husband that he could trust her. She bit back her protestations and put her wine glass down on the counter.

"I'll just check on Morgan," was all she said. "Why don't you take your drink through to the sitting room? The fire's lit and I won't be long."

Danny glanced at the kitchen clock. "It's getting on."

"It's only half past nine. What's going to happen? You'll turn into a pumpkin?"

There was no way Tara was letting Danny out of her sight now that she finally had him alone. She'd been waiting for this moment all day long. Through the pizzas and ice creams and the loud computer games she'd been counting down the minutes until it was just them. Her hair was freshly washed and teased into loose ringlets that softened her face, and her skinny jeans and fleecy pink sweater showed off her curves in an almost accidental way, while the tan knee boots with spiky heels suggested there might be more to her than just the wholesome girl next door. Tara had agonised over what to wear, changing her outfit several times until she was satisfied she was just the right combination of sexy and sweet. There had once been a time when Danny couldn't keep his hands off her. Hopefully, if she'd played all her cards right tonight, he might remember the magic they'd once shared.

Before he could make his excuses Tara turned and climbed the steep flight of stairs up to the small room under the eaves, knowing full well that, as she did so, Danny was treated to a view of her backside snugly clad in tight denim. She'd pulled a muscle in her neck trying to check that view in her bedroom mirror, but what she'd seen had suggested than the pain was worth it. By the time she'd kissed Morgan goodnight, her heart melting as always at the sight of him fast asleep, Danny was sitting on the sofa by the wood burner and looking quite at home.

This *could* be home for them, she realised with a jolt. They'd got on well today, hadn't they? For a few hours it had felt just as though they were a family again.

"Nice place," Danny remarked once she was sitting beside him, her boots kicked off and a glass of Chablis in her hand. "It was good of Richard to move out and let you have it."

"He's just a nice guy. He's helping out his mother by staying with her to pay the bills," Tara said, curling her legs beneath her and smiling up at him from under mascaraed lashes. Danny was so close she could smell his skin, and as she inhaled Tara felt a stab of nostalgic longing. Maybe this was the moment she should tell him that she was sorry and wanted to try again. Playing all these games was far too exhausting and she wasn't sure she could keep it up much longer.

But Danny was laughing.

"Come on, T! You don't really believe that do you? Richard's let the house out because he fancies you!"

Tara shook her head. "That's utter rubbish. I told you, Kursa can't afford the bills in her place so Richard's moved in for the winter."

"So that's why she was in the pub last night having a right old moan about her style being cramped because her son's suddenly moved in?" Danny was so amused that his sexy smile even lifted the injured side of his mouth. "Apparently she's going to ask for a refund on her online dating membership."

"But he was adamant!"

"Guys always are when they want to impress a woman," said Danny sagely. "Trust me on that. Richard wants to impress you."

Tara wasn't convinced about this – but maybe Danny was jealous? That was a positive sign surely? Feeling encouraged, she shifted a little closer to him until her knees were resting against his thigh.

"Never mind Richard," she said. "I'm more interested in us."

"Us?"

"Yes, us. You and me and Morgan. We're a family, Danny. That means a lot."

There was a silence after she said this. A log slipped in the wood burner. In the kitchen the dishwasher thrummed and swished. There was a drumming in Tara's ears as her heart began to race. This was it. The moment she'd been waiting for. What happened next was going to alter the course of their lives.

Then Danny sighed wearily, like a man who'd been holding his breath for a long time.

"Yes it does," he said quietly. "Our family used to mean everything to me, Tara, absolutely everything – and you know that. It meant everything until the moment you decided to take it away."

She did know it, and not a day went by when she didn't hate herself for putting it all into jeopardy. She wanted to say that she was sorry, that she wished she'd never done the thing she'd done. But how could she when, if not for that one selfish, careless mistake on a drunken night nine years and nine months ago, Morgan might never have been born at all? How could she regret something that had ultimately brought her more happiness and joy than she could ever have imagined?

No, the words she wanted to say were that she was sorry for opening her mouth and telling Danny the truth. That was her biggest regret. If she had only been able to keep the secret, to live with the constant dread of being discovered... That gnawing guilt was nothing, nothing in comparison to the horror of the destruction she'd caused by one desperate, bedside confession in the hospital. The irony was that it hadn't even been a full confession, because Danny hadn't wanted to hear what she'd had to say. He'd not even let her finish. Instead he'd turned his bandaged face to the wall and from that point on had refused to see her.

"Danny, I—"

He held up his hand.

"Please, T, don't make it worse. There's nothing I wouldn't have done for you or Morgan. I loved both of you so bloody much, Tara. You were my world. You meant everything to me. Morgan's my son. Mine. I didn't want to know anything else. Christ, do you really think I never guessed? That I never suspected?"

Tara couldn't look him in the face. This was *exactly* what she'd thought, until she'd tried to confess her dreadful, appalling secret. To discover that Danny had suspected for all those years had shocked her to the core.

"But you never said a word," she whispered. "Not one word. Why, Danny?"

He turned to face her and the grief etched on his face was worse than all the scars. With a growing horror Tara realised that the damage she had done to Danny was worse than anything a roadside bomb could ever have inflicted on him. He was a man with the courage to fight his country's enemies and live with the consequences – but he'd thought she was on his side.

"Do you really not know?" He reached out and touched her face, and she felt his sadness trembling through his fingertips. "Can't you guess?"

Tears spilled onto her cheeks. "You didn't want it to be true."

"Because I loved you Tara, so damn much, and I loved Morgan too. It didn't matter what had happened because I loved you and I loved him. Love him. He's my son and that's all I ever cared about."

Outside the thick harbour wall, waves rose and fell like sobs.

"I knew you'd had a fling," Danny continued, looking away from her now and staring into the glowing fire. "I'd always known."

"It didn't mean anything," she whispered. "It was stupid. I was lonely and flattered and I hated myself as soon as it happened. I never wanted to hurt you. "

"You might not have wanted to, but you did."

"And now you hate me." She hung her head. It was no more than she deserved.

Danny shook his head. "Oh, Tara, I don't hate you anymore. I did for a long time, especially when you tried to blurt it all out in the hospital. But it's history now, isn't it? And I've had a lot of time to think about it all and make my peace." He paused and then sighed. "Besides, there was blame on my part too. I neglected you, which doesn't excuse what you did, but I know it does explain it. My career came first and you were lonely. I'm not stupid; I've been in the army long enough to see how these things go. As for not knowing? Christ! It's the bloody army and gossip's always rife. Did you really think that the rumours about you wouldn't reach my ears? Or that people wouldn't love dropping sly hints my way?"

Tara was cold from head to foot. She really had thought that Danny had been oblivious.

"It was just the once," she whispered. "It didn't mean anything."

"Maybe not to you, but it does to me. I loved you, Tara. I wanted things to work and I blamed myself. I knew how lonely it was for you stuck in those Godforsaken barracks in Germany. I knew the other wives gave you a hard time but I hoped that we could make it work. When you said that you were pregnant I hoped with all my heart that it was the fresh start we needed. I prayed that Morgan was my son."

"I swear I thought he was yours," Tara whispered. "I so wanted him to be."

Danny's blond head nodded slowly. "But when I was away on that last tour he had the appendix operation and needed blood, didn't he? Then I came home injured and needed gallons of the stuff and that was when you realised the truth."

It wasn't a question.

"I didn't know for sure until then." Tara still recalled the horror of realising the truth. Funny how just with a quick Google search and a few clicks of the mouse you could change your world forever. She reached for her drink and took a huge gulp. A pointless exercise. All the booze in the world wouldn't make this go away. "I didn't know what to do."

"That was when you knew for certain he wasn't mine," Danny said bleakly.

"Morgan *is* yours in every way that matters!" Tara cried. "He's your son, Danny! Your son! He loves you."

"And I love him, Tara. I'd lay down my life for him, you know that, but you had an advantage over me. I didn't really know for sure until you turned up at the hospital and tried to blurt it out. I'd always hoped that I was wrong. I thought that if there was any doubt, you'd have told me at the time. Not seven and a half bloody years later!"

"I thought about it so many times but I was so scared. I tried in the hospital, Danny, but you wouldn't let me finish! You told me to get out!" Tara cried.

"I'd lost my fucking face, my arm and my career. Did you really need to take my son as well? Jesus, Tara. What were you thinking? That I'd just turn to the wall and die quietly?"

"Of course not!" Tara was horrified. "But I did think you might die, Danny. We all did."

"So you thought you'd unburden your soul just in case?" His mouth curled into a mocking smile. "How totally bloody selfish and how typical. If you said it, then it was out and a fact, wasn't it? I couldn't kid myself that I was being paranoid or had made a mistake. It was true. I lost everything that day and you damn-near made sure I lost my son too. Well, I won't let that happen, Tara. I won't. He's my son."

It had been a selfish act, Tara knew that now, but at the time she'd been terrified that a secret like that couldn't be put right. She couldn't have gone to her grave without telling the truth. But as for how the revelation would make Danny feel? If she was brutally honest, that hadn't figured.

She bit her thumbnail, a nervous habit she'd thought she'd outgrown. "What do you want to do?"

"Do?"

"Do you want to tell Morgan?" Tara felt sick to the pit of her stomach at this thought. Stability was key for their son and she couldn't imagine the consequences if he handled it badly.

Danny looked at her as though she was mad. "Why on earth would I do that? Apart from the fact that he's my son, no matter what the sodding DNA says, he's only nine. When he's older then we'll tackle it together, but not yet. Christ. That would be beyond cruel."

She nodded. "I agree. Thanks, Danny."

"Don't thank me," said Danny. "I love him and I'll always love him. That's never going to change."

Tears made his face shimmer.

"But you don't love me anymore do you? You look at me and all you see is a woman who betrayed you." Misery clawed at her throat. "I look at you, Danny, and I still see the man I fell in love with."

"Hardly. Bits of him are still in a sand dune somewhere," Danny quipped, but the joke fell flat and an awkward silence followed. Tara mopped her eyes on her sleeve. Danny was such a good man: honest and loyal and generous. Of course he couldn't bear the sight of her anymore. Of course he no longer loved her. She'd blown his world apart more effectively than any enemy bomb ever could.

"We have a history and we shared so many very special times," Danny told her, "but we messed up. We've both made mistakes, but if I'm honest I don't think I can ever feel the same way again. No way.

We're not the same people. Yes, I look at you and I still see the beautiful girl I fell in love with – but things can never be as they were. I'm sorry, Tara, but nothing you can say or do will make me feel the way I did."

Danny might have been telling her that their marriage was over, but all Tara heard was him saying that he still thought she was beautiful, and her heart leapt with a tidal surge of hope. Hadn't he just said that he'd made mistakes too? That as far as he was concerned Morgan was his son? Was he trying to say that there was a chance for them after all? The wine, the warm room and the scent of his very male skin just a fingertip's touch away made her dizzy.

"Are you sure of that?" she said and, acting on pure longing and instinct, leaned forward and kissed him.

It was as though she'd set light to touchpaper. Danny's hand gripped the back of her neck and his mouth closed over hers in a burning kiss. As he pulled her closer she could feel the heat of his chest through her thin sweater, and the sensation of his hardness against her loins made her head spin all the more. Instinctively Tara lifted her mouth to him, and his tongue plunged deeper into her mouth as he reached to cup her breast. She remembered all the other times he'd kissed her and all the places they'd made love, and she felt faint with longing. As though they had a will of their own, her shaking fingers began to unbutton his shirt, her hands slipping beneath the fabric to explore the smooth flesh of his chest and trace the whirls of golden hair.

Dimly, like a swimmer who's dived beneath the surface of a lake and can only hear the muffled world above indistinctly, Tara became aware of a voice calling her. At first it didn't register but slowly, breath by breath, she surfaced, until she broke away from Danny with a start.

Morgan.

"Mum! Mum! I feel sick!"

"The joys of being a mum," Tara said ruefully. "Give me a moment."

Danny's breathing was ragged and he couldn't look her in the face. Instead he made a big show of tucking in his shirt.

"Someone's had too much cake. You'd better go."

Leaving Danny flustered and dishevelled on the sofa, Tara shot up the stairs, smoothing back her hair and pulling down her jumper as she went. A quick glance in the landing mirror revealed bright eyes and a flushed face, but nothing that couldn't be explained away by the warmth of the fire and a few glasses of wine. As Dan had predicted, a surfeit of chocolate cake and pepperoni pizza were playing havoc with Morgan's tummy. It took a glass of water and a fair bit of soothing to calm him. By the time he'd drifted back off to sleep with his camera clutched tightly in his hand and Tara had returned downstairs, the sofa was empty and the sounds of the dishwasher being emptied and then restacked were coming from the kitchen.

Danny's back was to her but Tara didn't need to see his face to know that the heated atmosphere of earlier had popped like soap bubbles. The tucked-in shirt and brisk chink of china spoke volumes.

"You didn't need to clear up," Tara said. Her voice sounded flat even to her own ears.

"I think we both know that I did." Danny turned round and smiled sadly. "Look, Tara, about what happened just now… It was a very bad idea. We got caught in the moment and maybe a little confused by everything."

She raised one shoulder. "I'm not confused. I know what I want."

"So do I," said Danny, "and this isn't it. There's too much water under the bridge. Too many resentments and too little trust."

He couldn't trust her.

He resented her.

Tara was knifed to the soul with misery. She could hardly blame Danny, not when she'd betrayed him in the worst way possible. Tonight she'd tried everything she could to win him back: nostalgia, honesty, sex... And all in vain. He might still fancy her, he might even have fond feelings for her, but the harsh truth of the matter was that Danny Tremaine didn't love her anymore. The love was gone.

"I've loved being a part of Morgan's birthday today," Danny was saying, "and I hope I can come to the next one too, but we both know that you and I will never work as a couple. I've told you how I feel about being Morgan's father and I don't want to do anything that could upset that. I don't want to be an absent father just because there's bitterness between you and me. I don't want bitterness at all, for Morgan's sake."

Tara was once more on the verge of tears. As she looked across the kitchen she suddenly saw the rest of her life stretching out without Danny, and it was a very bleak feeling.

He was looking straight at her.

"I want to be Morgan's father in the real sense of the word. I want to be there for him, now and for the rest of his life. Stability is key for Morgan. Structure. Routine. We all know that. We've read the educational psychologist's report and we've seen Morgan's special needs statement. This isn't about us as a couple and the rights and wrongs of what we've done; it's about far more than that. If we took tonight to the ultimate conclusion and it all went wrong – which it would, because there's too much history – how would Morgan feel then?"

"It could always work out with us," Tara murmured.

Dan shut the dishwasher with a decisive slam. "If it was going to work out, sweetheart, you wouldn't have run off to Plymouth six months ago or found your way into another man's bed nine or so years before that."

The words were like a slap.

"I made a mistake, Danny! It could still be good with us! Give me one last chance to prove that," Tara pleaded. "You still fancy me, I know you do."

"Of course I do," he agreed firmly. "You're a very attractive woman. But Tara, I don't *love* you anymore. I choose to be Morgan's father and I choose to be your friend if you'll let me, but I can't make myself feel that way about you. God knows I've tried and I've wished that I could, because it would certainly make life more convenient – but emotions like that can't be forced."

"You loved me once," she said sadly.

He stepped forward and dropped a kiss onto the top of her head.

"I did and I will always cherish what we once had, but it's over, Tara. It's over."

"So that's it? There's no hope?"

"There's hope that we can actually work together now rather than being at loggerheads," he told her. "We need to move on and move forward, not just for our sakes but for Morgan's too. There will come a time when he has to know the truth – and I want him to hear it from us both, without bitterness and accusations. I want him to understand just how loved and wanted he is by us both."

"But we won't be together," Tara said quietly. "We won't be married."

"No, we won't." There was steel now in Danny's voice, and this was when she knew that it really was over. The last time he'd sounded so determined and set on his course was when he'd told her he didn't want her anywhere near him in the hospital. Dan had kept his word then and she knew he would now. He was a man of strong principles. When Danny Tremaine gave his heart he didn't give it lightly. He gave it with every fibre of his being. The same applied when he took it back. There were no half measures.

Danny had reached for his coat and shrugged it on before opening the little kitchen door and stepping into the dark, smoke-scented night. Pausing on the doorstep, he added gently, "Tara, I don't love you anymore and, if you're really honest with yourself, I think you'll find you no longer love me either – the man I am now or the man I was then. It's time we both moved on. Let's not waste the chance of finding happiness again."

The door clicked shut and Tara stood in the empty kitchen, her arms wrapped tightly around herself. She stared at the door Danny had just closed.

Let's not waste the chance of finding happiness again...

At the moment she couldn't imagine ever being happy again. Any hopes she'd cherished that she and Danny might work things out were well and truly dead, and for that she had nobody to blame but herself.

Her tears falling in earnest now. Tara turned off the kitchen light, sat at the kitchen table and wept until dawn's pink fingers streaked the sky.

Chapter 15

"I don't often hate my job," Tess Hamilton told Jules, putting her curly head in her hands, "but I have to say I come very close when it's time to organise the school nativity. Honestly, Jules, I'm a total wreck. Have you any idea just how many times I've been approached by irate parents who all think their child should play Mary or an angel? I'm starting to dread leaving my classroom at the end of the day because there's bound to be someone waiting for me."

It was late November and Christmas was creeping up on Jules. It was always the busiest time of her year and there was so much to do that if she thought too hard about it she would start to panic. The nativity play was a highlight and traditionally took place on the village green on the same night that the Polwenna Bay Christmas tree was lit. This meant that there was only a week to go. No wonder Tess was fraught. The shepherds were on strike because nobody wanted to wear a dressing gown, and Mo's old pony Bubbles had objected violently to wearing donkey ears and given Joseph a very sharp nip. Floods of tears had followed (Joseph) and then a steaming pile of pony crap (Bubbles). It did not bode well.

Following this afternoon's big dress rehearsal, the two women had headed through the village for an early supper in The Ship. It was supposedly a working dinner where they could liaise about the Polwenna nativity, but Tess was so stressed that most of their time together had been spent with Jules trying to calm her down. On top of marking, assessments, report-writing and trying to actually have a life of her own, taking charge of 23 children for the Christmas show was clearly taking its toll on the exhausted primary teacher, if the three gin and tonics she'd knocked back were anything to go by.

Jules had every sympathy because the same outraged parents had taken to doorstepping the vicarage as well. The Polwenna nativity play was a huge deal in the village – it even made *X Factor* look amateurish – and all parents were determined that their child should be the star. Those of the *Jeremy Kyle Show* persuasion were ready to knock her block off, while the Boden-wearing brigade were slightly more subtle with their offerings of wine from Waitrose. No matter what their methods, both sets of parents were equally convinced that their own offspring should have the starring role. Nobody wanted to see their little cherub with a tea towel on his or her head. It was tinsel or broke. Still, like Caesar's wife, the vicar of Polwenna Bay had to be above suspicion, and it was taking all of Jules's tact and determination to turn them away.

"The rehearsals are looking great though," she said, determined to cheer Tess up.

"You think?" Tess looked across the bar and gestured for another drink. "Even when Morgan insisted that it's *A Whale in a Manger* and then, rather than reading his set piece, stated that God doesn't exist, fact?"

Jules grinned at the memory. "You must admit that it was quite amusing. I thought Miss Powell was going to combust."

"In my dreams," Tess said gloomily. "Miss Powell's so stuck in the dark ages, it's untrue. Do you know she even told me that autism's just an excuse for bad behaviour? How am I supposed to work with that? She really hasn't got a clue how to handle Morgan. He totally winds her up. Maybe I shouldn't have made him the narrator."

"Bollocks," Jules said staunchly. "That was a brilliant idea and he's going to be fantastic. Alice tells me he already knows all his lines inside out. He's the perfect choice."

Tess nodded. "I think so. It's been wonderful to see his confidence grow since he's been here. He's such a character. It's nice that he'll be staying too, isn't it?"

Jules nodded. Tara and Morgan seemed settled into Waterside Cottage and Danny was by all accounts a frequent visitor. Maybe they were sorting things out as a family at last? This thought was bittersweet; it was what she'd wanted for him, but knowing that Danny was lost to her forever was the most painful sensation in the world. Jules prayed constantly for the strength to handle it and to do the right thing, but she still struggled.

"Another drink?" Tess was asking as, purse in hand, she rose to collect hers.

It was a tempting offer, given that the pub was warm and the fire crackling merrily in the big inglenook was crying out to be sat by with a glass of mulled wine. However, Tess was also meeting Nick Tremaine when he came in from sea. The two had shared a couple of dates and were in the first flush of a touchy-feely fling, and Jules wasn't sure she could face being around a loved-up couple right now. Besides, she also had the joy of a PCC meeting to contend with.

"Thanks, but I'm going to head back to the vicarage. I've got a meeting at half seven and a mountain of paperwork to finish."

"Fair enough; I know how that feels. Just take care that you don't get accosted by any parents on the way home! Maybe keep your hood up and go the long way around?"

"Don't even joke about it," Jules said grimly. "That's exactly what I'm going to do."

* * *

The cold hit Jules like a slap as she pushed open the pub door and stepped outside. It was a sharp November night with bright stars freckling the sky and a fat white moon floating above the sea. Some keen villagers had already placed fairy lights in their cottage windows, and as she walked through the narrow streets Jules noticed that the Pollards had been busy stringing up the Christmas lights. These were an ingenious combination of brightly coloured seaside buckets stuck together in pairs with bulbs inside. Just seeing them made her smile because they were so cheery and just so Polwenna. Making a mental note to ask Big Rog if there were any spare to decorate the church hall, Jules stomped up the hill to the vicarage – where she bumped into Alice, who was waiting patiently on the doorstep.

"Hello, love. I know I'm a little early for the PCC but I thought I'd give you a hand setting up," Alice said. She looked incredibly tired, Jules thought with a lurch of concern. There were deep bags beneath her faded blue eyes. Alice was such a dynamo that it was sometimes easy to forget she was actually nearly eighty.

"You should have called me. I'd have got here sooner and let you in," Jules said as she unlocked the door.

"I always forget you lock the place," Alice said, following her inside.

"Call me a paranoid townie but I just can't get out of the habit."

Jules made tea while Alice laid out the agendas and arranged biscuits onto plates as the members of the PCC drifted in, bickering gently over who was sitting where and what items on the agenda were the most important. Danny was the last to arrive, nodding at Jules as he took his usual place beside her.

She smiled at him. "How's things?"

"Fine." Danny didn't look at her, instead seeming to be intrigued by the last meeting's minutes. "How's your new friend settling in?"

"New friend?" Jules was stumped. Who was he talking about? "Do you mean Tess? She's fine. Stressed over the nativity play and Morgan's Richard Dawkins moments, but apart from that she's fine."

Danny grinned at the mention of his son. "Yeah, I had words with him about that." Then his smile faded. "I meant that writer chap you've been hanging out with."

"Oh! Caspar!" Or should she say Cassandra Duval? Jules was still a little star-struck from meeting one of her literary idols and trying to equate the uber-feminine bodice-ripping pink covers with the rather theatrical and very male Caspar. She'd spent a few afternoons chatting with him but generally he was flat out admiring Tara from afar and writing his novel. "He's fine."

"Jolly good," said Danny, but in the kind of voice that implied he'd prefer it if Caspar were six feet under. Jules was about to ask him what his problem was when Big Rog Pollard thumped his fist on the table and declared the meeting open.

Jules had a feeling she was shortly going to regret letting him be chairman…

"Item one on the agenda," Big Rog declared grandly, "discrepancies in the accounts. More sums of money have been deposited anonymously into the St Wenn's bank account."

"Why is that a problem?" asked Alice, frowning. "Surely that's a nice thing."

"Because it looks as though we're laundering money," Richard explained. "We have no idea what the source is, so it could have come from anywhere. Crime or drugs, for example. The accountants will be all over it and we could be heading for a tax investigation."

Alice's hand flew to her mouth. If she looked pale before, it was nothing to her pallor now.

"I've spoken to the bank and there's no way we can trace who made the deposits." Jules was exhausted trying to untangle it all. "There are all sorts of due diligent issues which I'll need to start looking into."

"It's that serious?" Alice asked.

"About as serious as it gets," Richard sighed. "No development here at all, I'm afraid, so I guess we just have to minute that as ongoing?"

"Already minuted," Sheila said proudly. "Next item?"

As the meeting progressed Jules listened with one ear while keeping a worried eye on Alice, who really didn't look too well. By the time they reached the final item on the agenda, the bishop's visit, she'd pleaded a headache and gone home. Jules didn't buy this for a second. Stoic Alice wasn't given to headaches and complaints; she was the kind who only took an aspirin if forced.

"Danny, would you go and check on Alice?" she asked, interrupting mid-flow Sheila's description of the tea they would lay on in Bishop Bill's honour. "I'm really worried about her."

"She looked bloody awful," agreed Big Rog, a grave expression on his weathered face. He tugged his whiskers thoughtfully. "Hope it isn't her heart. My old Ma looked just like that before she keeled over and died."

"Wasn't she coming up for eighty too?" asked Little Rog.

"She was, my boy, she was. Strong as an ox one moment and stone-cold dead the next. Tragic, it was."

"Thanks for that," said Danny drily. He pushed back his chair and reached for his jacket. "I'm sure she's fine, probably just all the usual stress of having to referee us lot, but I'll walk over and make sure she's all right. Then I'll text you, Jules, OK?"

She nodded gratefully. At least they could put the weird atmosphere between them aside for Alice's sake, which was something. Whether or not they would ever be friends again was another matter entirely.

Big Rog sneaked a glance at the clock. It was eight-thirty and way past beer time. "Any other business?"

"A Christingle service would be nice," Richard suggested. "Jo, my practice nurse, is really keen on the idea."

"Five-year-olds carrying candles?" Sheila pooh-poohed the idea instantly. "St Wenn's will be up in flames in minutes."

"It might be asking for trouble," Jules agreed, wondering if the church's insurance was up to date for this kind of thing. Another job to do.

"So why not use those fake flickering candles you get down Par Market?" This was from Little Rog. "Ma loves those, doesn't she Pa?"

"She does, my boy. Bleddy hundreds of them in our house. But we haven't had to call the fire brigade since she discovered them, which is good," said his father. "Buggers were threatening to charge us!"

"They did come out five times," sniffed Sheila.

"That's why I pay my taxes," grumbled Big Rog.

"Well you certainly got value for money," grinned Richard.

"I'll think about a Christingle with fake candles and speak to Tess." Jules privately thought that if she told Tess the children would need to decorate oranges, on top of everything else, her friend would freak. Polwenna Primary was a Church of England school and for Jules treading the fine line between being actively involved and interfering was proving easier said than done.

"Anything else?" Big Rog was getting twitchy now; it was definitely beer o'clock.

"Charity!" trilled Sheila. "After the huge success of the Polwenna Bay calendar we need to up our game and raise even more money for the church."

"I wouldn't call the calendar a success exactly," Jules said quickly, before Sheila could suggest something else that would give her even more grey hair. "We were lucky the bishop saw the funny side."

"It was perfectly decent," Sheila huffed.

"I'll say so!" leered Little Rog. "June was my favourite."

"March was better, son. What Patsy does with those buns!"

"I thought we could have a slave auction," Sheila said.

"Like in that *Fifty Shades* book?" Big Rog's eyes lit up. "Great idea!"

"Absolutely not," said Jules, horrified as the most gruesome image of Big Rog trussed up in bondage gear flitted through her mind. Lord, she'd need Dettol for her brain to get rid of that picture. "It's cake sales or nothing."

"Spoilsport," said Little Rog.

"I think we're forgetting something," interrupted Richard, "and that is that we don't actually need any more money coming in. We've got enough problems explaining our surplus away as it is. No, the only piece of any other business we need to worry about is finding out where the extra payments are coming from – and fast."

"And if we can't?" said Jules.

Richard took off his glasses and polished them carefully. His grey eyes were worried.

"Then, Jules, I'm afraid St Wenn's really is in trouble, and it will take a lot more than a calendar or an auction to save us. The bishop might overlook a daft calendar, but any suggestion of money laundering or improper accounting isn't going to look good for us."

Jules felt a cold sense of dread in the pit of her stomach.

"In that case," she told the group gathered around her kitchen table, "we'd better get sleuthing."

And with that final instruction the meeting closed, leaving Jules with a horrible sensation that time was running out for St Wenn's.

Chapter 16

Tara had lived in the village long enough to know that when the St Miltons threw a party it was well worth going to. No expense was ever spared: champagne flowed faster than the River Wenn, the food was always exquisite and the hotel would be beautifully decorated. This was never truer than for the annual Christmas charity fundraiser, which was always held on the last Saturday in November. The big cedar trees outside the elegant old house were filled with twinkling coloured lights and in the entrance hall an enormous Christmas tree had pride of place, reaching from the bottom of the sweeping Adam staircase right up to the dizzying heights of the cupola above. Tickets were hugely expensive but generally sold out like hotcakes, especially because the proceeds always went to a local charity. Tara was having to be super careful with her money, budgeting down to the very last penny of the child support from Danny and her wages, and there was no chance she could have attended under her own steam.

"Glad you came to work for me?" Sy asked her as they oversaw the unpacking of the evening's canapés. Miniature Yorkshire puddings with beef jus and horseradish, goujons of fish with matchstick fries, and mouth-watering retro-style lobster vol-au-vents were all being laid out beautifully on silver platters. Meanwhile, the pièce de résistance, an enormous meringue and cream fairy-tale castle, was just having the finishing touches added by Luke, Sy's sous-chef.

"It's just about bearable," Tara sighed, but the big smile as she said this told Sy just how much she appreciated the work he'd put her way.

It was wintertime now, hardly peak tourist season, and he probably didn't need an extra member of staff nearly as much as he'd implied. That was Symon through and through: quiet and thoughtful and very kind. After Danny, he'd always been Tara's favourite Tremaine sibling.

"Now that this lot's off our hands, I say we go and enjoy the party." With the last platter set out and the containers stacked, Sy looked relieved. He was such a perfectionist when it came to his food. No wonder he was rumoured to be about to receive a second coveted Michelin star.

Tara was shattered after working a double shift in the kitchen all afternoon and then a few more hours at the hotel. Morgan was staying at Seaspray with Danny, which had given her an opportunity to earn some extra funds. She'd hardly seen Danny since their kiss, which was fine by Tara. He'd made it clear how he felt about her, and she could hardly blame him. If Danny hated her it was nothing compared with the contempt Tara had for herself. The past could never be undone and the echoes that it would send into the future were terrifying. That Dan understood why she'd been lonely and bored was one thing, but to lose his beloved son was more than any man should have to bear. Her only comfort was that the young soldier she'd spent that one fateful night with seemed to have vanished. No amount of Googling or searching for him on Facebook had shed any light on his whereabouts.

She guessed that was a wrong she'd have to put right another day.

Leaving Sy to circulate, Tara changed out of her kitchen gear and into a little black dress. She put on a quick slick of make-up and dragged a brush through her hair, but when she walked into the party she felt underdressed. The other guests were all beautifully attired in designer clothes, the women freshly made up and with their hair lovingly styled.

Their wrists and necks glittered with jewels – real ones, Tara was sure, and worlds away from the Dorothy Perkins pendant she had picked out to wear.

She stood on the edge of the crowd, listening to old Jonny St Milton thanking whoever the generous mystery benefactor was who had already donated five hundred pounds to the charity. Applause rippled through the room and Tara joined in, trying to imagine what it must be like to have so much money that you could donate huge chunks to charity. Unless she had a major lottery win, she guessed she'd never know.

The raffle took place next, after which the band struck up a medley of Christmas music and the partygoers returned to the serious business of drinking champagne and eating canapés. Handsome men escorted glossy women onto the dance floor, where they twirled under the twinkling lights like *Strictly* stars. Chief among these glossy women was a tall and very slender woman in a crimson one-shouldered number that fell in immaculate pleats to the tips of her blood-red toenails. Her blonde hair was straightened to perfection and her nails were beautifully manicured, unlike Tara's chipped ones. It was Ella St Milton, granddaughter of the hotel's owner Jonny, and tonight's hostess. As usual she was surrounded by a crowd of admiring beaux who were hanging on her every word. One of these was Richard, Tara's dog-walking landlord, and Tara watched him from across the room with interest. He seemed relaxed and was chatting effortlessly, with none of the awkwardness that he sometimes had whenever she spoke to him. *He fits in here*, she thought with admiration. His air of gentleness and his ability to listen drew people to him with an ease she could only marvel at.

I'm just useless, Tara concluded sadly, *and it's all my fault. Nobody wants me here and I don't blame them.* If they knew the truth they'd hate her even more. How on earth could she make up now for all the mistakes she'd made? Danny was right: it was way too late. What was she doing back in this village?

Richard caught sight of Tara and instantly broke away from his group, mid-conversation, to join her.

"Hello, lovely tenant lady! It's a nice surprise to see you here." He leaned forward to kiss her. He smelled of fresh air and raindrops and salty sea breezes.

"I'm here by default," Tara confessed. "I've been helping Symon with the catering, so I've sneaked in through the back door." She glanced ruefully at her outfit. How come she'd never noticed just how faded and tatty her dress was? "To be honest I was thinking about just catching a cab home. I'm hardly dressed for this kind of thing."

"Nonsense, you look wonderful." Richard took her elbow and gently steered Tara through the chattering throng into the orangery, where waiters were circulating with flutes of champagne and glasses of hot mulled wine. Collecting one and handing it to her, he added, "I think it's time you had a night out. We hardly see you in the village."

"That's got a lot to do with having a nine-year-old and working nights," Tara sighed. "I think my partying days are over. I'll probably get a cat and take up knitting."

Richard looked shocked. "You're far too young to shut yourself away. I won't allow it. Come and enjoy the free champagne and mingle a bit. Everyone's having a wonderful time. Look at Alice dancing with that old rogue Jonny St Milton. She looks like a teenager."

Sure enough Alice, dressed in a long floaty grey dress and with her silvery hair piled up on her head, was waltzing with the elderly hotelier. They were lost in their own world and watching them made a lump rise in Tara's throat.

"They look so elegant don't they?" Richard remarked. "I can't imagine what our generation will look like when we dance at that age. OAPs headbanging could be asking for trouble."

"Or imagine them in a mosh pit!"

He winced. "The NHS will never afford all the replacement hips and knees. How about we make the most of being young and fit and take to the dance floor ourselves?"

Tara was on the brink of protesting that she had two left feet, when they were interrupted by the arrival of her peculiar writer neighbour. He was dressed from head to toe in flowing black velvet and clutching a sheaf of papers in his hand. He seemed to be making a beeline for her, and a huge manic grin crinkled his face as though he was thrilled to see her. This was a little disconcerting; they'd hardly exchanged more than the odd hello on their respective doorsteps.

"Tara! I never thought I'd see you here!" Caspar was at her side now and Tara couldn't help herself stepping back. His eyes were so bright. Surely he couldn't be drunk already? It was only early evening. "This is wonderful! Wonderful!"

It was?

"Err, nice to see you too," she said.

"I've seen you around the village," Caspar continued, oblivious to Tara's lack of enthusiasm, "and I've admired you from afar. In fact, you've inspired me to write one of the best books of my life. You're my muse, Tara!"

What on earth did a girl say to that? She was still struggling to think of a suitable reply when Caspar dropped to his knees and began to declare theatrically:

"Oh beautiful eyes, oh angelic face,

You're a beauty wild and free,

The eagle of my soaring heart,

The one who means the world to me!

Mistress of my eyes, I long for your smile—"

Tara couldn't help it; she started to laugh. The poetry was just so dreadful and he looked so ridiculous kneeling on the floor, with his arms raised to heaven and his eyes rolling like those of a dying horse, that giggles rose up in her chest like bubbles in a hot spring. The situation was absurd, and the more he recited his poetry the more comical it became.

"I'm sorry!" she gasped as Caspar's words petered out. "But seriously? What on earth are you on about? You don't know me, and if you did you'd never say I'm angelic. Is this a joke?"

"Don't you like the poem?" Caspar looked crestfallen and more than a little stupid kneeling on the floor. People were starting to look and, taking pity on him, Richard tugged the would-be bard to his feet.

"To be honest," said Tara, "I'm a bit creeped out. Are you a stalker?"

"A stalker?" His mouth fell open with shock. "I'm not a stalker! I'm a poet! I write from afar, like Petrarch to Laura, like Abelard to Heloise, like…"

"Like Stan to Slim Shady?" suggested Richard. "Maybe it would be better if you just stuck to writing the novels instead?"

Caspar threw his papers to the floor in a snowstorm of A4 and lilac ink, and slammed his fist against his heart.

"I have never been so insulted in my life! I'm a writer, a wordsmith, a bard. Not a stalker! This was poetry! It was Art!"

"I'm flattered, I really am," Tara said quickly. "It's very sweet of you."

"*Sweet!* Flay me to the quick with such a word," he gasped. "The *Belle Dame sans Merci*. I laid my heart at her feet and she has trodden it into the earth."

This sounded very messy to Tara and she felt awful. Oh dear. Weren't artists supposed to be sensitive and a bit mad?

"I will never get over this. Never!" Caspar wailed. "My great novel is nothing but an illusion. Not art but smoke and mirrors!"

"What on earth's going on?" Jules Mathieson, surprisingly sexy in black velvet and with a cleavage that made Tara want to race home and fetch her chicken fillets, was at Caspar's side, looking horrified at the poetic snowstorm. Then her hand flew to her mouth. "Caspar, you didn't show your latest muse the poetry did you?"

"Latest muse?" Tara asked.

"And there you were thinking you were special," Richard whispered, nudging her.

"It's how he writes," Jules explained as Caspar huffed out of the room. Even his cloak looked outraged. "Caspar needs a muse to inspire him, otherwise he has terrible writer's block. He's a hopeless romantic, you see, and his novels even more so."

"He writes romances? I had him down as writing gothic stuff." Tara was surprised.

"The cloak and the hair are very *Twilight*," Jules agreed. "Oh dear, I'm afraid this is all my fault. Since his girlfriend left him he's been very down, which meant he couldn't write. The hours we've spent talking about writer's block!"

"So that's why you've been spending so much time with him!" Richard shook his head. "We all thought there was something going on between you. Danny was convinced."

Jules looked stunned. "Something between me and Caspar? No way. I'm a vicar. Hardly muse material."

Danny might disagree, Tara thought. Intuition and that sexy black dress told her that men saw Jules as far more than just a vicar.

"I suggested that he admired somebody from afar and made them the heroine of his novel," Jules explained. She looked mortified. "What a muddle."

"I'm afraid I laughed at him," said Tara. "I'm really sorry."

"He'll survive," Jules assured her. "Honestly. He'll be over you in about twenty minutes and onto the next muse, I guarantee it."

"Story of my life," Tara sighed.

Richard threaded his arm through hers. "You can be my muse, Tara. After a few glasses of fizz I'm sure I can come up with a few couplets."

The rest of the evening seemed pretty tame after this episode, but Tara found that it flew by. She danced and drank champagne and, to her surprise, found that she was actually having fun. Richard was such good company that she quickly forgot to feel inadequate about her lack of designer clothes and just enjoyed chatting to him. It felt good to have a friend at last. Even their shared taxi ride back to the village was filled with conversation and laughter. When she lay her head against his shoulder and closed her eyes it felt like the most natural thing in the world. There was a strange fluttering sensation in her chest, which didn't go even after he'd said goodnight and brushed a chaste kiss on her cheek – a pleasant change from guys like Anthony who tended to lunge in for a Hoover-style snog and then try to barge their way inside for a "coffee".

Richard was such a gentleman, Tara thought – and, besides, he only saw her as a friend anyway. He had a kind heart and she was the single mum he'd taken pity on. That was why he'd rented her the cottage. There was nothing more going on. Anyway, he wasn't even her type.

Although, he did have the most amazing eyes – dove grey and with a dark outline around the irises – and that full and kissable-looking mouth…

Lord! Just how much champagne had she drunk?

Laughing at herself, Tara locked up the cottage and headed up the stairs, reflecting that pity and just-friendship or not, this had been one of the nicest evenings she'd had for ages. The fluttery sensation simply refused to go away.

It was only when she was tucked up in bed, with the light off and the heavy feather duvet pulled up to her chin, that Tara was able to identify the feeling. No wonder she hadn't recognised it; this was an emotion that had eluded her for a very long time.

She was feeling happy. Happy! The churning anxiety and that gnawing guilt had finally left her in peace and it was absolute bliss. Even the strange episode with Caspar hadn't spoiled the night. In fact she couldn't help but feel flattered. Nobody had ever written poetry for her before.

With a smile on her face, Tara Tremaine finally drifted into a sweet and dreamless sleep.

Chapter 17

Tuesday didn't start well for Jules. The shrilling of her mobile at five in the morning had dragged her from a heavy and exhausted slumber, the kind that only a vicar who'd been overseeing the nativity dress rehearsal could sleep. Having been deep in a dream where the Pollards had tea towels on their heads and Ivy Lawrence was hiding the tinsel, Jules awoke with her heart hammering and reached out blindly for her phone.

It was Caspar.

"Jules! I've done a stupid thing! A really, really stupid thing!" His voice was cracking with emotion.

"Like call somebody at five in the morning?"

"Ah, sorry about that. No, even more stupid. Oh God! If only I hadn't! I can't believe what I've done."

He paused and Jules yawned. It was still pitch black, for heaven's sake. She shouldn't be up this early. Even the seagulls were still asleep!

Caspar paused for dramatic effect, bursting for her to ask what this dreadful thing was. For a moment Jules was tempted not to ask, but then her vicarly instincts kicked in and she reminded herself that she was supposed to listen to her flock.

Maybe tonight she'd put the phone on silent?

"Go on, what have you done?" she asked dutifully.

"I've deleted my book!"

"What?" Jules couldn't believe what she was hearing. "The book you've been slaving over for the past twelve days? The one you said was your best yet? The one you'd nearly finished? The one I can't wait to read?"

"Err yes, 'fraid so. That one."

Jules sat up and rubbed her eyes. They felt as though somebody had tipped grit into them.

"Have you gone nuts? What on earth did you do that for?"

There was a heavy sigh. "After Tara laughed at me I couldn't bear to write another word. Every time I thought of my heroine all I could see was the scorn on her beautiful face. I detested myself and my novel even more."

It was early, she'd tossed and turned for hours stressing about the bishop's impending visit and not fallen asleep until the small hours, and Jules wasn't in the mood for self-indulgence.

"Of course she laughed at you. You behaved like a total idiot, Caspar. In fact you're pretty lucky she hasn't taken a restraining order out thinking you're some kind of deranged stalker."

"I thought she'd be flattered to be immortalised in literature," he said sulkily.

Jules sighed. "That won't happen now you've deleted the book. So, now you've told me, can I go back to sleep?"

"No! I need you to help me get it back!" Caspar cried. She could almost hear him tearing at his wild hair. "If I don't deliver it I'm in serious trouble. Come on, Jules, there must be a way."

"I'm a vicar, not Bill Gates. I've no idea how to do that. Anyway, I thought you said you wanted it gone?"

"No! That was just the artistic temperament in me." He was sounding more frantic by the minute. "Please would you come and help me? Please?"

The chink of sky between Jules' curtains was still inky with darkness. It was the middle of the night as far as her body clock was concerned. All she really wanted to do was burrow under the covers and go back to sleep, but Caspar sounded desperate and she was quite fond of him in a rather frustrated kind of way.

And besides, she really wanted to read the next Cassandra Duval book...

Wondering how life had led her to this crazy episode, Jules promised Caspar that she'd be straight over. Then she hauled herself out of bed, dragged a brush through her tangled hair and threw on her jeans, sweater and boots. She didn't bother with make-up; after all, there were only the seagulls to see her just-got-out-of-bed look.

It was still dark when she left the house. The lights of the fishing boats glowed as they steamed out of the harbour, and the moon still floated lazily above Ashley's house. The village was empty; nobody was up and about to stop Jules with requests or complaints, and so she was at Tide's End Cottage in minutes. She didn't even need to knock on the door, but instead found Caspar waiting on the doorstep.

The writer looked even wilder than usual. His hair was dishevelled, he was wearing only jogging bottoms and he had even bigger bags under his eyes than Jules, which was saying something.

"You look dreadful," she said.

"I've been up all night trying to sort this," Caspar said sadly as she followed him into his small sitting room, where the laptop glowed on the table. "I swear next time I'm writing it all by hand."

"Then you'd have called me over to Sellotape all the ripped-up pieces back together," Jules pointed out. "After fishing them out of the harbour, of course. The laptop isn't the issue here."

Caspar sank into a chair, his head in his hands. "You're right. Oh, what a curse to feel things as deeply as I do."

What a curse to be such a drama queen, Jules thought wryly.

Aloud, she said, "Put the kettle on and make me a coffee, for a start. Then you can think about some toast. I can't function on an empty stomach."

"Do you think you can help?" Caspar was at hand-wringing stage now. The advance he would have to pay back must be huge.

"If teenagers can hack into the Pentagon and bring telecom giants to their knees, then I'm sure we can find a deleted file," Jules said firmly. "How hard can it be?"

Two hours later she was starting to regret these confident words. Her eyes were gritty from lack of sleep and staring at the screen, her fingers ached and her brains were scrambled. She was awash with tea and stuffed full of toast, and her ears ached from Caspar's constant pleading, but she was no closer to finding the latest Cassandra Duval novel. By eight o'clock she was ready to tear out her hair and throttle the anxious writer. Using the excuse of having a sermon to prepare, Jules shut the laptop firmly.

"We'll try again later," she promised. "I'll give Richard Penwarren a call. He knows a lot about IT. We'll get it back somehow."

With his head drooping like a thirsty tulip, Caspar escorted Jules to the front door.

"Thanks for trying," he said, kissing her on the cheek. "I do appreciate it."

"We'll think of something," Jules reassured him. She patted his cheek soothingly. "Now go and get some sleep."

Leaving him standing in his jogging bottoms in the doorway, she stepped out into a crisp sunny morning and straight into Danny. The sun had turned his hair to gold and his breath smoked in the cold air. On seeing her, he inhaled sharply. He was holding Morgan's gloved hand and carrying a brightly coloured packed lunchbox across his chest. It was obvious from the shocked expression on his face that she was the last person he'd expected to see leaving Caspar's house. Jules was suddenly all too aware of her tangled hair, hastily thrown-on clothes and unmade-up face. Danny glanced from her to the bare-chested Caspar, and a fleeting expression of hurt flickered across his face, like cloud shadows passing over the valley. Then he nodded politely.

Oh Lord. He thought that she'd spent the night with Caspar!

"Morning, Jules, Caspar," Danny said with icy politeness. Tugging Morgan behind him at an army-style pace, he marched past them and up the slipway.

Jules was mortified. Leaving Caspar on the doorstep, with his shout that they must "try to do it again later" echoing after her, she scurried up the slope and into the narrow street.

"Danny! Wait for me!" she called.

"Slow down, Dad!" Morgan was saying. "Jules can't catch up."

"Exactly," she heard Danny mutter.

Jules increased her pace, something she would never have managed a few months ago. Still panting a little, she drew up beside him.

"Dan, it's not what you think!"

Danny shrugged. "It's none of my business, Jules. You can see who you like."

"I'm not seeing Caspar! For heaven's sake, Danny! You've got it all wrong."

He snorted and looked as though he was about to say something in reply but had thought better of it.

"Morgan, run ahead to the shop, will you, and ask Mrs Jago for Grand Gran's paper? And an apple for your lunch. I just need a word with the vicar."

"You don't want the paper. And I don't like apples. You just want to talk without me listening," Morgan said. "Fact."

"Yes, fact." Dan opened his wallet and pulled out a fiver. "Now go and get the paper."

"Can I have some sweets? Some Skittles?"

His father grimaced. "Mum will kill me but, OK then, one packet of Skittles. Now scram!"

As Morgan raced up the road to the general store, his dinosaur rucksack bouncing on his back, Danny turned to Jules. All the humour of seconds before had vanished.

"Don't treat me like an idiot, Jules." His voice was cold now. "I might only have one eye but I know what I saw just then. Do you really think I'm stupid?"

"Yes, if you don't listen to what I'm saying!" Jules caught his sleeve. "Slow down, Danny, and listen to me! I'm not seeing Caspar!"

But Danny just shrugged. "See who you like, Jules. It's none of my business, is it? You've made it pretty clear that you're not interested in me, so you're a free agent."

"Yes, *I* am but *you're* not!" Jules shot back. "Which we've been through a million times. And you always trot out the same old argument that there's something I can't know that would explain it all, if only you could trust me enough to tell me."

Her voice was raised and joltingly loud in the early morning. Net curtains twitched in cottage windows. *Great*, thought Jules. It would be round the village in seconds that the vicar and Danny Tremaine were having a row.

She took a deep breath. "Sorry. I didn't mean to shout."

He stared at her. "I probably deserved it. Anyway, I do trust you, but trust's a two-way street – and when I say that I can't tell you something, you need to know that I'm telling the truth."

"Just like I am now about Caspar," she shot back. "Dan, let me explain…"

"Explain? I'm not stupid. It's barely eight in the morning and you're leaving his house, looking like neither of you have slept. I don't think there's much to explain," spat Danny. "He's artistic, handsome in his own way, and you like his company. You don't owe me any explanations."

The hurt that lay beneath the anger in his voice was enough to flood her eyes with tears.

"Danny, I know you're upset but it really isn't what you think."

"So how about you tell me what it really is?" His voice had an edge of steel in it now and Jules's heart sank. "What were you really doing at his house?"

It was checkmate.

"I can't tell you. It's a secret."

Danny laughed, a bleak laugh. "A secret. I see."

"Danny, please! This isn't my secret," Jules said desperately. "Caspar needed help."

"In the small hours? Yeah, right." He shook his head. "It's all right, Jules. You don't have to spare my feelings. I thought there was something between us. Christ, I actually thought I was falling in love with you, but it wasn't real, was it? It was totally one-sided."

Jules couldn't keep quiet a second longer. All the months of eating her heart out for him, of crying quietly at night, of praying and praying for the strength to do the right thing, all those long lonely months finally took their toll.

"If you really think that of me then you're right!" she shot back. "It isn't real if you can judge me so quickly and write me off. Of course I'm not seeing Caspar. How can I when you know I love you? If you want the truth then here it is: Caspar's a bestselling romantic novelist, one of my favourites as it happens, and he's deleted the file containing his latest book. He called me in a panic because he needs to find it. That's why I was in his cottage, and if neither of us look like we've slept then it's because we haven't!"

Her chest burned and she was shaking. Danny just stared at her.

"Say that again? How you feel about me?"

Jules could have ripped her tongue out. Her face was on fire. "I... err..."

"Jules," Danny said softly. "Look at me."

Reluctantly she dragged her eyes from the pavement to meet his gaze. Her heart flipped over and over.

"Do you love me?" Danny asked. "Did I hear that right? I only have one fully working ear, remember?"

Jules was trapped. In the heat of the moment she'd told the truth.

"I love all my parishioners," she said quickly. "It's the greatest commandment."

His mouth curved into a smile. The blue of his eye was no longer arctic but a Caribbean hue. "Yeah, nice try, Jules. Let me think: Sheila and the Pollards and Keyhole Kate? You feel the same way about them as you do me?"

"Yes! No!" Wrong-footed, she searched for the right answer. What was she thinking, blurting out the truth? Luckily at this point, Morgan came scampering up, armed with *The Guardian* and a monster bag of Skittles, and she was spared any further explanation.

"Are you friends again?" Morgan asked her. "Dad thought you wanted to be friends with Caspar Next Door instead – but you don't, do you?"

"I'm friends with everyone," Jules said.

"Even Ivy?" Morgan's brow crinkled. "She's very mean."

Ivy was very mean, there was no denying it, and having a stern word with her was still on Jules's ever-growing list of things to do.

"Even Ivy," she said firmly.

"But you like my dad the best. Fact." Morgan tipped a pile of Skittles onto his palm and regarded her beadily. "My mum says so."

His mum. Tara. Jules felt as though she'd had a bucket of icy water thrown over her head. What was she thinking, telling Danny she was in love with him, when they both knew it was impossible? How could he and Tara possibly mend their marriage with her in the way? She was horrified with herself.

"I like you all," Jules told him staunchly, but Danny was laughing.

"But you like me best," he said. "You can't take that back now, Jules, no matter how much you might want to. Here, have some Skittles and stop looking so worried. Morgan hates the orange ones, so help yourself."

"I'm tired and I wasn't thinking straight," Jules protested. "Blame Caspar for that. Two and a half hours I spent trying to find that deleted folder. My words are coming out all wrong."

"Fibber," Danny said fondly. "Your words are coming out just perfectly. Don't look at me like that either. You and I are going to talk. You can count on that."

"Did you look in the trash?" Morgan asked, looking up from the important task of selecting orange skittles from the packet. "That's where all the deleted folders go."

Jules hadn't and she stared at him. "What?"

"If you haven't emptied the trash then that's where the files go. Fact. It's very simple," Morgan explained, with the same pity in his voice that Jules heard in her own whenever she tried to explain to her mother how to use an iPhone.

All those hours of searching the hard drive and the bloody book might still be in the trash? She could have wept.

"Looks like the missing book problem is sorted. You can pop back and tell Polwenna's answer to Shakespeare that all's well that ends well," Danny said. He checked his watch. "Look, I have to get this one to school or Miss Powell will probably put me in detention, but you are I are definitely going to catch up later. This conversation is not over, Jules. Not by a long way."

"There's nothing more to say," Jules said.

"You're wrong," Danny told her. "We haven't even started."

As he walked away, Jules stared after him. Her stomach was more tangled than the nets heaped on the quay. It was time to face facts. The feelings she had for Danny Tremaine were not going away. If anything, they were getting stronger.

There was only one solution – and no matter how painful it was, she had no choice but to acknowledge it and do the right thing. She could only avoid Danny for so long, and it was getting harder and harder by the day because every fibre of her being yearned for him.

Her heart was shattering in to a thousand pieces already but Jules knew that she had no other option. If she was to stick to her principles and live by what she knew to be right, then she was going to have to leave Polwenna Bay.

Chapter 18

"I don't understand it. My dear, you've been so happy at St Wenn's and such an asset to the village." The bishop leaned back in his chair and looked at Jules with a worried frown. "This is a very sudden change of heart. It's nothing to do with the *unfortunate* events of earlier on this year, I hope?"

It was Wednesday morning and Jules was seated in a big comfy chair in Bishop Bill's office, doing her best to balance a large cup of tea and a plate of biscuits on the arm. Her hands were trembling so much that she was in danger of spilling the lot. Plucking up the courage to make the appointment to see the bishop had been hard enough. Telling him that she wanted to leave the parish and find another post had been even more difficult.

"After all," he continued when she merely shook her head in reply, "although it was a little misguided, the calendar did raise a lot of money for St Wenn's – and I have to say that the accounts are looking very healthy indeed. You should be very proud of all that you've achieved."

Jules smiled faintly. After seeing the bishop, her next port of call was the main branch of her bank.

"Thanks," she said. "I am proud but I still feel that leaving is the right thing to do."

The bishop raised his teacup to his lips, took a delicate sip and replaced it in the saucer with a rattle. "You look tired, Julia, and you've lost weight. Do you think that maybe you're under stress? Perhaps a rest is what you need?"

All the rest in the world wasn't going to mend her broken heart, thought Jules, but the bishop didn't need to know this.

"No, it's nothing at all to do with that. I just feel that it's the right time for me to move on."

"Is this because of the audit?" The bishop wasn't buying her excuses. "If it is, then – and this is strictly off the record, you understand – then you really don't need to worry on that score. St Wenn's isn't under any imminent threat."

A week ago Jules would have been orbiting the moon with joy at this news. Today, however, all she could do was nod.

"Provided we don't find any issues with the registers, of course, and the audit makes sense," the bishop added. "But that's just a formality. Oh, and no more scandals of course, ha ha!"

What if their mysterious benefactor continued to make big donations? Jules thought with alarm. What an irony if somebody who really wanted to help St Wenn's actually became the church's downfall. For the hundredth time Jules wracked her brains trying to work out who this person might be, but as usual she drew a total blank. Beneath her teacup her fingers were firmly crossed. As long as she kept Sheila away from the slave-auction idea and the Pollards were kidding about a "butlers in the buff" fundraiser, then things should be fine.

"I'm sure everything will be perfectly in order." Jules sent up a quick prayer with this thought. "Whoever takes over from me won't have any problems."

There was a pause as the bishop gazed at her thoughtfully. The room was quiet except for the heavy ticking of a longcase clock and the buzz of traffic outside.

"Is this something that you feel comes from God? Or are you running away?" he asked eventually.

"Running away?"

"From a situation you feel that you can't escape? Or maybe someone?"

Jules looked up, shocked at his insight. "Is it that obvious?"

"Not at all, but it's not an easy path that you've been called to follow. It comes with many blessings but also many burdens, and sometimes you'll have to decide if those blessings are enough to compensate for the hard choices you'll make along the way."

She swallowed back the lump in her throat. "I love my job, and I know it's what God wants me to do. It's just that there's a conflict for me now and I think that leaving would be the best thing to do."

The bishop removed his glasses and regarded her with faded brown eyes that had doubtless watched many young clerics come and go. There was probably nothing that he hadn't seen before.

"The best or the easiest?"

"Both, maybe?" Jules wasn't sure. She loved Polwenna Bay and St Wenn's and Danny. Leaving these behind would be like losing a part of herself but, ultimately, if it cleared the way for Danny to resolve his issues with Tara, then that had to be for the best. "So, is it possible for me to leave?"

"All things are possible, Julia. You're not a prisoner in your parish. If you really do believe that God wants you elsewhere, then of course you're free to move on. But I would ask you this: make sure that it really is His voice you are listening to and not just the whispering of your own fears. Sometimes what God wants for us is the steep and rocky road rather than the smooth downhill one."

"So you're saying I should stay?"

He inclined his grey head. "I would suggest that you give it until the New Year. Let's get Christmas out of the way; it's always the busiest and most emotive time. Then come and speak to me again once you've had time to reflect."

"So I can't have some time off now?" Jules had been hoping that the bishop would put forward the idea of a locum filling in for her while she had a few weeks away. That would be enough time for her to write her resignation and think about her next move.

"I'm afraid not. There's nobody who could help out at such short notice and you'd be leaving St Wenn's without a vicar at Christmas. Of course, if you still feel that's the right thing…"

His voice trailed off but the meaning was clear. She could stay and deal with her issues or walk away and leave St Wenn's in the lurch. Jules could no sooner do that than she could just switch off her feelings for Danny. She was damned either way. As the conversation turned to the upcoming nativity play, the matter of her resignation having been gently but firmly put aside, Jules knew that she would have no choice but to go back to the village and tell Danny once and for all that there could and would never be anything more than friendship between them.

Then she could count the days until she left for good.

* * *

"One hundred, one twenty, one forty, one sixty, one eighty, two hundred… and four fifties."

The bank teller was busy with the customer at the head of the queue while everyone else fidgeted quietly and, in true British style, watched for anyone who might surreptitiously try to push in. Jules, sitting on the furthest side of the bank, checked her watch and sighed. She'd been due to see the bank manager over fifteen minutes ago and there was still no sign. It felt a bit like waiting for the dentist.

Shall I put that in an envelope for you?" the bank teller was asking.

"No thanks. Could you pay it straight in to this account please? I've got the details here."

"Certainly, Madam."

Although Jules couldn't see the front of the queue there was something familiar about the customer's polite and well-modulated tones. Cricking her neck she made out an elderly woman delving into a printed jute bag and pulling out a piece of paper.

"Sorry, Madam, I can't read the writing. What does that say? St Winn?"

"St Wenn's church. It's in Polwenna Bay. I've written down the sort code."

Jules was on her feet and at the counter before she even knew it. This was the mystery benefactor caught red-handed, she was certain of it!

But what she hadn't known was who this person would be, and it was hard to say who was more surprised – Jules or Alice Tremaine.

"Alice?" Jules's eyes were round with shock. "It's been you all along? You've been paying money into the account?"

Alice's face was ashen. "Jules! I can explain! I've just been trying to help."

"But you know the trouble it's been causing," said Jules in bewilderment.

Alice looked stricken. "Of course, but what can I do? If I have the money in our account Jake will see it or Jimmy will fritter it. He's been twice as bad since he came back from America. This was going to be the last donation, I promise. Giving it to the church felt like a good thing to do."

"In theory it is, but not like this." Jules was staggered. "Alice, where on earth are you getting all this cash from?"

A look of guilt crossed Alice's face. "I can't tell you."

Jules was starting to feel a little tired of the Tremaines' capacity for secrets.

"Oh yes you can," she said grimly. "I need to know everything. And so will our accountant. And the tax man. Do I need the police as well?"

Alice looked offended. "Certainly not! It's all perfectly legal and above board."

"Will you get a move on?" grumbled the next person in the queue. "Some of us have got homes to go to."

"Madam, shall I pay the money in?" asked the bank teller, looking nervously at Jules. The wad of money in her hand trembled.

"Yes," said Alice.

"No!" cried Jules. "Those deposits of yours look like money laundering. Any more and we'll probably have a tax inspection – at the least."

The notes were pushed beneath the window and Alice put them in her purse with great reluctance.

Jules shook her head. "I don't know what this is all about but I think it's time we had a chat."

There was a coffee shop across the road from the bank, a trendy affair that was all glass and steel and bleached driftwood, and which had a mind-boggling menu. Once they were seated, each with a latte and a cinnamon slice, Jules fixed Alice with a stern look.

"So? Are you going to tell me exactly what's been going on?"

It was like opening the harbour gates mid-storm. As Alice began to speak, her words gathered speed and her breath became ragged. Several times Jules had to tell her to calm down and take a sip of her drink. It was as though she was unloading a dreadful burden, and with every word she uttered her face seemed to become less pale and strained. Jules listened, her mouth hanging open, while her untouched coffee grew cool. She couldn't believe her ears.

"So now you know," Alice finished quietly. "I wrote *Blackwarren* just as a bit of fun. I never thought of publishing it until one of the women at the University of the Third Age did a talk about Kindle books. When I pressed the publish button on Amazon I didn't think anything more of it."

Jules was still not quite able to comprehend what she was hearing: Alice Tremaine, seventy-nine years old, pillar of St Wenn's and respected grandmother, was the secret author of *Blackwarren*, the steamy self-published novel that had been taking Polwenna Bay and, it now transpired, the rest of the UK by storm.

"I never thought it would earn any money, so when some came in it was a nice surprise." Alice gave Jules a half smile. "To be honest it was a bit of a distraction from everything at home with Danny and Tara. I'd always loved writing and everyone was on about that dreadful *Fifty Shades* stuff, so I thought why not?"

"Some distraction," Jules said. "I guess that's why you kept borrowing the laptop from Morgan?"

"Guilty as charged," nodded Alice. "I knew that nobody would ever guess I wrote the book – but I did feel dreadful when everyone was speculating, and having to pretend I was in the dark too. I thought that giving the money to St Wenn's would make up for that. When you mentioned that I might have caused problems I felt terrible about it. I was going to put this last bit in and then stop."

Recalling her earlier conversation with the bishop, Jules thought that *problems* was an understatement. *No more scandals*, was what he'd said. He might have a sense of humour and be pretty understanding, but the Church of England being subsidised by soft-porn novels probably wouldn't amuse him.

It could also mean the end of St Wenn's.

"You have to stop giving the money to the church," Jules said firmly, and Alice nodded.

"It's just that I wanted to make sure there was a good lump sum in by the time the bishop looked at the finances. I didn't mean to cause any trouble."

Jules reached across the table and squeezed her hand. "I know you didn't, but there might well be questions about where the money came from."

"I understand, and of course I'd stand up and tell anyone official who needed to know that it was me. But do you really have to tell the others I wrote the book?" Alice looked very upset at this thought.

"The PCC needs to know where the money came from," Jules said gently. "They're worried."

Alice bit her lip. "I know, but I'd hate to embarrass my family.

"They'd never be embarrassed of you."

"This is awful," replied Alice, glancing down, "but I'd also rather Jimmy didn't know. He's spending everything we have as it is. If he thinks there's an extra income stream he'll be twice as bad."

"I understand that," said Jules, "but I really think it's best to be honest. Besides, what will you do when the film companies start making offers?"

Alice laughed. "I hardly think that will happen, love."

"So what's the real problem then? You're proud of your work, your family love you and Jimmy will just have to behave. Why can't you admit you're the author?"

The older woman stared into her coffee cup. "I've also based Lord Blackwarren on somebody real. I'd rather he didn't know. It could be very… awkward."

Recalling the juicy scenes – lots of rippling torsos, throbbing manhoods and quivering thighs – Jules totally understood why. Although, then again, most men would be hugely flattered: Lord Blackwarren was sexy and hung like one of Mo's stallions.

"So spill: who is he?" she asked. "We're all desperate to know."

But Alice's lips were sealed. "That's my secret. Suffice to say that a lot of my book wasn't wholly fiction! Jules, promise me that you won't tell anyone it's me. Can't we pretend the book was written by somebody else? There must be someone who owes you a favour? Somebody who's prepared to say it's them? Someone who might plausibly have written it?"

Jules was just about to pick up her cinnamon slice. Her hand hovered over it as several pennies dropped.

"Do you know what," she said slowly, "I think there is. And, even better, he's going to be only too happy to help."

Caspar Owen was about to become very useful indeed.

Chapter 19

Avoiding Danny wasn't easy in a village the size of Polwenna Bay, but having kept her mobile set to silent and made sure that she was out on parish business as much as possible, Jules had managed to get to Friday without seeing him. The week had been hectic anyway. Much of it had been spent persuading Caspar to drop some hints that he was the secret author of *Blackwarren*, but she'd also had a packed Christmas schedule to keep her occupied. For one thing, there was organising the lighting of the Christmas tree, and then there was the nativity play too. For the past few days she'd been working flat out. Jules was still determined to resign, so she knew this would be both her first and her last Christmas in Polwenna Bay. Although it was a bittersweet occasion, she was determined to put her heart and soul into it.

The first Friday in December was traditionally the night when Polwenna Bay's Christmas decorations were lit. All week the Pollards had been busy stringing lights across the village, over the top of the fish market and along the quay, while the shopkeepers had dusted off their tills and goods in readiness for the influx of festive tourists. The pièce de résistance was the huge Christmas tree that had been erected on the green and smothered in white and blue lights to match those on the smaller trees either side of the harbour gate. The PA system was fully up and running now; earlier, big Eddie Penhalligan had been shouting "Testing! Testing!" at regular intervals, between which random snatches of Christmas carols had echoed across the valley. Stalls had been erected on the village green, too, including The Ship's makeshift stand selling mulled wine and hot toddies. Meanwhile there was great excitement over a huge and sumptuous Harrods hamper that had been anonymously donated for the raffle.

"It's the Polwenna Bay Angel again," Tess said to Jules as the two women strolled around the stalls. "It has to be. Who else would do something like that?"

"Somebody who doesn't want any fuss?" Jules suggested.

"Which rules out the usual suspects like Cashley or the St Miltons." Tess looked thoughtful. "I reckon it's somebody who doesn't want to be seen as generous. Somebody who likes to be miserable."

"Hmm," said Jules. "It's one theory, I suppose."

The Polwenna Bay Angel was fast becoming a village legend. Any anonymous donation was now considered to be the Angel's doing, and speculation as to his or identity was rife. Ashley Carstairs was a favourite, as was Summer Penhalligan. Both of them denied it though. Jules sighed. People denying things had become something of a theme around here, and she was tired of it. Denying her feelings for Danny was ripping her into pieces every day. It was getting harder, not easier. Would going away help? She could only hope so.

The night was dark and clear; stars twinkled above the crumpled rooftops and people's breath clouded the air. *Stop the Cavalry* belted out from the PA speakers, the scent of roasting chestnuts drifted on the breeze, and steaming cups of mulled wine warmed chilled fingers. The children had performed their nativity play beautifully and even Bubbles the pony had behaved for once. Proud parents held mittened hands and beamed, each convinced that their child was the star of the show. The number of pictures they'd uploaded to Facebook this evening would probably be enough to crash the social media giant, Jules thought. Tess was so relieved the play was over that she'd already enjoyed several visits to the mulled-wine stall, and Jules was feeling a little sick from overindulging in the mince pies. All in all, it was exactly what a village Christmas should be.

Visitors were still pouring into the village, fatly wrapped up in coats and scarves and hats. The streets hadn't been this packed since August and the green was rapidly filling up. Radio Kernow had arrived to broadcast the carol singing and the photographer from the local paper was snapping away merrily. Leaving Tess at the mulled wine stand with Nick, Jules wandered through the stalls to buy raffle tickets and a scoop of fiendishly hot chestnuts.

"Get on, Vicar!" Big Rog called from the top of a ladder. He was fiddling with the star at the summit of the tree. "What do you think?"

"It's a beauty," Jules said warmly. "I can't wait to see it lit up."

"Hope it does light up," muttered Little Rog, who was holding the ladder. "Not sure we should have bought these cheap lights from the market, Pa."

"It'll be fine, my boy," said Big Rog, giving the star a final tweak. "Proper job! He's ready!"

"Switch-on in five minutes!" Sheila barked at the Pollards. Clutching a clipboard to her bosom, she'd been issuing orders with military precision. "Vicar, we'll need to say a prayer just beforehand. Are you ready?"

"Just about," said Jules.

Sheila scribbled something onto her list.

"The mayor's here for the switch-on and the Salvation Army are ready. Time to get going."

Dutifully, Jules followed Sheila through the crowds and onto the small stage at the back of the green. In the flickering light of the stalls she made out the faces of her friends, rosy from the cold and smiling with the joy of the occasion. There was Silver Starr from the hippy shop, all decked out in a white fur outfit topped with glittery deely boppers, and by the tree were Ashley and Mo, wrapped in each other's arms and oblivious to everything and everyone else. They were closer than words could describe, and the sight of them knotted something in Jules's throat. Although she'd tried so hard not to, she couldn't help scanning the throng for that one dear face she longed to see – but of Danny there was no sign. Morgan and Tara were by the tombola with Alice, so he couldn't be far away. After all, Christmas was a time for families.

"You're on!" Sheila gave Jules a little shove in the small of her back. "The local TV people are here too! Don't let us down."

"No pressure then," Jules murmured to herself before taking a deep breath, stepping up to the microphone and welcoming everyone with an opening prayer. Several carols then followed, sung with enthusiasm if not very tunefully, before the mayor threw the switch. Jules held her breath, as did both Pollards, but she needn't have worried. Although there was a bit of a crackle and a flicker and an alarmed look on Big Rog's face, the village burst into light.

The magic of Christmas never faded no matter how old you were, Jules thought as she looked at all the delighted faces gazing up at the tree. The lights trembled and danced in the harbour too, filling the water with a galaxy of colourful stars. Her chest tightened. She was going to miss this place so much.

"Waste of electric if you ask me," muttered Ivy Lawrence, who was standing at the side of the stage, arms folded across her bony chest and a scowl stitched on her face. "And if those lights shine into my bedroom and keep me awake I'll be having words with you, Mr Pollard."

"Bah humbug," said Little Rog, winking at Jules.

"You can mock, young man, but I mean it," Ivy told him, wagging a finger at the tree. "That's a fire hazard too and a waste of good money."

It must be hard work being that miserable, thought Jules, watching the old woman elbow her way through the crowd and back to her lonely cottage. Everyone else seemed to be having a lovely time. What on earth had happened in Ivy's life to make her so relentlessly bitter?

"You look deep in thought," said Danny.

Jules jumped.

"I'm not that scary am I?" he asked. "I know I'm a dead ringer for the Phantom of the Opera these days, but after you've had a few mulled wines I'm sure I can't look too bad."

Dressed in a dark coat and hat that made his golden hair and blue eyes more pronounced than ever, Danny looked wonderful to Jules. He held out his hand.

"We need to talk."

The fizz of energy that shot through Jules when his fingers closed around hers could have lit the village. Almost as though in a dream, she stepped down from the stage and allowed him to lead her through the streets and down to the harbour. All her resolutions about staying away from him had dissolved like smoke from the chimney pots into the darkness. They walked right to the furthest edge of the quay and looked back towards the village, where lights flickered and swayed and music drifted on the night air.

"What do you want to talk about?" Jules asked.

He gave her a small smile. "The weather? Politics? Come on, Jules. You know. I want to talk about what's been happening between you and me."

Panic rose up inside her. She licked her lips nervously.

"Dan, you know where I stand on that. We've discussed it a thousand times and—"

He cut her off before she could finish her sentence. "Jules, I know what you're going to say about marriage and, believe me, I do agree with you. Marriage should be for life. But sometimes things happen that are so huge, you know that no matter how much you might wish it was different you can never go back. That's how it is for me and Tara. I've filed for divorce, Jules, and nothing you can say will change my mind."

"But Danny, why? What happened?"

"Just trust me," he said, softly but with such urgency that it gave her goosebumps. "I can't tell you why, but take my word that the reason is sound. I don't take love lightly, Jules. I never have and I never will. Just trust me when I say that there's nothing that can change the way I feel about her. Or," he stepped forwards until they were just a breath apart, "you."

Here was a love that Jules knew she could lose herself in forever. But at what cost?

She shook her head. "Danny, I can't."

"Please, Jules." His voice was an entreaty, pulling her closer, impossible to resist. "Don't overthink it or overcomplicate it. Just listen to your heart."

If she did that she would be lost.

His gaze continued to hold hers. "I'm not a saint, Jules, and I've made mistakes, lots of mistakes, but I have learned from them. I know what's important and I promise that if there was any way back then I would take it. All I ask is that you trust me."

"And all I ask is that you trust me enough to tell me the truth." Jules wasn't prepared to go down this road again. "Trust is a two-way street, Danny."

Dan looked away, staring out into the emptiness that was the sea. The blackness was only chased away now and then by the warm sweep of the Eddystone light.

"It's not my secret to tell," he said finally. "I made a promise that I would never speak about it and I can't break that promise, not even for you."

"Not even if I tell you that everything I hold dear, my faith, my life here, my future, depend on knowing that truth?"

He dragged his gaze back to her and Jules knew in a heartbeat what the answer was. He was silent for a long time and the unsaid words hung heavy in the air.

"It's all right, Danny. You've already answered my question."

On tiptoes, she brushed his rough cheek with her lips. It was as cold as the moonlight and she had the feeling that with each passing second he was growing even more distant. Her breath caught in her throat because at that moment she knew she loved him so much that if she stayed for a second longer it would be impossible to walk away. All she wanted to do was step forwards and kiss him, but that would lead her down a road she knew she couldn't travel. Not if she wanted to remain true to everything she believed in.

"I love you, Jules," Danny said brokenly. "Isn't that enough?"

Certain that he could hear the hammering of her heart and feel the same clawing grief, Jules could only shake her head and whisper, "And I love you Danny, but without total trust how can that ever be enough?"

Then she turned and walked away, leaving him alone on the quay. No matter how much it hurt, she knew what she had to do now.

She would call the bishop first thing in the morning. It was time Jules Mathieson left Polwenna Bay.

Chapter 20

In Tara's experience shopping was usually a great antidote to feeling fed up, especially on a frosty Saturday in the run-up to Christmas. The train ride to Truro had taken her through some of the prettiest countryside imaginable, and although it was a familiar journey she was struck by the beauty of the glittering pastures fleeting past the window. Now and then she caught a glimpse of the sea on the horizon before the tracks turned inland to head through moorland dotted with grazing ponies and the slumbering engine houses of long-quiet mines. Cornwall in December had a chilly beauty all of its own and it was hard to be miserable when the sky was denim blue, spiders' webs laced the hedgerows and the air was so sharp it made your nose tingle.

Hard to be miserable, yes, but as she was fast discovering, far from impossible. Pretty landscapes, wintry sunshine and shops crammed with velvets, sparkles and ribbons were wonderful, but not even these things were enough to ease the aching misery of waking up to find that your divorce papers had landed on the doormat. She'd been half expecting the Christmas cards and the junk mail, but not the legal documents served by her husband citing unreasonable behaviour. As much as she'd come to accept that her marriage was over, it had still been a dreadful shock to have the hard evidence in front of her. Tara had sat at the kitchen table staring at the papers, her mouth dry and with the room spinning around her. Then, as the reality of it had sunk in, Tara had wept for everything she'd lost.

Thank goodness Morgan was staying at Seaspray for the weekend and hadn't witnessed her meltdown, Tara reflected. Dan must have planned it that way; she knew he'd never want to do anything to upset his son. And Morgan *was* his son in every way that mattered. His natural father had been long off the scene by the time Tara had realised she might be pregnant with his child, and although she'd tried to trace him she'd had little success so far. She supposed she was storing up problems for the future, but surely as long as Morgan knew he was loved by her and Danny he'd be secure enough when the time came to handle the truth?

She hoped so with all her heart.

Did she wish she could turn the clock back? That was a hard question to answer. Morgan wouldn't be here if she hadn't cheated on Danny. Tara couldn't imagine, didn't want to imagine, a world without her wonderful son. But did she wish that Morgan was Danny's biological son?

Yes. There was nothing she longed for more.

Tara knew that when that day arrived she would have to explain a great deal. That was only right. It was her responsibility and Morgan had to hear it from her. Danny would never breathe a word, and for that she would always be grateful. He had the power to blow her world apart if he chose but, being an honourable man and a person of huge integrity, he would never put his grievances with her above Morgan's well-being – even if the cost of this was his own happiness.

Tara was no fool. She could see how Danny felt about Jules. He lit up like Polwenna's Christmas lights whenever the vicar was around; his laughter was easy and he looked young again as he bantered with her. Maybe it was because Jules had never known him as he'd once been.

Before the accident he'd had those golden Tremaine good looks that stopped people in their tracks. Broad-shouldered, muscular and with a smile that had melted hearts, he'd been the most handsome of all the boys – and when he'd been in his uniform jaws had literally dropped. Now people stared at Danny for all the wrong reasons. Perhaps only Jules really saw him.

At first Tara hadn't taken any of this seriously. Tara was used to being admired for her looks and attracting men as easily as candles drew moths, so she'd not been in the least bit worried about the plump vicar with the unmade-up face and home-dyed hair. When she'd visited Jules back in the summer it had been an exercise in weighing up any potential opposition. But maybe she'd been too quick to dismiss Jules. Or perhaps, Tara reflected now as she strolled from the station down into the city, she'd been too shallow to see what it was that Jules had to offer. Her integrity and honest friendship were oxygen to Danny. Like Jules, he was beyond judging people by surface appearances, and Tara could only conclude that he was genuinely in love with the vicar.

We were young when we met, Tara mused. *Maybe too young?* What had they really seen in one another, apart from the obvious flame of physical attraction? When you were in your teens this was everything, of course, but with more maturity and life experience you began to realise that there had to be more than that to sustain a relationship. Friendship. Shared goals. Easy conversation. Values in common. All these were suddenly far more important.

Anyone could see that Danny had found all of these things in Jules. Tara had seen it herself, hadn't she? Wasn't this one of the reasons she'd really come back? Because she had sensed a threat?

Tara caught sight of her reflection in the window of Boots and smiled wryly at herself. A slender brunette with wide-spaced eyes and a dusting of freckles across the bridge of her nose smiled back. *I feel like a different person now*, she thought wonderingly. *I see things so differently. Dan and I never really had anything in common, and I betrayed him in the worst way possible.* Of course their marriage was over. The miracle was that it had actually lasted this long.

The divorce papers were in her handbag and Tara slipped her hand inside, brushing the thick white envelope with her fingertips. She would find somewhere to have a coffee, sign them quietly and then let events take their course. Setting Danny free was the least she could do for him. It was the one thing that might tell him that she had loved him once and that she really was sorry. Maybe then he could move on and be with Jules. There was a faint ache in her heart at this idea, but it was just a feeble echo of what she had once felt. *My feelings have changed too*, Tara realised with a little flicker of hope. She was ready, perhaps, to be brave and to face a future without him. Maybe their divorce wasn't actually the end but, rather, the beginning of something even better for them both. This thought cheered her.

She took a deep breath. All around her, people were getting on with their lives, and she knew that it was time for her to move on with hers too.

Tara loved shopping and it had always been a great distraction from any worries, so this was partly why she'd headed to Truro. It had also seemed wise to keep away from the village today while her emotions were still running high. She might be starting to accept that her marriage was over, but bumping into Danny on the very morning he'd served her the divorce papers was more than she could cope with right now. It was best to have a little bit of distance, and if she could do some Christmas shopping too then so much the better.

Checking her bank balance on her phone, Tara was pleased to see that she was at least in credit, if not exactly wealthy. She could afford to pick out some nice gifts, and if she was careful she might even have enough to treat herself to a new lipstick or perhaps a top. There was nothing like new make-up and clothes to cheer a girl up.

Since it was the penultimate Saturday before Christmas, the pretty cathedral town was thronging with Christmas shoppers. The car parks were overflowing, the pavements bustled and there was an air of excited anticipation despite the cold. The Christmas market on Lemon Quay was doing a roaring trade and the surrounding coffee shops were crammed with shoppers enjoying eggnog lattes and stollen as they recovered from lugging their bulging carrier bags across the town. She caught a glimpse, too, of the traditional horse bus as it carried its passengers on a tour of the main streets. Piped Christmas carols floated out of shop doorways, competing with the cheerful strains of the fairground carousel and the shouts and laughter of delighted children as they rode its luridly painted ponies. As Tara wove her way in and out of the shops the pavements grew ever more crowded with Christmas shoppers, all wrapped up in winter coats and scarves, and hell-bent on shopping until the daylight faded.

By midday Tara's feet were starting to ache and the handles of her carrier bags were threatening to cut off her circulation altogether. The streets were even busier now; yet more shoppers had flooded into the city for an afternoon of present-buying. As she stood on the pavement outside Laura Ashley, trying to juggle her bags onto fingers that were slightly less blue, Tara was jostled and bumped by a surging human tide.

It was high time she stopped for a moment to get her breath back, find a coffee and put her signature on that sheaf of papers nestling in the bottom of her bag. She was deep in thought about this unpleasant but very necessary task when a man cannoned straight into her. Tara's shopping slid from her grasp and spilled onto the pavement – where she would have ended up too, if a pair of arms hadn't caught her and steadied her.

"Sorry!" gasped Tara. "I wasn't looking. Oh!"

She was taken aback because she'd been almost knocked flying by none other than Richard Penwarren. His grey eyes twinkled down at her from behind his trendy wire-rimmed glasses, and his mouth curled into a delighted if apologetic smile.

"Tara! Fancy bumping into you, and literally too. I'm really sorry if I knocked you for six. I was charging along and quite miles away. Are you OK?"

Tara was ridiculously pleased to see him. Since the St Miltons' party she'd been working as many hours as possible for Symon, and presumably the villagers' winter ailments had kept Richard pretty busy at the surgery. She'd hardly seen him lately. On the one occasion that she'd visited, because Morgan had had a sore throat, they'd been seen by a locum – and Tara had been amazed to feel a sharp stab of disappointment.

"I'm fine," she told him. "It's my fault anyway. I wasn't looking where I was going."

She started to bend down to retrieve her bags, but Richard was determined to pick them up himself and carry them for her too.

"I won't hear of it," he insisted when Tara protested. "Of course I'll carry your bags. Not only is it the least I can do after knocking you over, but I'd hardly be a gentleman if I let you struggle."

Tara thought briefly of Anthony, who'd been more than happy to let her lug half of Aldi up the steps to their house. Nobody could ever accuse Ant of being a gentleman, that was for certain. Richard, however, couldn't have been more different from her ex. He was gallant and old-fashioned in a way that made her feel very feminine and cherished.

"Thanks," she said, deciding to make the most of this because her fingers were throbbing. "That's very kind."

"Well, that's me. Kindness personified. I get no pleasure at all from sharing the company of a beautiful woman in exchange for carrying a couple of shopping bags! It also helps me hone my fine physique." He lifted her carriers as though they were dumb-bells and pulled a face. "Crikey, Tara, these weigh a tonne. What have you been buying?"

Tara laughed. "I've been on a mission. That's practically all my Christmas shopping there. Are you sure you're up to it?"

"I'll give it a shot. Now, where were you off to?"

"I was going to try and grab a coffee, but to be honest I don't think I'll have any luck." Tara could see that the nearest cafés were bulging at the seams. "I might just get a takeaway one instead."

"I've got a better idea," Richard told her. "I'm meeting someone for lunch and I've reserved a table at Casa Rosa. Do you fancy joining us?"

Tara knew the Casa Rosa. It was a pretty Italian restaurant down a narrow side road by the cathedral. Dimly lit with dripping candles in Chianti bottles and cosy red velvet booths, it was the perfect place for a romantic assignation. Presumably, Richard was meeting a woman there. She was surprised at how disappointed this made her feel.

The last thing Tara wanted was to feel like a gooseberry, especially on the very day she was having to sign her divorce papers.

"It's nothing fancy, I'm afraid; only pizza and pasta, but its good food," Richard added, seeing her hesitate. "I should imagine Dr Olsen, a colleague I'm meeting, chose the place mainly for the wine list. You know how medics can drink."

Actually Tara didn't, but at the mention of pasta her stomach rumbled loudly.

Richard laughed. "I think that says it all."

But Tara wasn't sure. Firstly she didn't want to crash a business lunch and secondly her bank account was a little depleted after all the Christmas shopping. A latte and panini would have been within her budget, but a meal in a smart restaurant wasn't an expense she could justify.

"It's my treat," Richard added swiftly, guessing the reason for her uncertainty. "Their tortellini is to die for, and as for the tiramisu... Well, let's just say that the cholesterol is worth it!"

He looked so hopeful that Tara didn't have the heart to refuse. Besides, she was hungry and Richard was great company.

"Damn. Tiramisu is one of my fatal weaknesses, just like that sticky toffee pudding you spoilt me with before," she said. "You obviously know that I can't resist an indulgent dessert!"

"Once you've tasted it you'll be powerless." Lifting her bags, Richard placed his hand on Tara's elbow and guided her carefully through the crowds. People stepped aside as though there was a magic bubble around her. The power of having an attractive and gallant man with you, she supposed.

Hang on. Did she just think that Richard Penwarren was attractive? How on earth had that happened? And now that the thought had popped into her head, Tara was unable to concentrate on anything else, especially with Richard this close to her. Just the sensation of his fingertips resting lightly on her elbow caused her pulse to pick up and the hairs on her forearms to ripple. When they waited to cross the road and he brushed against her, Tara was shocked to feel a sudden jolt of electricity. She didn't dare look at Richard, although she could feel him gazing down at her. Had he felt it too? And if so, what did it mean? By the time they'd reached the restaurant and Richard was holding the door open for her, Tara was starting to feel giddy. Just what was going on here?

"Aha, there's Dr Olsen." With his hand lightly on the small of her back now, Richard guided Tara across the garlic-scented interior. "Amanda! Sorry we're late!"

An ebony-haired woman seated in a dimly lit booth towards the back of the restaurant glanced up from scanning the menu. She had an expensive golden tan, the kind that came from winter sun in the Caribbean rather than a tube of Boots' best fake-it variety. Everything about her was groomed and expensive. Catching sight of Richard, she started to smile before she realised that Tara was accompanying him. Within seconds the two women knew exactly how the land lay. Richard might only think of Dr Olsen as a colleague, but Tara knew instantly that the glamorous Amanda saw things very differently.

"Amanda, this is my friend Tara," said Richard, once he'd kissed her and they'd said their hellos. "I bumped into her just now, so I thought she could join us."

"Lovely to meet you," said Amanda, air-kissing Tara. The look on her face said that she could have stabbed Tara quite happily.

"Likewise," Tara said.

After they were all seated and an efficient waitress had brought them their drinks, Richard grinned at Tara. "See, I told you Amanda wouldn't mind. We go years back, to medical school. I once hid a pig's head in her bed. It's an old med-school gag. I think she's just about forgiven me."

Amanda swirled her blood-red wine. "The jury's out on that."

He laughed. "I guess that means lunch is on me then? Ah well, I suppose I deserve it. It was a mean trick."

"Sounds it," agreed Tara.

"It was schoolboy stuff," Richard said. "The fact is, I used to fancy Mandy like crazy and I thought that would get her attention. Boys, eh?"

The irony was that all he had to do now was give her just one tiny bit of encouragement, Tara thought as she sipped her Prosecco. There was no need for a pig's head.

"In fairness we all did that kind of thing at med school when we were training to be doctors," said Amanda. She flicked a nonchalant gaze over Tara. "So, what do you do?"

Career one-upmanship. Tara couldn't win at this. Not that she wanted to win; after all, she wasn't competing with Amanda for Richard.

"I'm a mum," she told her. "I have a nine-year-old son who keeps me pretty busy."

"She's a fantastic mother," Richard said warmly. "Morgan's a credit to you, Tara."

His praise was a balm to her today. "Thanks. I'm proud of him."

"And when you're not being a mum, what do you do?" Amanda asked coolly.

Tara frowned. "I'm always a mum. If you're asking what I do to earn money, I'm doing whatever I can over the winter. At the moment I'm a waitress."

"How nice," said Amanda politely. "I did that once when I was a student. Can't say I ever enjoyed it though. Not really my thing."

Tara looked her straight in the eye. "I guess not. Waitressing takes good people skills and tact."

"A bit like a good bedside manner, Mandy," joked Richard, oblivious to the subtext between the two women.

Amanda looked as though she'd like to say more but was afraid to seem like a bitch in front of a man she wanted to impress. Tara was relieved. She wasn't here to upset anyone or fight them for a man. For heaven's sake! This was the twenty-first century, wasn't it?

Lunch progressed somewhat awkwardly from this point onwards. Amanda pointedly ignored Tara, and poor Richard worked doubly hard to make the conversation flow. Tara did her best to join in, but each time she opened her mouth Amanda steered the discussion back onto something medical, knowing full well that Tara wouldn't have a clue what she was talking about. By the time Tara was scraping her tiramisu bowl clean, she was feeling pretty low wattage. Excusing herself, she headed to the bathroom and stared sadly at her reflection.

"What are you doing with your life?" she asked herself. "How many more screw-ups, Tara?"

Richard was lovely but he was a doctor. Why on earth would he want to spend time with a soon-to-be divorcee and single mum? She had more baggage than Heathrow's Terminal Five. She must have been kidding herself to think he'd be interested. He'd been kind to her, that was all. Richard was kind. It was one of the nicest qualities about him. His thatch of dirty-blond hair, his misty grey eyes and his gently authoritative demeanour were attractive too, of course, but it was the essential goodness of him that Tara was so struck by. Why it had taken her so long to see it was anyone's guess.

She returned to the table with a bright smile pasted to her face.

"I'm going to head off now," she said lightly. "There's still a few bits I need to get and I'd better make sure I find them, or Santa will be in big trouble."

"Do you want me to come with you and carry those bags? We're all done here anyway," said Richard, rising to his feet.

"Actually, I'd like a coffee," Amanda interrupted, catching his arm with a manicured hand. "I'm in no rush. Besides, I wanted to pick your brains about clinical commissioning groups." She gave Tara a bright smile that had all the warmth of the deep-freeze aisle in Asda. "No disrespect, Tara, but I don't think it would interest you."

Tara was shrugging on her coat. She couldn't take any more of these games. She was too tired and totally beyond it. She was fonder of Richard than she'd realised but she wasn't up to matching Amanda's verbal missiles. Not on the day that her marriage had officially ended, anyhow.

"I'm sure it wouldn't," was all she said. "You guys carry on. Thanks for lunch, Richard."

"It's my pleasure. We must do it again," he replied.

"Maybe we could meet up in your restaurant, Tara?" suggested Amanda, deliberately misunderstanding and putting the knife in at the same time. She couldn't have marked her territory more if she'd stuck a flag on Richard's head. "You could tell us what's worth eating."

"All of it," said Richard. "The Plump Seagull is a fantastic restaurant."

"I can't wait to go," said Amanda, beaming at him. "And if Tara's there we'll have amazing service as well."

Tara had enough going on in her life without this kind of crap too.

"It was nice to meet you Amanda," she said politely.

"And you," Amanda replied, although the expression on her face said something entirely different. It was clear that for some reason she felt threatened by Tara, but there was no need. Tara knew when somebody was out of her league and Richard, however lovely, was certainly that. Besides, he'd just been taking pity on her. She was vulnerable and had read too much into everything. He was kind. That was all. There was nothing more – and the sooner she accepted that, the better.

Richard kissed Tara on the cheek. "I'll catch you in the village, very soon."

She nodded and then left the restaurant as fast as she could. Now that the lunchtime rush was over the coffee shops had cleared a little and Tara was able to find a quiet table in the window of one of them. Spreading out the divorce documents she took a deep breath before scrawling her signature.

She stared down at it. The dark ink was like a wound against the thick white paper. It was a shock to see the end of her marriage laid out in front of her. A shock and horribly real. Amanda's insults were nothing compared with this.

It was done. Danny had what he wanted and soon they'd both be free. *Free.* Tara shook her head. It sounded more like lonely to her.

As always, she hadn't seen what was right under her nose until it was too late.

It seemed to be the story of her life.

Chapter 21

"More tea, Bishop? Or maybe another slice of sponge? I made the jam myself, you know."

Sheila Keverne hovered at Bishop Bill's side. In one hand she was holding a teapot and in the other she was balancing a platter that boasted an enormous jam sponge oozing with clotted cream. Just looking at it was enough to make Jules put on a stone, so goodness only knew how the bishop must feel after being plied with several doorstop slices. His purple ecclesiastical shirt was looking very snug.

"No, thank you, Mrs Keverne." He placed his hand over his teacup before Sheila could slosh in more tea. "I'm awash."

"Surely there's room for some more cake? Or how about another saffron bun? All home-made, of course."

The bishop was looking a little green at the thought, but Sheila had been baking for days in preparation for this visit and wasn't going to give up easily. Before he could protest, she manoeuvred another gigantic slice onto his plate.

"*I'll* have some more cakey tea. 'Tis bloody handsome. Go on then, give us a saffron bun." Big Rog held out his plate hopefully, but Sheila was ten steps ahead. "You will not, Roger Pollard! Don't think I haven't spoken to your wife about your cholesterol levels. And don't *you* think you can ask for some and sneak it to your father," she added to Little Rog, who instantly looked guilty.

Jules decided it was time to start the meeting, before the bishop had a cream-induced heart attack or war broke out between Big Rog and

Sheila. Clearing her throat loudly, she shuffled the stack of papers in front of her and looked around at the gathered PCC members. Although she'd yet again committed the cardinal sin of calling a meeting on a Saturday evening, they were all present – with the exception of Danny, who was looking after Morgan. Jules hadn't seen Danny since she'd left him standing on the quay, and he hadn't been in touch either.

It hurt but it was probably for the best, especially in view of what she knew was about to take place tonight.

"First of all can I say how delighted I am to welcome Bishop Bill back to Polwenna Bay and St Wenn's," Jules began. "As you all know, the bishop visited us back in the late summer and we've been very concerned about the future of St Wenn's."

There was a ripple of agreement around the table. Not a great deal united Jules's Parochial Church Council, but the thought that St Wenn's might become a holiday cottage had certainly brought them together. Although Jules didn't always agree with their methods of fundraising – naked calendars and salacious novels weren't the most appropriate options, in her view – there was no doubt that they'd all worked as a team and helped to swell the bank account. The publicity had also increased the congregation and resulted in a few more marriages and christenings on the books.

"Don't keep us in suspense!" said Little Rog. "Tell us what's happening! We need to know."

"Quite right, my boy," nodded Big Rog, his eyes still fixed on the plate of teatime treats. "What's going on? We all know why the bishop's here, and it's not just for Sheila's buns."

His son sniggered.

"That'll do, my boy, that'll do," said his father.

Jules took a deep breath. This was her first announcement of the evening and the one she was looking forward to. The second, however, had caused her several sleepless nights and many long, rambling prayers.

"After a few very worrying months and a great deal of hard work from all of you here, I'm absolutely delighted to tell you that the team carrying out the review of St Wenn's found that, as a parish and a church, we *are* still viable!"

There was a cheer at this. Big Rog was hugging Little Rog, Richard Penwarren had relief written all over his face, Sheila was planting smackers of kisses on the bishop's cheeks, and Alice was beaming from ear to ear.

"The safe future of our church is down to you and your efforts," Jules said, once the cheering had calmed down sufficiently for her to be heard. "You should all be very proud."

"We couldn't have done it without you!" This was from Sheila – and it was just as well Jules was sitting down. Her biggest critic was thanking her? Tears flooded her eyes. What she was about to do was getting harder by the moment.

"Three cheers for the vicar!" cried Little Rog, jumping to his feet and flinging his arms around Jules. While everyone shouted their hoorays and then launched into a rendition of *For She's a Jolly Good Fellow*, Jules was highly amused to see Big Rog's hand shoot out to snatch a saffron bun during the distraction.

The bishop raised his hand. "I won't go over the same ground, but I will say that I've been very impressed with the work you've done here. Some of your methods were a little *unorthodox*, of course. First there was the calendar, and more recently we've had a certain author donating royalties to the pot—"

"Must write a book," mused Big Rog. "If that great girl Caspar can do it then it can't be too hard. Maybe my memoirs?"

"Could be dodgy, Dad," pointed out Little Rog.

"True, my boy, true. I was wild back in the day. Your mother wouldn't like to read it."

"How about the history of the village?" Sheila suggested excitedly. "Or the story of St Wenn?"

Jules had a sudden flashback to that autumnal afternoon at the well. She recalled the cool kiss of the water and the foolish request that had risen from her very soul. Even St Wenn couldn't have made her winter wish come true.

"All wonderful ideas, of course, but not needed quite so much now. Your church is very much staying open." Years of preaching in echoey spaces had given the bishop a booming voice when needed, and he wasn't afraid to use it. Instantly the chatter stopped.

"However, there will be one very significant change here at St Wenn's, and I know it will bring sadness to you all." He looked at Jules. "Would you like me to continue?"

That would be the easy choice, but since when had she ever plumped for the soft option? Jules shook her head and swallowed down the rising knot of grief.

"This is probably one of the hardest things I've ever had to do," she began, glancing around the table. As always they were gathered in the vicarage kitchen, which today looked like an explosion in a tinsel factory thanks to Sheila and the WI, who'd insisted that they always took care of Christmas decorations for the vicar. There was even a tree complete with flashing red lights, which right now were making the Pollards glow in a rather sinister fashion.

All eyes were on Jules. Big Rog had even abandoned his stealthy saffron bun mid-chew.

She took a deep breath. This had to be done.

"As of January you'll be looking to appoint a new vicar. I'm moving on."

There was a stunned silence.

"You're leaving?" said Alice finally.

Jules nodded. "Yes. I'll be heading back to the city."

"But we need you here!" This was from Sheila, who was dangerously red eyed. "You can't leave us now. You're our vicar."

"You saved St Wenn's." Big Rog shook his head in confusion. "You can't leave now, maid. Your place is here."

Richard said, "Is this because of the accounting? Are you worried about an investigation? I'll take total responsibility."

"It's my fault." Alice was white and looked every one of her seventy-nine years as she wrung her hands. "I made all the deposits into the account; it was me who wrote *Blackwarren*. Not Caspar at all. He was just kind enough to cover for me."

"Bleddy hell," breathed Little Rog, his eyes the size of dustbin lids. "That was you? You wrote that book? Get on, Mrs T!"

"Even I've read that," Richard told Alice. "You can certainly spin a yarn."

Big Rog was nodding. "Bleddy right she can. So go on then, Mrs T; how much cash did you make? Was it hard to do?"

"Who's Lord B?" demanded Little Rog. "Is it Teddy?"

"That's not the point! Jules is resigning and we can't let her!" hollered Sheila. Hands on hips and eyes blazing, she turned to the bishop and added, "That calendar was my idea, so if you're blaming Jules then you're wrong! You can't sack her for something that isn't her fault. She never wanted to do it."

There was a chorus of agreement. Bishop Bill shrank into his chair; the speed of his transition from guest of honour to vicar sacking villain had been so fast that the poor man's head was probably spinning.

"Nobody has sacked me. I'm resigning," Jules said firmly. "It's completely my decision."

"But why, my love?" Alice was mopping her eyes with a lace hanky. "Aren't you happy here?"

Jules felt dreadful. She loved Polwenna Bay and leaving the village was going to break her heart. But how could she tell Alice the truth? *I'm in love with your grandson, your married grandson, and I know that I need to give him some space if he's to make his marriage work.*

She couldn't look Alice in the eye. "It's the right thing to do."

"Are you sure?" Richard frowned. "It seems very sudden."

It hadn't been sudden enough, Jules reflected as around her the meeting descended into chaos. She ought to have left the minute she realised how she felt about Danny, instead of being arrogant enough to think she could handle it.

"It's a decision I haven't taken lightly," she said finally when, looking exhausted and upset, they finally quietened down. "I've loved it here and I'll miss you all, but please, respect my decision. I'll be here for Christmas and I'll do everything I can to make it a good one, but then I'll be moving on. It's the right thing. St Wenn's is safe too, so there are good things to celebrate."

"Don't much feel like celebrating," muttered Big Rog, rising to his feet. "Come on, son, let's go to The Ship."

Sheila grabbed her bag. "Wait for me, Mr Pollard. I'll come too." She looked at Jules reproachfully. "We know when people don't really want to be with us."

One by one they left the vicarage, subdued and hurt, and Jules felt terrible. Her announcement had ruined what should have been one of the biggest victories ever for St Wenn's. How was it that each time she tried to do the right thing she only succeeded in making the situation ten times worse? It was just as well she was leaving.

"That went well," remarked the bishop drily.

"I didn't think they'd take it quite this badly."

"I did warn you, Julia. Leaving mid-term is never a good thing for a pastor or her flock. People have invested in you and they feel let down."

She hung her head. "I know you did, and I feel dreadful, but this really is the best thing for everyone."

He raised a bushy eyebrow. "But is it really? I'm not convinced I know the full story, Julia."

And you never will, thought Jules. Her love for Danny Tremaine would be locked away in the furthest corner of her heart. She'd leave it there in the darkness, try not to revisit it too many times and hope that it would gradually fade away until one day it no longer existed.

Since the meeting had finished sooner than she'd anticipated, there was nothing to do except deal with the pile of saffron buns and some washing up – the only evidence that the PCC had been there at all. That could wait, Jules decided, until after she'd walked with the bishop through the village and up to the car park.

It was a chilly night, and as Jules locked the door the bishop gazed thoughtfully across the fairy-lit village and out to sea.

"I think we're going to have snow," he remarked.

"Seriously?" Huddled beneath her scarf and woolly hat, Jules reckoned it was certainly cold enough. The stars seemed very bright, but from the east a bank of low cloud had started to build. "I didn't think it snowed much here, though?"

"As a rule it doesn't tend to, but we have been surprised on a few occasions," he said. "Make sure you get some food in and have some salt for the path. Once it sets in here the village will be cut off."

Great, thought Jules. She'd be snowed in, broken-hearted and public enemy number one. Merry flipping Christmas.

She could only hope the New Year would bring some improvements.

Chapter 22

Tara untied her apron and hung it up with a sensation of relief. Her feet ached, which was hardly surprising given that she'd been on them since just after eight this morning. It was now nearly three in the afternoon, and she felt absolutely exhausted. In the run-up to Christmas The Plump Seagull had been booked solid by second-homers returning to the village and by local companies wanting festive meals for their staff. All this had meant a lot of shifts and overtime for Tara, which was great in some respects; however, it had also left her feeling shattered and smelling constantly like Sunday dinner, which wasn't so much fun.

The afternoon shift was still in full swing and Tara's head throbbed from taking orders, dealing with awkward customers and trying not to think about Danny. Actually, she reflected as she reached for her jacket, it was odd but signing the divorce papers seemed to have liberated her from some of her unhappiness. After months of regrets and doing her best to try and make things right – and failing miserably most of the time – it was something of a relief to know that the struggle was over. Maybe this way she and Danny could eventually find some peace and be friends. She would always love him, in her way. Besides, he was Morgan's father; biology didn't alter that. Dan was Morgan's dad and that would never change.

Another strange thing was this: instead of thinking about Danny, her mind was occupied with thoughts of Richard. She'd lain awake in bed on Saturday night and relived their meeting in Truro, seeing again the chivalrous way he'd carried her shopping and protected her from the bustling crowds. He'd seemed genuinely thrilled to see her, too. Was that because he was just a nice person? Or was there something more to it? Then she'd recalled Amanda, with her glossy groomed looks and dazzling medical career. Amanda and Richard were equals in terms of profession, income and even their shared university experience. Of course he wouldn't be interested in a single mother who waited tables. She was just dreaming.

"Table six ready. Come on! Let's get this out!"

Symon's shout across the kitchen and the chorus of "Yes chef!" from his staff yanked Tara out of her melancholy thoughts. There was no point brooding on all this. She'd ruined things with Danny a long time ago and thinking about Richard was just indulging her imagination. It was time she concentrated on what she did actually have – a son and a beautiful place to live – and stopped feeling sorry for herself.

"I'm off to collect Morgan," she called, and Sy nodded. Both literally and metaphorically, he had his hands full at the moment preparing festive food. Although The Plump Seagull was predominantly a fish restaurant, he was still paying homage to Christmas by serving goose with all the trimmings. Before she'd even started her waitressing today, Tara had spent two hours peeling chestnuts for the stuffing and another hour plating up the Christmas puddings. If she never saw a Christmas dinner again she thought it would be too soon. Maybe Morgan would be happy to have pizza instead?

Outside the warm fug of the kitchen the winter afternoon was bitingly raw. Thick clouds the colour of clotted cream had rolled in from the east to hang heavy on the horizon, and the village was bathed in a weird yellow light. Even though it was only early afternoon, lights were already shining from the cottage windows and smoke billowed from the chimney pots. All the old folk were muttering about snow and glancing at the ominous clouds. Tara could well believe that it might snow; it was one of the coldest days she could remember. She was already shivering and as she walked through the village to the school her breath rose in little clouds. Even the seagulls bobbing in the harbour looked chilly and fed up.

I'll light the wood burner when I get home, Tara decided. Caspar had taken a delivery of logs and in an effort to compensate for his bizarre behaviour at the St Miltons' party had offered to chop some for her. She rarely saw him outside the cottage, though: he seemed to be permanently inside sitting by the window, tapping away at his laptop with such intensity that it was as if he was in another world altogether. Perhaps he really was a genuine writer, rather than another pseudo artist who just liked to hang out in the village looking the part. He was certainly very cagey about what he wrote.

The daylight was fast seeping away and by the time Tara reached the school twilight had crept in and Christmas lights were glowing all the way through the village in a jewel-hued trail. Mums clustered around the gate chatting to one another as the children poured out in a torrent of brightly coloured coats and bobble hats. As usual Morgan was one of the last to leave, having left something behind and retraced his steps to retrieve it. On seeing Tara, his face broke into a joyful smile. At least *he* loves me, she thought as she folded him into her arms and dropped a kiss onto his head. Nothing else really mattered in comparison.

"Good day, sweetie?" she asked, taking his rucksack and PE kit.

Morgan shrugged. "It was all right. What's for tea? Is it sausages?"

She laughed. "It can be if that's what you want."

"Yes please!" Morgan looked delighted. "Grand Gran's making sausage stuffing on Christmas Day specially for me. Issie said."

Tara felt as though cold hands had grabbed her stomach and twisted it. "But Morgan, we're not at Seaspray on Christmas Day. We're going to be in our house."

"When we wake up and Santa's been. Then we'll go to Seaspray to be with Dad." He looked up at her with anxious violet eyes. "Won't we? Jimmy James's parents are divorced and that's what he does."

Tara was alarmed. Did Morgan think they would be spending Christmas with the Tremaines? No fear. Mo was likely to stab her to death with the carving knife.

"Not that I believe in Santa, Mum," Morgan informed her. "I know it's you. Fact."

Tara said automatically, "Of course it isn't. I'd never fit down the chimney."

Morgan gave her a pitying look. "Mum, that's just a story. Santa does not exist. Fact."

"Opinion, not fact." Tara shot back. She took a deep breath and plucked up her courage. "Sweetie, do you want to go to Dad's for Christmas dinner?"

"Of course. We always go there. Every year. At ten we go to church. Then we have dinner at half past one. I always have the red crackers and sit next to Grand Gran." Morgan started to pull at his hair, which was always a bad sign. "Then we go for a walk on the beach and then we come back for Christmas tea. There's a cake with five plastic reindeer and a Santa. I'll eat all the icing first. That's what we always do."

He was right; it was what they did. Or rather, it was what they used to do. Tara wasn't sure of the etiquette when a couple had filed for divorce, but she was pretty certain that being invited to your ex's family home for Christmas dinner wasn't standard practice.

"Of course it is and you'll go there like you always do," she promised him. Routine was key for Morgan and even if it broke her heart she would do everything she could to help him keep that structure in his world.

"Yay!" Morgan tugged his hand from hers and ran down the street, arms out like a plane and obviously delighted with the news. "Sausage stuffing!"

Tears prickled Tara's eyes. How could she deny Morgan a family Christmas just because she wanted him with her? Of course he should go to Seaspray. She'd miss him terribly but it was no more than she deserved.

Morgan had rounded the corner and was out of sight. Knowing that he was probably leaning over the river looking at the rushing water, Tara picked up pace, fully expecting to see him on the footbridge. When Morgan wasn't there she was taken aback. Normally he loved to watch the river; that was what he always did. Given that Morgan was a little boy who liked routines, she was alarmed not to find him there.

Tara looked around frantically. It was dark and the River Wenn was racing beneath her feet. Could an excited nine-year-old have fallen in? Surely not. Her heart started to rattle against her ribcage. "Morgan!"

There was no answer, just the roar of the wind as it picked up speed, slicing at her cheeks and whipping her hair across her face. There was a cold flurry of ice against her brow and she started shivering again.

It was snowing.

"Mum!" Her son's voice made Tara turn round abruptly. "Mum! Come quickly!"

Morgan wasn't under the bridge as she'd feared but was running towards her. His eyes were wide and frightened.

"Quick, Mum! You've got to come and help!" He launched himself at Tara, grabbing her arm and tugging for all he was worth. "She's on the floor and I think she's dead. Come on, Mum!"

Morgan was panting and full of panic. Tara crouched down and placed her hands on his shoulders.

"Morgan, take a deep breath and tell me what's happened. Who's on the floor?"

"Poison Ivy!" He yanked at her again, frantic for her to follow him. "Come on, Mum!"

Tara followed him back over the bridge, round the corner past the green and to Ivy's house. Unlike all the other cottages with Christmas trees in the windows and gaudy flashing lights strung over shrubs, Ivy's place was in total darkness.

"She's lying on the floor, Mum!" Morgan was saying as he hopped from foot to foot in agitation. "Climb over the wall and look through her window. Then you'll see."

"Is that what you just did?" Tara was stunned. "Morgan, that's really naughty. Why on earth would you do that?"

"Because it was a dare. If you can look in the wicked witch's window then all the kids play with you and you have friends," Morgan explained. "I don't have many friends. They all say I'm a freak, but Jimmy dared me to see the witch, so I did it 'cause I want friends. But now I think she's dead." He started to cry. "Mum, do something! She's horrible and mean but I don't want her dead."

Tara knew he was telling the truth and it broke her heart to think that Morgan had been having a hard time at school. They'd talk about this later, and she'd be having words with Tess too, but first of all she needed to find out exactly what was going on.

Her heart racing, she clambered over the wall and peered into the gloomy sitting room. It took a moment for her eyes to adjust, but then she made out the shape of a figure crumpled on the floor in the flickering light of the room's one-bar heater. Tara squinted and thought she could see the elderly woman's chest rising and falling, but she wasn't sure.

"Mrs Lawrence!" Tara slammed her hand on the window. "Ivy!"

There was no response. Tara tore across to the front door, only to find that it was locked. No matter how hard she rattled the handle, it refused to budge. Glancing up, she saw that the sash window on the first floor was slightly open. If she could climb up onto the porch using the trellis as a ladder, haul herself up the drainpipe and manage to reach the window, she could push the sash up and let herself in. It was worth a try. Ivy really didn't look too good. Tara fished into her pocket for her mobile, cursing under her breath when she realised she must have left it at the restaurant.

"Morgan, I need you to be very brave," Tara told her son, trying to sound calm. "Run to Mrs Jago in the village shop and ask her to call an ambulance for Ivy. Then she can ring Dr Penwarren and Mrs Keverne, who'll know exactly what to do. OK? Don't stop until you get there."

Morgan bit his lip, nodded and shot off into the darkness.

Gritting her teeth and plucking up courage, Tara hauled herself onto the windowsill and then stretched across to the porch. Her trainers scrabbled on the soft wood of the trellis and her hands clawed at the drainpipe, the icy metal scorching her palms. Several times she slipped, before finally managing to get a grip firm enough to pull herself upwards. She'd always been good at gym when she was at school, and she was still relatively supple now. Praying that the drainpipe would hold her weight, Tara pulled herself gingerly up onto the porch roof and held her breath.

Phew. So far so good.

In spite of the flurries of snow that stung her eyes, she inched her way forwards on her hands and knees, until her fingers reached the windowsill. Curling them around it, she slowly pulled herself up onto her feet. *Just don't look down*, she told herself as she tried to push the sash open. *Keep looking up.*

At first the frame didn't yield, but with another hard shove the aged mechanism decided to give and the sash rose upwards. Tara climbed through and onto the landing. She was so relieved to have made it in one piece that she could have cried.

Inside, the house smelt old, of things too long left shut and of absence. There was no warmth; even when she turned the hall light on, the place still had an air of dinginess and hostility. Tara shivered but not from the cold this time. No wonder Ivy was so miserable. Or had the house absorbed her unhappiness? There was a lesson in there somewhere.

Able to see now and negotiate the stairs, Tara flew down them and raced into the living room. Flicking on the main light she saw Ivy crumpled by the sofa like a rag doll. Her left leg was at an angle that made Tara feel queasy. It looked as though Ivy had fallen and injured her hip.

"Mrs Lawrence? Ivy? Can you hear me?" she asked, crouching down beside her and resting her hand on the old woman's chest. Thank goodness, there was a shallow rising and falling of those frail ribs. "Ivy? It's Tara, Morgan's mum. You're going to be all right."

Envelopes were scattered around Ivy like the snow that was falling outside. As she pushed them aside in order to kneel down, Tara saw that each one had a villager's name on it and contained a glittery card; none of them were sealed yet. Mince pies were also strewn across the floor, crumbs and icing sugar dusting the carpet just like the snow outside.

How weird.

"Tara? Tara Tremaine? Ivy's voice was thin and shaky.

Tara nodded. "That's me."

The elderly woman exhaled. "Thank you. Thank you."

Ivy's eyes were closed and her breath was coming in short gasps. At least her airways were clear, Tara thought with relief. She didn't dare move her, but she reached out and took Ivy's hand in hers. Claw-like fingers gripped her own as though Tara was a life raft that could stop Ivy from drowning.

"An ambulance is coming," Tara told her. "It won't be long."

Ivy groaned. Her face was twisted with pain.

"Silly old fool. Wanted… Wanted to get out before it snowed. Slipped and fell in here."

"Don't try to talk," Tara said. Ivy's lips were turning a nasty blue colour and she was trembling. Shock maybe? Cold certainly. Tara slipped off her jacket and lay it over Ivy.

"I'm going to see if I can find a blanket," she said, but the fingers clutched her arm even more tightly.

"Don't leave me," Ivy whispered. "I'm scared. I thought I'd die here all alone. Nobody would notice. Nobody would care."

"Of course they would," Tara said, but Ivy shook her head.

"No they wouldn't – and who could blame them?"

"Well, Morgan noticed," Tara said, although she decided not to reveal just how it was that her son had come to discover that Ivy had slipped. They'd be having some stern words about that later. She looked around the room. Picture frames were crammed onto every spare surface and a pretty woman smiled out of all of them. In some she was alone; in others a handsome man joined her, and sometimes there was a gap-toothed little girl too. "I can see you've got family. They would care. Is the girl in the pictures your daughter? I can call them for you if you'd like?"

A tear slipped down Ivy's papery cheek. "That's my daughter Beth. There's no point calling. She's gone to Australia. They left four years ago."

"That must be hard. It's such a long way. Have you visited?"

Ivy made a noise that was halfway between a sob and a hiss. "I told my daughter if she left then she was dead to me. I said some awful things. I didn't mean any of it, but she took me at my word and we haven't spoken since. She broke my heart and I'm a proud woman. I wasn't going to apologise. I sold our old family home and moved here. They don't even have my address."

It seemed to Tara that being proud was quite a lonely way to be, but she was starting to understand. "So you moved here to start again."

Ivy groaned again and a spasm of pain twisted her features. "I didn't know anyone here, and that suited me just fine. I'd rather keep myself to myself. People just let you down in the end, you see. All of them. Even the vicar's leaving."

"Jules is leaving?" Tara was taken aback. "Are you sure?"

"I heard Sheila telling Betty in the shop. So much for what she said about caring for the village."

Did Danny know about this? Tara frowned. Jules had seemed very settled. What had changed? Was this Tara's fault for coming back? Had her return been the catalyst?

Had she inadvertently brought Danny's world crashing down for a second time?

"People just let you down," Ivy repeated, in a whisper.

"They don't always mean to," Tara said thoughtfully. "Sometimes people make stupid mistakes that they know they'll regret forever. It's how they make amends for those mistakes that matters."

Ivy nodded and closed her eyes again. More tears seeped from beneath their lids. "Sometimes they don't even need to know you've made amends. It's how you feel inside that matters."

Tara's own eyes filled. She felt pretty dreadful inside. How could she ever make amends to Danny?

"Is that what these envelopes and mince pies are all about?" she asked.

"I wanted to do something nice for the vicar, so I was taking these to the church as a Christmas surprise. I was going to leave them there for her to find. I thought that it might make her change her mind."

"These envelopes with the money? But why?"

Ivy's thin lips twitched into a faint smile. "Because your little boy was right. Being nice to people is far better, and everyone does leave you on your own if you're unkind to them. That's my punishment. Like your little boy said, my grandchildren have left me. Well, I can't make my family happy but I thought I could try and make other people happier. At least I know my hamper will make Eddie Penhalligan very happy; that's something, I suppose."

Tara's head was spinning. Eddie had won the Harrods hamper when the raffle was drawn. The anonymously donated Harrods hamper. She stared down at the frail old woman lying beside her and suddenly the penny dropped.

"You're the Polwenna Bay Angel?"

Ivy tried to laugh but it turned into a horrible gargling sound. "Some angel."

"It was you all along? You donated that money to the charities? And made the cakes?"

"My house was worth more than I could have imagined so money is one thing I do have but without my family it's meaningless. And I love baking but what's the point without anyone to eat it all?" Ivy said sadly. "Anyway it's not nearly enough to make up for how I've behaved lately but it was a start."

"Sometimes," Tara said quietly, "making a start is all we can do."

They sat in silence for a while, each lost in thoughts about their own mistakes. By the time Sheila and the ambulance arrived, Tara had learned more from Ivy Lawrence that night than the old lady would ever know.

She would be grateful for the rest of her life.

Chapter 23

"How's he doing?" Danny asked Tara when she came down from tucking Morgan into bed. He was sitting in the armchair by the window and although the lights from the Christmas tree bathed him in a warm glow, his face was drawn. There were deep hollows beneath his eyes. He looked tired and sad.

She smiled at him. "You can go up and see for yourself. He's not nearly as upset as he was."

"Poor little chap. It must have frightened the life out of him to see Ivy on the floor like that." Danny pulled himself out of the chair, wincing slightly. "The cold's playing havoc with my leg," he explained, seeing her worried expression. "The sooner this snow goes away the better."

While Danny went to kiss Morgan goodnight, Tara tidied away the supper things and lit the wood burner. Then she curled up on the sofa with a glass of wine and watched the snowflakes whirling past the window. Already a fine powder had whitened the slipway and dusted the quay. Who knew, if it continued it may well settle and then Morgan could build a snowman. She'd make a sausage casserole with mashed potatoes and dumplings for him to enjoy afterwards. Real winter food. That should cheer him up. She could invite Richard over for lunch too, as a thank you for the one he'd treated her to.

Oh, who was she kidding? She wanted to see him and, short of inventing an ailment for herself and trundling down to the surgery, this was the best excuse she could think of.

She picked up her mobile and scrolled through her list of contacts, until she found his number. As it rang she tried to slow her pulse by taking measured breaths. This was ridiculous! It was only Richard she was calling. What had got into her?

"Hello? Richard Penwarren's mobile."

It was Amanda Olsen; there was no mistaking that clipped cut-class voice. Tara's thumb hit the end-call button instantly. If the glamorous female doctor was answering Richard's calls then it was pretty obvious what the situation was. Richard and Amanda's lunch date clearly hadn't ended once Tara had left.

Her disappointment was so intense that it was as if somebody had punched her in the solar plexus. Tara shook her head and then knocked back her glass of wine in one mouthful. How stupid she was being. Richard was a free agent. He could see whomever he chose. There was nothing going on between them anyway.

She was still trying to untangle her feelings when the pad of socked feet on worn wooden stairs heralded Danny's return.

"Morgan's got ten minutes' iPad time and then lights out," he said, sinking back into the armchair.

"Is he less worried now?" Tara asked. Morgan had been frantic to know whether Ivy would be all right. Following his own rather peculiar logic, he seemed to think it was all his fault for knocking on her window.

"He seems fine. I've told him he's going to be something of a hero. The paramedics said if Ivy had been lying there all night then she might well have caught hypothermia and not made it. It's thanks to Morgan that she's safe and warm in the hospital."

Tara thought about Ivy's cold and empty house and shivered. There'd been no Christmas decorations and no sound, just the echoing of regrets and the absence of a family she'd let slip away. Was this what Tara had to look forward to as well?

"He's been teased at school," she told Danny, trying to push these thoughts aside. "I had no idea, but I think the others have been making him do daft things to win their approval."

"Jules did mention that Morgan had been a bit silly during the nativity. She said she thought it was out of character," Danny said slowly. "Don't worry, T. I'll have a chat with him about it all. He generally seems pretty happy at school, so I don't think it's a major issue. There's enough of us Tremaines here to look out for him. He's got his family."

And Morgan *was* a Tremaine, was the unspoken part of this sentence. The past, the biological facts, her mistakes – none of this counted now so far as Danny was concerned. All he cared about was Morgan. His son. Maybe they would be able to move forward in spite of everything?

"We'll make this work, Tara," Danny told her quietly, sensing her train of thought. "We can move on from the past and do the best for Morgan. After all, he's what matters here. It might be too late for us but we can still make sure he has the best start in life possible."

He was right; it was too late for them but Tara felt at peace with this now.

"You're a good man, Danny Tremaine," was all she said.

He looked up and smiled his sweet, sad smile, the same smile that had once melted her heart and made her long to trace his lips with her own.

"Not good enough, I'm afraid. Anyway, you're not so bad yourself. Not many people would have risked their necks to rescue a miserable old boot like Ivy."

"She wasn't always miserable, Dan," Tara pointed out. "Nobody starts out that way. She was lonely and sad."

"True," Danny agreed. "I guess we're all a product of the hand that life deals us, aren't we?"

Ouch. The implied rebuke stung.

"Maybe it's how we play that hand that really matters?" she countered, but Danny just shrugged. His good eye was dark with sadness.

"Or maybe there's just no point in taking part at all if the dice are loaded? There are some games you can never win."

Outside, the Salvation Army were playing on the quay. The strains of *Silent Night* could be heard, pure and heart-achingly melancholic. She felt a sudden spike of guilt because this sadness was down to her, wasn't it? Her return to the village had turned his life upside down. But enough of the metaphors, Tara thought. It was time they were just truthful.

"This is about Jules, isn't it?"

There was a pause before Danny spoke. His voice was tight with misery.

"She's leaving."

Just those two simple words spoke volumes. Tara hadn't heard him sound so despairing since... well, since that dreadful day when she'd said the things she'd said.

Danny had turned his face away now and was staring out at the dark harbour, his gaze fixed on the lights halfway up the side of the valley where the vicarage stood.

"Ivy mentioned it." Tara watched him closely. His chest was rising and falling quickly and his fist was clenched. He was struggling to control his emotions, and in that moment she realised exactly why. Perhaps she'd known all along.

"You're in love with her." Tara wasn't asking him. It was obvious. Danny was in love with Jules. Fact, as Morgan would say. She waited to feel the same surge of jealousy that had overwhelmed her heart when Amanda had answered Richard's mobile, but there was nothing except curiosity.

Danny was nodding. "Yes. Yes, I am. It happened slowly and it wasn't something I ever expected or even looked for, but Jules is the one, Tara. She knows me, the real me, and she doesn't care that I've said and done some terrible things. She's been there for me when nobody else was. She's honest and kind and she has the biggest heart in the world. She's my best friend. So, yes, I love her – and I'm pretty certain she feels the same way."

Tara could guarantee this. Female intuition had told her as much weeks ago. Strange that the thought of Jules and Danny being romantically linked had been unbearable then, whereas now it made perfect sense.

"So why are you looking so sad?" she asked him, perplexed. "If it's because of me, you needn't worry. Our marriage is over and we both know that we can never undo the past. There's been too much that's gone wrong for us. I won't stand in your way. I've already signed the divorce papers."

"The divorce is why she's leaving," Danny said despairingly. "Jules thinks that she's the reason why we can't make our marriage work."

"But that's rubbish! Our marriage has been over for ages and it's nothing to do with how you feel about Jules."

"We know that, but she doesn't. Tara, see it from Jules's point of view. She has no idea what's gone on between us. She thinks we had a perfect marriage before I was wounded, and that you've had a hard time adjusting to my injuries."

She hung her head. "I led her to believe that, Dan. I'm so sorry."

"Tara, I'm not here to start throwing blame about," he said softly. "We've both messed up. The past isn't the issue. It's where we go from now that will count."

"But Jules doesn't know that." Tara was starting to see the problem. "Because you can't tell her the truth, she thinks she's breaking up our marriage."

"She's a vicar, T, and she feels very strongly that marriage is sacred. She marries people and teaches marriage classes. How can she do her job, fulfil her vocation, keep her faith – call it what you will – if she thinks that she herself has broken up a marriage?" His voice was full of anguish. "Nothing I can say will change her mind. She's resigned from St Wenn's and she's leaving after Christmas."

But there *was* something that Danny could have told Jules, wasn't there? One explanation that could help her to understand why there would never be any hope for his marriage. A more selfish man would have blurted out that secret, sharing it in the anticipation that he could trade it for his own happiness – but Danny was probably the most selfless person Tara had ever known. He had given his strength and his health and even a limb to do his duty for his country; he had stood by her even when he'd had the worst suspicions; and now he would protect Morgan, even if it cost him the woman he was in love with.

Tara's mouth was dry as she whispered, "You could tell her the truth."

His head snapped up. "The truth?"

"About what I did. What I told you. The real reason we'll never mend our marriage."

Dan's jaw was taut with determination. "I gave my word that I'll never mention that until you think it's the right time. I won't go back on what I promised. Not even for Jules. Morgan is my son, Tara, and I will always put him first. Always."

He would, Tara knew that – just as she knew that Danny would also keep his word. All the way through their relationship Danny had been constant. As a girl she'd thought it meant he was dull and staid; now that she was a woman, she knew his worth could never be measured.

And Morgan could never ask for a better father.

There was nothing more they could say. Minutes stretched. Tara searched for something she could offer as a solution, but the words withered on her tongue. All she could think of were useless platitudes. She was filled with sadness, regret and guilt, but those were no help to him either.

"I should go," Danny said. He was standing now and leaning on the frame of the door between the kitchen and the sitting room. He looked tired and his face was etched with new lines. Tara could hardly bear to see the effect of all this heartache on him. She didn't want him to leave, not like this. Surely there was a way she could make amends?

"You don't have to go, Dan. You can have a beer if you like?"

But he was already at the door, his hand on the latch. "I don't think it's going to help anyone if I start drinking now."

"OK, so I'll make some coffee. I've biscuits too."

He shook his head. "I'll get going. The path to Seaspray will be lethal if this carries on. Don't look so worried, I'm not about to hurl myself off the cliffs. Not yet, anyway."

Danny was joking but as the door clicked shut Tara wasn't laughing. She hated to see him so despairing. What a mess she'd made of everything. Morgan's life, Danny's life and even Jules's life – all three had been affected by her actions, even if they weren't all aware of it. How could she learn from Ivy? What could she do to put things right?

Outside the snow was getting heavier. Feathery flakes tumbled from the dark sky, landing on the steps outside and starting to cover the footprints left by Danny.

Tara wished with all her heart that she could cover over the mess she'd made of everyone's lives. There was a way, of course, and she realised now what it would be. Hadn't Ivy already shown her? The only question was whether or not she was brave enough to see it through.

Chapter 24

The snow was falling hard on Cornwall, gathering on cottage rooftops and settling on the bare-limbed trees. The trawlers down in Polwenna's harbour were iced like cakes, their mooring ropes frozen stiff, and the quay was covered in a plump white duvet. In the distance a man was walking a chocolate Labrador on the beach, and the dog's dark coat seemed to leap out against the whiteness. Elsewhere in the village, drifts were starting to build up against the garden gates and dry-stone walls. As Jules leaned her head against the cold window and heated the glass with her breath, the presenter on Radio Cornwall was interviewing a motorist who'd been stranded in his car up on the A30. The county was in the grip of a very unusual cold snap, and everything was grinding to a standstill.

It might look very seasonal, with the white vicarage garden only lacking a cheerful robin to complete the picture, but Jules could have done without this added complication. Aside from all the packing she still had to do, Christmas Eve was one of the busiest days of her year, and trying to negotiate Polwenna Bay in the snow was hard work at best and a recipe for a broken neck at worst. Driving to the cottage hospital to visit Ivy had been one of the most terrifying things she'd ever done. Her little Peugeot had slipped and skidded all the way, and several times Jules had thought she was a goner. She wouldn't attempt to leave the village again if this weather kept up. The steep main road out was treacherous already and only four-by-fours stood a chance of making it. Most of the villagers had adopted a siege mentality, stopping work for Christmas a day early and heading to the pub for mulled wine. Jules couldn't help feeling envious. Christmas might mean a holiday and a big roast dinner to them, but to her it was a huge amount of work.

Ivy was the Polwenna Bay Angel. Jules hadn't seen that one coming. People never ceased to surprise you, did they? The sad story of Ivy falling out with her own family, and of her stubborn pride standing in the way of making peace with them, had made quite an impression on Jules. It had made her reflect on her own situation too. Was she being proud? Was what she'd thought of as doing the right thing actually a sin of pride? Her temples thudded. How could she know for sure?

Give me a sign, Jules prayed. *Show me what to do.*

As she gazed out over the village, Jules ran through her mental list of things to do and ticked off those she'd managed to achieve. So far today she'd conducted two of her three services – one at a nursing home and then the carol service on the village green – before visiting Ivy and picking up some shopping for a couple of her elderly parishioners. Although it was only early afternoon, there was no time to put her feet up; St Wenn's needed to be ready for Midnight Mass.

Jules had checked the church several times since this morning, but no matter how high she cranked the thermostat the atmosphere was still arctic. Jules was becoming increasingly concerned that her congregation would be in danger of getting hypothermia. The heating was trying to do its best, but its asthmatic gasps of lukewarm air into the chilly depths of an ancient church were pretty ineffectual. Whilst in town she'd picked up thermal long johns to wear beneath her cassock, but she feared that the extra layer wouldn't be enough. Her hands had turned blue while she was setting out the carol sheets and in the end she'd had to retreat into the vicarage to thaw out.

If Jules survived Midnight Mass without getting frostbite then there would be the Christmas morning service complete with the Christingle candles, followed by dinner with the mayor at the Polwenna Bay Hotel, before she could even think about drawing breath. Everyone wanted a piece of the Reverend Jules Mathieson at Christmas. Still, busy was good. Busy didn't leave her any time to pause and reflect. Busy ensured that she didn't have a moment to think about how much she missed Danny or to feel heartbroken about leaving the village.

Jules traced a heart shape in the mist on the windowpane before rubbing it out and returning to her desk. She was feeling as bleak as the weather and there was no hope whatsoever of her circumstances thawing out. Even the bright fairy lights twinkling on the tree and the carols playing in the background couldn't lift her spirits.

If she was this unhappy on Christmas Eve, what on earth was it going to be like on New Year's Day when she moved out? Jules wondered sadly.

She was making a start on sorting out her books and papers in readiness for the move, wondering how on earth she'd managed to collect so much stuff in just ten months, when there was a knock on the door. Jules looked up in despair. Whoever had coined the phrase *no peace for the wicked* hadn't seen how hectic a vicar's life was. Abandoning her packing, Jules unlocked the front door, only to come face to face with the one person she had least expected to see.

It was Tara Tremaine.

"It's getting worse out there," Tara said, stepping into the porch without being invited, stamping her boots on the mat and peeling off her gloves. Snow had settled on her hood; as she pushed it away from her face an icy flurry fell to the floor. "I've lived in Cornwall most of my life and I've never seen it like this."

Jules pushed her hair behind her ears as she regarded Danny's wife. She was pink-cheeked from the cold and her hair was damp with melting snow, but she still looked stunning. Wearing a red duffle coat that hugged her curves, white skinny jeans and knee boots, she could have stepped straight out of a Marks and Spencer Christmas ad. In jeans and a fisherman's sweater, Jules felt tatty in comparison.

"Do you have time to talk?" Tara asked.

Jules was about to say that she was particularly busy today, but seeing that Tara was shivering it seemed rude to send her away without letting her warm up first. Besides, she was biting her lips and her brow was crinkled. Something was up. Was it Danny? Had something happened? Her stomach almost rose into her throat at the very thought.

"Sure," she said. "Come on in, but excuse the mess. I've started packing. Would you like a hot drink?"

"Coffee would be great. Thanks." Tara followed her into the kitchen, perching on the edge of one of the chairs that was the least piled with belongings. "Wow. You have been busy. You really are planning to move, aren't you?"

Jules flicked on the kettle and selected two mugs from the cupboard. "Absolutely. It's all happening here. Look, Tara, I don't want to seem rude but I've got a lot on today and a service to prepare for. What did you want to talk about?"

Tara inhaled deeply. Her hazel eyes were troubled. "This isn't easy for me. I'm going to tell you something, something really important, but I need you to promise me that it will never go any further."

"I can't promise that if I think it's something that's putting you or somebody else at risk," Jules said automatically, spooning coffee granules into the mugs and then pouring on boiling water.

"It's nothing like that. It's something really important that you need to know. Something that will make you understand why Danny can't be with me anymore and why, actually, I know that he's right to walk away from our relationship."

Jules shook her head. "You guys have a marriage and a child. There is every reason to stay."

"Even if the child isn't his?"

Stunned, Jules stood absent-mindedly pouring boiling water onto the worktop. She only realised what she was doing when Tara gently took the kettle from her and mopped up the spillage with a stray tea towel.

"Yes, I did just say what you thought I said," Tara told her, wringing the tea towel out over the sink. "Maybe you need a brandy in your coffee?"

"I think I need you to explain," Jules said. Her legs felt shaky and she sat down on a kitchen chair. She wasn't sure what it was she'd thought Tara had come to say, but she certainly hadn't predicted this.

Tara opened the fridge, fished out the milk and sloshed some into the mugs. Pushing a coffee across to Jules, she sat opposite her and took a sip of her own drink before starting to speak. "This isn't easy for me to say. The only other person who knows is Danny and that's a decision we made together. He would never breathe a word and he certainly wouldn't approve of me being here now."

Jules wrapped her hands around the mug. *Trust me* was what Danny had said; *there is no way I can fix my marriage.* Was this what he'd been alluding to? Was this why he'd been so bitter about his ex? Tara had cheated on him and Morgan wasn't his biological son? Her head was whirling. Danny adored Morgan. She'd never met a more devoted father.

It didn't make sense.

"What happened?" she asked gently. "If you still want to tell me, that is?"

Tara stared into her coffee. "If I could turn time back I'd do so many things differently, including taking my relationship with Danny for granted. I'm not proud of myself. What can I say in my defence? Not a great deal, except that just over nine years ago we were living on a base in Germany and I was very young. I hated living there, Jules. I didn't speak a word of German and the other wives were way older than me and really snooty. I hardly saw Dan. He was busy with his regiment all the time."

"You were lonely." Jules could understand that.

Tara nodded. "I was. Don't think I didn't love Danny, Jules. I did. He was the golden boy and I adored him. Should we have married so young though? Probably not, but we weren't thinking ahead. I didn't have a clue what army life would really be like. I thought it would be uniforms and parties and travel, not looking at four grey walls in a grey house and never seeing my husband."

"So what happened?"

"I had a fling." Tara dashed her hand across her eyes. "It was only the one time and it was so stupid. I hated myself the minute it happened and I swore it wouldn't happen again. You can probably guess the rest." She looked up and laughed bitterly. "I'm Polwenna Bay's answer to *The Jeremy Kyle Show*, aren't I?"

Although she was shocked – after all, this was Danny they were talking about – Jules had enough pastoral experience to know that these situations were never clear cut. It must have taken a great deal of courage for Tara to come up and tell her this.

"Of course you're not," she said gently.

"I hoped that I was wrong about my dates when I found out I was pregnant, but then Morgan was born a month early," Tara continued quietly. "I thought about telling Danny but I could see how thrilled he was with the baby and I couldn't bear to spoil that. I guess I was scared to in case he left. If Dan suspected anything he never said so, but looking back things were never really right with us. I think we only lasted as long as we did because he was always away on tours of duty."

"And are you sure about this?" Jules asked. "Lots of babies are born early."

"I wish I wasn't but there's no mistake. When Morgan had his appendix out I found out that his blood group was A. I'm a B; I know that from my caesarean section. Then Danny got hurt and he needed pints of the stuff, which was O."

"You've lost me."

Tara pushed her cup away and looked up at Jules. Her hazel eyes shone with sadness. "It means there's no way Danny could be Morgan's biological father. No way at all."

The two women stared at one another.

"And Danny knows this?" Jules whispered. His heart must have broken and the thought of this made her want to weep for him.

"When he was hurt in the roadside bomb we thought we were going to lose him," Tara said quietly. "I was so scared that he was going to die and I panicked."

"So you told him the truth." Jules wasn't asking. She'd seen this before. People often confessed the worst things at the worst times.

"I tried to but he went mad and starting yelling at me. He said he'd already lost his arm and his career and that he wasn't going to lose his son too." Tara dabbed her eyes with her sleeve. "It turns out that he'd always suspected but he'd never breathed a word because he loves Morgan. Danny didn't want to know the truth. I took away that choice and he'll never forgive me for it."

Jules passed her the kitchen roll. As Tara unravelled the tissue paper, Jules was aware of all her own assumptions unravelling as well.

"That's why he wouldn't let you visit him in the hospital?" Jules asked.

"Of course it was. Our marriage was over from the second I confirmed what he'd always feared. He'd lost everything then, don't you see? And then I took away the one good thing that he still had. That was when I knew our marriage was as good as over, even if it limped on for a few more months. There was no way we could recover. I know that now."

It was so much to take in. Jules felt as though, after months of stumbling around in the gloom, someone had suddenly switched on a spotlight and blinded her with the facts.

"Danny's an amazing father," she said. "He loves Morgan."

Tara blew her nose. "I know, and he *is* Morgan's father in every way that matters. It's not biology that makes a man a dad. He's promised me that he'll never mention it to anyone until we decide that the time's right, and I know he'll keep his word. Danny would rather break his heart than break his word."

Jules thought of all the times Danny had insisted that things between Tara and himself could never be resolved. He'd asked Jules to take him on trust but she hadn't been able to – and yet he'd never broken his promise. Now she finally understood why he was so adamant that he wanted to draw a line under his marriage.

"I expect you think I'm a real bitch, don't you?" Tara said sadly. "I wouldn't blame you. I don't like myself very much sometimes."

"Tara, I'd never think that. You made a mistake and you've paid for it terribly."

"Some mistake." Tara hung her head.

"A mistake," Jules repeated. "You're human. We all are and that means we mess up. All of us."

Tara laughed. "Even vicars?"

"Especially vicars," Jules said firmly, thinking about how much she had messed up by falling in love with Danny. "Tara, did you intend to hurt Danny? Did you set out to deceive him? Of course not."

"But I did those things. *I* did them."

"And I can tell you've regretted them bitterly. Danny has forgiven you, hasn't he? I've seen more peace in him lately." Jules paused. "Maybe it's time you forgave yourself?"

Tara nodded. "If I can salvage something good then I think that might be possible. I think that in time Danny and I can be friends. We're parents; that's the most important thing."

"You're married." This particular elephant had been stomping about the kitchen for far too long and Jules knew it was time they acknowledged it.

Tara fixed her with a clear hazel gaze. "Jules, you must understand this: our marriage is over. There is no future for Danny and me.

Nothing anyone says or tries to do can change that. Nobody has broken our marriage apart from me."

The atmosphere in the kitchen was as thick as the snow flurries outside.

"Why are you telling me this?" Jules whispered..

"Because Danny loves you," Tara said simply. She smiled across the table, and although there was sadness in that smile there was relief and warmth too. "He loves you, Jules Mathieson, and it's tearing him apart that you're leaving. He respects your beliefs; in fact, I know he loves you even more for holding true to your values, just like he does. He knows you would never agree to be with him if you thought there was hope for his marriage. But because he won't break his promise, he'll never tell you the truth about why it can't work between us. He thinks he has to watch you walk away. How could I let that happen?" She shook her head. "Hasn't he lost enough because of me without losing you as well?"

"And is there no hope for your marriage?" The vicar in Jules had to know the answer.

"None." Tara was adamant. "We've already filed for divorce. There's no going back. I don't want to go back. It's time to move on. What happened, happened and it was because of what I did and nothing to do with you. Danny finding you and falling in love with you is a happy coincidence. Please don't deny him happiness. He's so sad right now and he doesn't deserve it. He's a good man."

He was the best of men. The most noble and the most self-sacrificing. Jules's heart was starting to race. Was there hope? Dare she even start to dream?

"But what about you?" she asked.

Tara shrugged her slim shoulders. "I'll be fine. Danny doesn't love me. He's fond of me and we do have a history but we're not going to make it as a couple. I know that now and I've made my peace with it. I'm not proud of myself – but I am proud of Morgan and I can never, ever regret him. The most important thing is that we're both there for Morgan." She looked up and smiled at Jules with real warmth. "Actually, I ought to say that the three of us are there for Morgan. You, me and Dan."

Jules nodded slowly. The future, which had once seemed as cold and as empty as the icy world outside, was suddenly looking very different. She felt lighter too, as though a burden she'd not known she was carrying had been lifted. She wasn't to blame for Danny and Tara's marriage being over and she wasn't responsible for having to mend it either! The relief was immense. Was this a sign from above?

"And if you're worrying about what God might have to say," Tara added, guessing correctly what Jules was thinking, "I'm no expert but I think you should see my coming here as a sign that He wants you and Danny to be happy. I know I certainly do – I wouldn't have come here otherwise."

"Thank you," Jules said quietly. "You don't know what that means."

"I think you'll find I do. I've seen how Danny is when he's with you. Go and find him, Jules. He was going to take Morgan sledging." She exhaled slowly and then smiled. "I can't say or do any more now. It's up to you. Happy Christmas, Jules."

Once Tara had left, stepping into the snow and vanishing within minutes, Jules stood by the door for a moment. Her thoughts were whirling as fast as the flakes in the winter sky, and for a few moments she was unable to think straight. There was so much to take in and her heart was so filled with happiness that she thought she might float away.

Tara had set both Jules and Danny free.

If Jules had prayed for a sign then surely here it was?

Unable to wait a second longer, she grabbed her coat from the peg and headed out into the snowy afternoon.

Chapter 25

By the time Jules reached the village green, the snow was falling so thickly that she could no longer see the church or even the gate to the vicarage. Yellow cones of light tumbled from cottage windows and illuminated the dancing flakes before they descended onto the windowsills, pavements and walls to merge with the ever-higher drifts.

Against all this whiteness Polwenna's festive lights were doubly bright and its Christmas tree was a splash of acid green. The tree's limbs were iced with snow and its white and blue bulbs seemed to twinkle with just as much brilliance. Villagers scurried by in coats and hats, calling "Merry Christmas" to one another and exclaiming excitedly about the possibility of it being a white one. Children had made makeshift sledges from tea trays and were racing down any slopes they could find, pink cheeked and whooping with glee while adults watched anxiously.

Jules paused, her eyes screwed up against the glare. It was hard to work out which child was which, as they were all swaddled in thick coats and wearing bobble hats. It was nearly as difficult to differentiate between the adults. The figure standing slightly apart from the others, arms crossed over a generous chest, had to be Sheila in her official capacity as First Responder. Devastated not to have been first on the scene when Ivy was discovered, Sheila was probably desperate for another accident so that she could prove her worth.

Tara's visit might have lasted only ten minutes but it had changed everything. In light of her revelation, Danny's inability to give Jules a firm reason why his marriage was over suddenly made perfect sense. *Trust me*, he'd said, but she hadn't been able to. Trust was a two-way street and at the time she'd felt hurt that he couldn't share whatever it was with her. Now, though, she completely understood: it hadn't been his secret to share. She loved him even more for not going back on his word. Would she have been able to keep such a promise if losing Danny had been the price? Jules wasn't sure. Her fears for her integrity as a vicar seemed to fade away, though; after all, what were these in comparison to a father's love for his son? Danny loved Morgan. That was why he was prepared to sacrifice his own happiness. He loved his son totally and unconditionally. It was as simple and as uncomplicated as that, and Jules laughed out loud. Of course! Love. A father's love.

Wasn't this what Christmas was all about?

She'd been so busy stressing about the technicalities and the nuances of certain Biblical verses that she'd forgotten the greatest commandment of all. She'd overcomplicated the most important thing about being the vicar of Polwenna Bay. Yes, leading by example was part of it, as was being able to support and guide her parishioners, but most of all she had to love them.

And she did love them, Jules realised as she watched Big Rog helping his grandchildren onto a home-made sledge while Sheila lectured him. From Ivy to the Pollards to Caspar, she had come to care deeply about these people and this place.

But most of all she loved Danny Tremaine.

She saw him now, standing apart from the others at the foot of the hill and watching Morgan zoom down with Issie. Danny was smiling but there with an air of isolation and sadness about him that broke her heart.

He must have sensed Jules looking; almost immediately he turned his head, and for a moment they stared at one another through the snow. Her breath caught in her throat because, in spite of his injuries, Danny was still the most handsome man she had ever seen. Tall, broad shouldered and with that burning blue gaze that made her head spin. She couldn't speak or move; she was frozen not by the cold but by the knowledge that this was one of the most important turning points of her life.

Danny said something to Issie, who nodded and took Morgan's hand, tugging the small boy and the sledge back uphill. Then he joined Jules.

"You know, don't you?" he said softly.

Jules took a deep breath. "Tara told me everything, Dan. Everything."

He bit his lip and then nodded. "I never asked that, never expected it of her. She must really think highly of you, Jules."

"It's you she thinks highly of," Jules said softly. "She wanted me to understand that you and she were over. She understood that I had to know one hundred percent that it wasn't my fault."

Danny looked upset. "I'm sorry I couldn't tell you the truth. I wanted to so very much but it wasn't my secret to tell."

"I know that now but I didn't understand before what it was you were keeping back from me," Jules said. "I really thought that it was my fault you and Tara weren't back together. I thought that if I went away you guys would be able to sort it out."

His gaze never left hers. "Some things can't be sorted out, at least not in a neat and tidy fashion."

"I know that now," she said. "I should have trusted you and listened to what you were saying, Danny. I'm sorry."

His lips quirked upwards. "Somebody once told me that trust is a two-way street."

"Sounds like something a very wise person would say," Jules deadpanned, and he laughed.

"I won't argue with that – although the same person can be very stubborn at times."

"Only because I want to do the right thing," Jules said. "And that has to be by my faith as well as by everyone else."

"I know that and I wouldn't have you any other way."

She tilted her head up to look at him. Snowflakes were dancing all around them and settling on his eyelashes.

"So you still want me then? Even after I told you to walk away?"

He stepped forward and took her hand in his. "Jules, there's so much in my life that I owe to you. I'm not the angry person I was six months ago, and that's down to you. You've helped me become a better man. Tara and I have made our peace now and that's thanks to you too in so many ways. Forgiveness is also a two-way street." His gloved fingers squeezed hers. "I think you know the answer to your question. Maybe I ought to ask whether you still want me?"

"I've always wanted you," Jules said simply. There was nothing left now but to tell him the truth and lay her heart wide open. "Danny, I love you. I think I always have."

"Even when I made you walk up all those hills? You didn't love me then, as I recall. In fact quite a few of the things you said then were very unchristian!"

"Hmm, that's true. Give me a moment." She put her head on one side and narrowed her eyes as though reconsidering. "No, I'm afraid to say that I loved you even then, even though your route marches nearly killed me and you've totally ruined my carefully honed junk-food addiction."

She waited for him to make a joke back, but Danny wasn't teasing any longer. Instead he put his arm around her and pulled her close.

"And I love you, Reverend Mathieson," he murmured against her ear. "But I think you already know that. You're stubborn and bossy and have a terrible Dairy Milk habit, but I can put all that aside because there's nobody else in the world for me but you."

His lips were so close to hers that she trembled with longing.

"You're cold. Come here." Noticing her shiver, Danny drew her even closer. He was so tall that Jules's head didn't reach past his shoulder; instead she found she nestled perfectly in the crook of his arm, with her head resting against his heart. She could feel it racing against her cheek and in perfect time with her own. She gulped. He was so warm and strong, and he smelt delicious. He was Danny, her best friend and the love of her life. Finding him had taken her completely by surprise, but Jules had never felt so safe or so at home.

Everything about Danny Tremaine felt right. It always had and Jules knew with every cell of her being that she belonged here with him in Polwenna Bay.

"Warmer?" he asked, his lips pressed against her temple.

"Is it cold?" she whispered. "I hadn't noticed."

"Paraphrasing Four Weddings? Have you been at the mulled wine already?" Danny teased. "It's bloody freezing!"

His lips strayed from her temple to the corner of her mouth and it was the most natural thing in the world to turn her head and kiss him. The magic of it made her heart fill with joy. Jules felt his lips on hers and the strength of his arm around her. His mouth tasted of the cold and of snowflakes, and it was the most delicious sensation imaginable. She never wanted to let him go again.

Above them the snowflakes wheeled and danced. As Jules kissed Danny back, wrapping her arms around his neck and savouring the feeling of his mouth on hers, she knew with certainty that at long, long last she had found the man who made her heart and soul dance every bit as wildly as the whirling snow.

It was wonderful. Magical. Incredible. Just as she'd always known it would be.

She never wanted his kisses to end. It really was the happiest of Christmas Eves.

Chapter 26

Tara stood in the churchyard watching the snow whirl in across the sea from a flat grey sky. She huddled deeper into her coat, dug her fingers further into her pockets and tried desperately to ignore the growing sensation that the whole world was being buried alive. The snow had blurred the lines between the sea and the beach, and as the flakes became thicker the village's jaunty Christmas lights and the glowing windows of the cottages were gradually being erased.

Speaking to Jules just now had been one of the hardest things Tara had ever had to do, but also one of the best. Tara had steeled herself for a reaction of horror and disgust, but she hadn't found that at all. She hadn't seen judgement in the other woman's eyes but instead compassion and warmth. *You made a mistake*, Jules had said, *and you paid for it bitterly*. And in setting Danny free, Tara realised suddenly, she had done exactly the same for herself. They could both move on now. Ivy was right: putting others first really did change you.

Before the snowfall had thickened Tara had stood by the churchyard gate and watched Jules run out of the vicarage, towards the village. From this vantage point she had seen Jules join the figures by the village green and had watched as one dressed in black had peeled away to join her. Tara wasn't sure whether it was snow or tears that had smudged her vision when she'd seen the two of them embrace. Her pang of loss had mingled with a strange glow of contentment that she had done the right thing, and she knew this would help soothe her aching loneliness.

By the time she'd wiped her tears away with a gloved thumb, the snow was starting to blow in horizontally. Blinking, Tara could only make out more whiteness. Unable to face returning to her empty cottage, she'd decided to turn left and walk back through Fernside Woods, past Mariners' View and back down over the cliffs. After all, Morgan was spending the night at Seaspray – she couldn't have denied him that – so there was nobody who would mind or even notice if she stayed out for a little while longer. Everyone was with their families or together with friends in the pub, drinking mulled wine and settling in for a Christmas Eve session. Waving to Little Rog Pollard, who was valiantly sweeping the path to the church in readiness for Midnight Mass, Tara had set off on a stomp that would hopefully clear her head and put her in a better frame of mind.

The lane that led from St Wenn's to Fernside was a tunnel of snow. The trees were laden with it, and the fresh white carpeting creaked beneath her boots. Except for this there was an eerie silence, as though everything had been paused. Emerging from the woods she realised that the world as she knew it had vanished completely. The snow was now billowing in clouds and stinging her face: a blizzard had surrounded her, as quiet and as deadly as an advancing army.

Where was she?

Unnerved and disorientated, Tara glanced left and then right. The sharp wind bore down on her, stinging her face and making her eyes water. Should she turn left here? Or was it further on? And if so, how much further? She knew that she needed to change direction where the cliff path began, but in the blankness it was impossible to see where that path started. Tara had no idea where she was. The lights of Mariners were hidden, and only feet away the cold sea frothed and foamed over needle-sharp rocks. Her heart started to race. Was she literally footsteps away from tumbling into oblivion, or was the solid path hiding somewhere beneath the whiteness?

How could she tell?

Her lungs were on fire and every breath she took burned. The more the snow swirled, the less certain she became. Her steps were increasingly tentative. Should she turn now? Or carry on straight ahead? As she was trying to decide, another heavy flurry came, bewildering her all the more. For a moment she thought she could see the lights of the village just ahead, and she almost increased her speed before fear made her hesitate. What if the welcoming glimmer wasn't Mariners but the Eddystone light luring her to her doom like the wreckers of old? Instead of stepping onto the firm path and safety, she would spin into the snow, falling and falling with the air rushing over her and her own terror rising to meet her, as sharp and as certain as the rocks below...

Tara's heart was rattling against her ribs and her breath came in short gasps as the cold snatched at her lungs. She paused and forced herself to be calm. The cliffs that she knew so well could turn from friend to enemy in the blink of an eye or the flurry of a snowstorm. To panic here could be fatal. All she had to do was stop and retrace her steps. That was the sensible option: just turn around and follow her footprints back to Fernside and safety.

But the elements had other ideas; all traces of her passage from the woods had already been erased by the ceaseless snowfall. Blinking in the whiteness, Tara realised with growing alarm that her eyes weren't playing tricks on her: her footprints really had vanished. She tried to tell herself that there might yet be a little shimmer of the pattern from the sole of her boots, but all evidence of her passage through the empty world had faded away.

Tara spun on her heel. Which way to safety? How could she get home before the cold began to seep into her bones and her eyes grew dangerously heavy? How long did she have before she was buried alive in this swirling snow? And who would even notice that she wasn't there? Nobody would miss her.

Nobody would care. She was like Ivy.

In her indecision the heel of her boot slithered and Tara fell forwards, slamming her knee into the granite lurking beneath the snowfall. She heard the rip of denim and the rush air pass her lips as she gasped. Crimson bloomed against the whiteness, just as shocking as the stabbing pain. Tears stung her eyes and for a moment she knelt on the path, too defeated and too afraid to move as the snow pillowed around her, blanketing her world in white. Then she pitched forward and curled into the duvet-like softness. She was so, so tired and so desperately sad.

The tumbling flakes swirled and blurred. Faces and figures seemed to lurch out of the nothingness, fading and dissolving just as she began to hope that there really was someone out there. She was lost in a nightmare in which she was plummeting into thick nothingness, her screams destined to die in her throat. Nobody would ever hear her sobbing. In despair she closed her eyes...

"Tara! Tara! It's OK. You're safe now."

Tara's eyes opened slowly as a dog bounded through the whiteness, the snow clinging to its chocolate fur. A rough tongue licked her face and then a figure emerged from the swirling storm. Strong hands on

Tara's shoulders pulled her upwards until she was engulfed in the warmth of human contact.

"Good boy, Watson! You found her! Well done!"

It was Richard who was holding onto her so tightly. His face was close to hers and she could feel the warmth of his skin and his heart beating through his thick fleece. Eyes the same grey as the sky locked with her own as Watson's shrill barks of excitement shattered the stillness.

Had she stumbled over the cliff edge and not noticed? Or was she free-falling right now? Tara's stomach was certainly somersaulting – and her pulse was skittering too – as, astonished, she drank in the sight of Richard. His sandy hair was ruffled, his skin glowed from the cold and his nose was pink, but he'd never looked so beautiful to her.

"Richard?" she whispered, her hands rising to cup his face in disbelief. Was he real or a snowy dream? "What are you doing here?"

"Looking for you," he said simply, his voice softer than the falling flakes as he rested his forehead against hers. "And I've found you, thank God. I've been frantic."

Now she knew it was a dream, for how would he have noticed she was gone? It was Christmas Eve and everyone was excited, wrapping presents by their wood burners or out sledging or busy preparing the next day's dinner. People were with their loved ones, which was just how it should be at Christmas. Who would have realised that she was missing? Nobody in Polwenna Bay, that was for sure, and certainly not Richard. No, he was with Amanda.

"Why would you be frantic? I've only been gone for ten minutes."

"Tara, it's more like almost an hour! There's a blizzard going on, in case you hadn't noticed, and you're out in the freezing cold and all alone. What were you thinking?"

She shook her head. "I just wanted to walk home, but the weather came in so fast and I was so confused out here. It all looks the same."

Richard was pulling her to her feet. "It certainly does. It's bloody treacherous to be up on the cliffs in this weather. Thank God Little Rog had the sense to ask Danny what you were playing at by going for a walk in the snow, or we'd have had no idea you were out here. I came straight out to find you."

"I'm fine," Tara protested.

"You're very far from fine," he said, in a voice that wouldn't be argued with. "You've fallen, you're disorientated and above all you're desperately cold, possibly hypothermic. Oh Christ, Tara, don't you realise how serious this could have been?"

Tara was starting to. "I'm so sorry. I really didn't mean to cause any trouble."

"It's not that." He shook his head. "Oh, Tara, don't you understand? I could have lost you."

She stared up at him. Snow dusted his eyelashes.

"Lost me?"

"Lost you," Richard said quietly. He wrapped his arms around her and held her tightly. "I'm taking you home, Tara, and I'm not letting you out of my sight."

A million and one questions were flittering through Tara's mind, whirling and spinning like the snowflakes tumbling from the now darkening sky.

"There's something I need to know," she began, but he shook his head.

"I need you to do something for me first." Releasing her, Richard rummaged through his rucksack and pulled out a flask. Pouring a cup of hot tea, he said, "I do think you're mildly hypothermic. I need you to drink this – and I've also got some Dairy Milk here, to help you get your strength back."

"Yes, Doctor," Tara teased, but he was looking so serious that she did as she was told. Besides, after a lifetime of dieting this was no time to turn down a medicinal chocolate bar.

The tea was sweet and hot. While Richard called Danny to let him know she was safe, Tara sipped it and little by little her energy levels began to rise. By the time she'd finished two cups, the sleepy sensation was retreating and she felt far more like her old self.

The shaking hands and racing heart she wasn't sure she could explain away quite so easily, though…

"Your knee has quite a nasty cut but I don't think it needs stitches," Richard was telling her, frowning thoughtfully as he peered at the injury. "I'll dress it once we're back."

Tara had totally forgotten her knee. The sensation of Richard's strong and skilled fingers on her leg were working miracles in terms of pain relief. Nurofen should be very afraid.

Once her tea was finished and she'd eaten several squares of the Dairy Milk, Richard took her hand and slowly they picked their way back through the snow, following Watson away from the cliffs and towards the village. As Richard's fingers knitted with hers, Tara dredged up her courage to broach the topic she feared the most.

"Richard, are you seeing Amanda?"

"What?" Richard stopped so abruptly that she cannoned into him. "Absolutely not! What on earth makes you think that?"

Err, apart from that she clearly fancies you rotten and wishes me on the moon? Tara thought.

Aloud she said, "She answered your mobile the other day."

"I left it in Casa Rosa and she picked it up for me," Richard said simply. "Thankfully it's just my personal mobile, not my work one."

His fingers squeezed hers. "My mind wasn't actually on the phone that day, though. I had something else I was thinking about – and, before you ask, it wasn't Amanda."

Tara was appalled by the surge of relief that came from learning this. Her heart had been shredded at just the thought of Richard being with Amanda; the reality would have been unbearable. She was about to ask him what it was that his mind had been dwelling on when his eyes, those kind eyes that spoke so much about the goodness and true worth of the man, locked with hers. Then his warm mouth met hers and Tara found that she already knew the answer. It was the sweetest and tenderest of kisses and, as she melted into him like the snowflakes that were melting on his coat, she knew that no kiss before had ever felt so right. She wanted to kiss him and kiss him until the world and the snow faded away.

Eventually they broke apart and smiled at one another wonderingly. Richard reached for her hand and raised it to his lips. She felt the heat of his mouth through her glove, and the strength of her longing to feel his lips on hers again made her feel dizzy. Richard, mild-mannered Dr Richard, kissed in such a way that it turned her bones to lava. Without doubt, a passionate nature lay beneath his gentle exterior.

"Tara, I'm not very good at this," he said softly. "I'm not a war hero, or particularly handsome, or dashing – no, don't try and speak, let me finish – and I don't have a huge house and lots of money. But what I do have is a heart that's spilling over with love for you."

She was lost for words. Richard might not have the medals or the uniform or the scars to mark him out as a hero, but in her eyes this was exactly what he was. He'd rescued her in so many ways that, if she were to try to explain it, she wouldn't even know where to begin.

"I knew from the first moment I met you by that well that I wanted to spend the rest of my life with you. It doesn't make sense, I know, but everything inside me was telling me so." He raised his eyes skywards in embarrassment. "I even went back and wished for you. Does that sound crazy?"

She touched his cheek. "No crazier than if I told you that I wished for true love that very same day, and moments later you arrived. Well, technically I suppose Watson arrived first, but I don't think we'll count him!"

"I wouldn't. He has terrible breath!"

They smiled at one another, but the smile quickly started to slip from Tara's lips as a new and horrible fear took hold. Richard didn't really know her, did he? Not the real her, the one who had betrayed Danny all those years ago. If he knew what sort of a person she'd been, would he still be here beneath this snowy Christmas Eve sky, telling her that he was in love with her? Or would he run back to Amanda as fast as he could?

Tara knew that if Richard really wanted to be with her then he had to know the truth. There could be no more secrets.

"There's something I have to tell you," she said. "It's going to be hard to hear and it could change everything. You might not feel the same way about me afterwards – but I need you to know."

A shadow crossed his face. "You still love Danny, don't you?"

She thought about this for a moment. "I'll always love Danny, but I'm not *in* love with him anymore. If I'm honest I haven't been in love with him for a very long time."

He nodded. "But there's someone else you love. Caspar?"

"Caspar!" Tara's exclamation was so loud it was a miracle she didn't cause an avalanche. "Hardly. No, it isn't another man. Not like that, anyway. It's Morgan, my son." She stopped and inhaled shakily. This was it. Time to tell the truth. "Richard, I'm not the person you think I am. I'm a bad person. I—"

He put his finger on her lips.

"Tara, I think I can guess what you're trying to tell me, and I don't need to know any more than that – not unless or until there's a time and a place when you feel it's right. That's in the past. That's who you were then. I love the woman standing here now. The wonderful mother. The good friend. The brave woman who risked her neck to save a grumpy pensioner. I'm in love with *her* and nothing you or anyone else can do or say will change that. I love you, Tara. You."

He knew. He'd worked it out for himself and he still loved her? Tara was blown away.

"The question is, though," he added quietly, "whether you could come to love me?"

Come to love him? In answer she rose onto her tiptoes and pressed her lips against his.

"I already love you," she said softly. "It crept up on me slowly, until I couldn't hide from it or escape it anymore – a bit like this snowstorm. I love you, Richard Penwarren, and you *are* my hero in every way." She bent down and patted the dog. "You too, of course, Watson."

And suddenly the cold and the snow and the darkness melted away, because Richard was kissing her and kissing her and kissing her. Then, hand in hand, they walked through the still white world and into the cottage, where they shut the door and curled up in front of the wood burner, the heat of their feelings and the passion of their kisses warming them almost as much as the flames. They talked and kissed and talked some more until their lips ached with smiling and kissing and their eyes grey heavy with the heat of the fire.

Bathed in the glow of Richard's love and the Christmas-tree lights, Tara lay in his arms and gazed drowsily through the window towards St Wenn's. The snow had finally stopped and she could just make out the church, a gentle beacon of light in the darkness as the villagers gathered for Midnight Mass. She thought about Jules and Danny, and her heart was glad for them. There was Yuletide magic in the air tonight, that was for sure.

"Happy Christmas," she whispered, snuggling into Richard's arms.

"Happy Christmas to you too," he murmured back, dropping a kiss onto her temple.

Whether or not she believed in St Wenn's Well, all their winter wishes had come true, Tara thought as her eyes began to close. There was no doubt whatsoever in her mind that it was going to be a very happy New Year.

She could hardly wait to see what it was going to bring.

The End

Epilogue

Christmas Day

"I hope everyone's hungry?"

The Seaspray dining table was piled so high with food that Alice Tremaine could hardly be seen above the roast potatoes, honey-glazed carrots and mountains of Morgan's beloved sausage stuffing. In pride of place was the enormous turkey, its skin crispy and golden. The bird was so heavy that both Jake and Ashley had been required to manoeuvre it from the Aga to the dining room.

Just looking at it was making Jules's mouth water. She was very glad the heavy snowfall meant dinner with the mayor was cancelled!

"Gran, you do know that there are only fourteen of us eating? Not fourteen thousand? I'd better get stuck in," teased Nick, gesturing at the laden platters. As his hand stole out to swipe a roast potato his grandmother slapped it playfully.

"Wait until we're all seated, Mr Greedy! Besides, we haven't even said grace yet."

"I think we have the perfect person here for that job," Danny said, squeezing Jules's fingers, which were entwined with his beneath the table. He'd hardly let go of her since yesterday afternoon – and, he'd whispered as they'd stood outside St Wenn's after Midnight Mass, he intended never to let her slip away again. Recalling this filled Jules with more warmth than any crackling fire or glass of hot mulled wine ever could. Danny's kisses, the soft snow flurries and the calls of "Happy Christmas" from the villagers had made it the best Christmas Eve ever.

Jules knew she should never doubt her boss; His plans were always perfect, after all. Even so, she was amazed at just how wonderfully everything seemed to have worked out. All her prayers had been answered, and as she smiled at Danny the love she saw on his face made her heart melt like snow in bright winter sunshine.

The blizzard of the previous day had buried Polwenna Bay beneath a downy blanket, and the scene reminded Jules of the festive window display in Patsy Penhalligan's bakery, with its cluster of gingerbread cottages topped with white. Opening the curtains on Christmas morning to find the world transformed into a living Christmas card had made Jules laugh for pure joy because it had looked so perfect. Even taking the Christmas service in a church several degrees colder than the world outside couldn't stop her lips from curving upwards. Happiness and her new thermal underwear had kept her warm, at any rate, even if St Wenn's heating had decided to give up.

But the snowfall hadn't been the only magic. Early that morning Jules had phoned the bishop, and in church she had announced that she would be staying in the parish after all. Telling her parishioners this and experiencing their delighted response had been the best Christmas present ever. Or the second best, she decided, squeezing Dan's fingers in return.

"I'd love to say grace," she said to Alice.

"You have to wait until my mum and Richard get here," Morgan told her sternly from his seat directly opposite the dish of stuffing. "They are seven minutes late. Fact."

"Your mum and the doc!" Issie giggled. "I never saw *that* one coming!"

Morgan gave his aunt a pitying look. "It was obvious. They always look at each other just like Nick looks at dinner. So do Dad and Jules. Fact."

Jules's face matched the festive scarlet tablecloth. And there she was thinking she'd made such a good job of hiding her feelings. Maybe she wouldn't be taking up poker in the New Year…

"And you look at Mo that way too," Morgan told Ashley kindly, just in case he felt left out.

"That's because I could gobble her up, covered in horse hair and straw or not!" Ashley said, winking wickedly at Mo. His wife rolled her eyes but her cheeks turned very pink. The electricity between those two was so strong you'd probably get a shock if you stood too close, Jules observed. It was yet another amazing Christmas gift that Ashley was with them for Christmas dinner today. Jules sent up a silent prayer of thanks. There were so many blessings to count.

Issie was busy making puking gestures. "All right, all right. I'm getting depressed by all you loved-up people. When's it my turn? I made my wish at St Wenn's Well too, and so did Granny. Where are our fit men?"

"Issie, that was just a bit of nonsense," Alice chided, but Issie grinned.

"Don't fob me off, Gran! I'm gagging to know who Lord Blackwarren really is. I know you couldn't have made that up and I'm going to find out!"

Alice seemed very interested in the turkey all of a sudden. Since being outed as the author of the steamy *Blackwarren* novel, she had achieved as much local fame as her notorious ancestor, Black Jack Jago – and although Alice claimed that this was the end of her writing aspirations, Jules wasn't convinced. Caspar Owen had already insisted on having his copy of Alice's book signed and was making noises about becoming her literary agent. If Caspar had his way, Lord Blackwarren's, ahem, *sword* was not about to be hung up!

"Jake, carve this will you, love? The others will be here in a minute," Alice said.

Grinning at Issie, her eldest grandson did as he was told. Soon plates were being piled high with tender slices of turkey.

"You made a wish at St Wenn's Well? What did you wish for?" Danny asked Jules softly. His voice was light and as full of teasing fun as her champagne glass was full of bubbles, but the way his thumb was tracing circles on her palm told her that he already knew the answer to his question.

She smiled at him, remembering the way the wish had floated from her heart, as natural and as pure as the cold water that had laughed and whispered over the rocks. "Something that means the world to me."

"Good for St Wenn," Danny murmured, leaning over to brush her lips with his. "I'd have gone to the well months ago if I'd known she was this effective."

"Even Dad's got a secret woman," Issie was saying now, the full beam of her blue-eyed attention on Jimmy. "Don't deny it, Dad! I heard you Skyping her last night. *Merry Christmas! I love you baby!* Is she from your commune in California? Is that where all your money's going? On a hippy chick?"

Jimmy Tremaine, who'd only just sneaked into the room after a merry hour celebrating Christmas in The Ship, spluttered into his Buck's Fizz.

"Don't be ridiculous! I was, err… watching telly!"

"Yeah right," scoffed Issie. She waggled a finger at him. "Don't think you're getting off that lightly or that you're forgiven for not taking me to San Francisco. It's Christmas, so I won't push it, but I think it's high time I had some winter sun. Even bloody Zak's jetted away to the Caribbean."

"He is recording an album there," pointed out Jake as he passed a heaped platter of turkey to his grandmother.

"Must be hell for him in the sunshine with all that rum and those bikini-wearing girls on tap," grumbled Issie, tossing her blonde braids indignantly. "I'm going to make up for it after Christmas and have some adventures all of my own *and* find a fit guy. Just you lot wait and see."

"Little Rog will be gutted," said Nick, followed by "Ouch! Get off!" when his sister walloped him over the head with a cracker. "Granny! Tell her to stop!"

"Would you think they were in their twenties?" Alice sighed to Jules. "I wonder why I do this sometimes. Maybe I should have saved myself the effort and booked us all in at Symon's?" But she was smiling as she said this and Jules knew that really Alice was loving every minute of having her family gathered around her for Christmas. Seaspray was ringing with voices and laughter, which was exactly as the big old house should be. The tree was twinkling like the sea below in the bay, and the huge pile of presents beneath it was as colourful as the Polwenna lights. There were several gifts there with her name on too, and Jules felt the wonderful glow of knowing that she was loved and accepted and part of it all.

How could she ever have survived leaving Polwenna Bay and Danny? It would have broken her heart. Sitting here now, with her hand resting in his, Jules felt as though all her Christmas presents had come at once.

Thinking of Christmas presents, Jules had already opened one earlier. It had been left for her in the vicarage porch and, like something from *Alice in Wonderland*, was tied up with a red ribbon and labelled *Read me!* Such a flamboyant gesture could only have come from one person. Once Midnight Mass was over and Danny had headed back to Seaspray after a thousand kisses, Jules had curled up in bed to open the gift. She'd been taken aback when she'd realised she was holding Cassandra Duval's latest manuscript.

The Reverend's Renegade Heart

Flipping open the first page, Jules had swiftly found herself transported into the eighteenth century and a small Cornish town peopled by wreckers, smugglers and feisty tavern wenches. The occupants of this oddly familiar town were the flock of the hero, who was none other than the dark and brooding Reverend Julian Matthews. With a heart full of passion, a secret and savage past fighting in the colonies and a crypt full of smuggled goods, he was as torn and tortured a hero as any reader of romance could long for. He was perhaps not quite as *energetic* as Lord Blackwarren, but the good Rev was soon flung headlong into a passionate love affair with the squire's daughter, Tana, and tempted by the sultry Eleanor. Jules couldn't help herself: she was hooked. She'd been unable to stop reading, no matter how heavy her eyes grew. By the time Santa had circled the globe, the snow had finished falling all around and the daylight had started to steal over the rooftops, Jules had devoured every page. Caspar was right – it was his best book yet. The descriptions of the "fictional" town were so vivid she could taste the tang of salt and hear the seagulls cry. The hero, an injured soldier turned vicar, was so plausible and familiar that she kept shaking her head in disbelief. That she had played a small part in helping Caspar create this was a humbling thought.

I hope you like it, Caspar had written beneath THE END, *because this book wouldn't exist without your help and friendship. I also hope you like the hero. In him two people have come together to make one perfect whole… I wonder where the inspiration for that came from? x*

A war-hero vicar? Who could ever guess where Caspar got his ideas? Yet now, amidst the chatter of the excited Tremaine family, Jules glanced at Danny – best friend, hero and love of her life – and knew Caspar was absolutely right. With Danny she felt a completeness and a peace that she could never have imagined before. Even if she spent the rest of eternity with him, it would still never be long enough.

"Here we are! Sorry to keep you waiting, but the roads have been appalling!"

The dining-room door flew open and Richard Penwarren appeared. His nose was red from the cold and his glasses were steaming up in the warmth. Laughing, Tara slipped them from his nose and wiped them carefully on her sleeve, before replacing them tenderly. She looked different, Jules thought. Softer somehow and less spiky, as though all her sharp edges had been smoothed away like sea-washed pebbles. Tara's mouth was curling upwards rather than being set in its usual determined line, and her eyes shone. The brittle energy that Jules had come to associate with Morgan's mum had vanished completely; instead she looked like a woman who'd let go of a huge burden.

"The path is really slippy. I thought we'd never get up. It's just started snowing again, too." Tara was stepping back to allow Richard to push a wheelchair into the dining room. "Jake, we'll need a load more salt if this carries on, or else we'll never get Ivy back. Either that, or we'll have to borrow the quad bike."

"I can't possibly ride on a quad bike! I… Oh! Actually, why not? It could be fun and, anyway, what's the worst that could happen? Falling and hurting myself?" laughed a voice that Jules recognised – although she'd never heard it sound so jovial before. No, this was a voice that was usually heard complaining, so Jules did a double take when she saw Ivy Lawrence in the wheelchair. Either the Christmas sherry was very strong indeed or Ivy was actually smiling. Surely not? Charles Dickens and Cassandra Duval combined couldn't make that up!

"Welcome to Seaspray, Ivy," Alice said warmly, bending down and kissing her guest's cheek.

"Thank you for inviting me," Ivy said – and, sure enough, the boot-button eyes that usually glared at anyone rash enough to get close were creased with smiles rather than criss-crosses of ill temper.

Morgan, wide eyed, was hiding his camera under the table. "I promise I won't take any pictures of you," he said quickly when he saw Ivy looking.

"You can take as many as you like, my dear," Ivy reassured him. "If it wasn't for you I might not have even seen Christmas." She winked at Issie. "Let's see if I do break that lens. Or maybe, just maybe, I'm not quite so much of a wicked old witch as I was?"

Issie squirmed. "I'm sorry about saying that."

"Don't be. You were right," Ivy said. "I was behaving like a wicked old witch and I'm sorry. I'd like to make amends, if I can."

"Well, I certainly think people have appreciated your gifts to the village. You really were a Christmas angel," Summer said. "My dad was thrilled with the hamper."

"The cakes you made were wonderful," Jules told her.

"And Polwenna benefitted a lot from your donations to the Christmas lights fund," Jake added.

But Morgan was confused by this change.

"You're not cross I looked in your window?" he asked cautiously, his camera still out of sight.

"Cross? You saved my life, young man," Ivy told him. "If you hadn't done that, who knows how long I would have been on the floor with my hip dislocated? You're a hero. Just like you father and," she smiled up at Tara, "like your mum is for rescuing me."

"Absolute fact," Danny assured his son. "It's OK, mate, you're not in trouble."

"Anyway, you're not a wicked old witch," Tara said firmly to Ivy, helping Richard move a chair and seat their guest at the table. "Did your daughter think that about you when you called her earlier? Did your granddaughter? Or were they thrilled to hear from you?"

A solitary tear slipped down Ivy's cheek. "I just wish I hadn't left it so long."

"Sometimes it takes a while to say the things that mean the most," Danny said quietly, looking at Jules as he spoke.

"But it's never too late to put things right. Or to start again," Tara added, reaching for Richard's hand.

The doctor pulled her close, nodding. "And what better time to do all that than at Christmas?"

Jules nodded. "Some secrets have to be shared and truths told if people are to be happy."

"I don't have a flipping clue what you lot are going on about but I'm starving. Can we please eat now?" Nick pleaded, looking longingly at the food.

Alice laughed. "We're all here now so why not? Jules, would you do the honours?"

"Absolutely," Jules said.

She put down her glass and smiled at the people gathered around the table, people who had become so dear to her since she'd moved to the village. And, of course, Danny was the dearest of them all. Her heart overflowing with love, Jules bowed her head to say grace, and the thankful prayer came as easily as breathing.

As the snowflakes kissed the village Jules knew with all her heart that winter wishes really did come true.

Ruth Saberton is the bestselling author of *Katy Carter Wants a Hero* and *Escape for the Summer*. She also writes upmarket commercial fiction under the pen names Jessica Fox, Georgie Carter and Holly Cavendish.

Born and raised in the UK, Ruth has just returned from living on Grand Cayman for two years. What an adventure!

And since she loves to chat with readers, please do add her as a Facebook friend and follow her on Twitter.

www.ruthsaberton.co.uk

Twitter: @ruthsaberton

Facebook: Ruth Saberton

Printed in Great Britain
by Amazon